LUNAR RISING

HOWLING STORM

MIANKE FOURIE

◆ FriesenPress

One Printers Way
Altona, MB R0G 0B0
Canada

www.friesenpress.com

Copyright © 2024 by Mianke Fourie
First Edition — 2024

All rights reserved.

No part of this publication may be reproduced in any form, or by any means, electronic or mechanical, including photocopying, recording, or any information browsing, storage, or retrieval system, without permission in writing from FriesenPress.

This is a work of fiction. Unless otherwise indicated, all the names, characters, businesses, places, events and incidents in this book are either the product of the author's imagination or used in a fictitious manner. Any resemblance to actual persons, living or dead, or actual events is purely coincidental.

ISBN
978-1-03-919708-4 (Hardcover)
978-1-03-919707-7 (Paperback)
978-1-03-919709-1 (eBook)

1. FICTION, ROMANCE, PARANORMAL, SHIFTERS

Distributed to the trade by The Ingram Book Company

To my girls who don't need saving and who would kick the butts of every bad guy, this book is for you. It doesn't matter how broken you think you are, you can always be your own hero.

PROLOGUE

"Where the hell is your daughter?"

I shoot upright in my bed. The bellowing voice, coupled with screaming and noises of destruction coming from somewhere in my home—where I live with my parents—makes my heart want to climb out of my chest. My head feels foggy, and my brain struggles to grasp what is happening. A loud crashing sound has me flinging my covers from me, and my senses are honing in on shouting… or is it screaming? I'm not sure.

I dart out of my room and into the hallway, but the sounds are coming from all directions. I run to the end of the hallway to the massive window looking onto the front of our property; I look out, hoping to see what is going on, and all I see is chaos erupting. There are a lot of wolves running around and looking frantic, and others I don't recognize rounding them up. I don't know why, though. Why are there so many wolves at our home anyway?

A commotion coming from the left side of the house, near the front door, makes my blood run cold. "Mom? Dad?" Where the hell are my parents? I cannot shake the feeling of needing to get to them.

A roar rings through our entire house, sending chills down my spine. The panic I see on the frantic wolves' faces starts to build in my chest.

"Mommy!" I call now, freaking out a little.

I run through the hall to my parents' room, bursting through the door. The room is empty, but the contents are thrown all around. What the hell is going on?

"Where the fuck is she?" The voice from earlier bellows from the foyer.

"Please, Alpha Jace, what do you want with our daughter?" That's my father's voice, and he sounds completely terrified.

I sneak down the hall as silently as possible. I need to see what is happening.

"You will not speak directly to the Alpha. You will speak to me!" A man with dark hair and an ugly scar on his upper lip snarls at my father, making him step back from the fierceness in his voice. The man standing next to "Scarface" looks menacing and very intimidating.

A growl leaves Scarface's chest, and my mother sinks to her knees, pleading now. "Please don't take her from us."

The menacing one looks down at my mother with disgust and kicks her away from his feet. "You have two choices here. Either give your daughter to me willingly, or I kill you and take her anyway."

I gasp, the sound leaving my throat almost mouse-like; they look my way, Scarface and the intimidating one smiling when their eyes fall on me.

"Bring her to me," the menacing one tells Scarface, his voice sickly sweet.

My body seizes, and I'm frozen to my spot from the fear that's now actively pumping through my veins. I scream when Scarface grabs me by my arms and yanks me out from behind the wall I tried to use to hide. His face is even more frightening up close. He walks with me, my arms still in his grip, squeezing me incredibly hard. He throws me to the floor in front of the menacing one.

I assume this is the Alpha; his aura practically screams it. "Well, aren't you a pretty little thing," the Alpha purrs, crouching in front of me.

I bite down on the scream trying to force its way out of my throat. The air rushes in and out of my lungs at an alarming rate, almost choking me. I scoot backward, needing to get as far away from him as possible. Everything in my body screams danger.

He lets out a disturbing laugh and grabs my chin forcefully. "I can't believe it; now I can go ahead with my plan," he declares. The way the Alpha looks at me makes me extremely uncomfortable. "You are going to be a good little slut, aren't you?" My eyes narrow at the degrading name he calls me; no one has ever talked to me like that.

"No, leave me alone," I whisper, trying to show my defiance but failing miserably.

He narrows his eyes at me, then drops my chin with a flick of his wrist and slaps me across the face. The sting of the slap doesn't get a chance to register before my father growls and lunges at the Alpha, but Scarface tackles him to the ground and grabs him by the throat, looking up at his leader.

The Alpha nods, and Scarface rips my father's throat out, then turns to my mother and kills her swiftly.

I let out a howling scream at the sight of my parents in front of me, uncontrollable tears streaming down my face. The Alpha laughs viciously and grabs me around the waist, hurling me off the floor and walking out of my childhood home.

CHAPTER ONE

TYLER

"What do you mean the event planner can't make it today?" I grit through my teeth to the person on the other side of the phone as I listen to yet another problem. "Well, sort it out, Sebastian! I don't care if you can't find him. Sort. It. Out."

I throw my phone on my desk, not bothering to hang up. This fucking festival is going to be the death of me, I swear. I need everything to be perfect. It's what everyone expects from an Alpha. I sigh, *an Alpha King*, I remind myself. I roll my eyes and let out a growl.

The Blood Moon Festival is an annual occurrence for all the packs on the West Coast. It celebrates the changes we've all had to go through, and what we've had to endure to get to where we are today—and the peace created between all our packs almost 150 years ago.

My family was at the forefront of the peace treaty, because we had evolved to where our wolves weren't separate beings anymore. They still have the ability to influence our thoughts and actions, but we are one with our wolves, which means the shift doesn't control us.

After the treaty was signed, the heads of each pack elected my great-grandfather King of all Alphas. I took over from my father about five years ago when he unexpectedly died from a heart attack.

The death of my father is still difficult to deal with. My mother feels that I need to talk to someone about my grief. I laugh to myself bitterly. I'm the fucking Alpha. I don't need to talk to anybody. I just need to deal with it.

I furrow my brow and scold myself inwardly. How the fuck did my thought process go from the festival to me dealing with my damn feelings. "I fucking hate this time of year," I mutter aloud as I pace my office floor. I walk over to my desk and grab my phone—no news yet from Kayden and the setup at the festival grounds. I brush my hair out of my face. I fucking need a haircut, but it will have to wait.

I unlock my phone and text Kayden. Nothing. I sigh, gritting my teeth.

Why is it so difficult for this fucking pack to answer me? I know I'm not one of the most patient people out there, but that's how I am. You can't call me "people" though. I'm a werewolf-vampire hybrid. My parents fell in love illegally—my mother being a hybrid herself and my father a wolf. Vampires and werewolves were never allowed to fall in love: it was against the laws of our world, not to mention lethal, since someone would kill them if it happened. The case with my parents was unique since hybrids were considered an abomination; now, you get more hybrids than you think. Yet another lovely thing added to this peace treaty and the festival. ACCEPTANCE.

I sit at my desk, trying to calm my nerves but mostly my temper. I close my eyes, rub my hand over my face, and take a deep breath.

Knock, knock, knock.

"Enter," I grit through my teeth, my hand still covering my face.

The door opens, and Layla enters my office. Layla is my sister and the mate of my Beta, Kayden. Layla is a few inches shorter than me, with shoulder-length blonde hair and always a witty smile on her face. "Aww, look at the grumpy wolf," she teases. I growl at her irritably, and she laughs at me.

"What do you want, Layla?" I say, forcing myself to sound not as irritated as I feel. I don't have time for this.

"Kayden just texted me," she says, her voice still sounding playful as she sits in one of the chairs in front of my desk. "He said he is still busy at the festival grounds; there are a few hiccups."

"Great, just fucking great," I growl again, slamming my fists on my desk as I stand. "I'm going over there to handle this shit myself. Why is everybody so incompetent today?" I yell, as I storm out of my office.

KAYDEN

The grounds surrounding the Lunar Packhouse still amaze me each time I come here. They're bathed in rays of sunshine, and the fields are green as far as the eyes can see. The landscape looks like someone painted it; with the diversity of the hills as it rises and falls, it almost looks like it's breathing. The most beautiful forest is at the edge of the open field, whatever side you look. We are secluded, and our location is perfect because there isn't much place to hide when trying to attack the Packhouse.

Once a year, with every rising blood moon, we have this festival to ensure every pack that's a part of our treaty is happy, and if there are any problems, we sort them out before the week is out. Admittedly, I wouldn't say I like this time of year. All the different packs that will be in our territory grind my gears. I hate formal gatherings. They're stiff and uncomfortable. It screws with my peace of mind, and I'd much rather take the serenity of it all.

Shoving my hands in my pockets, I huff out an irritable sigh. I'm strolling along the outlined path towards the area where we will raise the tents and set up for the coming week. The festival starts tonight, and I'm responsible for ensuring everyone else does their job.

"Ugh," I groan again, pulling my hands over my face in frustration. Tyler will be here any minute, and heaven forbid something is out of place. The man is a bloody hound regarding events like these. Everything must be in order. Every detail needs to be perfect, or else it drives him insane.

"Yo, Logan!" I call to one pack member, who's busy untangling massive heaps of rope. The frown on his face shows that this task is getting to him. "Please tell me that the main tent and its necessary equipment are already raised and sorted out?" I expectantly ask, when he looks up at me eventually.

The guy looks confused and scratches his head. "I thought Eddy was in charge of that assignment."

"Oh, for fuck's sake." Why the fuck am I saddled up with this shit. I walk over to where the main tent is supposed to stand with fleeting hope, but just as I thought, the pile of material is lying on the ground. Less than fifteen hours remain before this bloody festival starts, and the main tent is nonexistent.

"Where the fuck is Eddy?" I ask Logan. "Alpha Tyler is on his way, and this shit isn't near ready!"

"Kayden!" Tyler's deep disappointment is evident in his voice as he approaches. "Not on my way, buddy, already here."

"Great!" I roll my eyes, huffing out a sigh. *Here we go.*

"Alpha!" Eddy squirms. "W-we are almost done, I swear-"

"Pathetic idiot, just shut your mouth and do your damn job, then I won't have to deal with this. Fuck." Tyler gives him a dismissive look and walks toward me. "How's everything going here?" he asks, the anger in his voice evident.

"Well, as you can see, everything is standing except for the main tent." I gesture towards the pile of folded material on the ground.

Tyler looks around at the already standing smaller tents, then he eyes the material on the ground, and you can practically see the vein in his neck throb. "Why the fuck is this taking so long?" he grits through his clenched jaw, the muscle ticking. "Didn't we establish everyone's role in this?" he yells, looking at all the pack members nearest him. "Who's in charge of raising this tent?"

Silence.

"Really, do I have to ask again?" he asks venomously, his hands balling up in fists, knuckles turning white. "KAYDEN!" Tyler bellows, as his eyes turn red and his canines elongate.

Jeez, temper, temper, I think to myself. "Tyler, calm down, man. We will sort this out," I say, unfazed.

Tyler takes a few deep breaths, and his eyes and canines return to their usual color and size. He roughly rakes his hand through his hair and stares at me. "I can't handle this shit now, man. You know how the Alphas of the other packs can get. I am not in the mood for their criticism."

"I know. I'm also not in the mood for their shit. Especially Jace. That guy makes me want to gnaw on my own wrists." I roll my eyes, my tone flat and laced with irritation.

Tyler chuckles and rubs a hand on the back of his neck. He closes his eyes and sighs heavily. "Tell me about it. Please sort this shit out. I'll see you at the house."

Tyler turns on his heel and walks off. Pack members move—or rather, scatter—out of his way. That man needs to get a hold of his temper.

CHAPTER TWO

ABBYGAIL

I wake up on the cold cell floor in the basement. "Ouch." I touch my side, and it stings. I'm confused for a few seconds before remembering where I am and what happened. "Shit." I breathe out. My neck feels wet when I touch the area, making me wince.

The fucking bastard marked me. *Again*. Grunting, I try to push myself up from the floor. I yelp as I push on my hand, and it shoots pain through my whole body. Fuck, he must have broken my wrist.

It's hard to take count of all my injuries since there is little to no light in the basement. Jace was in one of his torturous moods again. I try to remember the details from what happened earlier, but my head hurts so fucking bad and bile rises in my throat.

Being awake is tiresome, so I scoot backward on my ass, using my one good hand. Every movement makes me bite my tongue to keep from crying out; I just want to lean my head and body against the wall. I need the stability of it to keep me from throwing up. When I finally rest against the wall, the basement door squeaks open, making me squint as the light hits my face.

It's hard to determine who is at the door, so I close my eyes since the squinting isn't helping my throbbing head. Jace probably isn't done with me. I'm exhausted, and my body aches too much to care.

Someone hurries to my cell door, and I slowly open my eyes to see Julia standing on the opposite side. Julia is Jace's mate and the only one who ever shows me an ounce of sympathy and care. She is short, with mahogany brown hair and hazel-colored eyes.

She fumbles with the keys and unlocks the gate. "Fuck, Abby, look at you," Julia curses and approaches me slowly. She kneels beside me and places a bottle of water at my mouth. I take a sip and wince. Shit, my lip is busted. I take another sip and another, this time more. I didn't realize I was so thirsty.

"J-Julia…w-what are you doing-" I cough and wince again, grabbing my side with my uninjured hand. I groan and try again. "What are you doing here?" Fuck, it even hurts to talk. "If Jace finds y-"

"Shh, please, just listen," she whispers so low I can barely hear her. "Jace is on his way down here; please don't antagonize him. His mood is particularly dark, and I think something is happening, but I'm not sure what. He's especially pissed off at you."

"You weren't there last night, were you?" I scoff.

She looks at me, confusion clear on her face. Of course, Julia wasn't there. Jace likes to make it known that he doesn't care for Julia by his side, so he deliberately excludes her. Mate or not, Jace does not care. Sure, Julia is less likely to be beaten to a pulp when he loses his mind—but hey, that's why he has me. If he craves violence and an outlet for said violence, he has someone he takes it out on. So, when is Jace *not* pissed at me? I don't even have the strength to last through another one of his beatings, let alone antagonize him.

"Please, Abby, just keep your eyes on the ground and don't say anything," she pleads. She knows precisely what Jace is capable of.

I nod, and she gets up quickly. Moving out of the cell, Julia locks the gate behind her and hurries out of the basement. As soon as the basement door shuts, I let out a strained sigh. Shit, I'm so bloody tired. I lower myself to the floor and close my eyes, the earlier events coming to my mind in vivid images:

The ballroom was full of people, so beautifully decorated, everybody dressed nicely. The theme was gold and black. Chandeliers hung from the intricate ceiling. Candles lit everywhere. Soft music played in the background. I would find it uniquely beautiful if I wasn't held here against my will. Jace liked to flaunt everything he owned.

I made my way through the people standing around, talking, laughing, and enjoying themselves with a tray in my hand. The flimsy waiter's outfit Jace made me wear made me so uncomfortable. The damn thing barely covered my ass, let alone my boobs. I hated these events; I hated being treated like a slut. I was one of those things Jace liked to flaunt.

Now and then, I felt some asshole grab my ass. Of course, I could say nothing and do absolutely nothing, as I was a slave and an Omega to the Timber pack. Jace's pack. I sneered inwardly as I thought of how I got to be here. Jace kidnapped me from my home six years ago, killing my parents in front of me.

I must keep out of my head, or I'm going to get in trouble, I thought to myself. I was expected to smile and wait on everybody there. If the guests wanted to touch, they could. I guess I should be glad that that's all they were allowed to do. Jace was very possessive, although I wasn't his mate. I hated his guts.

A shiver ran down my spine, as if my body tried to warn me. I turned and found Jace watching me. I lowered my eyes at once. I didn't want to give him a reason to harm me. I shifted the tray to my other hand and moved through the crowd again.

As I passed a group of highly respected pack members, I heard them talking about me. "I don't even know why Jace lets the vermin touch our food and drink," a woman with a remarkably high tight ponytail, dressed in a sleek black dress, said, as she eyed me and took a sip of her champagne.

"Veronica, really. What do you expect a slave's job to entail?" the man opposite Veronica said while laughing. He was short, with a receding hairline, and not one of the fittest pack members, if you catch my drift.

I pulled at the silver collar on my neck, on display for everyone to see my status. I lowered my eyes as they laughed, and I turned around quickly. I needed air. I couldn't listen to them talk for one more second. As I turned around with my tray full of champagne, I slammed straight into Jace and Owen.

Everything happened in slow motion. I watched as the liquid in the champagne glasses toppled over and spilled all over Jace's shirt and Owen's pants. The glasses fell from my tray and smashed on the ground.

"Alpha J-Jace, B-Beta O-Owen, I-I'm so sorry, p-please forgive me," I trembled as I tried to apologize, and I dropped to my knees and started to clean up the mess I'd made. To my absolute horror, I heard those entitled bastards behind me laugh, and the next moment, a roar rang through the ballroom.

Jace bent down and grabbed the front of the collar around my neck. He wrenched it upwards, and I could feel it cut into my skin. He forced me to look up at him, but I kept my eyes down. I don't dare look at him.

"YOU CLUMSY PEACE OF SHIT!!" he screamed at me, "YOU TRY TO EMBARRASS ME IN FRONT OF MY PACK!" He slapped me so hard I tasted blood. "Take her to the basement," he snarled to Owen before he threw me to the ground.

"With pleasure." Owen grabbed me by my hair and pulled me up to him. "Come on, sweetheart, time for some fun," he said with a sickening grin. That grin and excitement in his voice made me tremble, and I felt my chest constrict with fear. He dragged me out of the ballroom and down to the basement, throwing me onto the cell floor, and slammed the door shut behind me.

Shit, shit, shit. I've done it now. My whole body started to shake more as I heard the basement door open again.

JACE

The ball is in full swing, and I am enjoying it. Everything is as I want it to be. *This is what a gathering is supposed to look like*, I think to myself with a smirk. They respect me: on the other hand, I force their respect, but who cares?

"What's so funny?" I hear Owen, my Beta, ask.

I look at him out of the corner of my eye. "Just liking that I have the most respect of all the packs."

"Hmm, I like the way you're thinking," he says, evil glinting in his eyes. "It's so much fun enforcing said respect."

A smile stretches across my face at his statement. "That's exactly right."

"Speaking of respect," Owen says. "What do you think the festival will be like this year?"

"Ugh, I *really* don't fucking care, Owen. That piece of shit Alpha King's time is limited," I sneer.

Owen looks at me, intrigued now. "Oh yeah, what do you have planned?"

"Still working on it. I'll fill you in later." I dismiss Owen, having spotted Abbygail in the crowd.

I zone out as I see her walking around in that tiny nonexistent shitty outfit I made her wear. I love humiliating her. She does not need to know her worth. My mind suddenly goes to the prophecy I overheard about six years ago, and it makes my hair stand on end. I know if it's to come true, I will be fucked.

I see some of the men grab her ass, and it turns me on, fuck I love to share.

Abbygail turns and sees me looking at her, and she casts her eyes down at once. *Good slut, just as I taught you.*

She moves away quickly, weaving her way into the crowd of wolves surrounding her. I laugh out loud, turn to Owen, and say, "Let's go have some fun with our little slave." The smile creeping on his face is priceless.

Making our way through the different groups gathered around the room, we eventually spot Abbygail, where she's serving a high-ranking wolf in my pack. His eyes are glued to her breasts. This certainly won't do. I quicken my step, and just as I want to reach out to grab her, she turns without warning and smashes into me and Owen.

All the champagne on the tray she is carrying spills on my dress shirt and all over Owen's pants. Laughter starts to ring out, and I am livid. A thunderous roar leaves my chest, and the whole ballroom is immediately quiet. She starts to tremble, and her stuttering apology is driving me insane. "YOU CLUMSY PIECE OF SHIT," I scream at her, "YOU TRY TO EMBARRASS ME IN FRONT OF MY PACK!"

I want to wring her neck for disrespecting me in front of everyone. I pull back my hand and slap her across the face. Abbygail yelps, and before she has time to right herself, I grab the front of her collar and force her face up to me. Lucky for her, she keeps her eyes down. She's going to pay for this.

"Take her to the basement," I snarl to Owen. That evil smile from earlier spreads across his face as he drags her out of the ballroom by her hair.

I look around, and everybody staring at me or in my direction looks away so quickly you will swear I burned them with my eyes. "Well, either you enjoy the rest of the party, or you get the fuck out!" I grab a napkin to clean off the mess on my shirt. The music starts playing again, and everybody continues their business.

"Alpha Jace, it's so nice of you to join us tonight. We utterly enjoy these prestigious gatherings you plan," Veronica coos as she seductively places her hand on my chest. In normal circumstances,

I would enjoy this behavior and praise, but now my thoughts are only on how I will make that stupid slut pay for what she did.

"Now is unfortunately not the time for this shit, Veronica." She looks taken aback, but I don't give a fuck of what she feels. I have things to do. I turn on my heel and storm out of the ballroom.

I walk into the basement where Abbygail is. She is sitting in the farthest corner of the cell with her legs pulled up to her chest and her arms tightly folded around her, trembling. I can't help but get turned on again as I see her so pathetic. I unlock the cell door and step in, all actions meticulously slow. I am deliberately taking my time. She tries to push herself back to move as far away from me as possible, but that won't work. There is nowhere to go, and that thrills me.

"Well, well. Who has been a bad slut?" I ask slowly, my voice dark while I stalk towards her. Her breathing becomes shallow and strained, and I can smell the fear radiating from her. The smile that stretches on my face is terrifying, if I have to say so myself.

"P-Please sir, it w-" she tries to apologize again, but I grab her by her hair and pull her off the ground.

Abbygail yelps when I yank her up, her pain sending enjoyable shivers over my skin, and I snarl in her ear, "You need to keep your fucking mouth shut, little slut. You would not want to anger me even more, would you?"

I move my free hand to her pretty collared neck. Fuck, I feel myself getting hard as I stroke her neck, and I see the goosebumps I leave on her flesh. "Look at this pretty neck and my mark I left here," I say, sliding my finger down and circling the fading mark. "It's not as visible as I want it. Let's fix that, shall we?" I feel her shiver, and I snicker.

I lower my mouth to her neck and bite into the flesh of the existing mark again. It hurts more each time you mark a wolf that's *not* your mate; it leaves the mark prominent, which is exactly what I want. It's an old tale, and no one is exactly sure where and when it started, but the legend goes that the Elders, at the beginning of our existence, placed a curse on the mating mark. You are only allowed to mark *your* mate, and only once. If you mark anyone other than that, you cause them extreme pain, which could kill them—especially if you keep marking them, making the consequences that follow pretty severe.

This was to prevent males from marking females for their taking and to prevent fighting when one male marked another's female before the mate bond set in.

I, in particular, don't really care that Abbygail belongs to another, because I will claim her as mine no matter how many times I have to mark her.

She screams and tries to push me away, knowing I've ruined her for a future mate. The more I mark her, the less her chances will be that *when* she finds a mate, they will want her.

"You are *mine*, to do with as I please. Do you understand?" I growl, making her whimper again, but she doesn't answer me.

I throw her to the ground and kick her in the ribs when she hits the floor. She lets out a cry of pain, which fuels me. I kick her again, this time hearing bones crack. I bend down, grab the front of her collar, and yank her up again.

"I think this isn't tight enough, don't you think, little slut," I state flatly, and she shakes her head at me, imminent fear in her eyes. A cackle leaves my throat, and I spin her around and push her forcefully against the wall.

She tries to fight me as she pushes away from the wall. I push her back harder this time, take her wrist, and twist it behind her back. *SNAP.* I hear the bones break in her wrist, making her scream again. I lift my head, let it fall back, take a deep breath, and close my eyes as her scream rings through the basement. I can't keep the delighted smile from my face even if I wanted to. I grab the collar and make it tighter.

"P-Please, Alpha Jace, it's hard to breathe," she gasps, barely above a whisper.

My anger gets the best of me, and I spin her around and slap her again. "Did I give you permission to speak?"

Abbygail shakes her head and winces as I grip her hair again, tighter this time. The pleasure I get from dominating Abbygail is indescribable. If I can break her before she meets her destined mate, that will make things so much easier.

"If. You. *Ever*. Disrespect. Me. Again," I sneer through gritted teeth, "The consequences will be much worse. DO YOU UNDERSTAND?" She nods, and I let go of her hair. She falls to the ground, and I storm out of the cell, locking it behind me.

If I don't leave now, I will surely kill her.

CHAPTER THREE

TYLER

"Layla!" I call out to my sister. "LAYLA!!" Where could she be? I grit my teeth in frustration. She's never nearby when you need her, but let something happen that you do not want anybody to know; Layla will be the first one there.

Entering the Packhouse, I walk through the halls, searching for her. "Really?!" I throw my hands in the air, feeling exasperated. I find myself in the middle of the mansion's west wing, turning to look down each hallway. *I give up.* I make my way back to my office.

"You called, brother." Layla's voice comes from behind me, and when I turn to look at her, she smiles lovingly as she leisurely walks up to me. I sigh heavily and frown at her.

"Where were you?"

"Here and there," she answers, sounding mischievous. She folds her arms before her, the smile never leaving her face. "What can I do for you?"

"Why do you think I always need something when I call you?" I ask, feeling annoyed.

"You never just call me to chit-chat, Ty. It's not in your nature," she says with a raised eyebrow. "What do you need?"

I stare at her for a few seconds, unable to argue with her reasoning. "The main tent isn't raised yet, and the packs will be here in a few hours. The damn caterer is missing, and there are a few things I need to sort out before this festival starts," I sigh. "I need you to—please—sort out the catering. Kayden will sort out the grounds and the tents, but I cannot be at seven places simultaneously."

Layla bursts out laughing, and I find myself feeling extremely irritated by her action. "What the fuck is so funny?" I growl at her, my eyes narrowing.

"Nothing, noth-" Layla's bent over, wheezing.

What the fuck is so funny? "Layla," I grind out, my jaw ticking. "You are getting on my last nerve."

"Oh, calm down, sour wolf," she says, wiping the tears from her face, still laughing. "It's just that you always scold me when I try to help you, and now you sound so desperate."

Fighting the urge to snap at her, I close my eyes, taking a few deep breaths as I try to rein in my temper. "Fine, don't help. I'll sort it out myself," I say slowly and turn to walk off.

Layla grabs my arm. "Oh, come on, Ty, it was only a little joke. Maybe you should try to laugh a little. That temper of yours is getting out of hand."

I just stare at her. "Are you going to help or not?"

"You know I will always help you," she scoffs.

"Thanks." I give her a small smile and walk off before she can say anything else to flare up my temper again.

I walk into my office, and Kayden is waiting for me. Kayden and I have been friends for so long that I can't even remember a time he wasn't by my side.

He is a big guy—not as tall as me, but almost. He has long dark hair and a full beard. Tattoos cover his left arm completely. He could have been a badass biker—if he wasn't a wolf. He always wears ripped jeans and T-shirts, no matter the occasion. Layla must nag his ear off for him to dress "appropriately," as she puts it. I, on the other hand, don't care, and usually dress more or less the same.

I was thrilled when I found out he was Layla's mate. I obviously had to ensure he understood that his body would disappear if he ever hurt her.

"Hey, Ty," he says, looking at something on his phone as I walk past him.

"And?"

"Hello Kayden, how's your day been?" he says sarcastically. "Well, thanks for asking Tyler. It's been a rough day, but I pushed through, and I triumphed." He punches his fist in the air.

I glower at him and huff. "Don't push me, Kayden. I'm already struggling to keep my temper at bay."

Kayden lets out a snort and rolls his eyes at me. I shake my head and look at him expectantly. "Do I need to ask you again?"

"You are insufferable, Tyler. Do you know that?" He looks at his phone again before tucking it in his jeans pocket. "Yeah, everything is sorted out. The main tent is up, and everything is ready."

"Great." I huff a sigh of relief. One less thing to worry about. "What time are the packs arriving?"

"Around 6 pm, I think," Kayden says as he checks his watch.

This is going to be a long fucking week. I want it over with. Some of the Alphas will stay in our Packhouse, which makes me extremely uncomfortable. I know there has been peace and trust for a long time, but something isn't sitting well with me. I have this nagging feeling something is at play.

Fuck, I can't go around suspecting people, and there is no proof that something is wrong.

"Hey, Kayden," I say as Kayden is leaving my office. "Keep your eyes open this week. I have a feeling we will need to be on our feet. So just a heads up." Kayden frowns and gives me a confused look. "I'm not sure what it is," I tell him, "but I have this nagging feeling something is amiss."

He stares at me for a few more seconds before he gives me a nod and then leaves my office. I sit back in my chair, cover my face with my hand, and rub my forehead. I hope everything will run smoothly this week.

CHAPTER FOUR

ABBYGAIL

The creaking of the cell door wakes me, and I jump when the door slams shut again. I don't know precisely when I fell asleep, but it wasn't a good night's rest. Deliberately slow, heavy footsteps echo in the cell, getting louder as they move toward me. I lie completely still, not daring to open my eyes. *Please don't let this be another punishment session*, I plead inwardly.

A hand grips around my neck, pulling me up from the floor. I gasp as the pain from my ribs and broken wrist shoots through my body. Shit, every part of my body hurts, and if it isn't enough that the damn collar tied around my neck is to its limits—I can barely breathe, and this asshole isn't gentle with his grip on my neck.

"Ah, the little slut is waking up, I see." I hear the voice, and my body starts to tremble at once. I can't bear to open my eyes. Fuck, it's Owen, and I know what's coming. I hate when they see me tremble or my body reacts without permission. I don't want to give them the satisfaction to see me scared, but it can only take so much. "I haven't had my turn with you yet, sweetheart, and I look forward to it."

I gasp, trying to drag air into my lungs as his grip tightens around my neck, and I feel a slight pinch on my arm. *Shit, shit, shit.* I'm panicking now, which only makes the poison spread faster.

"P-Please, Beta Owen. P-Please don't do this. I'm so s-sorry. I-It won't happen again," I plead through gasps of limited air, but he ignores me and injects me with wolfsbane again. With the amount of wolfsbane running through my veins, my senses aren't working like they should. Sometimes, I can't believe that I'm still breathing.

"First, we need to make sure this pesky healing of yours doesn't work," he says as I scream, the wolfsbane burning its way through my body. He throws his head back and laughs maliciously, a sound which I have become used to. I know my pleading will do nothing, but I still try every time. Maybe, just maybe, this time he will leave me be.

He looks at me, and I can feel the evil radiating from his body, see it behind those black, dead eyes. I swear I only see a semblance of life behind them when he tortures me.

Owen pulls me closer so his mouth is at my ear, sending a shiver through my body. He reaches out, grabs my broken wrist with his free hand, and squeezes.

I try my best not to scream, but it just rips through my lungs while agonizing pain shoots through my wrist, and tears stream down my face.

"Let me hear you beg, you worthless piece of shit," he sneers in my ear. I can't think straight, and it will be better if he just kills me now.

"P-Pl-" I can't even finish the word as the pain becomes unbearable.

He throws me to the ground, and I scream again as the pain in my side comes to make itself known. I gasp for air, to breathe through the pain, but it's becoming difficult. I see black spots as my vision blurs, which isn't good. Owen won't be overly impressed if I pass out now. That will mean more punishment when I regain consciousness. Everything is hazy. I can't hear him speak through the fog I'm trying to fight in my head.

"Get on your fucking knees!" I barely hear his command.

I struggle to focus, pulling on the damn collar. Owen fists a handful of my hair and he yanks me onto my knees.

With his free hand, he unbuckles his belt, his other hand still in my hair and holding me in place.

"N-No, please, no, please-" I struggle against his hold.

"OWEN!" The voice ringing out in the basement makes Owen stop. "WHAT THE FUCK ARE YOU DOING?"

Owen growls and lets go of my hair, and I fall on my ass.

He fastens his belt, and the creepiest grin spreads on his lips when he turns around and greets Julia. "Luna Julia, I was just seeing to her injuries. She has a broken wrist, and this bite looks quite nasty."

"I bet you were," Julia sneers at him. I can hear the disgust in her voice. "Well, you can leave now. Abbygail needs to get cleaned up. We are leaving in a few hours."

I have never felt so grateful for Julia in my life. She just saved me from that bastard and his disgusting "play time," as he calls it. I don't have the strength for this anymore.

Owen unlocks the cell door and walks out of the basement past Julia, giving her a smirk. "See you in a few, little slut," he says without looking at me.

Julia practically runs to my side when Owen's footsteps die out, worry plastering her face. "Abby, oh fuck, come on, let's get you out of here," she says, as she takes in my appearance.

I get up slowly, with the help of Julia, and limp out of the basement towards the bathroom area. I don't even want to look at myself in the mirror. "Where-" I wince as I ask Julia where we're going. Don't get me wrong, I will go fucking anywhere so I don't need to be in that basement.

"Abby, please, don't talk. Let's get you cleaned up." After a few seconds, she looks around to ensure someone isn't eavesdropping and whispers, "It's the Blood Moon Festival at the Lunar pack. We need to get you ready. Jace wants to take you with us this time. Fuck knows why, but I didn't see the need to piss him off more."

I nod in agreement and hobble alongside Julia. I must stop a few times along the way, the pain unbearable for one, and I need to catch my breath.

"That bastard." Julia fumes after I stop for the umpteenth time to catch my breath. I look at her, confused. We all know Jace is a bastard, but that isn't new. It's a redundant statement if you ask me. "He tightened the collar, didn't he?"

I just nod to her, not having anything else to say since she already knows the answer.

"Don't worry, I'll fix it as soon as we get in the bathroom."

Terror rips through me at the thought of Jace seeing my collar loosened. He will lose his mind, and then we both will get into trouble. "No, ple-" I groan. "No, please, leave it. I don't want to get you in trouble."

"Abby, I can't leave that fucking thing around your neck so tight. Your lips are starting to turn blue. If I must, I'll take my punishment, but this is enough."

I turn to her, tears building in my eyes, squeezing her hand in thanks.

Taking in the image in the mirror in my room, I don't even recognize myself anymore. My cheek is red and swollen. My busted lip is so sensitive that it bleeds again when I make the slightest movement with my mouth. My wrist is broken, and at least three ribs, *I think*.

My side looks like a deer trampled me. The bloody mark on my neck just below the collar looks like an inflamed mess.

Julia has done an excellent job cleaning me up, but nothing will heal after being injected with wolfsbane. Luckily, the bruising on my face isn't as bad as the other times. They can be real brutal shitheads if they want to be.

Julia wipes my wounds slowly and carefully, cleaning them; when she gets to the bite, she sighs, the sound so deep and remorseful, and I see pity in her eyes.

"I'm ruined, Julia. No wolf will want me." The tears are running freely now as she keeps wiping the dried blood from my neck.

"Shhh, Abby, don't say that…" Julia trails off, her own voice wobbling. She can't even finish her sentence, knowing the chances of a wolf wanting a marked mate are slim.

I shake my head slowly, trying to rid myself of the memory. I don't need pity; I need to get out of here, but the all-looming question arises again. It's the one that breaks my spirit every time. *How?*

I look down at my wrist, now strapped in a wrist brace. This will be a problem when Jace wants me to wait on him and the pack. I'll just have to manage; I can't stand another beating. Julia has loosened the collar just a little, hoping I can breathe better and Jace will not notice.

I pull at it again, this fucking thing is still so tight—but at least I can almost breathe now. I roll my eyes. *Way to see the bright side, Abby.*

Okay, enough staring at my broken and bruised body. I can't put this off any longer. Grabbing my top from the bed, I pull it on with difficulty. Next, my pants; this action proved less demanding and not as painful. I take another glance at my reflection in the mirror. *Let's get this fucking week over with.*

Leaving the room, I hastily make my way to the front door to wait for Jace and the pack like I was instructed just after Julia had finished cleaning me up.

Staring out of the open door, I wonder what the other packs are like. It's the first time Jace is taking me out of the confinement of this Packhouse, and honestly, I'm a little excited.

I'm ripped from my thoughts when I hear Jace, Owen, and the rest of the pack approach. I lower my head and place my hands behind my back like I was taught. This action isn't sitting well with my wrist, which is throbbing in protest. I grit my teeth and try to keep my composure.

"You better be sure that everything is packed and ready to go because, so help me, if you missed something again, there will be hell to pay!" Jace's demanding voice booms through the halls.

"Yeah, pretty much. It looks like there's one more plaything to pack," Owen says as he stands in front of me now, his breath warm on my face, and I have to keep from flinching.

He places his finger under my chin and forces my head up. My back goes rigid; he enjoys toying with me like this, and he gets a rise from the thought of punishing me when I fight to keep my eyes from meeting his.

But I keep my eyes lowered and stay as still as I can.

"Come on, sweetheart, give us a little kiss," he coaxes and drops his head to kiss me.

"Owen." I hear Jace snarl. "Back off, now." Owen watches Jace for a few seconds and then drops his finger from my chin. A sigh of relief leaves my lips before I can stop it, and I cringe inwardly. *Fuck.*

Jace pushes Owen out of the way and comes to stand in front of me, scowling. I just know he is because I've felt that scowl a million times. He hooks his finger in my shirt collar and plays with the fabric.

"Tsk, Tsk. I don't give you these so you can hide them, little slut," he says, ripping my shirt in one swift movement, exposing the mark and the collar around my neck. "Everybody needs to see that you are a slave who is marked." Jace trails his fingers over the mark before turning and walking out of the Packhouse, saying over his shoulder, "Come on then, we have a festival to attend."

CHAPTER FIVE

LAYLA

Walking into the kitchen and noticing the buzzing of people getting the food and drinks ready makes me extremely happy. I found the event planner, who was freaking out over all my brother's demands. I convinced him to get his act together and effectively avoid dealing with his Alpha, especially if said Alpha was under pressure. Next, I sat with the chef to review the menu for the week and any other concerns he may have.

I take out my phone and unlock it to text my overbearing brother. He *really* is a sour wolf.

> Ty, everything is sorted out with the caterer. The chef has all the details for the menu for the week and the food got sorted for the rest of the packs. You can chill now.

It wasn't even five seconds, and my phone pings.

TY: Thanks

Is that it? Really? *Ugh, he drives me up the wall.* I don't think anything will ever soften that man's heart. He is too set in his ways. It got worse after our father died. Personally, I believe Tyler has never really dealt with the pain and loss. He looked up to our father and always hung on every word our father spoke.

He only retreated further into himself when he got older and the Alpha duties got more strenuous.

My phone rings, and I'm pulled back to reality. "Hello."

"Lay." I hear Kayden's voice on the other end of the line.

"Hey, my love, how are things at the festival grounds?"

"Everything is ready, eventually. How's everything on your end?" Kayden asks, but something in his tone is off.

"What's wrong, love?" I ask, sounding concerned.

"Tyler is worrying me. He told me to keep an eye open this week. He says he has a bad feeling."

"Ugh, fuck." I sigh. My brother is usually always right about things like this. Still, I hope it's just his nerves and the fact that he is overworked that makes him paranoid.

"I know," Kayden says.

"Well, the best thing is to do as he says and keep your eyes open. Hopefully, nothing will happen, and he is paranoid from a work overload," I say, changing course and walking towards my brother's office. "I'll see what I can find out, see what is bugging him."

"Thanks, Lay. Let me know."

"Love you," I say as I reach my brother's office, knocking on the door.

"You too," Kayden says before disconnecting the call.

Nothing. I knock again, this time a little harder. "WHAT?" Tyler bellows from behind the door.

Great, I was hoping (to no avail) that his temper and mood would improve when everything was going according to plan—but it clearly hasn't.

I push open the door and see him sitting at his desk. His hair is messy, and papers are strewn about his desk. "Ty, what are you still doing in here?" I ask, exasperated.

He looks up at me as if I just threw shit at him, asking such a stupid question. "What does it look like I'm doing?" he says—rather calmly, to my surprise.

"You are supposed to get ready for the Alphas and their packs' arrival. That's what it should look like. You look like shit." I cross my arms in front of my chest and tap my foot. He glances at my tapping foot and slowly up at me before returning to work.

Ugh, I love my brother to death, but he knows how to piss me off. "Tyler!" I say, raising my voice somewhat. "You need to shower right now and get dressed for this bloody event."

Silence.

"Tyler, don't make me drag you out of here!"

He snorts and puts down his pen. "As if *you* can drag me out of here, or anywhere for that matter."

"Don't be snarky with me, Mr. Big Alpha man," I say sarcastically. "Will you just go get ready?"

After about 45 minutes, Tyler comes back into his office. He's dressed to impress and looks less disheveled. The shower must have done him good because the scowl on his face is missing, and overall, he looks much better. Even his mood has improved.

Okay, maybe just a little, but nonetheless, it's better than nothing.

I really do have a handsome brother. He is built like a brick wall, around six foot four, with dark blond hair, broad shoulders, and ripples of toned muscle. He has the most unusual eyes: one the deepest green and the other light blue, almost white. We don't know why his eyes differ in color. Mom speculates that there must be a unique part of his hybrid nature that they thought died out along the lines and only reappeared again in Tyler since there are so many differences between her and him.

Almost any women who interact with Tyler swoon at his feet. It's funny watching them melt when he speaks, trying to get his attention by touching his arm or anything in that manner, and other times a little pathetic since he doesn't pay any of them any mind, but hey, they can't really help themselves. Most of them see the power he wields, drawing them in. Who wouldn't want to be mated to the King of all Alphas?

He loves clearing his mind by sparing with the warriors, which is good. Usually, he's out there for four to five hours a day, but since he started planning for the festival, he doesn't have the time, which adds to his frustration.

I didn't get the split gene; I'm wolf through and through, with no sign of my mother's vampire bloodline. I'm relieved I didn't because I see the shit Tyler must deal with daily. I think that's why he has such an extremely short temper. Maybe if he finds his mate one day, she will temper the beast within.

"Are you even listening?" Tyler asks, irritation prominent.

"Sorry," I giggle. "Got lost in my own thoughts again. What did you say?"

"I asked if you've heard from Kayden?"

"Oh, yeah, he's just about done with everything."

"Okay, that's a relief," he huffs, and I can see relief rolling off him.

"Speaking of Kayden," I say casually. Tyler eyes me, his brow raised, as he buttons up the last few buttons of his dress shirt. "He says you asked him to keep his eyes open this week. Is everything okay?"

Tyler throws his hands up in the air in an exasperated move. "For fuck's sake, why can't *my Beta* keep anything to himself," he says, emphasizing "my Beta."

"Oh, come on, Ty, you keep forgetting 'your Beta' is my *mate*," I scoff, making quote markings in the air with my fingers. "We don't keep secrets from one another."

"This fucking mate bond is pissing me off; that's all I know," he scowls, gritting his teeth and making his jaw tick.

"Yeah, keep saying stuff like that. When you find your mate, it will bring you to your knees. Mark my words," I laugh teasingly.

"That will never happen," he scoffs.

"What? The fact that you will find a mate or that it will bring you to your knees?" I ask, one eyebrow raised.

"Be realistic, Lay. Nothing is supposed to bring me to my knees—nothing except death," he responds, his tone dark now.

"Stop changing the subject. What's going on? Do I need to be worried?"

"Layla, I'm not sure, okay? All I know is I have this chill that keeps running down my spine, and it's making me more nervous than I would care to admit," he groans. This is truly bothering him. "Just drop it, please. I promise I will let you know if there is something to be worried about."

There's not much that can scare my brother. Sure, he loses his shit at just about anything, but this is something totally different.

"Okay, fine. Only because you made a promise," I agree as I stand and approach my brother.

I give him a peck on the cheek and walk to the door, "I'm going to go get ready."

"Hmm," he hums as he looks out the window. "You go do that."

I sigh; I just know this will be an eventful week.

TYLER

What is it with my sister? It's like she can read my damn mind. Kayden sharing everything with her does not help the situation much. I don't know why this nagging feeling keeps lingering, but it's driving me insane.

Maybe I'm just overreacting. I sigh as I close my eyes and lean with my hands on each side of the window. I don't need trouble now. This week needs to go down without a hitch. The fact that my sister can pick up on my tension is nerve-wracking. I can't place my finger on it. I just know it's tying me up in knots.

Pushing away from the window, I return to my desk and grab my phone. I hit speed dial, and the phone rings on the other side. Wouldn't it be nice if we could mind link like most of those werewolf shows? It would make my job so much easier.

"Yeah?" Kayden answers.

"So, you thought it best my sister comes and asks me what the situation is with this shit feeling that's bugging me?" I ask, slightly annoyed.

"Oh shit, that wasn't my intention, man. I swear, I'm just concerned about you. You haven't been yourself these past few weeks. Your temper is extremely short-"

"It's always fucking short, Kayden," I snap.

"Okay, shorter than normal then. The pack walks on eggshells around you. You are really scary to deal with." Kayden adds quickly, "If someone doesn't know you."

"So?!" I don't need this lecture. Fuck, what am I, *nine*? I don't need to be told off by my Beta.

"*So*," he mimics me. "How can you run a pack on fear? You need their love and loyalty, man, not their fear. They already have a fear of the fact that you're half-vampire. Your temper and attitude aren't helping the situation."

"Have I ever harmed anyone? Have I ever given them a reason to fear me?" I grit out, my rage just beneath the surface. "I'm trying my best here, Kayden, what the fuck more do you want from me!"

"Calm down, Ty, I'm talking to you as your friend, not your Beta," he cautions. I know he's only trying to help, but it's like my brain won't let the words sink in.

"Fine!" I sigh. "I can't promise anything, but I'll try to keep my temper at bay."

"That's all I'm asking, man."

"Yeah." I desperately want to change this subject. "Are you ready? The Alphas will be here in a few minutes if they aren't here already."

"Yeah, all dressed up. These fucking suit and tie events grind my gears, and you know that."

"True, but it comes with the position, Kayden, so suck it up."

"Humph," he huffs over the phone. "Well, you better get down here; some of the packs are pulling up. I'm at the front door."

"Be right there."

I disconnect the call, grab my suit jacket, and head for the front door, where Kayden is waiting to welcome the Alphas and their packs. *Let's see how this day will unfold.*

CHAPTER SIX

JACE

I smirk when we pull up to the Lunar Packhouse. This is the start of a new beginning. I can feel it.

I look over at my mate next to me. She's staring aimlessly out of the other window. Her cold demeanor toward me isn't something new. I don't know why I've been granted a mate as weak as Julia. I clench my jaw, trying to rid myself of the irritation building within. The lengths I have to go to exclude Julia from almost every major event is starting to get on my last nerve. I don't know why I keep her around. She's too caring to be a mate to an all-powerful Alpha, a soon-to-be King. Her caring and loving nature is such a weakness.

People should fear you. They will get this wild idea that you owe them if they don't. That's my opinion, and I've never been wrong. My father made sure he drilled that into my head each time he beat me within an inch of my life for trying to care for something, and I've learned that he was right—right up to the moment I ripped his throat out without an ounce of remorse.

This plan needs to go off without a hitch, and soon, I will reap the fruits of all my hard work.

I might be getting ahead of myself, but I know what I want, and Julia *will* learn to play the part. She thinks I overlooked the fact that she loosened Abbygail's collar, but I didn't. I have more pressing matters to worry about. For instance, I have the perfect trump card for overthrowing the current Alpha King.

Julia gives me a sideways glance, and I turn my gaze away from her to look out of my window as the car stops.

Following the pathway up the stairs, my eyes fall on the front door. As expected, Tyler and his bitch Beta await to greet the Alphas. The feeling of disgust overpowers the irritation, and I know, without a doubt, that I will never stoop so low. When I am in charge, there will be a change of order and how the hierarchy will follow. That will be my first order of business.

Smiling wickedly, I look down at Abbygail, who sits at my feet where she belongs: on her knees, hands in her lap, head and eyes cast down. So beautiful. My mark and her collar are visible for everyone to see through her ripped top. Did she really think I would not notice?

Well, I noticed, and I fixed it.

I reach out to take her collar and lift her head, but she flinches when my hand comes into her view. *Oh no, no, no, that is unacceptable.* "Did you just flinch at me?" Venom drips from my tone. "We will deal with this little mishap later on."

The softest whimper escape from her lips, and I laugh harshly. "You will stay in the car and wait until I send Owen to come and get you. Do you understand?"

Abbygail balls her uninjured hand into a tight fist, her hand shaking before she nods.

Her lack of manners infuriates me, and I grab her jaw harshly and force her head up. "I asked you a question, little slut. You answer me properly now."

"Yes, Master Jace," she struggles to say, her breathing coming in short, fearful bursts through her nose. A satisfied grin pulls at my mouth when she answers correctly, and I drop her face.

"Is that really necessary, Jace?" Julia asks with a sneer on her lips and disgust in her eyes.

"You want some of this treatment, *my mate*?" I say sweetly, the grin turning wicked. "I can always arrange it if you are eager to go against me."

Julia stares at me for a few seconds before exiting the car and slamming the door behind her. Rolling my eyes, I let out a frustrated growl.

I follow suit soon after, and the moment I step out, I smile broadly, inhaling the air that will soon be mine. I take in the view of the Lunar Packhouse. They've made modifications since I've been here last. The east wing was expanded, and the training grounds have been enlarged. The mansion itself is old Victorian architecture and a beautiful landmark.

Hmm, alright. I can work with this. It's a mansion on the edge of a forest—thankfully, far from any prying human eyes. Cliché, I know, right? We are werewolves, after all.

I pull on my suit jacket and fasten the button to look my best. Julia joins me on the right, and Owen stands on my left-hand side. Well, let's get the greeting part over with.

We walk up the stairs and stop directly in front of Tyler and Kayden.

I eye Kayden as he steps forward. "Good afternoon, Alpha Jace," Kayden bows his head slightly and forces a tight smile. I nod my head in acknowledgment. Why the fuck would Tyler let his Beta greet me first? *Show some respect, fuck.* I curse inwardly as I size Tyler up.

"Good afternoon, Luna Julia." This time, with the same gesture, but his smile is genuine, he takes her hand and kisses it.

She smiles slightly, then eyes me to see my reaction. *That's right, you better not look happy*, I think to myself.

I narrow my eyes as I look at Kayden. I can't react badly at this stage; he didn't show me any disrespect. Acting like nothing is wrong between us is an art we have perfected over the years. So, for now, I will continue with this act until it's time to strike.

"Beta Owen," Kayden bites out. Owen glares at him.

I turn to Tyler. "Good afternoon, Alpha King Tyler." I bow at the waist. I fucking hate to submit to this bastard. *Just wait*, I sneer inwardly. "You remember my mate and Luna from the Timber pack, Julia?" I gesture to Julia, who also bows at the waist in front of Tyler.

He just nods at me and then at Julia, no fucking emotion whatsoever in his eyes. Not saying a single word. The whole interaction is pissing me off more and more.

A growl slips through my teeth, and he quirks an eyebrow. I clear my throat. "My Beta, Owen," I say quickly, gesturing to my left. Surprise washes over me at the amount of intimidation I feel, just from that small twitch of his eyebrow.

"Welcome," Tyler finally says. "Please make yourselves at home and enjoy the festival. The Alpha meeting will start in 60 minutes at the main tent on the festival grounds. If you don't know where it is, please don't hesitate to ask Kayden or my sister, Layla, who is apparently late," he states and steps out of the way so we can enter the house. "Please follow Sebastian. He will show you where your quarters are." Tyler then gestures to his Gamma.

I nod and follow Sebastian down the hall with my entourage. As soon as we are clear from Tyler and Kayden, I beckon to Owen. "Go and fetch Abbygail from the car and bring her to your room. I will call for her later." Owen nods and turns on his heel. "Oh, and Owen, don't you dare touch her. We must make an everlasting impression tonight." I smile wickedly.

His eyes glint maliciously, that wicked smile he gets forming on his lips before he turns and walks off to do what I asked.

This is going to be so much fun!

CHAPTER SEVEN

ABBYGAIL

Silence surrounds me as I sit in the car, calming my soul. I can't remember the last time I felt at peace. Well, the nearest to peace as I will get in my situation. I don't know how long this will last, but I enjoy every moment.

The silence is disturbed by a loud growling sound, which makes me look down at my stomach. Shit, I haven't eaten in four days. My stomach growls again, and this time, I hunch over, swallowing the bile that rises in my throat. My stomach cramps heavily, and I feel lightheaded. I take deep breaths through my nose and blow them out slowly through my mouth as I try to keep from fainting.

Fainting is not an option, especially not in front of Jace or Owen. That would be catastrophic.

I frown at that stupid but very accurate thought—like it's my choice not to eat anything. I snort and laugh bitterly. Taking a few more breaths, I feel the feeling of nausea and lightheadedness fade when I hear footsteps approaching and I know my serenity is over. *Here we go.*

The door is wrenched open, and Owen stands before me. I can only see his legs and shoes, but I know it's him. I can sense it.

I frown when nothing happens after the door opens. What the hell is he waiting for? The suspense is killing me, and not to mention, I can feel his eyes burning through me.

After what feels like an eternity, he spits, "Hands!"

"N-No, please no. P-Please don't shackle my hands," I whimper.

My chest tightens, and it feels like I am going to have a panic attack. I can't stand it if my hands are tied. I can endure most of the shit they throw my way, but the fear I associate with when they restrain me is indescribable.

He lets out a deep, terrifying growl. "Don't push me, little slut. Don't you dare disobey me. I have strict orders not to touch you and find it exceedingly difficult not to. So. Do. Not. Tempt. Me." With every forced syllable, a shiver runs down my spine, and he barks out again, "Hands!"

I lift my trembling wrists to him, and he places two silver shackles around them. He tugs on them to pull me out of the car, making sure they are incredibly tight.

I yelp from the pain that shoots through my wrist, where the shackle bites into the wrist guard.

"Oh please, stop with that pathetic yelping. Come on, you're sleeping in my room," Owen announces excitedly, and I feel the bile rise in my throat again.

The claustrophobic feeling creeping around my chest is chilling. I am tied to the bedpost in Owen's room, pulling on my bindings in the hopes they wouldn't bite into my wrists so much when I hear the bedroom door open, and Julia enters the room. Looking up, I see a slight smile on her face. I smile back, looking confused when I see what she is carrying. What the hell is that supposed to be?

Julia's smile turns apologetic. "You need to put this on, Abby. Jace wants you with us at the Alpha meeting in fifteen minutes."

"What? Why?" I ask, dumbfounded. He never takes me with him anywhere. It scares him immensely that someone will see me who's not supposed to—or that my mate will see me.

The latter isn't possible, I have decided I do not have a mate. Jace decided my destiny: to be a slave to a dominant dictator with no regard for any life whatsoever.

"I have no idea, Abby. Something is happening here, and I'm not sure what, but he is planning something." She wonders as she furrows her brow.

I look at the fabric in her hands again. You have got to be kidding me. What is Jace playing at? That thing will barely cover my body. Why he likes to put me on display is beyond me. *Ugh, fuck.* I don't actually have a choice, though.

I nod, and Julia walks over and unties my hands from the bed.

I get up from the floor slowly and take the flimsy outfit from her. When I'm in the bathroom, I look down at the sheer fabric and let out a strained sigh before I put on the stupid thing. Shaking my head, I look at myself in the full-length bathroom mirror. This outfit makes me think of the one Jasmine had to wear at the end of the Aladdin animated movie, when Jaffar had captured her.

Fitting, isn't it? I think to myself.

The satin bikini top barely covers my boobs. The long satin and organza skirt hangs so low it barely covers my hips and crotch area. It has a slit that runs up to my hip. My bruised ribs are visible, as are my collar and the still-inflamed mark. I laugh to myself. More fabric will not appear from me staring at myself.

I comb roughly through my hair with the brush I found on the counter. This will have to do. It's not like I can do anything else, and you know what, I don't want to. Fuck this.

I open the bathroom door and step out into the room. Julia stares at me as she evaluates my scars and black and blue skin. She sighs. "That bastard is getting on my last nerve. I don't know his intentions, but I guess we will find out soon."

"No doubt about that," I laugh dryly as I roll my eyes.

Julia walks towards me, and my gaze falls on the chains in her hand. My eyes become vast, and I step back.

"I'm so sorry, Abby. You know what he'll do if you aren't 'properly dressed'—his words, not mine."

"I know." I nod once, letting out a shaky breath.

Closing my eyes, I bite my cheek to stop trembling as Julia shackles my wrists again. Next, she takes the silver chain and fastens the top part to the front of my collar. The bottom of the chain is secured to my shackles to keep my hands together. Another chain is attached to the front of my collar like a fucking leash.

I hate this. I hate feeling helpless. I hate this fucking pack. I hate that I am treated less than shit. I. Hate. *All of it*. My eyes sting with tears, and one rolls slowly down my cheek. Julia reaches up and wipes my tears from my face.

"I'm so, so sorry, Abby, I don't even know what to say anymore…"

I open my eyes and see the tears in Julia's eyes. She steps closer to me and hugs me softly.

"It's going to be okay, Abby, I promise," she says after a few minutes. I frown at her. How can she say that? It's *not* going to be okay. I have nowhere to go, and I have no one that will ever love me. I feel defeated. I lower my head and shake it slowly as the tears now run freely down my cheeks. "Shh, I promise you everything is going to be okay," Julia soothes when I look up at her. She smiles softly, and the determination in her eyes is unmistakable. "Okay?" she presses as she looks me dead in the eye.

I nod slowly, but I'm not getting my hopes up. They've been shattered too many times.

She wipes the tears from my face again. "Now come on, we will be late and don't want that."

Julia takes the chain from my collar and leads me out the door.

Julia walks into the Alpha meeting five minutes later, with me behind her. I keep my eyes down, but I can feel the people staring at me, especially the males of all the packs—and now the Alphas. The occasional hiss and sharp intakes of breaths plague my ears, coupled with some wolf whistles. It makes my skin crawl.

Julia leads me over to where Jace is sitting, bowing her head slightly when we reach him. "My mate," she acknowledges him, and he smiles wickedly at her.

"Luna Julia, you brought me my little pet. How sweet of you," he purrs as if he did not order her to bring me. He surely is a manipulative bastard.

Jace grabs my face with so much force I can't stop wincing. "It's so nice of you to join us, little slut," he pronounces loud enough so everyone can hear before dropping my face harshly.

Jace grabs the chain from Julia, twists it around his hand, and yanks it towards himself. I instantly stumble closer to him. I tremble again, and he only laughs at me. "On your knees, little slut," he orders.

I do as I'm told. Jace will *not* be happy if I disobey him in front of his peers.

I sink to my knees, but he keeps the chain taut, forcing my head up. I lower my eyes at once, and he throws his head back as he laughs.

All the other Alphas are just staring as he interacts with me. Some smile in approval, others show pure disgust, but no one intervenes. As much as I hate it, I know no one will say anything because Jace is one of *the* most feared Alphas. I don't know anyone else who is more feared.

As the thought takes life, a looming presence enters the tent, and everyone falls silent immediately. The scent of the unknown presence that fills my nose is overwhelming. *Hmm.* It invades my mind, and my nose lifts into the air of its own accord as I inhale the scent deeper. It smells of Old Spice and cedarwood. It's intoxicating. It fills all my senses, and I can't think straight.

I shiver, feeling goosebumps cover my skin; the presence's sweet smell and pure strength and dominance are refreshing. Jace shifts uncomfortably in his seat. I tilt my head, not understanding why his demeanor changed, and then it hits me.

Jace is highly uncomfortable, or he's afraid. He's scared of whoever is entering the tent. Well, I was so wrong. There is someone else more feared.

I smile inwardly at the thought that Jace can fear someone. It makes my heart soar. I don't even know who the presence belongs to. I am curious to see for myself, but the fear of Jace is stronger. Jace's hand holding the chain starts to shake, but only slightly, before he gets a hold of himself. It is brief, but I have seen it.

He unwinds his hand from the chain, and I can lower my head. The sting where the collar cut deeper into my neck is now screaming at me, and I can feel tiny droplets of blood there. Nothing new.

Jace moves his chair closer to the table, and I glimpse his face. He doesn't look happy and still has a hint of fear in his eyes. *Well, this is going to be interesting,* I think to myself, as the man with the absolutely intoxicating scent draws nearer.

Within seconds of the presence entering, the people start mumbling, and there is tension in the air that wasn't there before. What the hell is going on?

Owen and Jace's faces light up with pure evil joy at what's unfolding at my back.

CHAPTER EIGHT

TYLER

After we greet all the Alphas and their packs, Kayden and I make our way to my office. The Alpha meeting is in a few minutes, and we need to review a few details before starting.

"Do you have everything you need?" Kayden asks me as I make my way around my desk.

"Hmm, looks like it," I grab my folder with the agenda inside. This is going to be a long fucking night. I'm already tired, and it hasn't even started yet. I wipe my hair out of my face and groan. I forgot to get a bloody haircut again, fuck. I will get to it tomorrow.

"What do you think of Jace and his piece of shit Beta?" Kayden asks, as I rummage through some of the papers on my desk, looking for my pen.

I sigh, feeling somewhat irritated. "Jace is pushing his luck; that's what I think."

"Other than being a pain in the ass with his shitty attitude, why do you say that?" Kayden laughs.

"The fucking bastard had the nerve to growl at me." I find my pen and look at Kayden; the look on his face goes from laughing to full-blown anger.

"What?" he spits. "And you did not rip his throat out?"

I laugh at him—like, really laugh—which makes him stare at me. "You asked me to keep my temper in check, and I am trying, but I must admit it took a lot not to slam his head into the floor."

Kayden is still staring at me. "What?" I ask, confused.

"Did you just laugh at my temper tantrum?" he asks, surprise still covering his face.

"Yeah, so? I don't know what the big deal is. Can we get going? We are going to be late, and that alone is making my blood boil," I state as I roll my eyes and make my way to the door.

In fact, it is a big deal. I can't remember the last time I laughed like this. My beast feels at ease, and it's very confusing. I haven't felt like this since...

You know what? I don't think I've ever felt like this.

I shake my head to myself and look at Kayden, who places his hands in the air and shrugs. "Fine, fine. Let's get going."

Kayden and I make our way to the main tent. I am confused when I hear the wolf whistles, growls, and chattering from the tent. Why the fuck would any Alpha wolf whistle at another's mate? That kind of insult will break out into a full-blown war.

We enter the tent, and everyone goes quiet. I don't know if it's from fear or respect, but at this point, I don't really care.

I enter the tent before Kayden, moving towards my seat, when I'm stopped dead in my tracks. An unfamiliar scent hits my nose, and I inhale sharply. Kayden slams into my back in full stride and curses.

"Umph, Fuck! Ty, what the hell?"

"Can you smell that?" My voice is hoarse, unrecognizable.

Kayden sniffs the air. "No, not really. What do you smell-" he breaks off mid-sentence when he hears me hiss.

I can feel my eyes change color, and my canines elongate, pushing past my lip. I try to inhale deeply to get myself under control, but the more I inhale, the more the unknown scent fills my lungs. I grab Kayden's arm and push him in front of me. My grip on him is harder than it needs to be as my body starts to shake.

Kayden turns and looks at me, confused. I look up at him, and he sees my eyes and fangs as I pant.

"Tyler, what the fuck is happening?" he asks in a hushed tone, looking around to see if anyone can see what's happening to me.

I hunch over slightly; I am fighting this attack on my senses to the extent that it feels like I'm losing my mind. I need to get a hold of myself, or someone will think I am weak with me keeled over like this, trying to catch my breath. "F-Fuck," I grunt, forcing with everything in me to get a grip.

I manage to get a hold of my senses and straighten up, still gripping Kayden. "I don't know what's going on, but-"

The scent hits me again; this time, one word hits me like a bullet to the chest. "MATE," I growl so low my whole body vibrates.

Kayden's eyes widen, and it looks like the wind is knocked out of him. "What?" he hisses. "Where?"

I shake my head, not wanting to look around just yet. I must get my senses under control.

What the hell is happening to me? My vision clears slightly; my irises still rim red, and my fangs aren't pulling back. "Fuck," I snarl again. This really isn't the time for this, whatever *this* is.

Kayden looks around the room, confused. "I don't see any new females other than the ones mated to some of the Alphas," he says, low enough so only I can hear. "People are starting to stare, which isn't good, Ty. You need to get a grip. We can deal with this later."

I nod, letting go of his arm, and straighten my spine. I make my way to my seat. I look around, seeing the confusion on everyone's faces about what they just witnessed and my appearance.

Fortunately, no one says anything. They probably think I lost my temper. I've never been so happy to have a short temper, and that I'm known for it.

I look to the right, where Jace sits with the biggest smirk on his face. He moves his hand, and my eye catches the glimmer of the chain he's clutching. I frown, following the length of the chain, and my heart stops beating.

Attached to the chain sits the source of my sensory overload. I grip the back of my chair so hard my knuckles will pop out of my skin at any second. I visibly swallow, taking in the sight in front of me.

She sits on her knees in front of Jace, her back towards me with her head bowed and her hair hanging in front of her face. The scent coming off her smells of cherries and magnolias. The chain in Jace's hands connects to the collar around her neck. Her shackled hands are in her lap in a submissive position.

There is an angry-looking bruise on her right side over her ribs. The clothes she has on barely cover her fragile body. There are scars visible on her back from what I can only assume is whipping.

I look back up to Jace, who cocks his head at me, almost as if he is challenging me.

My hands start to shake violently, and I feel my control slipping. I must get out of here. Some fresh air may make me think more clearly. I can't attack Jace in front of all the packs. This will surely put an end to the peace treaty. "Kayden," I force out. "I need to leave. *Now*."

Kayden looks rattled, which is unlike him. He nods and addresses the room. "We are going to take a ten-minute break. When we return, we will resume the meeting."

"The damn meeting hasn't even started yet, and you need a fucking break," one of the Alphas spits at Kayden. Before I can collect my thoughts, a growl rips through my chest, and the whole tent shakes. I stalk towards the man who dares to speak.

Kayden grabs me from behind and turns me towards him, placing his arm around my neck and forcing my head down. "Ty, don't do this," he pleads through gritted teeth. "You need to calm the fuck down!"

He drags me from the tent as my body shakes from the anger. We walk—or more so, Kayden drags me—back to the house and into my office.

I rip myself from his hold and snarl at him, fangs all the way out, my eyes engulfed in red. I am *not* in control, and I can feel it slipping further away from me. Kayden holds his hands up in defense in front of him. "Ty, come on, man. Get a hold of yourself."

I growl again and lunge at him. Kayden dodges my assault and grabs his phone from his pocket. He dials a number, never taking his eyes off me. "Lay, babe. Yeah, we have a problem," he states as I snarl again, throwing a chair at him.

What the fuck is wrong with me? I have never, and I mean never, lost control like this. I struggle to rein in my temper, and I've always thought I had a good hold on it. Then it hits me: this isn't because I lost my temper; this is because my beast—the wolf inside me—is trying to get out after catching the scent of our mate.

Shit. I'm fucked. I can't let this control me, and this is only because of some fucking mate bond. I haven't even seen her face, and everything is spinning out of control. I hear the office door open and shut. "What the hell is going on in here?"

I whip my head to the person who entered the office, tilting my head; I stalk towards her, still snarling.

"Ty?" I hear her say softly. "Calm down, please," she pleads.

"Lay, be careful. I don't know if he can hear you," Kayden warns as he moves between us.

I stop in my tracks and grab my head, *fuck Tyler, you need to get a grip*. I close my eyes and fall to my knees, breathing heavily.

Layla walks around Kayden cautiously as she approaches me. Kayden holds on to her protectively, his eyes wary of me.

I let out a howl so loud the windows in my office shatter, and I drop to my hands as the last thundering sound leaves my body. My vision slowly returns, my fangs returning to their normal form.

I stay like this for a few minutes, panting.

I feel Layla's hand lightly touch my shoulder. "Ty, what the hell was that?" Catching my breath, I sit up slowly.

Kayden steps forward. "He felt the mate bond," he sighs, shoving his hands in his pockets.

Layla whips her head around to look at Kayden and then slowly back at me. "Where is she?" she nearly shrieks.

I look at her, pain and sorrow washing through me. The images of her on her knees in front of Jace play in my head repeatedly. "In the main tent," I groan, rubbing my face with my hands.

"Well, what are you waiting for? Go and get her!" Layla exclaims.

Kayden looks at Layla and shakes his head slightly. "He can't babe. The situation is… Complicated," he says somberly.

Layla frowns in confusion. "I can't see why we can't *un*complicate it. You've found your mate Ty-"

"Babe, she belongs to Jace." Kayden places his hand on Layla's shoulder.

"I don't understand. Is she Jace's mate?"

"No," I snarl, slamming my fists on the floor, feeling my beast make itself known again.

Kayden sighs heavily. "She's his slave, babe."

Layla only stares at me blankly. "Shit," she whispers, barely audible. I feel my anger build at Kayden's words, and I slam my fists on the floor again, sending a crack along the tiles.

What the fuck am I going to do?

CHAPTER NINE

JACE

I watch as Tyler and Kayden enter the tent. The next moment, Tyler stops dead in his tracks. His Beta slams into his back, Tyler's eyes turn bright red, and his fangs elongate as his nostrils flare.

So fucking predictable. The prophecy is correct: I have the Alpha King's mate.

The next thing I know, Tyler hunches over and struggles to get a hold of his senses and wolf. I've only heard legends of hybrids finding their mates and that it knocks the wind out of them.

It's ten times stronger when a hybrid meets his mate than a regular werewolf.

I am going to bring this kingdom to its knees. This is priceless. I watch as Tyler composes himself and walks over to his chair.

Now for the punchline, he looks around, and his eyes fall on Abbygail on the ground on her knees in front of me. I can't help but smirk, seeing the look of pure venom on Tyler's face when he sees her. He makes eye contact again, and I cock my head, challenging him to act.

"Kayden, I need to leave. *Now*." Tyler snarls at his Beta.

Good, I've got you rattled. Everything is going according to plan, and all I must do is sit back and watch. I laugh to myself. *This is going to be so easy.* A deep growl rattles the tent and pulls me from my thoughts. Kayden grabs Tyler and forcefully drags him back to the house.

Now is my moment to cast doubt. If I'm going to take over this role, I must plant some unwanted seeds.

I rise slowly and turn to the rest of the gathering. "As you can see, our 'King' is losing control, and he's placing us all at risk," I mock, quoting King. "We must reconsider our ancestors' choices and choose a new King." Silence falls all around me as everybody watches me. "Maybe we must look at this as a sign. We can't have a King who can lose his shit and kill without knowing it. We need to be responsible for our people. The hybrids may be the end of our existence."

My words die out, and I can hear them talking amongst themselves. A deep voice rises above the murmurs. "Careful, Jace," one of the older Alphas warns. "There is loyalty in this room, of which *you* apparently know nothing about."

"Really, Albert? You're going to sit there and talk about loyalty when we have a King who can't even control himself long enough to conduct a meeting?" I counter. I look around the room and hear the people start to talk amongst themselves again. I smirk as I sit down.

A howl rips through the tent and the pack grounds, making everyone's hair stand on end. I look around frantically—*what the fuck was that?*

Thirty minutes after the howl ripped through the festival, Tyler and Kayden walk back into the tent. I can tell from the vein throbbing in Tyler's neck that it's taking everything for him to keep his composure and wolf at bay. The vampire side, not so much. His fangs push out slightly as soon as he enters, and his irises are rimmed red.

He closes his eyes, takes a deep breath, and almost chokes on it. Tyler's fists ball at his sides as he exhales slowly. His eyes open, and nothing about his appearance changes. I can't help but feel the triumph of this moment. This is even better than I imagined.

"I'm sorry, it took a little longer than we expected," Tyler says, his voice shaking. "There were a few…" his jaw clenches, "unforeseen circumstances."

"Alpha King Tyler, what was that howl we all heard?" Albert's mate asks, looking concerned.

"That was me, Sonja. I do apologize. It seems the blood moon is extremely strenuous on me this year," he grinds out, sounding strained. "Now, let's get on with business, shall we? I am here now to discuss the peace treaty-" He glares at me. "And make sure we uphold the peace between our packs," he struggles to say.

This whole ordeal is taking its toll on Tyler, and everyone can see it clearly. He stops now and again and grips the table hard; I can see the battle raging inside him. "Kayden, please continue," he grinds out again, breathing heavily.

An hour later and we are done with the meeting. I am impressed. Tyler held his composure the entire time. That is saying a lot, especially for him.

This is going to be so good; let's see how far we can push him while there are still people around. After all, the goal of this assignment is to force him to crack.

I stand up as everybody leaves and call Tyler, "Alpha King, please, before you go. I want to introduce you to someone!"

CHAPTER TEN

ABBYGAIL

The howl that rings out makes my blood run cold, but at the same time, I'm not scared. Jace is startled, and that is something you do not see. I can't help the smile that spreads across my face. Jace is scared. Jace, flabbergasted, is the best sight in the world.

The Alpha King had left in quite a fuss, and everyone was confused and murmured to each other. The next thing I know, Jace is on his feet, yanking my body up by the chain. I don't think he even realizes that he did it.

As he addresses the gathering, the chains rattle against my collar and shackles. The noise from it brings unwanted attention to me. Some bastards who wolf-whistled when we walked in are now eyeing me lustfully.

A cold chill runs down my spine, and I shiver. *Please sit your ass down, Jace*, I plead inwardly.

I don't like the way they stare at me. I feel them undressing me with their eyes. Not that it will take them exceptionally long, as there isn't much left for the imagination.

I hear someone answer Jace, and the warning in his voice is clear as daylight.

What is he trying to do? Why would he go against his King?

It becomes clear, and a soft gasp escapes my lips. This asshole is trying to create doubt in all the packs, which only means he's trying to overthrow the current Alpha King. Okay, everything makes sense now, but what's still unclear is what I am doing here. Why would Jace risk it? Why would he flaunt me like this? It's one thing when he does it in his territory, but it's not his, so what is the reason?

I'm so lost in my mind that I don't hear the Alpha King and his Beta return. I snap back to reality when I hear his voice as he addresses the Alphas.

His voice is rich and deep, raspy even, but strained. I frown; why would he sound so strained? A delightful shiver runs over me as I listen to him talk. Holy crap, he has a handsome voice, and out of nowhere, sadness overtakes me.

What the hell are you doing, Abby? I scold myself. *Why are you even listening so intently to this man? This will only hurt you more.* I can't have a mate or a normal relationship, so why would I be crushing on someone I haven't even seen? Not to mention that he is way out of my league anyway.

I sigh as I zone out, not wanting to listen anymore. Why do I keep doing this to myself? I keep on hoping, but it will never happen. I feel so weak and drained. I still haven't had anything to eat, and now my heart feels like it will die inside my chest. The feeling is so heavy I think if I just give in, it will crush me.

Now, *that* would be a blessing.

The sound of Jace's voice forces me back to the present. He stands and clears his throat. "Alpha King, please, before you go. I want to introduce you to someone," he almost sings. His whole body radiates anarchy.

"Jace, I am sorry, but-" the Alpha King grits out, barely finishing his sentence when Jace wraps his hand around the chain and yanks me to my feet.

The force he uses to pull me up from the floor makes me choke, and I gasp for air as I grab the chains. I rise to my feet, stumbling a little, and cough as the air pushes through my tightened throat. Jace grabs my chin forcefully and forces my head up to him. As soon as he does this, a low, deep growl vibrates through the room again.

What the hell is going on?

"Jace," I hear the Beta of the Lunar pack warn. "Be very careful of your next move."

"Look. At. Me." Jace growls.

I shake my head no. "P-Please, sir, I d-don't want punishment. Please don't make me do it," I plead as I tremble, ignoring the pain in my side.

"NOW!" he bellows, and my gaze shoots to his crazy eyes. I whimper when he narrows his eyes before his face lights up with pure malicious delight. "Now, Your Highness," he mocks. The sarcasm drips from his voice, and he looks back at the Alpha King. "Meet my little slut—oh, sorry, I mean, Abbygail."

With that, he spins me around to face the Alpha King, but I instinctively lower my eyes. You aren't allowed to look royalty in the eyes when you are an Omega, let alone a slave. Apart from that, I can't bear to make eye contact with him.

To see the disgust in his eyes as I've seen it in so many aristocrats' eyes. A slave is the lowest form of being in our world. Surely, that's why he sounds so angry. What else can it be?

"Little slut, did I give you permission to lower your gaze?" Jace sneers in my ear from behind me. I shake my head quickly. "Then lift your fucking eyes." He grabs a fist full of my hair and yanks my head up.

I yelp from the pain in my scalp, my gaze moving up the Alpha King's body and falling on his eyes. I stare into the most beautiful, odd-colored eyes I've ever seen, and his scent hits me again. I inhale sharply, and my knees go weak as one word rings through my head so loud I think my head will explode.

MATE!

I fall to my knees, my head spinning so fast I feel nauseous. My chest tightens, and I gasp for air. The mate bond hits me like a solid concrete wall. I have a mate, and he's the King of all Alphas and a hybrid. I can't wrap my head around that. It doesn't feel real. This must be some mistake or a cruel joke.

I haven't fully regained control of my mind and senses before Jace wraps his long, slithering fingers around my neck and forces me to submit to him.

Please, no, not in front of my mate.

I have no choice but to give in to his control. I've never been able to resist him, not since he marked me. What the hell am I going to do?

CHAPTER ELEVEN

TYLER

The events unfolding before me must be a sick joke, right? This can't be happening right now. Am I in one of these twilight zones? Fuck, it must be, because this can't be real.

I watch Jace yank my mate up from the floor and hear her choke. That fucking collar is so tight it's cutting deeper into her flesh. My body trembles, my wolf howls so loud in my mind, begging to rip Jace apart.

I can't lose control. If I do, Jace will get his way, and he will overthrow me, and the whole peace treaty will be null and void. An ice-cold chill runs down my spine, and the realization hits: this is why I had that spine-chilling feeling these last few weeks. It was Jace. The bastard is antagonizing me so that I will lose it, and he can convince the packs that I am dangerous.

Over my dead body.

He grabs her face, and a growl slips past my lips. I hear Kayden speak, but it sounds so far away.

"Jace," Kayden warns as he watches me from the corner of his eye. "You better choose your next move carefully."

Jace forces her to look at him, and I hear her pleading not to be punished. What the actual fuck? I take a shaky breath, closing my eyes to keep a hold on my now almost nonexistent self-control while it feels like my wolf claws at the edges of my mind. "NOW," Jace screams. Abbygail's whole body trembles when she looks up at him.

My fists ball up at my sides, my claws digging into my palms, my vision bleeds red, and I feel my control slipping. Kayden picks up on it. He folds his hand over my shoulder and digs his claws into the flesh just below it. "Please, Tyler, keep your mind clear. Don't let him provoke you," I hear him plead.

I grunt in pain as Jace lifts his gaze to me. "Now, your highness, meet my little slut—oh, sorry, I mean, Abbygail," he laughs as he whirls her around to face me.

She drops her eyes as soon as I see her. Jace snarls in her ear, "Little slut, did I give you permission to lower your gaze?" She shakes her head quickly, and he grabs her hair and forces her head up to face me. "Then lift your fucking eyes."

Her eyes fall on mine, and I stumble a few steps back as the mate bond fully hits. I grunt and fall to my knees; my head is spinning. I can't think straight. "*MINE!*" My wolf howls, and I grab my head.

Kayden kneels beside me instantly, looking worried, "Ty?!"

I shake my head at him and stumble to my feet. I look at my mate, and she is on her knees; the bond must have hit her as it hit me. Jace grabs her by the throat, forcing her to submit to him again. I stare at her, confusion spreading across my face. Why is she submitting so quickly when she just felt the mate bond? I look at the collar, and the reason for his control over her becomes abundantly clear.

HE FUCKING MARKED HER!

My control slips completely, and I rip out of Kayden's hold, lunging at Jace, ready to rip his throat out. Kayden and Sebastian rush after me and tackle me to the ground, grabbing my shoulders and pulling me back.

They aren't strong enough to keep me in place. They plunge their claws into my shoulders again, pinning my arms behind my back, forcing me to my knees. I snarl viciously and hear Kayden above the haze in my mind. "GET THE FUCK OUT OF HERE, JACE!"

Jace looks at me, satisfaction dripping from the smile on his face. He grabs the chain on my mate's collar and drags her from the tent.

"CALL LAYLA!" Kayden yells at a pack member as I struggle against their hold. My vision is still red as blood. My wolf is forcing his way out, and I don't have any control.

"She's on her way, Beta Kayden." The pack member's voice breaks through my frantic mind, fear filling the air.

I look around frantically, still struggling, and see people enter the tent and stare at me.

By the looks on their faces, this isn't a pretty sight. Jace accomplished his mission tonight. The packs see their King growling and snarling like a bloody wild animal while his Beta and Gamma have him pinned to the fucking floor.

"TY!" I hear my name. "TYLER, COME ON, CONTROL. YOUR. WOLF!"

Kayden? No, it's Layla.

I'm really struggling to get my wolf under control. "Lay?" I shake my head as I groan.

"Yes, Ty, it's me." She touches my face and pleads, "Please, please, come back to us."

The memory of my mate pleading to Jace not to punish her is brought to my mind when I hear my sister's desperate voice. Everything goes red, and I push forward, letting out a bellowing roar. Layla falls back on her ass, and everything goes black.

KAYDEN

"FUCK!" I yell as Tyler sinks to the floor, unconscious. I pace the floor by his body. Sebastian feels for a pulse and nods at me. I let out an exasperated sigh. "*Fuck!*"

"What did you do, Kayden?" Layla fearfully asks as she scrambles to her brother's side.

"I-" I start to say when, out of the corner of my eye, I see movement. I look up and stare straight into some of the Alphas and pack members' faces who have come to see the commotion. "Oh, mother fu-"

"Kayden!" Layla cuts me off. "You need to deal with this situation quickly. It's really bad," she angrily whispers while cradling her brother's head on her lap. My ordinarily calm and nonchalant demeanor is slipping; Layla is right. This is really, really bad. I start pacing again when Layla and Sebastian hiss at me.

"Kayden!"

"Now will be as good a time as any." Layla looks around as the different pack members start to walk closer.

"Anybody who isn't part of the Lunar pack, please leave the main tent," I say so everyone can hear me.

"Beta Kayden, if I may?" Albert speaks. "Jace is out for blood, and this will be very hard to explain to all the other packs who weren't here to witness what happened."

"Alpha Albert, I know. Please cooperate with me and help me get these people out of here. I need to do damage control, and it's challenging to do that with an audience." I close my eyes and pinch the bridge of my nose.

Albert nods. "EVERYBODY OUT!" he bellows. "NOW!" Within seconds, everyone except some Lunar pack members scatter like someone is shooting at them. Well, that's precisely what we need. I thank Albert as he leaves the tent and turns to look at Layla.

"Remind me to never get on Albert's bad side." I kneel next to her as she holds on to Tyler. I place my hand on her cheek, and she leans into my hand before kissing my palm.

"What did you do to Tyler, babe?" Tears form in her eyes.

"I injected him with wolfsbane, my love," I sigh. This will surely upset her, and I am right when she starts to whale on me.

"You fucking did what!" she screams at me. "How can you do that to Tyler, Kay? What is the matter with you?"

"Layla, please calm down and listen to me," I implore, brushing her hair out of her face.

She raises her eyebrows. "I'm listening."

"This wasn't an easy decision, first of all, and secondly, you didn't see him react when he only caught her scent. He didn't even see her yet, Lay. Then, look at what happened in his office. This is something we haven't seen before," I say as I stand up.

"Jace is out for blood. You should have seen the smug look on his face when he saw Tyler buckle as the mate bond hit them. It brought them both to their knees. I only brought the wolfsbane as a contingency plan, and I'm glad I did. We would be in a full-blown war if I didn't inject him. He would have ripped Jace's head from his body."

Layla frowns as she listens to what I am telling her. "This doesn't make sense, Kay. You said Jace looked smug when the mate bond hit them?"

"Yeah, it was like he was waiting for something like that to happen when he spun her around to look at Tyler," I affirm, pacing again.

"Will you please stop pacing, babe? It makes me nervous, and my nerves are already shot," she sighs.

"Sorry, babe." I smile at her apologetically. "It keeps me calm at this stage."

"Um, Kayden," I hear Sebastian say. I almost forgot all about him.

"Shit, sorry, bud. You can leave if you want to. I think everything is semi-under control now." I turn to him, and he shakes his head as he looks not at me but at Tyler, stirring. Oh fuck, how is this possible?

"Babe, please move away from Tyler before you get hurt. You know he will never forgive himself if he hurts you, and I might just kill him if that happens."

"Fuck," she curses under her breath. "How much wolfsbane did you give Tyler?"

"Ten fucking milliliters," I say, exasperated.

"WHAT?!" she snaps. "THAT AMOUNT CAN KILL A NORMAL WOLF!"

"He's not a normal wolf, is he? And I didn't give him the whole ten ml at once. I pushed the syringe slowly so as not to overdose him. When he eventually passed out, I saw the syringe was empty."

"Kay, if he cannot control his beast, or wolf, or whatever, what are we going to do?" Layla says, concerned.

"We need to restrain him until he can regain control, babe. If we don't, there will be hell to pay, and believe me, we don't want that right now."

Layla chews on her bottom lip as she watches Tyler slowly regain consciousness. "Fine, but he's going to kill us when he's himself again, do you know that?"

"Yeah," I let out a strained breath. "We'll deal with that problem when we get to it, but for now, we need to do whatever is necessary for the pack and this damn peace treaty—which Jace has shit on."

"Kayden, please, not now," Layla states as she closes her eyes in frustration.

"Fine, *fine*," I counter, shrugging. "Just my opinion, though."

"Kay!" Damn it, I love how stubborn she can get. My little feisty mate. *Shit, Kayden, now's not the time to get turned on*, I scold myself.

Tyler stirs and groans. We are running out of time to get him to the house and secured. "Okay, bud, let's move him to his office. We can brainstorm there, away from prying eyes," I tell Sebastian, who nods, and we hoist Tyler off the ground and move toward the house.

CHAPTER TWELVE

ABBYGAIL

I stumble behind Jace as we go to his sleeping quarters. My head is still spinning. What the hell? The mate bond that hit me was crippling. I can't concentrate; everything happens in slow motion, yet it happens too fast to grasp.

I shake my head. *Focus, Abby.* I will myself to get a grip. I didn't even notice that we weren't walking anymore. I look around to take note of my surroundings when *smack*, Jace's backhand comes across my face, and I feel the sting on my cheek as I fall to the ground.

"Answer me, Abbygail," Jace seethes. What the hell did he ask me? Fuck, fuck, *fuck*.

I look around frantically, and we are in his room, *alone*.

Where is Julia? I can't be alone with Jace, not with what happened in the main tent. I whimper and scoot backward until my back hits the wall as he stalks closer. I look up at him. His eyes are wild.

Jace grabs the chain connected to my collar and drags me across the floor to his bed. This is bad; this is unbelievably bad. Jace removes the chains and shackles from my wrists, grabs me around my throat, and pulls me up from the floor before he throws me onto his bed. He straddles my hips and pins my hands above my head swiftly.

A dangerous smile spreads across his face, and a chill runs down my spine. I tremble beneath him, and his smile gets wider. He dips his head down, stopping mere inches from my lips. "How does the mate bond feel, little slut?" Jace asks, dipping down further to my collarbone. He drags his nose against my neck, inhaling deeply and stopping below my jawline.

I shiver again, covering my whole body in goosebumps. "Do you *really* want me to repeat myself a third time?" he whispers.

I struggle against his grip, but it's no use. His hold on me gets tighter, and my broken wrist screams in protest. His free hand slides down my side; the wickedness sparks in his eyes and spreads across his face as he lifts his head to look at me.

A blood-curdling scream rips from my throat when he pushes down on my side, where he broke my ribs, his eyes closing in pleasure from the pain he's causing. My heart races as the fear envelopes my mind, tears running down my cheeks without mercy. My chest constricts, and my breathing becomes irregular.

"N-no, please sir, p-pleas-" I pant. *Shit!* I start squirming below him, and he only laughs at me.

"Squirm as much as you like, little slut." Jace snickers, and drops his head to my neck again. "You are *MINE*," he growls dangerously.

To my absolute horror, he licks at the mark he left just below my neck and bites down again. My back arches in pain, and the scream that leaves my mouth this time sounds foreign. Black spots appear in my vision as I hear a faint howl in my mind. My wolf makes herself known just before everything goes dark.

The absolute cold that seeps through my body wakes me. My head feels like there is too much fog and confusion. My memory is hazy, and I can't recall what happened. My whole body aches.

I move slowly and grunt from the pain radiating off my side. Moving a little more, I feel my hands tied behind my back. I pull against the restraints, wincing. My fucking wrist. This is getting tedious. The fucking wolfsbane should've burned off by now.

I open my eyes slowly. It's dark in the room, with a little light spilling in from the bottom of the door. I listen intently, not wanting Jace to know I'm awake.

I look around and see I'm in his bathroom. The yelling and screaming coming from the other side of the door make me keenly aware that I'm not alone with Jace anymore. I frown. Is that Julia? Closing my eyes, I try my best to focus on my hearing.

"YOU ARE FUCKING INSANE!" Julia screams.

Who the hell is she screaming at? My eyes snap open when I hear Jace's voice.

"Julia, you better watch your tone with me," he seethes. Has she lost her damn mind? She knows what Jace is capable of, yet she is screaming at the top of her lungs.

"YOU FUCKING KNEW ABBYGAIL WAS HIS MATE, DIDN'T YOU?"

"Julia," Jace snarls his warning.

"Oh-h," she laughs. "Don't you *dare* snarl at me, Jace," she grits, her voice trembling.

"Julia, I will not warn you again." Jace's voice sounds venomous. "I will not tolerate this disrespect!"

"I don't give a fuck what you will or will not tolerate, do you hear me. You will get all of us killed because of your fucking obsession with Abbygail and this fucking kingdom."

Jace growls, his thundering footsteps moving towards, I can only assume, Julia. A slap rings out, and my heart stops. He's going to kill her. I've never seen him touch Julia, not even lovingly.

"Did you just FUCKING SLAP ME," Jace's voice rises, and it is deafening.

"YES!" Julia yells. "If you ever touch me again, *I will fucking kill you in your sleep.* Do you hear me?"

I hear Jace retreating as he snickers. "Feisty, I like it. Now this Julia, I would fuck." What the hell? I furrow my brow. Where did that come from?

Smash! Something shatters against the bathroom door, and I jump, wincing again. "Fuck," I grunt.

Suddenly, it's deathly quiet. "Ah, my little slut is up and ready for round two."

"Jace, if you touch Abbygail again, you *will* be sorry," Julia snarls.

Jace snorts. "Listen, sweetheart, you are my mate, and therefore I will give you the courtesy to do as you please. But if you dare interfere with my plans, you will not see the light of day again." This time, I hear Jace's footsteps and a loud thud as Julia gasps. He probably is pinning her to the wall as he threatens her. "DO. YOU. UNDERSTAND?"

She gasps, "Yes."

Another thud as Julia hits the floor when Jace releases her. "Now, I'm going for a run to clear my head," he snarls, just before the door slams shut behind him.

LAYLA

I pace the floor in Tyler's office. How is this even possible? Nothing is making any sense. I look to the back of the office, where my brother is chained to the wall. He struggles against the restraints around his wrists and neck. I can hear the sizzling sound every time he moves. We had to dip the chains in wolfsbane, and Kayden had injected him again.

Why isn't it working? The chains are deadbolted to the wall, but I'm afraid they won't hold him. Why is he reacting like this after he found his mate? I have never seen anything like this.

"Ty," I say softly. "It's me, it's Layla. Please come back to me. You need to get control of your wolf, please."

His head snaps up, his irises still red as blood, his fangs long and sharp as they glisten in the moonlight shining through the broken windows, his fingers claw-like. Tyler lunges at me with an angry snarl, pulling on his restraints again, the metal whining under pressure.

I step back quickly, his swinging claw missing me by inches. Fuck! What am I going to do?

What if the Alphas want to see him? Nobody can see him like this. Our whole family's reputation will be flushed down the drain.

Kayden told me what exactly happened after the meeting. My blood is boiling. I want to rip Jace's heart from his chest and feast on it in front of him while he lies at my feet, dying. I can't believe he is putting my brother through this hell. I should have expected something like this. Jace has always been power-hungry.

But I can't understand how he knew Abbygail was Tyler's mate. No one knows beforehand who their mate is. It's a very sacred bond between two wolves. It's done this way precisely for the reason we are dealing with now. How will I get my brother to come out of this haze?

I start pacing again. I'm wracking my brain. This is impossible. We need to figure this out quickly.

A thought crosses my mind, and I don't know if it's smart or idiotic.

Julia.

I know Julia always says she doesn't support how Jace handles certain situations if not all of them. If I can only convince her to sneak Abbygail out of Jace's room, there might be some sliver of hope. Maybe, just maybe, Abbygail can get Tyler out of this haze. Shit, Kayden will lose his mind if he finds out what I'm planning to do. Well, he'll just have to find out afterward. I can't sit back and watch my brother and our pack get destroyed by Jace. My father would have wanted me to act. No, I am sure he would have ordered me to.

Okay, I'm going to do this, fuck please let this work.

CHAPTER THIRTEEN

ABBYGAIL

The bathroom door opens, and Julia flicks on the light, which makes me squint as it hits my eyes. Gasping, I grit my teeth and move to sit up.

"Abby, you are going to hurt yourself. Let me help you," Julia says somberly, crouching down next to me and helping me to at least sit on my ass. "Here." She takes a water bottle from her back pocket and cracks it open. My eyes water, and my throat is so dry it feels like sandpaper.

She holds the bottle to my mouth, and I gulp it down. "Easy, easy, you are going to choke on it."

I don't care. My thirst is too overwhelming. I close my eyes as the cold liquid runs down my throat, and after a while, Julia takes the bottle from my mouth when I nod at her.

"More?" she asks, and I shake my head.

"No thanks."

Julia forces a quick smile and sits down next to me. "I'm so sorry, Abby."

"What for, Julia?"

"For everything that's happening to you. I tried standing up to Jace, but I failed miserably."

"You have nothing to be sorry for, really," I groan as I turn to look at her. "You are the only one that has ever shown me any ounce of kindness. I can never repay you for that."

Julia scoffs. "Look at you, Abby, how can you say that? Jace must have hit you harder than I thought."

"I haven't seen myself in a mirror after the last time Jace had his hands on me, but I must be radiating beauty," I joke, but Julia gives me a look of absolute sadness.

"Abby, please, look at what *my mate* did to you. Look at the trouble he is causing for you and yours."

My mate. The sound is foreign. I have a mate.

My excitement is short-lived when I realize I can never seal the bond with him. Jace had made sure of that. Tears start to form in my eyes, and I close them to stop them from falling, but it's no use.

"You really don't have to worry about that, Julia. We will never seal the bond. For one, I'm already marked, and he is the Alpha King. He will never want me. I'm tarnished, weak, an Omega. Secondly, Jace made me submit to him in front of my mate. That brings my chances to zero," I whisper, lowering my head.

Julia sits next to me quietly; she looks heartbroken. I feel like someone is reaching into my chest and squeezing the crap out of my heart.

We sit like this for a while, neither wanting to move or say anything. The silence is doing us both good. I shift and gasp, feeling the broken bones in my wrist scrape against each other, and the lingering pain is killing me.

"Are you okay?"

"Under the circumstances, yeah. My wrist and side are not happy with my current position, though. I don't understand why I haven't healed yet, or even partially. The wolfsbane is supposed to be out of my system by now."

"Abby, Jace injected you again last night after you passed out. I walked into the room when he was on top of you. I lost my shit. I screamed at him and threatened him-"

"I know, I heard you." A broad smile forms on my face for the first time in… Forever. "I am so proud of you."

My statement confuses her as she cocks her head slightly and furrows her brow. "You heard all that?" She blushes, and I nod. "I'd kept everything built up for so long. It just came out."

"That was awesome. I wish I could have the courage you have. Maybe I wouldn't be in this mess then."

"Abby, you know that's not true. Do you not see the courage you have? I don't think I would last as long as you if I'm ever in your position. Jace is a sadistic bastard. I think this is why he kidnapped you."

"What do you mean?"

"I think Jace must've known that you are Tyler's mate. I think he has been planning this for quite some time. I've heard whispers of a prophecy, but I'm not sure." Julia scratches her head, staring ahead of herself, her eyes darting, and she frowns.

I struggle to wrap my head around what Julia just said. What is she talking about? What prophecy? About whom? I shake my head slowly; what the hell is going on? That's all I've been asking these last two days.

"Come on." She pulls me out of my thoughts when she stands up. "Let's get you off this cold floor and clean that damn bite mark." She helps me up, and as soon as I'm standing, my head starts to spin and I feel nauseous. I sway and sink to my knees again as my stomach growls loudly. I inhale and exhale slowly as I fight the hunger pains and the bile that threatens to leave my throat. Not that there will be anything to throw up, though.

"Fuck, Abby. When was the last time Jace gave you something to eat?" Concern clouds her voice.

"Don't remember," I breathe out.

Julia growls, more to herself than to me. "Come, there is some fruit and crackers in the room, and water."

Sitting on the floor beside the bed, I feel much better. Julia gave me something to eat and more water. She cleaned my wound and put an ice pack on my aching ribs. There isn't much she can do with my wrists tied behind my back, though. She tried to remove the shackles, but Jace locked them in place.

I didn't mind; the fact that I have eaten something makes everything a little more bearable. Food is such an underrated thing—when you get so little of it, you have more appreciation for it.

Jace has been gone for quite some time, and I am getting restless. The anticipation for his return is weighing on me, and Julia frowns, picking up on my uneasiness since I can't stop glancing at the door.

"Relax, Abby. When he goes for a run, he normally stays away for the entire night. Maybe you should try to get some sleep. I'll keep an eye on you, okay?"

I nod; maybe she's right. I didn't get much sleep in the last few days, and I can feel it. I lie my head back on the bed and close my eyes.

Knock, knock, knock.

I lift my head and watch as Julia walks to the door, the same confused look on her face as I have on mine. She opens the door and gasps. "Lady Layla, what are you doing here?" Julia asks, surprised, bowing her head at the person on the other side of the threshold.

I can't see this Lady Layla from where I sit, and I think that's precisely Julia's intention. She wants to shield me from more harm.

"Julia, I need your help," Layla says softly. "It's urgent."

"Anything, Layla, what do you need from me?" Julia answers without hesitation.

"Where is Jace?" Layla almost snarls.

"He's out for a run and won't return for a while. Why do you ask?"

There's silence for a few minutes. "Can I come in?"

"Um, I don't think that's a good idea, um-" Julia is now stumbling on her words. I roll my eyes. *Way to keep it cool, Julia.*

"Please, Julia," Layla pleads again. "I know Abbygail is in there; that's why I'm here."

Julia sighs as she nods and steps aside so Layla can enter. Who is this Layla, and what does she want with me? My head is starting to hurt. This day is getting the better of me.

Layla steps into the room and gasps when she sees me on the floor. *Yeah, not a pretty sight.* None of them knows what I have endured, but that's just part of my life, and I shouldn't complain.

"You must be Abbygail." The surprised look morphs into a kind smile as she slowly approaches me. I push my body back fearfully. Her eyes seem kind and loving, and her whole demeanor is soft and gentle.

I've been fooled so many times by a gentle approach, but for some reason, hers feels real. This makes me relax a bit as she cautiously approaches me like I might disappear if she moves too fast. She kneels next to me with tears in her eyes. I frown at the sight of her tears. Did I do something wrong here?

She lifts her hand and touches my face softly with only her fingertips. The movement startles me, and I'm frozen to the spot, only staring at her. "Who are you?" My voice barely above a whisper.

She smiles softly. "How rude of me. I'm Layla. I am Tyler's sister."

I frown. "T-Tyler?"

"Your mate, Abby," Julia says when I look at her.

I lower my head, still frowning. "Oh," I mumble, more to myself. Why is she here? Why must I be reminded of something I can never have? This is more tortuous than anything Jace has ever put me through.

Layla looks at Julia and then at me again. "Why aren't you more excited? I don't understand. If what Kayden tells me is true, then you and my brother have an exceptional mate bond. Can't you feel the pull like he does?"

The pull? What pull? All I feel is sadness. I don't want to hear about this anymore. "No, I don't feel any pull. Please just leave me be. I don't know what you want from me."

Layla rises abruptly like someone just slapped her across the face. She stares at me and then turns to Julia. I can't look at her anymore. "I don't understand. Why can't she feel the pull of the bond?"

Julia sighs again and steps closer to me. She bends down and swipes my hair off my shoulder towards my back. Layla gasps, and her hand moves to her mouth. The look on her face is pure horror.

She kneels by my side again and brings her hand to the mark on my neck. She touches it lightly; maybe she thinks it's a hoax or something as she brushes her fingers against it.

I wince, and she removes her hand quickly.

"H-How many times has he marked you?" she asks the horror still in her eyes.

Swallowing, I wrack my brain. How many times *did* he mark me, though? "I, um, I can't remember…" I trail off. I feel so overwhelmed at this stage, and I look at Julia bewildered as Layla sits beside me, crying.

"It's okay, Abby. Layla has a mate of her own. She feels the sadness from the thought that you can't connect to your mate," Julia reassures me.

Layla smiles sadly at Julia's words. I purse my lips. "I don't know what you want me to say or what you want me to feel, but can we please not talk about this anymore? I'm tired, and my body hurts. Can you please just let me rest?"

Layla sighs, "I'm so sorry, Abby. May I call you Abby?" I frown at her as I nod. "But I can't. That's why I'm here. I need your help."

My help? What the hell can I do? I have no say in any matter, and I have no status. How on earth can I be of any help to anyone?

"What do you mean, Layla?" Julia asks, sounding somewhat intrigued.

"It's my brother. He is trapped in a haze in his mind. I think his wolf has taken over and is trying to break free and get to Abby. I believe he can't get control of his wolf because he hasn't connected with Abby and her wolf-"

"M-My wolf?" I look at Layla like she is crazy. "My wolf has been dormant since the day Jace first marked me. I can be of no help to your brother. I am ruined." As the words leave my lips, I remember hearing my wolf howl faintly in my head just before I passed out. I thought it was a dream, but now I'm unsure.

"Abby, please, I beg of you, please just try and talk to him. Maybe your voice can pull him back to us. Please just try," Layla pleads.

My chest is starting to feel tight again. I can't do this. If I leave this room and Jace finds me gone, he will undoubtedly kill me. Nothing is stopping him from doing that now; he achieved his goal. He has broken me, and now my mate.

At that thought, I feel a sharp pain in my heart as the image of my mate broken and hurt runs through my mind. The anger brewing in my chest is indescribable. The pull on my heart is so powerful it feels like someone is about to rip it from my chest.

My body behaves weirdly, and I feel my canines elongate slightly as a soft snarl leaves my lips.

Layla stands up quickly and moves to where Julia stands.

"Did you just see that?" Layla asks, surprised.

"Yeah, seems like someone is starting to feel the pull."

"But did you see her eyes shift color?"

Julia frowns. "That's not possible, that only happens to..." Julia trails off as she watches me intently.

"Hybrids..." Layla gasps. "Abby's a fucking hybrid!"

The shock on Julia's face is nothing compared to the shock I'm feeling. This can't be true though, can it? There's no way I am a hybrid. I can't recall my parents being different from one another. I surely would have noticed it. I wrack my brain, but I can't recall anything about them. How is that even possible?

"Does Jace know?" Layla asks Julia.

"I don't know, perhaps, but everything is making sense now. This is why Jace keeps her away from the world," Julia says as she kneels beside me.

"Did you know you are a hybrid, Abby?" she asks almost accusingly. "Why didn't you tell me?"

"I swear, Julia. I didn't know. I don't think you are right, though. How can I be a hybrid? Hybrids are supposed to be strong and fearless. Aren't they supposed to be a dominant breed? What about me screams dominant, fearless, and strong? Nothing!"

"Hey, Abby, don't be so hard on yourself. You know this isn't true," Julia claims, grabbing my face and turning it to look at her. "This is why Jace is always injecting you with wolfsbane; it's to keep you weak, not because you are. Don't you get it? He's afraid of you, Abby, and I think his fear spiked when he heard that prophecy."

"What prophecy?" Layla asks, sounding surprised.

"I'm not exactly sure. I just know right before Abby came to us-"

"I did not come to you, Julia. I got kidnapped," I interject.

"Kidnapped, sorry," Julia apologizes, flicking her eyes at me, and looks at Layla as she continues, "Jace came home one day after he went for a run, and he was pale. It looked like he had seen a ghost. When I asked him what happened, he mumbled something about a prophecy and that we were ruined. I tried to ask him again a few days after he brought Abby to our Packhouse, but he acted like he didn't know what I was talking about."

"Hmm, well, this is interesting. I think this tidbit of information will be useful in the future, but for now, we must get my brother back if we want to use it," Layla says, a spark in her eyes.

Everything is getting out of hand, these two sound like they will throw Jace out on his ass, but they forget I'm linked to him. I don't have power over him. If he makes me submit, I will have no choice but to obey. I don't know how I am going to get out of his grip.

"You forget that Jace owns me, and if he finds me gone, there will be hell to pay. And you do know I'm going to be the one who is going to have to pay for it. Jace is never going to release me."

"She's right," Julia says somberly. "He hates Tyler, and his main goal has always been to take whatever Tyler has. I'm afraid that if he isn't going to get his way, he has one way to break Tyler completely if all else fails..."

"He'll kill me," I affirm the words that none of them want to say out loud.

Julia and Layla only stare at me as the realization sets in.

"Fuck!" Layla curses, pulling her hand through her hair. "What are we going to do? I can't take you from here now. This will not just break my brother. I fear it will kill him."

I sigh after a few minutes of silence; I've made up my mind. Now is as good a time as any to regain some control of my life. "Well, we will just have to deal with that problem when we get to it, won't we?"

Julia and Layla look at each other as if I've lost my mind. What else do I have to lose? If the only thing I can do for my mate is get him out of the haze, then I must try.

CHAPTER FOURTEEN

KAYDEN

"**F**ind me some fucking answers!" I yell at the three men who are standing in front of me.

"Yes, Beta Kayden," they answer in unison as they turn and hurry out the door.

I am standing in the dining area of the Packhouse. I had to call a pack meeting to inform them about what was happening and why their Alpha wasn't present. The dining area is the only place big enough in the Packhouse, where I wouldn't be too far away if Tyler decided he didn't want to be tied up anymore.

The pack was understandably worried after hearing rumors about what happened, and I assured them that they didn't need to be concerned. Of course, I didn't give them all the details, and I especially did not tell them what's happening with Tyler now. I can't spread fear in our pack; it will only make us vulnerable.

Some of the other packs are already getting restless. They can sense uneasiness and change in the air. They aren't exactly sure what it is, but it's in their nature. When a wolf senses weakness from a rival pack, they attack to claim the territory.

I'm hoping with everything in me since we are a higher evolutionary being, that they will remember the treaty and regard it in the same sense as us. We can't afford a war now. Our leader is out of commission, and that will be our downfall. I must keep all the packs at ease and ensure everything is in order in our house. There's no doubt in my mind that the people who witnessed what happened in the main tent haven't told their Alphas and the rest of their pack members.

"Fuck." I drag my hand through my hair, almost forgetting the pack before me.

"Beta Kayden," Roy, one of our warrior wolves, says. "Do we need to set up a perimeter and establish a contingency plan if there's trouble stirring?"

"No, Roy. Not just yet. I am still trying to figure out what precisely happened tonight. I know that Jace is trying his absolute best to rattle us and weaken our pack and our resilience. We simply can't show any force now. It will just fuel his motivation, and with our Alpha's current state, it will not fall in our favor. We need to be in stealth mode. Keep your ears to the ground and your eyes open. If any of you hear something, please report it directly to me."

"Yes, Beta," the pack says.

"You are dismissed," I say loudly, and they leave the dining room.

I flop down on one of the chairs, resting my face in my hands. I'm not even sure how we will get out of this mess. My watch pings, indicating it's time to give Tyler more wolfsbane. "Oh fuck, if we don't solve this fucking problem soon, Tyler will kill me."

I stand and go to Tyler's office; halfway down the hall, thrashing and chains clinging against each other fill the space. He's going to hurt himself. The thought of injecting my friend again makes me sick. I take the small vial of wolfsbane out of my back pocket along with the syringe, pulling up ten milliliters into the syringe before I go into the office.

I hate this. I push open the door and stop dead in my tracks when I see Layla in the office with Julia and Abbygail.

"What the actual fuck is going on Layla?" I state flatly, making all three women jump at my voice.

"Hi, baby." Layla smiles as she runs to me, throwing her arms around my neck and kissing me deeply. I can't help but fold my arms around her and pull her closer. I deepen the kiss but pull away after a few seconds to catch my breath.

I clear my throat and eyes, Julia, before returning my attention to Layla. "What is going on here, and what are they doing here?".

"Don't be mad, okay? I had an idea, and I was hoping to execute my plan before you found out, but I'm not so lucky, am I?" A mischievous grin on her face.

I just look at her, my eyebrow raised, silently urging her to get to the point.

"Well, I thought that if I can get Julia to help get Abby here, we can maybe get through to Ty. I mean, it doesn't hurt to try. What if Abby's voice can break through Tyler's haze? If we can get him back, we can devise a plan to get her away from Jace."

"Fuck Layla, Julia is Jace's mate. What were you thinking? What if this is a trap for Jace to get in here and kill Tyler? Have you thought about that?!" I snap at her, and she narrows her eyes at me.

"Kay, do you really think I'm that stupid? I know Julia, she didn't choose her mate. She's the one who has been caring for Abby when Jace had his rage fits. If it weren't for her, Abby would be worse off."

I look up at Julia again, and she gives me a small smile. I don't know if I can trust her. My gaze falls on Abbygail, but she doesn't look at me, keeping her eyes down. She is scared; I can smell it coming off her.

"Okay, what exactly is your plan, my love?" I ask, sighing defeatedly. Looking at Abbygail again, I frown, seeing the inflamed mark on her neck and her hands tied behind her back. She reeks of Jace.

"On second thought, don't tell me. I don't know if this is going to work."

"And why not?" Layla asks stubbornly, placing her hands on her hips.

"Babe, if that wound below Abby's collar is what I think it is, Tyler's wolf will overpower him completely. It's not too hard to imagine what he will do if he gets free from his restraints. Secondly, she reeks of Jace. That's risk number two. And why would you bring her to him tied up? Don't you think that alone will send him over the edge?"

"P-Please, Beta Kayden, I am willing to try. If this," she takes a deep breath and looks at me, "if this can help him, I will do anything that is needed."

I sigh heavily and rub my hand on the back of my neck. The tension can be cut with a knife at this stage. "Fine, just give me a minute. Your plan will work better when Tyler's in a weakened state, and we need this in our corner, especially with the earlier-mentioned problems."

I let go of Layla and make my way over to Tyler, still thrashing against his restraints. His neck and wrists are burned to a crisp and bleeding from the chains cutting into his skin. The wounds are going to scar, and then Tyler's really going to have my head.

I grab his claw-like hand and force his arm away from me as I plunge the needle into his arm and empty the syringe. I step back quickly out of his reach.

Tyler snarls at me before letting loose a thundering roar as the wolfsbane burns through his veins. Within a few seconds, he slumps to his knees, growling weakly. A second growl sounds behind me, and I frown as I turn around quickly, seeing Layla and Julia holding back Abby.

I watch as her eyes change color. I see brilliant white bleed into the green in her irises, which still rims her eyes.

"What the fuck?" I manage to force out. Are my eyes deceiving me? Did that really just happen? "Layla?"

Julia steps in front of Abby. "Hey, hey, Abby, look at me," she pulls Abby's face towards her, and Abby glares at Julia. "It's okay; Kayden is trying to help Tyler. You need to calm down, okay?"

While Julia talks Abby down, Layla walks to me. "Isn't it awesome," she asks, glee in her voice. "Abby's also a hybrid."

"Lay, she's not just a hybrid," I say slowly, not taking my eyes off Abby. "She is one of the rarest bloodlines of hybrids."

"What, how do you know that?" Layla asks, surprised. Julia turns to look at me as Abby's eyes return to the normal emerald color, and she gets a hold of her wolf.

"Wh-what?" Abby asks, bewildered. Layla looks from me to Abby with the same bewilderment on her face.

"Okay, wait, Abby, you first," Layla states, holding her finger in the air.

"Huh, what do you mean me first? I have no idea what he's talking about."

"I know, I wasn't talking about that. I thought you said your wolf is dormant."

"She is, or she was. I don't know what just happened."

"Your wolf must have been woken up when the mate bond hit, but she couldn't make herself known with Jace's dominance. I think when Kayden injected Tyler, your wolf wanted to protect him," Julia says slowly.

"Hmmm, sounds about right," I chime in.

"And you," Layla says suddenly, looking at me. "How do you know about her bloodline being rare? That's just a myth, isn't it?" Not sure of herself now.

"Did you see her eyes, Lay? Only the rarest of hybrid's eyes bleed from one color into another."

I see the gears in Layla's head spinning. "Oh no, Lay. I know what you are planning, and this will be a disaster."

"Just listen, okay? If what you're saying is true, we have a good chance to get rid of Jace," Layla blurts quickly, afraid I will cut her off. Layla looks over at Julia apologetically. "Sorry, Julia, but I think you will agree."

"Sure, of course, but don't you think we need to know more about the bond between these two and its capabilities? I don't think we should show our hand before we know all the facts, and besides, we don't know how much Jace knows," Julia agrees, a hint of sadness in her voice.

"Okay, sounds good. Let's deal with our first problem, and then we can start our research," Layla sighs, nodding towards Tyler. Layla chews her bottom lip for a few seconds, then turns and looks Julia dead in the eyes. "We can trust you, right?"

"Layla, how can you ask that? You know what she has done for me." Abby frowns at Layla.

"I do. I have to ask, you know. To make sure. It's no use if this question hangs in the air," Layla eyes me as she finishes her sentence.

Jeez, why am I always the bloody bad guy? If Julia were to betray us, we would surely perish at Jace's hands, which doesn't sit well with me. I hope Layla knows what she's doing.

CHAPTER FIFTEEN

ABBYGAIL

Watching the interaction between Layla, Kayden, and Julia is exhausting. I look at Tyler out of the corner of my eye; at that moment, he lifts his head, his red eyes falling on mine, watching me with his head tilted. I gasp as I feel myself pulled towards him, my feet moving on their own accord.

The other three are still planning my escape while I'm slowly going to Tyler. My heart is pounding. Fuck, what if I can't help him? What if he rips me to shreds if I cannot get him out of his haze? Well, maybe that is my only way out. I sigh, keeping my eyes on him. He slowly tilts his head to the other side, watching me intently.

"Abby!" Layla yells.

She runs to me, grabs my tied wrists, and pulls me away from Tyler. I yelp, which does not sit well with him, as he lets out a deep, vibrating growl, baring his teeth in a vicious snarl.

Layla glances over at Tyler. "Are you insane?" she asks me while watching her brother before coming around and placing herself between me and him, staring at me now. "We don't know what he'll do."

"Isn't that why I'm here?" My brow furrows. "What did you expect of me if it wasn't to interact with him?"

"Well…" she trails off, the wheels spinning in her head. "I don't know exactly. Maybe just talk to him."

"And what would you like me to say precisely?"

"How do I know, Abby? Think of something," Layla says, sounding annoyed.

"Maybe you should leave us-"

"There is no way in hell I'm leaving you alone. I can't let Tyler hurt you, Abby. He will never forgive himself and rip *my* head from my body for allowing it," Kayden speaks up.

I close my eyes in frustration. "Okay, fine, you can stay, Kayden."

"No, Abby-" Layla starts to say.

"Please, guys, I can't do this with an audience. You'll just have to trust me," I plead.

"Fine," Layla and Julia say in unison.

"We'll be right outside, okay?" Julia gives me a hesitant smile, but it doesn't reach her eyes. I thank them as they leave Tyler's office, closing the door behind them. Letting out a shaky breath, I look at Kayden again. I don't know this man, and now I'm looking to him for some semblance of reassurance.

Kayden gives it to me without missing a beat when he smiles and nods towards Tyler. Inhaling deeply, I straighten my spine and release a shaky breath, turning to Tyler.

"Abby, wait," Kayden speaks up, walking closer, stopping me.

"Kayden, please-"

"No, listen. We should cover that mark with your hair and maybe get these shackles off you so we don't antagonize Tyler."

"Hmmm, okay. If you can get the shackles off me-" I don't get a chance to finish my sentence when I hear them clang on the floor.

"Shit," I breathe out a sigh of relief when I can move my arms again. "Thanks."

"No problem." Kayden smiles at me, stepping back. "Remember to cover that mark."

I nod as I pull all my hair over my shoulder. I take another deep breath, letting it out slowly, calming my nerves as I reach Tyler. He pulls weakly on his restraints, snarling at me as I get closer.

"T-Tyler," my voice shaking. "Please listen to my voice. I know you don't know me, but please let me help you."

To my surprise, Tyler inhales deeply and closes his eyes as I talk. Is this actually working?

I walk closer to him, getting mere inches from him. I lower myself onto my knees to be at eye level with him.

He doesn't move.

"Tyler?" I reach out to touch his face. I'm really being bold today. Calling this man by his name and not addressing him by his title as someone of my rank should.

My fingertips graze his skin, which sends a spark through my body. The next moment, his eyes flash open, and a snarl rips through his chest before he grabs me by my throat. I gasp for air, grabbing his wrist, his claws cutting into the back of my neck.

"ABBYGAIL!" Kayden screams, running over to us.

"N-No," I choke out. "Stay b-back."

Bursting through the office door, Julia and Layla run toward me when Tyler tightens his grip on me, making me choke again.

"ABBY! Julia yells.

"SHIT!" Layla screams. "KAYDEN, WHAT THE HELL ARE YOU WAITING FOR. YOU NEED TO GET HIM OFF HER."

Kayden steps in front of them, effectively stopping them, and grits out, "She said to stay back, babe. Please don't get close to them. If you are going anywhere near them and he harms you, I won't be able to control *my* wolf."

"But-" Layla stumbles.

Tyler growls as he tilts his head at them, yanking me closer, his grip tightening.

I'm inches from his face when his eyes flick to mine. Tyler snarls aggressively at me, baring his fangs, and snaps his jaw. Holy crap, this is it. My mate is going to rip me apart.

Before I can decide my next move, a fire I've never felt before burns through me.

The feeling is empowering. I have no idea where this is coming from, but my canines elongate, and my vision changes. Looking up at Tyler, his eyes staring back at me with so much anger, I can feel it vibrating through me. Making eye contact, I feel my wolf stir, and a growl rumbles from deep within my chest.

"Tyler!" I yell. "You are hurting me; please let me go."

His grip on my throat loosens at once. He closes his eyes and shakes his head a few times.

I feel his struggle with his wolf as his grip tightens and loosens every few seconds. "Look at me," I plead with every ounce of my being. "Look at me, Tyler, please. I'm right here. You are in control."

His grip tightens again. *Oh fuck*, this isn't working.

The panic builds in my chest before I feel my wolf's presence, stronger than ever. *Please help me*, I plead to her silently.

I feel her acknowledge my request. I close my eyes, and as I open them, a thunderous rumbling comes from my chest. "*You need to take fucking control!*"

Tyler inhales sharply and groans, this time in frustration, as he releases me and slumps forward. I gasp for air as I fall flat on my ass. He lifts his head slowly; his eyes pinned on mine. The red drains and his beautiful eyes regain their color. His fangs retract completely as he pants.

I rub at my throat, coughing. I watch as the realization of what happened hits Tyler. His eyebrows pull into a deep V shape as he frowns, eyes jumping between me and the other people in the room.

"What-" he groans, shaking his head slowly.

"Tyler?!" Layla yells from behind me as she comes running toward us. "Are you really back?"

She throws her arms around her brother, and he winces when the chains burn him again.

"Fuck, Layla," his voice hoarse and weak. "Careful."

"I'm sorry, Ty. I'm just so glad this worked. I was so scared, but it actually worked," Layla cries into her brother's shoulder. I am stunned out of my mind; did I just do that? Maybe some of Julia's words ring true. I shake my head slightly, and I look at Tyler again. He is watching me intently.

A blush creeps up my cheeks, and I look down immediately, playing with my fingers on my lap.

I'm so lost in my thoughts that I don't see Layla coming for me next. She slams into me as she throws her arms around my neck. "Abby," she cries, a broad smile on her face. "You did it."

The moment Layla slams into my side, I gasp and let out a loud groan.

"Shit, Abby, I'm so sorry. Are you okay?"

I pant as I put my hand up, trying to breathe through the pain. "I'll be okay in a minute, shit."

"Abby?" I hear his rich, baritone voice speak my name, and it's as if my pain disappears instantly.

I close my eyes and tilt my head back as his luscious voice fills my ears. "Hmmm," I hum, feeling drunk on this high his voice leaves in me.

The room goes completely silent, and I open my eyes quickly, realizing I did that in front of everybody—the blush on my cheeks deepens. Lowering my head, I feel silly, but I dare a glance in Tyler's direction. I look up through my lashes, and he's straining against his chains to get to me.

"Release me," he commands without taking his eyes off me. The command reverberates through his office, and Kayden stiffens.

"Ty, I don't think that's such a great idea," Kayden says warily, which makes me look at him, and I see the worry in his eyes.

"Kayden," Tyler warns. "Release. Me. Now," he asserts slowly, his temper flaring.

My hand shoots up to my neck, where the mark is hidden beneath my hair, knowing that if Kayden releases Tyler, he will want to seal the bond. I look at Layla, my eyes wide as the fear creeps into my chest and seizes my heart. Layla steps in between me and Tyler when she sees my terrified face.

"Fuck," she hisses. "Release Tyler, babe."

Kayden looks at Layla bewildered but she doesn't take her eyes off Tyler. Kayden does as Layla says and releases Tyler.

He falls to his hands, groaning. Tyler gets up slowly, his eyes burning through his sister. As soon as he is on his feet, Layla steps back, shielding me from Tyler.

"Julia," Layla calls.

Julia doesn't need to hear the rest as she is beside me instantly, helping me to my feet.

Kayden moves to stand almost in front of Layla, but she lightly pushes him to her side.

"It's okay, babe. He will not hurt me. *Right?*" she asks Tyler, her eyebrow raised.

"Layla," Tyler says venomously. "Get out of my fucking way, *now*."

Tyler takes a few steps towards Layla but stumbles and sinks to his knee, pushing on the floor with his hands as he stables himself. He takes a few breaths and rises again, a little steadier on his feet. He narrows his eyes at Layla and Kayden when they don't move. "MOVE!" he bellows, taking another step closer.

The tension in this room is about to burst at the seams when a chill runs down my spine, and my body stiffens. I look at Julia, horror on my face. She barely has time to register when we hear a malicious cackle behind us.

I spin around, and all the color drains from my face.

CHAPTER SIXTEEN

TYLER

"Tyler," I hear faintly. "*You need to take fucking control.*"

It comes through the fog in my head as the sound rumbles through my body. That sweet scent from earlier hits me, and my wolf backs off, feeling semi-content now.

I grab this opportunity and take back my control. I feel my canines retract. I lift my gaze, and I'm met with the most gorgeous emerald eyes. I can't look away from them. The fog clears from my head entirely, and before I register what the hell is happening, my sister collides with me, causing the chains around my wrists and neck to burn me.

Shit, this feels like it's been happening for a while. The burns are raw. I scold my sister, but she only smiles at me as she cries. Layla leaves me and slams into Abby, throwing her arms around Abby's neck. I hear her gasp and groan loudly, the need to protect her pulling at my chest. I can't get to her because of these fucking things on me. I frown; why didn't Kayden release me?

"Abby?" I say, and she closes her eyes at the sound of my voice. She hums, content, and tilts her head back like she's liking what she's hearing.

Her head snaps back, and her eyes open quickly when she realizes we all have seen her little gesture. Fuck I need her, I need her body against mine. I need to take in her intoxicating scent when she is in my arms. I need to seal the mate bond. My wolf is pounding in the background to claim our mate. *Well, you need to sit your ass down*, I snap at my wolf.

"Release me," I command Kayden. I don't dare take my eyes off Abbygail, scared she will disappear if I do, but no one is doing anything.

"Ty, I don't think that's a great idea," Kayden says warily. I see Abby turn to look at him.

I crinkle my nose as her sweet scent gets a bitter taste to it. Inhaling the air around me, I immediately recognize the fear mixing with her scent. I don't like the thought of my mate fearing me. Nothing is making sense. My Beta isn't following orders, and now my mate is frightened.

"Kayden," I warn. "Release. Me. Now," I demand slowly, my temper flaring to the surface.

Why won't he help me get to my mate?

Abby's hand grabs her neck and looks at Layla with big, fearful eyes. I need to get to her; I need to hold her. I need to show her that she does not need to fear me.

Layla's voice rips into my thoughts as she curses and tells Kayden to release me. I feel relief until my sister steps in between Abby and me. What the actual fuck is going on here? My head is spinning. Everything happening now is pissing me off. Layla is the one who urged me to get to Abby, and now she's trying to keep me away from her.

Kayden does as Layla says, and when I fall to my hands, Layla backs up to shield Abby from me, calling Julia.

Jace's mate? Why is she here? She rushes to Abby's side, and my anger rises.

I am losing my patience. "Layla," venom drips from my voice. "Get out of my fucking way, now."

If I must plow through them to get to Abby, I will. I move towards my sister, and I feel the wolfsbane still burning in my veins. *Shit*. My knees buckle, and I sink to one knee, steadying myself on the floor with my hands. I take a few deep breaths; this isn't happening right now.

I stand, steadier this time.

"MOVE!" I bellow at my sister, taking a slow, calculating step closer to her. Abby stiffens, and then a horrible cackle rings through my office.

I will know that shrill cackle from anywhere. *Jace!*

Jace strolls into my office with his Beta and five more of his pack members. Shit, this isn't good, I can't fight. I'm too weak from all the bloody poison running through my veins. I'm going to kill Kayden; he will regret doing this to me. I know I'm being irrational, but I am the fucking Alpha King, and I am too weak to protect my mate or my pack.

"Well, well, isn't this a pretty sight," Jace sneers, looking at Julia, pulling his face in disgust. "The ultimate betrayal, isn't it, my conniving mate."

"For this to be a betrayal, I would've had to be loyal to you first, and we both know I'm not," Julia spits, moving in front of Abby. "Which reminds me, this is as good a time as any. I, Julia, renounce you, Jace, Alpha of the Timber pack, as my mate."

"Oh, you're going to regret saying that you bitch." Jace huffs, a grunt slipping past his lips when their bond snaps, and nods to his pack members to move forward. "Bring that bitch and my little slut to me," Jace says venomously.

Kayden snarls at Jace as he steps forward. "Leave, Jace, or you're going to regret it."

Jace lets out a blood-curdling laugh that rings through my office, and the sound alone sounds like nails being dragged down a chalkboard. "No, you are massively outnumbered, and I don't think you stand a chance now, do you?"

"Your pathetic Alpha can't even keep himself up straight, let alone fight. What kind of Alpha King gets brought to his knees by a measly slave?" Owen laughs, evil pleasure glinting in his eyes, which spreads to his face when he smiles.

A deafening roar rings through my office as Kayden lunges at Owen. He hits him square in the jaw, and Owen's head recoils backward like a spring. Kayden lands two more blows to Owen's face and two more to his abdomen before anyone can react. Owen grunts in pain as he doubles over.

Four of the five pack members from Jace's pack tackle Kayden to the ground. It takes three to pin him down while the other grabs his throat with his claws ready to slice on Jace's command.

I watch in horror as my Beta struggles against his opponents, and the one with the claws grips harder, drawing blood.

"NO! Please," Layla screams, falling to her knees, crying.

I glare at Jace, and he smirks at me. He is challenging me to attack him. Fine, I'm done playing his game. I'm ready to rip him limb from limb.

I growl, moving towards them, but my body betrays me as I stumble and fall against my desk, grabbing hold of the corner to steady myself.

Jace bursts out laughing again. "Pathetic," he snarls as he spits on the floor before me.

"Why are you doing this?" Irritation is evident in my voice. "I know we don't see eye to eye, but why risk everything to go to war? You know your pack isn't strong enough. Did you think you could get to me through my mate?"

Jace smirks at me, crossing his arms in front of his chest as he looks from me to Abby. His smile spreads wickedly across his face. "I have nothing to explain to you, so let's get this over with, shall we? I see I still have much doubt to plant in the other packs, so this time, you are lucky. I'm not taking your throne from you today, but know it's inevitable…"

He looks around the room, and his eyes rest on Abby again, trembling behind Julia. He lifts his hand and beckons her towards him with his finger.

"Here! Now!" he commands her in his Alpha voice.

"Jace, don't you fucking dare touch her…" I warn, knowing my threats fall on deaf ears. I don't care, though; I will die fighting for her.

Abby walks towards Jace slowly, fighting the hold he has on her. The fear on her face is breaking my heart. No, I can't let this happen again.

I step in front of Abby, softly touching her cheek. Sparks shoot into my hand and up my arm. We both inhale sharply; she closes her eyes, and tears run down her cheeks. Abby leans into my touch before she moves away from me.

"I'm sorry, Tyler," her voice barely above a whisper. "I don't have a choice, and even if I did, I would still go if it's going to keep you out of harm's way." She smiles sadly.

"Abby, please, don't do this."

Am I pleading? It's the weirdest feeling, and I realize I will drop to my knees to beg her if that is what she wants.

She shakes her head at me and hesitantly approaches Jace while I try to keep my head from spinning.

What did she mean she had no choice? Jace isn't her mate. I can't grasp this concept as Owen grabs her and brings her to stand before Jace.

"Hold her arms behind her back," Jace orders Owen, and he doesn't hesitate as he pins her arms. Jace turns them sideways so I can see both of them. He shoves her hair from her shoulder while she struggles against Owens' hold.

Jace fists a handful of her hair; a wicked smile spreads on his mouth as he glances at me and then back to Abby before he strokes the back of his fingers down her neck.

My eyes fall on her neck, and the memory from the tent hits me as I see the mark just above her collarbone. Jace chuckles and, with a swift movement, bites down—on the same mark he has left multiple times, by the looks of it.

Abby screams horrifically, but Owen puts his hand over her mouth as Jace bites down harder. She's shaking from the pain of being marked so many times. My wolf thrashes, and I am ready to release him if that will get her away from Jace.

I step forward just as Jace pulls back from Abby's neck. Her scream dies out, and she collapses in Owen's arms.

Something's wrong, really wrong. Jace watches me intently, grinning maliciously as I feel my wolf whimper and retreat. A crippling pain shoots through my head and heart simultaneously, and all my strength leaves my body. I fall to my knees, struggling to breathe, and my vision blurs.

What the hell is happening to me?

"And there it is—the mate bond curse. It spreads in a hybrid when another marks his mate," he laughs again.

I try to stand, but I am too weak. This can't be right. It must be the wolfsbane that's still in my system. I groan, feeling my consciousness slipping.

No, Abby, I must save her. "Kayden," my voice is so weak it's barely audible. Kayden struggles again, and Layla is torn between us. She looks from Kayden to me, and I fall to the floor. As Jace turns around to walk away, he stops and turns back to me. "Oh yeah, and if it hasn't been clear before, *she's mine*," he snarls, baring his canines at me.

And with that, his minions let go of Kayden, and they are gone.

Layla runs to Kayden, sobbing. He grabs her and folds her into him protectively. She clings to him as if he's life itself. Which he is. I should know because mine was taken from me, and I can do nothing to stop it.

Julia runs to my side; she grabs my arm and pulls away quickly. "Layla!" she calls out, her tone alarmed.

Layla ignores her as she grips Kayden tighter. "You stupid, bombastic bastard," she cries into his chest, "how dare you decide to leave me? What if-" she sniffs. "What if they killed you?"

"Shhh, baby, shhh," Kayden soothingly coos as he strokes her hair, keeping her pressed to his chest. "I'm sorry, I wasn't thinking clearly."

"Layla!" Julia yells. "Something is wrong here."

Layla lets go of her death grip on Kayden and runs over to where I lie. She touches my face and pulls back instantly. "Fuck, you're burning up!"

"N-no k-kidding, little sister," my voice shakes, and my whole body trembles uncontrollably as the fever takes hold of me.

CHAPTER SEVENTEEN

LAYLA

Tyler smiles at me weakly and closes his eyes. "No, *no*, Tyler, don't you dare close your eyes. You need to stay awake. Please, just stay awake." Panic envelopes me. Grabbing onto my brother's scorching shoulders, I shake him. He groans and opens his eyes slightly. A sigh of relief escapes my lips. "Babe, call the pack doctor, now!"

"On it, babe." Kayden nods, his phone already in his hand.

Julia places her index and middle finger on Tyler's wrist. The seconds ticking by are killing me. She lowers her ear to his chest and stays like that for a minute. She lifts her head and looks grim.

"His pulse is feeble, Layla, and his heartbeat is irregular. We need to move him out of here. I don't think we have time to wait for the doctor."

"How do you know Julia? What if it's just because of the wolfsbane in his system?" I'm searching her eyes for a hint that this might not be as grim as she is making it out to be, but there is none.

"I've had some medical training before I was mated to Jace. I wanted to become a doctor, but he forbade it," Julia admits sadly.

Howling Storm

How can someone be so selfish? Jace will be the downfall of his entire pack, and his plan will not have any room in the rest of our lives. I promise this to myself as I look at my brother. If I must fight to my dying breath, I will.

I nod at Julia, and Kayden's already on the phone with Sebastian. If he knows what's good for him, he will hurry.

Tyler grunts again, his back arching off the ground, his face contorting in pain as he lets out a blood-curdling scream.

Horrified, I look at Kayden, and the tears sting my eyes, pleading for him to do something because my mind is drawing a blank. "We don't have time to wait, Sebastian… No…. You are asking too many unnecessary questions…. Sebastian!" Kayden's voice is getting louder as his irritation grows. "You are pissing me off, man… tell Adam to meet us at Tyler's room and then get your ass here, NOW!"

I look at Julia as she monitors Tyler's vitals. I don't know what the hell is going on, or what, precisely, we are dealing with. What did Jace mean?

"We can't wait any longer, guys; if we don't move him now, he will die," Julia jumps to her feet and starts to push the desk and everything blocking our way to the side.

She bends down opposite me as Kayden bends down by Tyler's head. We need more help. My brother isn't a small guy. I look at the two of them, questioning our next move, when Sebastian enters the office. "Adam is already in Tyler's room setting everything up," he says as he kneels at Tyler's feet.

"Okay, that's good," Kayden says with a nod. "We'll lift him and move to his room on three." The three of us nod in unison as Kayden starts to count, "One, two, three…"

We lift Tyler off the floor in one smooth motion. He moans in protest. My heart isn't going to survive this. My brother is in so much pain. Why couldn't he find love like an average person, which is pure, easy, and free?

I sigh, remembering my father's words. "*Love is an untamed force. When we try to control it, it destroys us. When we try to imprison it, it enslaves us. When we try to understand it, it leaves us feeling lost and confused.*" Nothing is easy in life if it's worth fighting for.

We move slowly through the Packhouse while Tyler slips in and out of consciousness. I move like someone else is controlling my body. I have never felt like this. My joy and easiness in life are slipping like my brother's state of being. The hallway feels like it will never end, never reaching our destination. We will never get to the doctor, and my brother will die in my arms.

A sob slips past my lips. *Damn it, Layla, pull yourself together.*

I push all the negative images from my mind and focus on getting my brother to Adam as soon as possible.

I've never quite liked the feeling when stuff is out of my control, so this whole situation is like an itch in my brain I can't scratch. After we got my brother to the doctor in time, I retreated to the farthest corner of Tyler's room, and all I could do was stare at how Adam examined Tyler.

It's been thirty minutes, and the look on Adam's face mirrors Julia's when she told me we should move Tyler—a look which she still wears.

She's next to Adam, trying to help as best she can. After a few minutes of whispering amongst one another, Adam turns to me. "Lady Layla, I'm afraid this isn't good news."

"Just say it, doctor, please. I can't take the suspense anymore."

"He is really weak; his heartbeat is irregular, like Julia said, but I can't exactly pinpoint what is causing it-"

"We had to inject him with wolfsbane to weaken him. Can that be what is causing this?" I ask hopefully.

"I'm afraid not." He shakes his head and looks at me again, worry etched in his eyes. "I've never seen a wolf's system react this way with wolfsbane. This is something entirely different. He will surely die if we can't find the cause of this illness."

Tears are now freely running down my face. "WHAT?" I can scream at him, and anyone who says my brother won't make it. Damn them all. "I don't care what you have to do, Doc, but you are going to keep my brother alive if it's the last thing you do, or I'm holding you responsible for his death," I whisper to him, and he looks taken aback.

"Lady Layla, that's unreasonable. I am doing everything I can."

"Then do more than what you are doing now!"

"Lay." Kayden steps in front of me. He rests his hands on my cheeks, wiping some of the tears still running down my face with his thumbs. "Placing unwanted pressure on the good doctor here isn't going to help Tyler. You need to calm down and think clearly. Let Adam do some research and see what-"

I look at my feet when an idea hits me as Kayden speaks. "What was that?"

Kayden looks confused, tilting his head as he frowns. "I said Adam will do everything he can-"

"No, no, not that. The part about the research." I'm looking up at Kayden now, who's still confused as hell.

"Yeah, I said let Adam do some research-"

"You are a genius," I interrupt him again as I stand on my tip toes and give him a quick kiss on the lips. I pull out of his hold, and he stands there like an idiot, still holding the same position when I was still in his grasp. He looks at me when his brain catches up with what just happened, but I'm already out the door, yelling to Julia to follow me.

KAYDEN

My mate is more of a whirlwind than anything else sometimes. She's so difficult to keep up with. I stare at her where she strides, already halfway down the hall and calling out to Julia. Julia looks just as confused as I am. She shrugs her shoulders as she turns to Adam. "Please call if you need any help with him, doctor. I am always eager to help."

Adam nods to her as he walks back to Tyler. Julia forces an awkward smile in my direction before going after Layla.

"How does it look, Doc?" I ask more for comfort than anything else. Tyler's condition hasn't improved in the last ten minutes since he spoke to Layla.

Adam turns to me and shakes his head. "I don't know what I'm dealing with here, Kayden. I can't treat something that I can't diagnose. I have never seen anything like this. How did this happen again?"

I sigh and rub my eyes, explaining to Adam what happened when Tyler caught Abby's scent.

He listens intently and frowns here and there but never interrupts me. I finish my story with what happened when Jace marked Abby in front of Tyler, and I can see the wheels in Adam's head spinning.

"Interesting," is all he manages to say, his frown never leaving his face. He clears his throat and rechecks Tyler's vitals.

"What did this Jace say? Give me his precise words."

"Um, something along the lines of *the mate bond curse that spreads in a hybrid when another marks his mate*," I answer slowly, trying to recall that moment.

Adam narrows his eyes and frowns again; I wish I could read the damn man's thoughts. It's driving me insane.

"Abby-" Tyler whispers in his unconscious state.

I rub at the back of my neck. *Damn it.* I had totally forgotten about her. If I know Jace, he will undoubtedly torture our future Luna until she's inches from death. For Pete's sake, I can't leave Tyler's side now; on the other hand, if Tyler finds out I'm standing around his bed while I could be searching for Abby, he will lose his shit.

"Um, Doc, I'm stepping out for a bit. Please call me if he wakes up."

Adam nods as he writes down his observations, not once looking at me. As I leave Tyler's room,

I pull my phone out and dial Sebastian's number. "We need to find Abbygail and get her to Tyler ASAP," I tell Sebastian as soon as he answers his phone.

"Agreed."

I am itching for a fight, and the timing can't be any more perfect to rid myself of all this tension. I stop by our suite and grab my baseball bat. *Let's crack some skulls,* my wolf howls in my mind with anticipation.

CHAPTER EIGHTEEN

ABBYGAIL

"...and the prophecy was obvious: I can't let that happen."

"I still don't understand where you could've heard it. Don't get me wrong, I am stoked that we are taking what is rightfully ours—but where did you hear this?"

At first, it sounds like someone is speaking underwater. It's muddled and unclear, but as my other senses return to life, so does my hearing.

The voices around me are so loud now it sounds like someone is screaming. What the hell? It's the second time I've heard someone discussing a prophecy regarding me. Okay, so we have established I'm a bloody hybrid, and it's apparent as hell that Jace knows. The bastard seems to know more than he's letting on, which is terrible, because he is always one step ahead of Tyler and his pack.

Speaking of Tyler, why hasn't he come to get me yet?

That's if he still wants me. Shit, the memory of Jace marking me in front of Tyler haunts me. I cringe inwardly. Maybe he doesn't care where I am.

Where am I, though?

The bite mark on my neck is throbbing, and I let out a soft groan as I feel the strain on my wrists and shoulders. Why does it feel like someone is pulling me apart at the seams? I crack my eyes open slowly, trying to focus. Shit, this is so uncomfortable, and the pain is becoming unbearable.

I look up at my wrists tied above my head, down at my toes barely touching the ground. I am hanging from a fucking ceiling like a damned shot buck. So we must be in a dungeon. Since the floors are mucky, and the place reeks of iron and mold.

Cold seeps into my skin, and I groan again, which gets the attention of the bastards in the room with me.

"Ahh, at long last, the sleeping slut awakens," Owen laughs sinisterly.

"Now, Owen, you are speaking to the ruined Luna of the Lunar pack. Show some respect," Jace snickers.

Anger begins to boil in the pit of my stomach, which has never happened before. Whenever Jace has me in these situations, I usually retreat into my mind, never standing up for myself, but I've had enough. "Fuck you," I grind out, looking Jace dead in the eyes.

I wish I could take a picture of Jace's expression and show it to everyone. It's priceless. His eyes jump between mine, his brain not fully understanding what just happened.

He and Owen are quiet as mice at first, Jace's sarcastic smile melting off his face as if I had thrown acid on it. He looks at me like I've spit in his food and am trying to feed it to him—shock, and then pure hatred. Honestly, the look on his and Owen's faces is so satisfying. Here I was, thinking that nothing could silence these two, and all I had to do was drop two little words.

It takes about two minutes for my words to sink in, and his eyebrows pull down so deep into a V-shape that it almost rearranges his face. I stare at him, never blinking, not showing an ounce of fear. Never again will this man make me feel useless. I don't care if he kills me. I have nothing to lose.

"What. Did. You. Say?" Jace utters every word so slowly it sounds like a hammer dropping as his voice becomes louder. My little spat earns me a slap across the face, splitting my bottom lip and the force making me spin. Jace stops me and grabs my face as I taste blood from his assault. I glare at him, and he glowers, challenging me to do it again.

Fine, you piece of shit, I accept. I pull my face from his grip, looking him up and down, and spit my blood in his face as I laugh at him. "You heard me, Jace. Fuck. You," I mimic his tone of voice.

He lets out a fierce growl, and it's clear that his control is slipping. Let's see how he feels when nothing is in his power. Owen is still dumbstruck in the corner, which isn't even surprising, as he usually takes a few minutes to catch up. Maybe I'm just being mean, but hey, I don't give a shit.

"You do not scare me anymore, you worthless piece of wolf shit." My confidence soars with each word I speak, and I love it. I know I'm unable to fight back or escape from here, but I will never be made silent by these assholes.

Jace loses it, and I mean *loses* his shit completely. I look at him, and a fit of laughter consumes me. Jace grabs the hunting knife he carries on his belt and pushes it against my throat, drawing blood. "How fucking dare you speak to me that way? I will kill you. Do you understand me!" he practically screams at me.

"Frankly, I don't give a shit anymore. Do as you wish, but you will never control me again. Never." He roars in frustration as he slices the blade across my side twice.

I grit my teeth; I will not scream and give him the satisfaction. The tears run down my face like the blood against my side.

He smiles wickedly at me. "We will see about that slut," he almost spits the word. "Owen, get me the whip." His eyes never leave mine. I lift my chin to show him I will not back down; he will not break me.

Owen hands Jace a whip, and Jace's eyes almost turn black as he anticipates the pleasure he will get from what he's about to do to me. Jace spins me so my back is to him.

He cracks the whip a few times next to me before the first hit slices across my back, and I scream.

I want to kick my own ass for letting the scream leave my lips, but my body is tired. With the wolfsbane still in my system, I can't heal properly, and this damn mark he keeps giving me is draining me.

I scream again as the blows fall on my back. Jace doesn't wait for the sting to linger before letting the blows fall continuously down on my back.

I don't even count how many lashes he gives me. I'm starting to see black spots as the whip comes down on my back non-stop. I've lost a lot of blood—between the wounds on my side, the mark, and now the gashes on my back. I slump in my chains, and Jace lets out a malicious laugh.

"Where is your fire now, little slut?" Jace asks gleefully. He lifts his arm to bring the whip down on my back again when the door to the dungeon bursts open.

Jace turns around just as a bat connects with his face. He grunts, and he slumps to the ground. Owen roars and lunges at the person who hit Jace. His roar is short-lived when he's also knocked out, falling on Jace, who is still out cold.

"Abby?" Kayden calls to me, and I try to answer, but I am so fucking tired. I want to go to sleep and sleep until I don't feel any of this anymore. "Abby, hey, come on. No, no," he says as he grabs my face, lifts it, and lightly taps me on my cheek. "Hey, stay awake-"

"Tired," I manage through the fog that's starting to cloud my mind.

"I know, hey, come on, Tyler needs you. He's dying, and he needs you," he says, but his words sound foreign.

Tyler dying? How the hell is this possible? Did they give him too much wolfsbane? "What?" The fog must be fading, as I can think a little clearer.

"That's it, come on, stay awake… Shit, Sebastian, come untie her." Kayden sounds stressed. Are there more of Jace's pack members he's worried about, or can Tyler really be dying?

"Where's Tyler?" I ask weakly, as Sebastian lets me down from my restraints on the ceiling. My feet hit the ground, and I know I will kiss the floor when my knees buckle—but Kayden keeps me up.

"Fuck Abby, Jace has done a number on you. I'm going to lie you down on your side, okay? I need to look at these cuts," he says as he lies me on the floor. "Sebastian, give me your shirt." Sebastian pulls off his shirt and hands it to Kayden as he kneels on my other side. Kayden is trying his best to keep me from bleeding out as he bundles up Sebastian's shirt and pushes it against my bleeding side. I groan when he increases the pressure. "Just hold on, Abby. I need to stop the bleeding before I can move you." Kayden looks tired, and I know the feeling.

"Sebastian, make sure these two assholes don't leave this room. We will deal with them later," Kayden grits out through his teeth, and I feel the pressure on my side increase again, making me cry out. Kayden pulls back slightly and says, "Shit, the bleeding isn't slowing down, and you aren't healing."

"W-wolfs-bane," I stutter, I'm getting cold, and I know that isn't good. "Kay-Kayden, I'm cold," I manage through my chattering teeth.

"Fuck!" he breathes out. "Bud, we need to move her to the doctor now."

"I know, her back isn't looking so good either. How do you want to do this?" Sebastian says.

"Abby, can you get up and walk if we support your weight? We can't carry you otherwise. Your back is mostly ripped to shreds, and I don't want to cause you any more pain," Kayden asks me.

I nod weakly, and they help me get to my feet. I groan as I get up. I don't know how far I can go in my current condition; my legs wobble, and I sink to the floor.

They steady me quickly, Sebastian on my right and Kayden on my left side, still keeping pressure on my wounds with the shirt.

We walk into a massive room in the Packhouse, even more significant than the one Jace lived in. I hop alongside Kayden and Sebastian, each supporting me from a side.

"Doc!" Kayden calls out, and a middle-aged man comes walking out of the bedroom part of this enormous room.

"This is Abbygail, the girl I've told you about. We found her hanging from chains. Jace has whipped her beyond tomorrow and gave her two deep gashes on her side with a hunting knife," Kayden states.

Adam walks closer rather quickly at the sight of me. Kayden removes the shirt he's been holding to my side and frowns as he looks at my wounds. "I swear, these gashes were so deep I could see bone," he says, looking confused.

Some strength returns to my body, and my wounds start healing slowly. The wolfsbane must be leaving my system. In his angered state, Jace must have forgotten to inject me with the poison again. It's been a while since I've felt my body heal, and it's euphoric.

Adam examines me while I'm hanging onto Kayden and Sebastian, frowning as he walks around me to inspect my back. "Hmmm, it seems we just need to get you cleaned up. Your healing ability works rather fast, the fastest I've seen in quite a while," Adam walks back around and watches me intently.

"There is still a lot for me to learn about myself," I smile shyly, my strength returning more with every passing second. Kayden lets go of me, and so does Sebastian. I know they, too, are just as confused as I am.

I lost so much blood a few minutes ago, and now my wounds look like they are about three weeks old. I roll my shoulders as the pain subsides completely, the bruising on my ribs fades away, and the pain in my wrist is gone within seconds. Removing the wrist guard, I smile as I flex my fingers. A real smile feels almost awkward on my face: I'm out of practice.

"Come on, Abby. I'll get you some clean clothes, and you can take a shower to clean up. We need to get you to Tyler as soon as possible," Kayden says as he pulls on my arm, leading me to the ensuite bathroom. "Oh, before you go clean up, let's get this garbage off your neck," I turn, and Kayden takes the collar off me.

I am so wrapped up in this feeling of being free and able to breathe properly that I forgot about Tyler. Crap, what kind of mate am I? Kayden's words ring in my ears again, and I feel nauseous; this cannot be true. Why is there so much bad shit happening?

CHAPTER NINETEEN

LAYLA

"Where are we going?" Julia pants as she runs up to me. She looks around, and I laugh at her confusion. We are standing outside our pack's very intimidating library; the walls are covered in rows of books and scrolls of old.

I push open the door and step inside, inhaling deeply. I love that classic old book smell. It calms my nerves. There isn't a lot that can unnerve me, but these last couple of days are taking its toll on me. On all of us. I push open the big glass door, Julia on my heels, and my phone vibrates in my back pocket. Taking it out, I smile at the name on the screen.

Took him long enough.

"Hi babe, sorry for running out on you. I—what? You found her? Where—"

I listen intently as Kayden tells me what happened with Abby and where he found her.

The fact she's healing so quickly is astonishing. The excellent news is refreshing for once.

Julia waves her hands in front of me, shrugging. I mouth Abby's name to her, and her eyebrows raise. *Shit,* she mouths back.

"Okay, so where is she now… Great, give her some of my shorts and one of Tyler's T-shirts," I say, smiling. "Okay, babe… Yeah… The library… I'll tell you when I find what I'm looking for… The Elders? Yeah, I'll do that… Hmmm… Okay, talk to you later."

I smile again as I hang up. That man of mine, nothing slips by him; I thought he would be clueless, but he knows me better than I know myself. I tuck my phone back in my pocket and look at Julia, who is still watching me, her eyebrows raised.

"So, Kayden and Sebastian went looking for Abby and found her in the dungeon with Jace and Owen. He says it wasn't a pretty sight. She had deep slices on her side, and her back was ripped up from the whipping Jace had given her, but when they got her to Adam, her wounds looked like they were three weeks old."

"What? Really? Well, that's something new. What about Jace and Owen?" The worry Julia is trying to hide still shows in her eyes. As much as I hate Jace and his stupid ass Beta, I understand her concern. Renouncing a mate like Jace never goes off well. The threat he made against her still hangs over her head.

"They're still alive. Sebastian locked them in the room where they kept Abby. Kayden had to knock them out, though," I say as I watch her reaction.

To my surprise, she shrugs. "Well, they should be glad they aren't being filleted. Jace is poking a sleeping bear. It's not my problem anymore."

"I second that," I say, nodding in agreement.

"I'm tired of being associated with him and his wicked ways, Layla. I can't take it anymore," she sighs as she closes her eyes and pinches the bridge of her nose.

I touch her shoulder comfortingly, smiling softly. She smiles back and takes a deep breath before releasing it in a huff. "So, will you tell me what we're doing here?" She turns slowly, looking at the remarkably high, decorated ceiling and taking in the beautifully decorated shelves and intricate flooring.

"Okay, so when we were in my brother's room, Kayden said something about research, and it hit me. We don't know anything about the prophecy you mentioned or about this unique bond between Tyler and Abby. So, I was thinking, where else can we find out what we need to know other than here?" I shrug and motion towards all the books and scrolls. "And if all else fails, we can speak to the Elders."

The Lunar pack library is vast in information. We have all the lore, myths and legends of our kind—and especially the oldest to the latest prophecies written here. I'm sure we will find what we're looking for.

"Okay. One slight problem, though. I am not sure what the prophecy says. I only know Jace was spooked, and then all this happened."

"The only way to find out is to ask Melissa, our librarian, if she has maybe heard of this or if she can point us to where we need to look. We need to start somewhere, Julia. We are running out of time. My brother will die if we don't find out how to fix this."

"I know," Julia sighs again. "Come on, lead the way." She motions forward with her hand. I smile at her and move towards the counter in the middle of the colossal library.

Behind the desk sits Melissa, her glasses halfway down her nose and a frown as she pages through an ancient book.

She's a beautifully aged woman, with long salt and pepper hair braided down her back. She has warm blue eyes that are wrinkled at the corners from always having a smile on her face.

Melissa looks up as we walk up to her. "Lady Layla, it's so nice to see you again. I wondered why you haven't visited us in the last few days. I normally have to force you to leave," Melissa teases.

"Hi Melissa, thanks. It's been rough these last couple of days. I don't know if you've heard all the commotion."

She chuckles. "You know I don't have a clue what's happening in the real world unless *you* tell me. I'm too busy adding the latest information and updating the current prophecies and everything else."

"That's exactly why we are here. I wanted to ask if you know anything about a prophecy regarding a hybrid, or pure bloodline hybrid, or anything in that vein—I'm not entirely sure what exactly we are looking for—being mated to the Alpha King and what that mating bond might entail?" I look at Julia next to me, and she nods, looking back at Melissa, who's frowning now.

"Hmmm, let me think." She taps her index finger on her chin. It takes seconds for her eyes to widen, and she moves to her computer, typing vigorously. "There is one that was delivered to me about six years ago. This specific prophecy is sacred, though. How have you come to know about it?"

The look on Melissa's face is of worry and shock. If this is a sacred prophecy, then I assume only the Elders and the one delivering it should know about it—with the exception of the librarian, of course.

"Maybe we should talk in your office, Melissa. There are a lot of ears listening in, and we can't afford anyone else to know about this until we find what we need to know. So, if you don't mind?" Looking around the room, I catch a few people looking away quickly.

Melissa nods and makes her way to her office, beckoning for me and Julia to follow her. We follow her to the office, and I close the door behind me when we all are inside. "Please sit." Melissa motions to the chairs in front of her desk. She looks at me expectantly as she takes her seat.

"This needs to stay between these four walls for now, please, Melissa," I ask, and she nods as she moves closer to the desk. "Tyler isn't doing so well-"

"Excuse me?" she interrupts, her voice louder than it should be. "What's wrong with our Alpha?"

"Melissa, please, calm down and listen," I impatiently tell her. She nods, but the tension she's feeling is showing in her face and body. I need her to keep her mind clear and help us; otherwise, we are screwed.

"Okay, so like I said, Tyler isn't doing so well. We need all the information you can give us about the prophecy regarding his mate and any information on a mate bond between two hybrids, one with a pure bloodline."

Melissa's eyebrows almost disappear into her hairline; she's struggling to keep her composure, and that is noticeably clear. She nods slowly. "May I ask some questions?"

I sigh heavily. I knew this was inevitable. "Go ahead."

"What do you mean our Alpha isn't doing so well?"

"I don't have a definite answer for you, Melissa. If I can find out what I need to know and how to save him, I can give you a proper answer, but until then, I can't."

"Hmmm, I'll take that. Secondly, how did you come to hear of the prophecy about the Alpha King and his mate?"

"From Jace, my mate, and Alpha to the Timber pack," Julia answers before me, guilt coming from her in waves.

"Ex-mate," I correct Julia, who smiles at me in return.

"Excuse me? How is that possible? No one is supposed to know about these," Melissa confirms my suspicions.

"All I know is that he came home one day, pale as a ghost, saying something about overhearing a prophecy and that we were screwed if it was to come true," Julia says again.

Melissa shakes her head slowly, now rubbing her temples. "That's impossible, I don't—Shit!" she exclaims. Realization covers her face as she stares past us.

"What?" Julia and I ask at the same time, sitting forward.

"Excuse my language. The prophecy was delivered by an unknown wolf crossing into neutral territory. The warriors patrolling our borders summoned the Elders to the clearing. The wolf delivering it asked specifically for Tyler, but he couldn't be there. The warriors smelt an intruder and went after him but lost his scent in the river."

Turing, I look at Julia; she has the same dumbfounded expression on her face as I'm sure I have on mine. Everything is falling into place and starting to make sense. Hopefully, I can say the same about my brother and his situation.

"Okay, so what did the guy say?" I hesitantly ask, afraid to hear the answer.

Melissa turns on the computer on her desk and pulls the keyboard closer to her. She starts typing as soon as the screen comes on. She narrows her eyes at the screen, searching for the specific prophecy.

"Here it is."

"I thought all prophecies were written on scrolls," Julia says.

"We need to keep records this way as well. Do you know the devastation we would face if anyone tried to challenge the throne, attack our territory, and burn down all our records?" Melissa laughs as she turns the screen to us so we can read the prophecy for ourselves.

> A MEANINGFUL CHANGE IS ABOUT TO TAKE PLACE, AND THERE IS A UNION THAT WILL BRING THE COMMUNITY IMMENSE JOY.
>
> THIS UNION WILL MEAN DISTINGUISHED POWER AND WILL SOLIDIFY THE REIGN OF THE ALPHA KING'S HEIR. HE WILL BE KNOWN THROUGHOUT HISTORY AS ONE OF THE GREATEST ALPHAS TO HAVE RULED, WITH THE PURE-BLOOD LUNA BY HIS SIDE.

She will bring calm to his temper and peace to his iron fist. She will tame the beast within the Hybrids. The pure-blood Luna with raven black hair and emerald eyes which change as she changes, bleeding a pure brilliant white into the emerald green. Their mate bond will hit like an earthquake.

Beware, a threat is lingering; when another marks a destined Luna, the consequences can be fatal.

"Fuck," I whisper, falling back in my chair. I look over at Julia; the expression on her face is blank. Everything in this prophecy sounds so simple, but it's far from it. Well, we have established that it can be troublesome if another marked a destined Luna, but it doesn't mention how to fix it.

Melissa tilts her head at me; I probably need to explain. Maybe she has the answers we need. I let out a heavy sigh and sit forward in my seat again, resting my elbows on my knees. I rub my face with my hands before I intertwine my fingers.

"Melissa, here is our problem. Tyler met his mate two nights ago in the main tent. Her name is Abbygail, and she's exactly how the prophecy describes her. They were brought to their knees when they saw each other as the mate bond hit them." Melissa gasps as I talk, but she never interrupts me. "The problem is Jace marked Abby. Multiple times. Tyler lost control of his wolf when he saw she was Jace's slave. Jace was the one who overheard the prophecy. How he found her is beyond me." My tears are shallow, and I swallow hard.

"Anyway, we couldn't get my brother to control his wolf and had to restrain him. Abby was the one who got him back, but Jace came and took her from Tyler and marked her again in front of him." My voice starts to shake. I'm struggling to get the words out, so I look at Julia for help. Seeing my distress, she squeezes my hand.

"Wait, you said Jace is your mate." Melissa looks accusingly at Julia.

"*Was* my mate. The key word being *was*: and it wasn't by choice, but yes. I do not want to be affiliated with that bastard ever again. We only told you that part because it's necessary for you to know all the information," Julia says sternly.

"I understand. Forgive my inappropriate behavior, please. Please continue," Melissa apologizes.

Julia nods and continues, "After Jace marked Abby in front of Tyler, he stood there waiting like he knew something was going to happen. When Tyler fell to his knees, gasping for air, grabbing his chest, Jace mentioned something about the mate bond curse that spreads when a hybrid's mate is marked in front of him, or something like that."

I clear my throat, finding my composure, "Tyler immediately had a fever, his body burning up, he's weak, his heartbeat is irregular, and Adam can't do anything for him." I let out a shaky breath, my tears stinging again, "Please tell me you have the information we need to save him?"

Melissa leans back into her chair and says nothing for what feels like forever. I am about to ask her if she heard me when she answers slowly. "Where is Abbygail now?"

"Kayden saved her from Jace. He almost killed her," I state. "She's with them."

"Okay, that's good. Because the answer is in the problem, but Layla, you need to listen carefully, and you need to be one hundred percent sure that Abbygail is his mate—"

"Trust me, Melissa, she's his mate. What the prophecy described is exactly what we saw. Her eyes bleed from a pure white into her emerald green," I reassure her.

"Okay, so listen up," she says as she explains what we must do to save Tyler.

CHAPTER TWENTY

ABBYGAIL

How can something so trivial feel so good?

The warm water is running over my face and healing body, and it feels incredible. I've always believed that water also has some healing properties. Why else do you feel so much better after a shower?

I scrub away the dirt and blood and the last six years' worth of disgust I am feeling. I wash my hair and condition it. *Shit*, when's the last time I had time to pamper myself and my hair? I'm astonished that my hair didn't all fall out after the assault my scalp has suffered. Why do they always go for the hair? I mean, that's just ridiculous.

I can't seem to get myself to leave the shower, but when the water gets colder, I have to force myself to get out. I didn't mind the cold, but more pressing matters are waiting.

Shit, Tyler. I need to see him, I think as the water runs over my face and I close my eyes. Kayden has me worried. How is it possible that Tyler is dying?

I sigh, knowing I can't stay like this forever, although I want to; I turn off the water and step out of the shower, grabbing a towel.

The material is soft and fluffy as I wrap it around my body. I towel dry my hair with another and look around for what I will wear when there is a knock on the door.

I jump at the sound, "Ye-" I clear my throat and speak up, "Yes."

"It's Kayden. I've brought you some clean clothes."

"Oh, thanks." I move to the door quickly and open it a few inches, and he pushes his hand through the gap to give me the clothes.

"You're welcome-" he's cut off by someone yelling for him before speaking to me again. "Abby, Layla is back; she needs to talk to you. It's urgent."

"Oh, okay. I'll be right out," I say, closing the door again. I let the towel drop to the floor and pull on the shorts, which would fit perfectly if I hadn't lost so much weight from imprisonment. I will need to do something about that. Next, I pull on the T-shirt, which I'm practically drowning in, and Tyler's scent hits me, making me inhale it deeply. Oh shit, this man's smell is going to be the death of me.

I step out of the bathroom, and I'm met with a pacing Layla, Julia standing in the corner, leaning against the wall with her arms folded across her chest.

Layla's pacing stops when she spots me, and a broad smile spreads on her face when she says, "Wow, Abby, you look way better."

"Thanks." Feeling a little self-conscious, I push some of my still-wet hair behind my ear. "Kayden says you need to speak to me."

"Have you seen Tyler yet?" she asks, and I frown. I already feel guilty about taking a shower before going to him.

"No." My voice is just above a whisper as I look at my feet. "I- I know I should've gone to him first, but-"

Layla walks over and pulls me into a quick hug before stepping back and giving me a sad smile. "I'm not accusing you, Abby. I am glad you could get cleaned up before seeing him. I have to tell you something before you go to Tyler, or rather ask you. I know it will be a lot, but I-" she says as she begins to cry.

"Hey, it's okay, Layla. Tell me what you need me to do." I smile softly, wiping the tears from her face.

"Don't just say that. You might feel that I am asking too much, but I need you to consider it, please, Abby," she pleads.

"Just tell me, Layla, what do you need me to do?"

"We went to the pack library where all the prophecies are kept. We spoke to Melissa, who showed us the prophecy about you and Tyler," Julia says, stepping closer. She looks worried, and that is making me unnerved.

"You guys are starting to freak me out. What's going on? What do you need me to do, Layla? Just say it."

"You and Tyler need to seal the bond, but there are complications with your situation."

They couldn't miss the blood draining from my face when I step back, my breathing becoming uneven. My mouth instantly dries up, making me swallow visibly, my eyes wide.

"It's okay, Abby. I know it scares you, especially with all you've been through, but trust me, my brother is a wonderful man. He will always love and protect you. You will be his entire universe." Layla steps towards me, her eyes soft and caring.

"I think so too, it's just…" I look at my feet again, touching the mark on my neck.

"Don't worry about that now. We'll deal with that when it's time," Layla says almost hesitantly, this time not looking at me—which is strange. It's like she's hiding something from me. I don't want to push her, though; now's not the time, so I make a mental note to ask her later about whatever it is she's not telling me.

"Okay." I nod, letting my hand fall to my side. "Are you going to tell me what you need from me?"

Layla glances at Julia, who nods encouragingly. Layla looks back at me and takes a deep breath. "Melissa, the librarian, has a theory, and we think it might work, and if it works, Tyler might be able to 'heal' if you will, to the extent that you two can seal the mate bond."

I raise my eyebrows and hug my arms around my chest; this is getting on my nerves. Can't she just spit it out? *For Pete's sake, tell me already.* Layla notices my uneasiness. "Shit, sorry, it's even more difficult to say than I thought, it's going to sound ridiculous, but you need to let Tyler feed on you," she says, blushing profusely.

"Um, what do you mean feed? Like drinking my blood?" I am dumbfounded. Werewolves don't need blood to survive. Vampires do. But then I tilt my head as the logic Layla was hinting at hits me: I'm a hybrid, and so is Tyler.

"But why my blood? How can my blood save him? I know we are supposed to be mates, but how can this work?" I ask, feeling my head spin.

"Well, Melissa did some research on your bloodline. She says that your bloodline traces back to the beginning of our existence. To both the original vampire and werewolf, which is extremely rare," Layla says with a frown. It's like she's also struggling to believe the words she just told me. "It's rare because, like you know, hybrid relationships were frowned upon and the children of the love affairs were killed. The concept of the 'pure bloodline' was considered a myth until now." Julia explains further when she sees the confusion on my face. "That's why your blood can help Tyler, and adding the fact that you are mated to him makes your blood so much stronger."

Shit, this is still something I need to wrap my head around. "Oh," is all I manage to force through my tightened throat.

"I know this is asking a lot, but Abby if this works, you will be able to save my brother-"

I hold my hand up to stop Layla from blabbering. "I'll do it. Tell me what you want me to do, and I'll do it." I give her a small smile, trying my best not to look as scared as I feel at this very moment.

"You will? Really? Oh, Abby, thank you!" She almost jumps on me, her smile wide.

"Yeah, no problem." It's a huge problem. Doesn't this then count as sealing the bond? I'm not even sure how this works.

"What is it, Abby?" Julia asks. "You look like you are about to throw up."

I let out a strained laugh, "Um, not sure. Does this not count as sealing the bond, though?"

"No, it doesn't. You, um," Julia giggles; the sound is weird. I've never heard her laugh before. "Sealing the bond requires both of you, um, to be naked, and… you know." She wiggles her eyebrows at me, and I know exactly what she means.

Shit! I blush bright red; my cheeks feel like there's fire underneath my skin. I quickly look down at my feet again. "Shit, I, um, I forgot about that part," I laugh nervously.

"Yeah, so like I said, we'll talk about that later. Unfortunately, yours won't be so easy," Layla says in her cryptic tone again.

A few minutes later, I slowly walk into Tyler's room. Layla has given me the gist of what I need to do. I am so nervous my hands are trembling. *You can do this, Abby, stop freaking yourself out.* I shake my hands a few times and take a few breaths as I round the corner of his bed, and the wind is knocked out of me when I see Tyler.

No, this isn't right. His skin is deathly pale and clammy, his breathing is shallow, and his face contorting in pain every few seconds. Tears sting my eyes, and I place my hand over my chest, hoping it may help keep my heart from breaking.

"Tyler," I whisper, too afraid I will hurt him if I speak any louder.

"Can I help you-? Oh, Abbygail, I'm so sorry I didn't recognize you. Layla filled me in on what you want to do. I'll give you some space." Adam says, setting down his notes and walking to the door.

"Doctor, wait." I turn to him. "Is this going to work?"

Adam stops and looks over his shoulder. "I don't know if anything else is going to work. If you don't try, he will probably not make it." With that, he leaves the room, closing the door behind him.

"No pressure," I mutter to myself.

I go to Tyler's bedside and sit down slowly, not wanting to cause him more pain. This is all my fault. A tear runs down my cheek; if Jace didn't find out about the damned prophecy, Tyler wouldn't be in this mess.

Tyler stirs when I sit down, groans, and opens his eyes slowly. Oh, my soul, how am I going to do this? He is going to think I've lost my mind. Feeling self-conscious, I pull my hair over my shoulder and play with the ends to keep my hands busy. "Tyler?" I say quietly again.

His eyes search for mine when he hears my voice; he inhales weakly and frowns. "Abby. Is that you?" he questions, his voice raspy.

"Yeah, it's me."

He smiles weakly. "How?"

"Kayden came and got me away from Jace and Owen." I'm careful not to tell him all of what happened. He can deal with it later when he is stronger.

"Good," he sighs and closes his eyes again.

"Hey, hey, no, open your eyes. I need to speak with you, please." I scoot nearer to him, touching his face lightly. Shit, he's burning up, but that tingling I feel every time we touch is just as strong as ever.

"Hmm," he hums. "Tired."

"I know, but Layla has an idea on how to get you stronger, and I'm here to see if it will work, so listen, okay."

He hums again, not opening his eyes. I get off the bed and move to his head, sitting down again, this time by his head with my back to the headboard. "You need to feed from me, okay?" Feeling silly, I blush. It's stupid, I know, but it sounds so weird.

Tyler opens his eyes again, frowning. "No, Abby, no." He shakes his head weakly.

"We don't have time to argue about this." My fangs elongate, and I bite into my wrist, tasting blood. I lower my wrist to Tyler's mouth, but he turns away. "Tyler, please. This might save you."

"*No.*" He tries to sound stern, but it doesn't do much in his weakened state, and I won't budge.

"I hear you're used to getting your way, but you'll lose this fight." I shove my bleeding wrist in his mouth, knowing full well that he doesn't have the strength to fight me.

He wants to turn his head from me again, but I gently place my free hand on his other cheek and keep him in place. "Drink," I say firmly.

He looks up at me, and I nod. He hesitates for a few seconds, but it's inevitable. The vampire in him has tasted blood. I feel his fangs scrape on my wrist before he bites deeper to make the blood flow freely. He swallows slowly, taking another suck on my wrist.

I stroke his hair softly while he drinks from me, and after a couple of minutes, I have to lean back on the bed's headboard, feeling a little dizzy. I haven't healed all the way, and this is draining me more than I thought it would. I don't know how much of my blood I am supposed to give him, but I'm starting to feel tired, and if he doesn't stop now, he will drain me.

My wrist slips from his lips, and his hand shoots up, grabbing it, and pushes it back against his mouth, gripping me hard, drinking deeper still.

"Tyler, you need to stop now. I'm feeling lightheaded," I whisper, and to my astonishment, he slows, and his grip on me loosens.

He licks at the two small holes he left on my wrist, and within seconds, they close. I really hope this works. I watch Tyler as I move to sit by his side again.

"How do you feel?" Closing my eyes, my cheeks red again. Why the hell am I still blushing? This is ridiculous.

I hear movement, and my eyes snap open when I feel his hand touch my face softly. I look into his beautiful, mismatched eyes. He stares at me intently. His smile is gorgeous, the corner of his mouth pulling up slightly, and I glimpse his fangs pushing just past his lips.

Oh fuck, if I weren't sitting down, I would melt. My eyes roam over Tyler's exposed torso before falling on his face again, taking in every inch of his features. His jawline is chiseled to perfection, with stubble starting to show. Every muscle is toned, and don't even get me started on the low-cut V of his hips disappearing into the hem of his sweatpants. This man is absurdly handsome. Without thinking, I lean into his touch and inhale deeply.

"I feel better; thank you," his deep, rich voice caresses my ears.

"I'm so happy this worked." I smile shily. "I'll call Layla and Kayden; they must be worried sick." I rise from the bed, turning to walk to the door, when I feel strong arms snake around my waist, pulling my back against his chest. Tyler pushes his nose into my hair, inhaling deeply.

"Hmmm," he hums.

I gasp, jumping, "Tyler? What are you doing out of bed? Please-"

Tyler spins me to face him and pulls me against his chest again before I can even finish my sentence. "I have wanted to do this from the first moment I saw you," he says, his voice even lower than usual as he cups my cheek and drags his thumb over my bottom lip.

His breath hitches in his throat when I pull my tongue over the spot his thumb was moments ago.

I take in the sight of him, his hooded eyes not moving from my mouth. Tyler's grip tightens around my waist when a moan slips past my lips, making me blush again. He groans low in his throat, and it feels like my stomach is making a flip as moisture builds between my legs.

Shit, we can't go down this path now, not with his sister and his Beta just outside the door, able to walk in any minute—and to be honest, everything about this is freaking me out a little.

I place my shaking hands on his bare chest. *Oh fuck, this feels so good.* I close my eyes, taking a shaky breath and inhaling his precious scent, pushing him from me lightly. "I, um, I don't think you're strong enough for this yet, and I am not sure I'm ready."

Tyler tilts his head slightly and slowly looks up at me, a low, frustrated growl vibrating in his chest. This is exactly why we cannot do this now. We don't know each other. How can he possibly be feeling like this towards me? *It's just lust from the bond*, I tell myself.

I push against his chest again, a little harder this time. He groans and huffs as he drops his hands from me. Tyler sways, and I grab him around his waist, dipping under his arm so I can support his weight, his arm around my neck.

"This is exactly what I'm talking about. You are too stubborn for your own good," I growl at him, and he chuckles.

"Did you just laugh at me?"

"Yeah, you're feisty, aren't you," he teases as I help him back into bed.

"Only when I have to deal with stubborn Alphas that don't listen," I say playfully, covering Tyler with his duvet. "I'm going to get your sister and your Beta. Please don't get up again."

"Yes, ma'am," he laughs softly as I walk to the door, and I throw him a scowl over my shoulder before opening it. I quickly step out of the way as Layla stumbles into the room, almost falling on me.

"What the hell?" I exclaim. "Were you listening at the door?"

Layla gives me a wolfish grin. "Um," she laughs, rubbing the back of her neck, and shrugs. "Maybe."

I cross my arms, feigning shock. "This was *supposed* to be a private moment. Tyler's awake and waiting for you," I motion toward the bed as the blush creeps up my neck again.

"Hey, little sis," Tyler's voice comes from behind me in his bed. He sounds stronger—but not yet to the point where he is able to… *um, yeah, I'm not going there now.*

I didn't think it was possible, but Layla's face lights up even more. This girl's emotions are going to give me whiplash. She runs past me, and I see Kayden walking in slowly, his hands in his pockets. He looks like someone awaiting a scolding. It's strange to see him like this. Is he scared of Tyler? What kind of Alpha is Tyler if his people are afraid of him?

I shudder to think—if he is that frightening to his Beta, what will he do to me?

Stop it, I scold myself. This man hasn't hurt me yet. I know what he did in his haze, but that doesn't count. I think. We need time to get to know each other, that's all.

Time, *hmmm*, I really do have time now. *I'm free and have time with my mate*, I think to myself as I absentmindedly rub my neck where the collar used to be. I smile to myself; I will never forget this feeling. I don't ever want to lose it.

Looking over to where Layla almost tackles Tyler, my smile widens even more, knowing I can at least bring joy to this mess I've caused. "Ty!" Layla almost sobs as she hugs her brother, then shoves his shoulder lightly when she pulls back. "This shit needs to end, my heart can't take anymore."

"What?" he asks innocently. "Like I asked for this," he laughs, and the guilt I was feeling previously comes rushing back. I lower my head, feeling more ashamed than I did before.

Damn it.

"Earth to Abby, Hello!" Layla laughs, waving her hand to get my attention. "Why are you zoning out so much?"

I look up quickly, and all of them stare at me, even Julia, whom I didn't see pass me when she entered the room.

"Sorry." I blush again. This is starting to irritate me. I didn't know I was capable of looking like a bloody tomato ninety percent of the time. "Got lost in my thoughts."

"Yeah, we kind of guessed that." Layla rolls her eyes at me. "So what's running through your head so much?"

"I, um…" I rub my neck again, my eyes falling on Tyler, his dark eyes looking through me, or at least that's what it feels like, and I look away quickly. "Just never thought I would be free, and the feeling is awesome." I won't reveal my guilt for placing Tyler and all of them in harm's way.

Tyler tilts his head at my statement, narrowing his eyes, silent, not saying a word. That's very unnerving. I clear my throat and walk to the foot of his bed, avoiding his eyes. I can feel him watching me, and the memory of his arms around my waist and his body so close to mine stirs feelings in me that I didn't know I could feel.

I feel flustered. *Ugh, what the hell?*

Tyler watches me for a few more seconds before turning to Kayden. "So bud, this was an interesting couple of days, wasn't it?" he says, folding his arms across his chest, looking very intimidating.

"Yeah," Kayden huffs, pulling a hand through his hair. "I'm sorry, man. You know it was necessary."

Tyler lifts an eyebrow, his arms still crossed over his chest. After about a minute, he slowly smiles. "You did good, my friend. You kept this pack safe when I couldn't, and most importantly, you got my life back." Tyler looks at me as he says the last part, and I get the feeling he isn't talking about his actual life. My eyes find my feet again, and the lingering blush deepens.

Kayden's mouth hangs open for a few seconds before he clears his throat and frowns. "You're not mad at me?"

"No, I'm proud, actually. Not many people have the guts to do what you have done," Tyler chuckles.

"I think I am losing my damn mind. I really thought you would have my head for all that happened," Kayden sounds shocked.

"Don't tempt me, though," Tyler laughs, the sound pleasing, throaty and deep. "How did you manage to get Abby from Jace? You need to tell me what happened." Tyler looks at me and then back at Kayden, his face serious again.

"Well, I called Sebastian, and we followed Abby's scent. It was laced with pain and fear; the smell was so strong you couldn't miss it. We tracked them to the basement. I had to grab my baseball bat from my room because if I had to fight that shithead, I would've killed him," Kayden huffs before he continues.

"I busted through the door as Abby's screams rang through the entire dungeon. It wasn't a pretty sight, man. I'm glad you weren't the one to find her; that would've caused a war." Kayden whistles as he raises his brow at Tyler.

Tyler watches Kayden as he speaks. Now and then, he glances at me, his eyes emotionless—or, I'm struggling to read the emotion behind them.

Why is Kayden telling this to him now? It's so unnecessary. "Kayden, please, Tyler doesn't need to hear this. Please just leave it, it's over now."

"No, Abby, he needs to know."

"Fuck," I mutter, crossing my arms over my chest when Kayden continues.

"Anyway, I busted through the door and knocked them both out with the bat. Abby here," he says, pointing at me with his thumb, "was hanging from her wrists. Jace had cut her with his knife on her side, and he whipped her so bad her back was ripped open."

As Kayden speaks, I watch Tyler's expression, his anger at the latter part of the events clear on his face. He crosses his arms over his chest to hide his balled-up fists. This is precisely why I don't want him to know. Tyler looks at me, and he frowns. "I don't understand. How are you standing there—and having just fed me your blood—if you were injured so badly?"

"Well, we moved her to Adam as soon as we could, and when we got here, the bleeding stopped completely, and her wounds were almost completely healed. We think it has something to do with the fact that she is of a pure bloodline descent," Kayden says.

"What?!" Tyler exclaims. "What did you say?"

"I, um, I'm a hybrid," I mutter again, and his eyes flash black before returning to their normal color. Heat pools at my core at his reaction, which throws me off guard as I stare at him.

Tyler catches me staring, and the half-smile on his lips speaks lustful volumes. I avert my eyes quickly. Shit, this man is driving me crazy. I can't decide if the mate bond is making me feel this way or if it is my feelings.

"Show me," he almost grumbles.

"I-I, um, I need some fresh air." Swallowing, I step backward, Tyler's eyes still on me. He makes me tingle all over when he looks at me that way, and I need to get some distance.

I have mixed feelings, and now he wants me to show him I'm a hybrid, but I can't. Not now, not with everyone watching. If he has that lustful look in his eyes just from finding out I'm a hybrid, then showing him will not keep him in that bed.

I turn and walk out the door before anyone can stop me.

I rush from Tyler's room and make it a few feet from the door before stopping in the middle of the hall, exhaling my breath, and leaning with my back against the wall. *Shit.* I take a few deep breaths, sliding to the floor.

"You, okay?" I jump at Julia's voice. "Jeez, Abby, relax," she says as she comes to sit next to me.

"I, um," I laugh nervously. "I don't really know." I pull my hand through my dry hair and rest my head against the wall, closing my eyes.

"Your emotions are going haywire. You know you can still talk to me, right?"

Turning my head to Julia, frowning, I say, "What do you mean my emotions are going haywire? Don't get me wrong, you are accurate, but how do you know?"

"Abby, I can smell it coming off you in waves," She smiles knowingly and sniffs the air. "For example, confusion, some fear but the good kind, and then," she sniffs again and laughs softly, "arousal and then a fuck load of confusion again."

I laugh as I cover my face with my hands. "Shit, are you serious? Can anyone smell that?"

"No, just if they are in close proximity to you, but you know you can mask your emotional scent, right?"

"What? No, I didn't know that."

Julia laughs again. "There's a lot you need to learn; masking your scent will come when your wolf is stronger and you two act as one."

"This day keeps getting better and better, doesn't it?" I say sarcastically, staring at the opposite wall, and I sigh. "I don't know what to do about these feelings I get when Tyler watches me. The way he looks at me makes certain parts of me 'hot,' if you know what I mean. Don't even get me started on when he pushed up against me and then when he wanted me to show him I'm a hybrid. I can't think straight."

"Wait, what? When did this happen?" Julia almost squeals, a smile stretching across her face.

I cover my face again. "Right after he drank from me, I stood up to call you guys in, and he came up behind me, wrapped his arms around my waist, and, um, pulled me against him, smelling my hair."

"And? Did he kiss you? Come on, Abby, spill the beans."

"I thought I would get this type of questioning from Layla, but you are just as bad," I laugh at her. "No, he didn't. He spun me to face him. I don't know. Maybe I offended him or something because his eyes were dark and hooded as I pushed him away. So, I don't know."

Julia stares at me like I just slapped her. She hits the palm of her hand to her forehead. "Fuck Abby, really? Have you ever been in a situation with a guy like that?" She sees the look of horror on my face as I shake my head before looking down at my hands.

"Shit, sorry, I…"

Julia can't finish her sentence; she knows what happened to me in the six years I've been with them. I'm lucky enough that Jace never went that far, but the other stuff was just as bad.

"It's okay, really. I, um, I haven't, though. Other than what happened with Jace and Owen, I haven't ever been with someone like that, no."

"I'm sorry, Abby, I'm so insensitive. My excitement for your happiness is so overwhelming that it slipped my mind," Julia apologizes, not looking at me.

"Julia, please, don't feel bad. I'm not mad; I wish I could forget, but it's like a dark cloud hovering over me. I don't even know how I can give my everything to Tyler without this getting in the way."

"Well, if you ask me, you need to tell him so he knows what he's dealing with. I believe he will be patient enough and support you," Julia smiles reassuringly, taking my hands in hers.

I huff, "That man embodies impatience and stubbornness, and I don't even know what else."

"You barely know him, Abby. How can you say that?" She laughs delightfully.

"Hey, don't laugh. In Tyler's weakened state, nearly dying, he tried to fight me when I wanted to give him my blood. He even tried to use his Alpha voice on me. Can you believe it?" I say, exasperated.

Julia laughs wholeheartedly, and it rings through the hall; it sounds so genuine and pure, making me feel at ease.

Maybe she's right; maybe with the mate bond, I can forget what happened—or at the very least, it won't get in between me and Tyler. I will get the courage to tell him.

CHAPTER TWENTY-ONE

TYLER

"So, you sure you're feeling okay?" Layla asks after Abby leaves abruptly. *Where is she going now?* This woman just can't stay put. "Ty?" Layla asks expectantly, and I realize I'm not listening to her.

"Yeah?"

Layla watches me, her eyebrows raised. She's lying on my bed, propped up on her elbow. Kayden leans against the bedpost with his arms crossed over his chest, seeing that I wasn't listening. I look at him for help, but he shakes his head and shrugs as he laughs at me.

Shit, what did she say?

"I asked you if you're sure you are feeling okay. It seems your head left with Abby. You are so whipped," she laughs teasingly.

"Careful, Lay, my temper might be tamed at this time, but I am still your Alpha," I joke, leaning my head against the headboard, my back propped up against my pillows.

"I have to agree with Layla. You are totally whipped. Ever since you saw Abby, your head has not been clear," Kayden chuckles.

"Hey, can you blame me? That woman knocked the wind out of me and screwed with my senses. I honestly thought I would never find my mate, and can you believe it? Layla was right." Eyeing my sister at the last part. Her mouth drops open, and I chuckle.

"Huh, did my ears deceive me? Did you say I'm right about something?" she says, surprised.

"Hmm, don't rub it in, though. You said it would bring me to my knees when I meet my mate, and it literally did."

She bursts out laughing. "You're right, I did. See, don't mess with me. I know what's good for you."

I huff, gesturing to my bed and my situation. "Yeah, it was *really* good for me. It nearly fucking killed me," I tease Layla, not noticing Abby and Julia re-entering my room.

A soft gasp makes me look up. The look on Abby's face nearly breaks my heart. Shit, my big fucking mouth and shitty sense of humor. She looks from me to Layla before pulling herself together, the guilt on her face only evident for a few seconds before she hides it again. I thought I saw it on her face earlier, but I wasn't sure. We need to address this later when we are alone. I can't let her feel guilty for what happened.

"So, I think we must let Tyler rest for a while, don't you think?" Abby says, walking to my bedside.

"Yeah, you're right; Tyler is looking pale again. Maybe you should stay and look after him," Layla says mischievously.

Abby blushes bright red. She shifts her weight from one foot to the other, chewing the inside of her cheek, clearly uncomfortable.

I sigh, closing my eyes to hide the slight irritation behind them before saying, "Lay, thanks for coming to see me and looking after me when I couldn't, but I am capable of looking after myself." I despise it when someone lingers and faffs over me. It drives me insane.

I throw the covers off me and get out of bed. "Let me walk you to the door."

The strength I was feeling earlier is now almost gone. I take two steps before my heart slams against my chest, and I gasp for air. My legs give in and slump against the bed. Abby's blood is supposed to be the cure. What the hell is happening now?

"Tyler!" Abby yells, running to me. Kayden and Layla are at her side as soon as she kneels beside me.

"I'll call Adam." Julia hurries out of the room, and within seconds, she returns with Adam on her heels.

"Please give me some space," Adam says as he and Kayden help me to get back on the bed.

My energy is completely drained, and I struggle to breathe evenly. The pain I felt in my office after Jace marked Abby is back, not as bad, though, more so lingering in the background.

I feel so stupid. No Alpha wants to be seen as weak and incompetent, and here I am, being pathetic.

Adam takes my wrist, checking my pulse as I try not to look at Abby and the disgust she must feel being mated to me.

My thoughts fade into nothingness when pain shoots through my head again; I guess it decided the background wasn't good enough. I grunt, grabbing my head as my breathing quickens.

"The blood is supposed to work. Why didn't it work?" Abby asks, her voice sounding small and afraid.

The pain moves from my head to my chest, and my back arches off the bed, making me grit my teeth, suppressing a scream. I don't want to frighten Abby more than I already have. "Lay, t-take Abby," I grunt again. "T-take her out of here." I grit my teeth when the pain crushes my chest again.

"NO!" Abby almost growls and pushes past Kayden and Adam. She lifts my head and slides into the space, resting my head on her legs. I am covered in sweat, and the little bit of strength I have left is disappearing.

She strokes my cheek. "I am not letting you die. Do you hear me?"

Her confidence and authority are unmistakable, and to my astonishment, there is no trace of disgust or regret anywhere in her tone. She bites down on her wrist again, drawing blood. I don't have time to stop her before she pushes her wrist to my mouth, and I taste the sweet liquid, filling my mouth and running down my throat.

I drink deeply, unable to resist the pull of her blood. The action comes naturally; the taste is almost as delicious as her scent. I need this to survive, but for how long? I can't depend on my mate to survive, not like this. How will I ever be able to protect her and my pack? If anyone finds out about this, they will think I'm weak, placing her in even more danger.

With every swallow, my strength returns, and so does my anger at the thought of anyone hurting Abby because of me. I tighten my hold on her arm and bite deeper so the blood will flow more freely, my energy returning with every mouthful of blood running down my throat. I'm getting drunk on euphoria and the strength her blood is giving me.

"Ty...TYLER!" Layla yells. "You need to stop; you're going to drain her. Stop Tyler!" She tries to pry my hands from Abby's arm, but it proves futile since I have a death grip on it.

Abby sways and slumps backward against the headboard, her wrist limp in my hands.

Fuck, what have I done? My fangs retract, and I let go of her. Adam's beside her quickly, his hand at the back of her head, keeping her up and feeling her pulse.

"She's okay," he says after the longest three seconds of my life, then turns to Julia. "Go get her some juice and something to eat. She needs to build her strength up after this feeding."

Julia nods and hurries out of my room to the kitchen. I move out of the way so we can lie Abby down. Adam takes some pillows and places them under her feet, elevating them.

"Abbygail, can you hear me? Hey... There you go, come on, wake up." He taps her lightly on the cheek. She opens her eyes slightly, her face pale.

"Tyler," she whispers, and I lower my head, relieved, a tear running down my face. Am I fucking crying? Are you kidding me? What is this woman doing to me? This beautiful creature is waking up emotions I forgot I had. It's refreshing but also unnerving. I can't remember the last time I cried.

"I'm here. I'm so sorry, Abby. I didn't realize I was taking so much." I'm on my knees beside her on the bed, wishing I hadn't taken so much from her.

She lifts her shaking hand and places it on my cheek, wiping the tear away with her thumb. "It's okay, just as long as you're better, it doesn't matter." She smiles weakly.

Leaning into her hand, I frown. It's so cold that I look at Adam, who sees the worry on my face.

"It's normal. You've taken much of Abbygail's blood, and she's still healing from her injuries. You and her need to find a balance, that's all."

After a few minutes, Adam sighs, looking pained at what he needs to say next, "I'm afraid until we find a permanent solution to your predicament, you will have to feed from Abbygail regularly."

"What? NO!" This is ridiculous.

Layla catches my attention when she loudly groans, the absolute horror of the situation playing on her face. She avoids my eyes before looking at me, recognition behind hers. "Layla? Do you want to tell me something?" I snap at my sister.

Regularly feeding on Abby is something I'm struggling to process. I can't expect her to do this, not after what she has been through, and definitely not if *this* will result in me feeding on her each time. Letting go of Abby's hand, I get off the bed slowly. I can't push my body to the limit; the blood only lasts so long, and Abby is in no position to give me more.

"This is what the prophecy means, oh shit," Layla mutters under her breath, before speaking up. "I—we—went to the library asking about the prophecy Jace overheard and about the bond between you and Abby. The prophecy warns about fatal consequences if another marks your mate."

"What!" My temper is flaring. "Why didn't you tell me this? Don't you think this is information that is crucial to know!" I ball my fists at my side and walk towards my sister. How can she not tell me this, or even Abby? We have the right to know.

"Tyler, please, don't be angry with Layla. It's my fault, so please direct your anger at me. I am the one doing this to you," Abby's voice comes softly behind me, making me stop dead in my tracks. I look over my shoulder in her direction and find her leaning against the bedpost, unsteady on her feet, her eyes cast down.

My anger disappears at once, and I move to her quickly. Hooking my finger under her chin, I lift her face.

"Look at me, Abbygail." My voice is stern, and her eyes slowly make their way up to mine. "I will say this only once, so you better listen carefully. You're not at fault, and I'm not blaming you. Do you understand me? This happened because Jace wanted to take what was mine. I don't want you to feel guilty about any of this or blame yourself, *ever*."

Tears form in her beautiful emerald eyes, and she nods slowly, but my words do not convince her. "Still, I'm so sorry this is happening to you and your family. I wish I could just disappear and take all this shit from you. I–"

"I would rather die than have you disappear from me again. You are my world, Abby; you are destined for so much greatness. Do you not see that? Do you not know your worth?"

She looks confused at my words; of course, she doesn't know. Jace has ensured she will always feel less than she is.

This is pissing me off. My anger churns in my stomach, threatening to spill to the surface. I close my eyes and take a few deep breaths; Abby's soft hand wraps around my wrist, still holding her face up, and at her touch, my anger dissipates. My eyes snap open, and I frown at her hand before finding hers again.

"Did you feel that?" Her eyes are wide with surprise, and I nod.

This has never happened before; nothing can rein in my temper except for me, which takes a lot of hard concentration. For the first time, I can think with a clear mind, my anger not getting the better of me.

I ask Layla what the prophecy says, never taking my eyes off Abby. My mind is numb as she recites it to me while Abby's face is expressionless.

Why wasn't I told about this? If I had known about this beforehand, I could've searched for her, and all this could've been avoided.

"There must be some mistake. I don't think the prophecy is about me. This must be a joke. I am not strong enough to be a Luna, never mind a Luna to an Alpha King…" Abby's voice trembles before she trails off.

"Oh, believe me, Abby, the prophecy is definitely about you and my brother; everything said there describes you to a tee," Layla states.

Panic erupts in my chest when Abby glances at me before sinking on the bed. "Are you okay?"

She gives me a small smile. "Yeah, um, I'm just struggling to wrap my head around this. It's overwhelming. I'm trying my absolute best not to freak out here. A few hours ago, I was a slave to someone who let me believe I am not worth the air I breathe, and now you tell me I'm supposed to be Luna to one of *the* most powerful packs that ever existed, and it will be historic?" Abby's voice climbs an octave at the last few words.

"Basically, yeah, but there's more," Layla cringes. She looks around the room just as Julia returns with an orange juice and a granola bar. She hands it to Abby, who shakes her head to show she doesn't want it, but I take it from Julia.

"What is it you said to me? I'm too stubborn for my own good. Right? Well, the same counts for you, my love." Abby gasps when she hears my endearment, looking up at me again, and I smile lovingly at her. "You're going to eat and drink this. If you don't, I will feed it to you."

Abby stares at me for a few seconds, stunned. She laughs softly and takes the items from me. "Okay," she says without arguing.

Fuck, that's the first time I've heard her laugh, and the sound of it is light and magical. I'm too hyperfocused on these small details, but this woman constantly surprises me. Abby opens the juice and takes a few sips from it, closing her eyes, and a soft moan slips past her lips. I watch her like I've never seen anyone drink liquid before. With her, it's different, graceful, sexy even.

Watching her, I swallow hard when certain parts of me twitch, and my dick hardens. I swallow hard again, *fuck*, I'm getting hard just watching her drink juice. I'm being ridiculous.

Abby eyes me suspiciously, and I'm sure she smells my arousal when her nose twitches. It *really* isn't the time for this, and I rip my eyes from her and focus on Layla instead.

"What is it, Layla?" Clenching my jaw, I close my eyes, which is of no help because I only see Abby. That little moan she let out rings in my ears, turning me on even more. *Fuck!*

"Melissa says the only way you can 'cure' this is…" Her eyes jump from mine to Abby's, and she sighs. "You have to mark each other, but there's a catch." When I look at Abby, the fear on her face at the thought of being marked again makes me want to kill Jace even more. White hot fury is now replacing my arousal.

"Lay, you better get to the point. My patience is wearing thin, and my head is starting to hurt. Tell me how we can fix this."

I move to sit next to Abby, resting my elbows on my knees and pinching the bridge of my nose.

"I'll get right to the point then. Abby can die if you mark her, but it's the only way. If she is strong enough, she can survive, but it's so rare there isn't much information on it," Layla's voice is shaking now.

"Excuse me? So, what you tell me is it's either me or her?" I snap, narrowing my eyes at my sister. I must be dreaming. What kind of sick joke is this? Finding my mate only to be cursed with this situation, and now I'm told that I should choose between myself and her. There is obviously no choice to make. I will not take her life to save mine.

Layla must know where my thought process is leading because the tears are already running down her cheeks. "Tyler, Abby is strong, she can survive this." Layla turns to Abby now. "Right, Abby?"

The horror on Abby's face is indescribable. Her hands are trembling, and her breathing is picking up. I sense it a few seconds before it hits her.

"LEAVE," I bellow in my Alpha voice. No one can resist, and that's exactly what I need. Everyone moves out of the room quickly, leaving me alone with Abby.

CHAPTER TWENTY-TWO

ABBYGAIL

My chest tightens, and I'm struggling to breathe. My vision is blurry, and all the voices around me sound like they're talking underwater. I faintly make out Tyler's bellow, and all I know is that I can't get this panic attack to subside. I have no control as the tears stream down my face and my chest compresses. A boa constrictor might as well be around my body, crushing me to death.

I hear the door close, and my panic attack hits like a volcano erupting. I pull my knees up to my chest and fold my arms around my legs, crushing them to me. It feels like I'm drifting in space and have nowhere to grab onto. Through the panic in my mind, Tyler calls to me. His hand firmly clasps the back of my neck, and his other strokes my cheek.

"Hey, my love, breathe, okay? Everything is going to be okay; just breathe."

To my astonishment, my body obeys his command. I inhale deeply and let it out slowly, repeating the process again and again until I feel the air rushing to my lungs.

"That's it, you can calm down now, breathe," Tyler soothes. My body relaxes, my breathing slows as I come out of my panic, and my vision clears.

He lets go of my neck and picks me up, placing me in his lap and folding his arms around me. I lean into his chest, my tears still running down my face.

I wake to light snoring beside me, and it takes a few minutes for my brain to catch up. I'm still in Tyler's arms. I must've fallen asleep last night because I don't remember getting into bed with him. He's holding onto me for dear life, or that's what it feels like.

I'm burning up. The heat from this man should be illegal; it could start forest fires. It's suffocating, and yet it feels like home.

This beautiful specimen sleeping so soundly next to me—or rather, more on top than anything else—is mine. However, I don't know for how long. Layla's words play in my head again, and with that, the panic threatens to return. "Shit," I whisper, placing my arm over my eyes, making Tyler stir.

I don't want to wake him. He needs the rest. How long has it been since he last fed? I don't even know what time it is. *Damn it!* This is why I'm burning up against him; his fever must've spiked again. I gently wiggle out of his arms and sit up. Reaching over him, I grab his phone, press the button, and the time pops up on the screen.

Fuck.

"Tyler, hey, come on, you need to wake up," I lightly shake him after placing the phone on the bedside table again. He only moans but doesn't open his eyes. I touch his forehead with the back of my hand, and he is searing hot. Damn it, how could I let this happen again?

Getting off the bed, I run to the bathroom, take one of the towels from the shelf, wet it thoroughly with cold water, wring it out, and run back to the bed.

I get back onto the bed and sit on my knees beside his large body. Tyler is still not moving, so I roll him on his back to place the wet, cold towel on his forehead. As soon as the cold touches his skin, he hisses, and opens his eyes slowly.

"Oh, thank goodness, you're awake," I sigh, relieved, dabbing the towel across his face. He forces a weak smile, but I know he's trying to hide his pain from me. "How are you feeling?"

He groans, "I'm okay. Just need to rest. Don't worry about me, okay?"

"Pfft, yeah, right." Rolling my eyes, I feel his pulse, and it's not as weak as the day before, but still not strong enough. "Please, don't lie to me. I can obviously see that you're suffering. Come on, it's time to feed." I shuffle closer to his head and bring my wrist to my mouth.

Suddenly, Tyler grabs my wrist with more force than I thought he could muster at this time, which makes me jump. "No, Abbygail. I've had enough. I'm not drinking from you again."

"What do you mean? You need my blood to survive, Tyler. Please don't be difficult. I don't have the strength to argue with you." I really didn't. Thinking of Layla's words again, this is inevitable. It's either me or him—but like she says, maybe I am strong enough.

"I'm not being difficult, my love. I don't see the point of drinking from you when we both know I will not sacrifice your life for my own. I will never put you in harm's way, *ever*. There is no argument here. My word is final."

He lets go of my wrist, his eyes stern, though I can see the toll this is taking on him.

"Oh really." I'm getting pissed off now. "Your word is final, is it? So, you're saying I mean the same to you as I did to Jace, just someone you can boss around without me having a say in the world!"

Tyler grunts as he struggles to sit up. He reaches for me, but I turn away from his grasp, getting off the bed. I'm fuming.

"I'm tired of being treated like I have no say, like what I want and need doesn't count. This is bullshit!"

I am full-on yelling now. I know it's not the time for this and that Tyler doesn't need the stress, but everything is coming out in waves, and I can't seem to stop.

"Abby, babe, plea-"

I glare at him, and to my surprise, he stops talking. "Don't, okay, just don't." I move to the opposite side of the room, leaning with my back and head against the wall, Tyler's eyes never leaving me.

It's so bloody frustrating.

I slide down the wall until I'm sitting on the floor, my knees pulled up, and cover my face with my hands as the damn tears run down my face.

Clearing his throat, Tyler rests his hand on my knee. I didn't hear him get up.

"Babe, please don't cry. I've made up my mind. You've been through so much. How can I possibly take your life from you when you just got it back? I am supposed to protect you, not hurt you-"

"You are hurting me now," I snap irritably.

Tyler looks taken aback and removes his hand from me, and frowns. "What, how, I-"

"You are hurting me by deciding my future, *our* future for me. I know I'm not what you want in a mate, and you must think I'm weak with all my issues and everything. I'm not even something remotely attract-" A sob slips past my lips, and Tyler grasps my chin rather firmly between his index finger and thumb and pulls my head up. I resist looking into his eyes, and he grips my chin a little tighter, making me look at him, and when I do, his usually abnormal-colored eyes are almost black.

"You don't ever talk about yourself like that again, do you understand me? You are everything I never knew I needed. You have ripped my world apart, and all I want is you. I'm struggling to think clearly. Don't you understand, Abby?" His voice is low and gravelly, and heat stirs and pools low in my stomach. His stare is so intense I start squirming.

He rests his other hand next to my head against the wall and dips his head down to me, our lips almost touching.

My heart is beating a million miles per second, and I am going to hyperventilate from the anticipation of what's about to happen. "I need you more than I need to breathe," he nearly pleads.

I feel his breath on my lips as he talks. *Damn it, this feels good.* He watches me for a few seconds before he closes the gap and places a light kiss on my lips, and my breath catches in my throat. As soon as his lips touch mine, an electric current runs through my body. He pulls back slightly, that alluring crooked smile turning my thought process into a puddle before kissing me again, this time a little harder, more hungrily.

A moan slips through my lips, and he groans, leaning into the kiss even more. Tyler pulls back from me again, both of us breathless, and gets up, stumbling a bit. He pulls me up from the floor and pins me against the wall, not hurting me once.

"Abby, you are driving me insane," he breathes as he leans his head against mine.

He cups my face with both hands, watching my mouth. I take a shaky breath, placing my hands on his chest; without thinking, I pull my fang over my bottom lip, and he growls deep in his chest.

"Fuck," is all I hear before his lips are on mine again, he kisses me deeply, fiercely, a moan escaping my lips again, and he takes this opportunity to deepen the kiss.

He slips his tongue into my mouth, making me gasp again, pushing his body closer to mine, slipping his hand behind my back, pulling me to him, and holding me in place. I've never been kissed like this, and it's incredible. I kiss him back with all the fire burning in me. My body responds to his every touch, to the delicious sound I pull from his chest. I push myself closer to him, his hard cock twitching against me through his sweatpants.

The realization of the situation I find myself in makes itself known, and it's like I'm being woken up from a dream. This is moving too fast; my heart is pounding against my chest. I push against Tyler's chest, and he pulls back from me slightly, both of us trying to catch our breaths.

I swallow, blushing when I look at him. "We, um," I pant, "we can't do this. You can't overexert yourself, please."

We don't move from our stance, his breathing heavy as he watches me intently. He closes his eyes and leans his forehead against mine again. "Hmmm, maybe you're right. I'm sorry if I overstepped my boundaries," Tyler grumbles, his voice reverberating through me, giving me goosebumps.

Shit, I need some distance between us. I lightly push him from me and move to the other side of the room, opposite him. Sighing, I swipe my hair out of my face, my back to him.

The chemistry between us is so strong I'm finding it difficult to stay this far away from him, especially when he looks at me the way he does.

After a few pregnant minutes, Tyler chuckles, but it sounds off. He's leaning against the wall, his arm folded over his chest, gripping his ribs when I turn to face him again.

"You feel it too, don't you? The absolute need to be with me, like I feel with you. The difference is you, apparently, have more control," Tyler groans weakly, sliding down the wall when his knees give out.

"Damn it, Tyler!" Running to his side, I catch him as he slumps.

"Fuck, I'm sorry, my love. I wish I could make you feel how much I want to be with you, but our time is limited."

"This is so much bullshit, do you hear me? You will not leave me this easily!" I grit out, bringing my wrist to my mouth. I bite down on it, and as soon as I taste blood, I force it into his mouth. "You will not deny me the right to be loved. We're done arguing about this. You don't have the right to decide if I want to live or die; that is my choice. So, drink my damn blood, get your strength back so we can discuss this fucking problem."

I don't know where I got the absolute badass attitude from, but I like it. I will never feel sorry for myself again, and Tyler will just have to deal with me being in charge of this decision. I will not be made a widow before we even have a chance to start our lives together.

Tyler grabs my wrist, pulling it from his mouth. "Abbygail, I said no," he commands, pushing me away, and stands, staggering, moving away from me. "You need to leave."

I get to my feet, livid, walking to him slowly.

"Tyler, so fucking help me, you have two choices." My eyes change color as my anger rises, my fangs protruding past my lips. He said he wanted to see me turn, so here it is. "You either drink from me willingly, or I chain your ass to that fucking bed and force-feed you until you are strong enough. There are *no* other options." My voice has a different tone to it. I'm challenging my mate and his wolf. I will not budge.

Tyler narrows his eyes at me, folding his arms across his chest, breathing labored. "Are you challenging my authority, Abbygail?"

"Yes," I snarl.

A growl ripples through his chest, and his eyes get a red hue to them. This fucking man is really trying to assert his Alpha dominance on me. *Well, tough luck, buddy. You are stuck with a mate who will not back down ever again. Let's see who wins this fight.*

I can't quite pinpoint why his Alpha voice doesn't work on me—maybe because of my bloodline or because I'm his mate. I don't really care at this time. Looking him dead in the eyes, still walking to him, I tilt my head and cross my arms.

He stands his ground, not moving an inch as I draw closer. I stop before him, my chin tipping back when I look at him.

Tyler towers over me, my frame so much smaller than his. His shoulders are almost one and a half times my width.

I place my wrist to my mouth and bite into my vein again—it had already healed shut. I pull my wrist away and lift it just enough for him to make some effort to come to me since I would need to stand on my toes to reach his mouth.

"Drink."

"No." He clenches his jaw, the muscle ticking once, twice. The hunger behind them is dangerous when his eyes fall on my dripping blood.

"Are you really going to waste my blood, let it drip on the floor? Am I worth that little to you?" I ask slowly, raising my brow.

Tyler growls again. "Fuck Abby, you aren't playing fair."

A sly smile appears on my lips. I nudge my wrist closer to him. Tyler bends down, slides his hands under my ass, grabs it, and lifts me off the ground in one smooth motion. He guides my legs around his waist, and I lock them behind his back.

Tyler groans, takes my wrist in his hand, his fangs elongating, and pulls it to his mouth. His eyes still narrow as he bites down, and I gasp from the sting.

He closes his eyes, and a deep, satisfied moan sounds from his throat when he starts to drink. I can feel his strength return when his grip on me tightens. Suddenly, Tyler turns us, walking until my back slams against the wall, pinning me there while he hungrily swallows down the blood.

After a few minutes, he pulls away from my wrist, licking at the two small holes, and tingles run through my body.

He drops my wrist, and his mouth finds mine again, kissing me urgently, his tongue pushing its way into my mouth.

I can't help but moan, and he grabs onto my hips and pushes me down as he pushes his pelvis upwards, grinding against me. I tangle my fingers in his hair as the heat in my crotch drives me insane from him kissing me this way. I feel his need for me, and I can't help but grind against him in return, making him growl dangerously, gripping me tighter, his fingers digging into my skin.

"Fuck, Abby," he pants, biting my bottom lip. "I don't want to lose control with you. I don't want to scare you away from me. I think we need to slow down and discuss our situation like you said."

"Hmm," I hum into him, gripping his hair tighter. "Are you thinking clearly now?" I mock him seductively. I pull away from his lips with difficulty, my hands still in his hair as I smile. "Don't you feel so much better now?" I tilt my head to the side, lifting it a little.

"Don't push it, my love. Not many people have the guts to square off with me like you did just now." He smiles proudly at me. "You are so hot, taking charge like that."

I laugh shyly. "Well, don't be an ass, then I won't have to get mad at you and take charge. If you want to make stupid decisions, don't blame me for not going with it."

"Oh really, stupid decisions, hey." He lets me down, and as soon as I stand on my feet, he bends down, kissing me on my forehead, smiling against my skin. "You wanting to chain me to the bed sounds promising, but I would prefer it the other way around—and not in these circumstances," he confesses and walks to his closet.

I stare after him, my mouth hanging open slightly, his statement catching me off guard. I laugh nervously, not sure why the thought of him chaining me to a bed and having his way with me isn't freaking me out more. I thought that I would feel uneasy, but it only makes me hot and bothered. He turns and sees the look on my face and chuckles. "Are you okay?"

"Hmmm," I hum.

How is this even possible? How can I feel so empowered after being free from Jace for only a day? How can I feel so much sexual desire for this man after what Jace and Owen put me through?

It must be the mate bond slowly taking effect, and Tyler is so good to me and my state of mind. It feels like I've known him for much longer than I do.

Tyler grabs a shirt from his closet and pulls it on quickly. "Okay, my love. Come on, we need to talk about our situation and figure out a solution," he asserts, walks to me, grabs my hand, and pulls me toward the bed. And without hesitation or protest, I follow him.

We sit on the bed opposite each other, me with my legs crossed, my hands in my lap, watching him as my nerves start to eat at my insides. We will surely talk about the mark Jace gave me, and I'm afraid it will set off his wolf again.

Without thinking, I pull my hair over my shoulder where the mark is, my hands trembling. I can't handle seeing the disgust in his eyes and the rejection that will surely follow. My heart feels heavy as the silence continues, neither of us saying anything.

Tyler notices my mood change and my anxiety. His eyes follow my every movement, even when I pull my hair over my shoulder.

"Hey, babe. It's okay. You don't have to hide it. I will be fine. You're here with me and keeping me and my wolf calm. It's amazing not to worry about losing my temper or control." He smiles warmly at me.

I am flabbergasted. There's no disgust or rejection in Tyler's eyes. He's actually smiling at me, his face caring, and it warms my heart. I visibly relax and smile back at him.

"Are you sure?"

"Yeah, I feel at ease and calm, to the point where it feels foreign. So, let's start there, shall we?" Tyler mutters, his shoulders tense as he reaches forward and removes my hair from my shoulder, tossing it to my back. The mark is visible even after it's healed.

Tyler looks at it and reaches over to touch it, but I move back quickly without even thinking, clasping a hand over it to cover it. He frowns, tilts his head, narrows his eyes, and clenches his jaw, suppressing a snarl. Without warning, Tyler pulls me to him in one swift movement, my legs on either side of him as I sit in his lap.

"Don't, my love, it only screws with my wolf, and I can feel him getting riled up," he says slowly.

"I-I'm sorry," I stutter, my head still spinning from him, moving me so fast. "It's a reflex. I, um, didn't do it on purpose."

"Hmm," Tyler hums in acknowledgment, watching me, his eyes still narrowed and pinned to the mark on my neck.

I swallow visibly, his eyes catching it. "Don't move," he growls so low that the sound vibrates through his chest and into mine.

I nod once, and Tyler lifts his fingers to the mark again; my body stiffens as he runs them over it. He traces every line of it, and I don't know how I feel about him touching it.

The fact that this happened to me makes me feel dirty. The fact that my mate must see this on me is disgusting. Why he doesn't show the same emotion as what I am feeling is beyond me.

Tyler's eyes fall on mine again, but I can't bear to look at him. I'm ashamed, so I turn my head, sighing, "I'm sorry."

Tyler pulls my face to him, and there's only love in his eyes. It confuses me. I frown, not understanding how he can show love in this instance.

"Why are you apologizing, my love? You've done absolutely nothing wrong."

"I-" I start to say, but my words fail me, and I just huff.

"What is it?" Tyler asks, his eyes pinning mine, and I can't look away.

"It makes me feel filthy, ashamed, and disgusting. How can you stand to touch me?" The sadness in my heart is overwhelming.

"That's not what I see when I look at you." He smiles lovingly at me and slides his hand into my hair, his palm resting just below my ear, stroking my cheek with his thumb. "I see a gorgeous, strong, caring, loving, and extremely gutsy woman. Touching you proves extremely difficult-"

I lower my eyes at that part. "I knew it," I whisper.

"Will you please let me finish before jumping to conclusions," Tyler says, somewhat annoyed. "Touching you proves to be extremely difficult because when I touch you, I want to pin you to this bed and fuck you until you scream my name."

I gasp, and the heat pools between my legs again.

"I want to claim every inch of your body and soul," Tyler mutters, watching me squirm with every word.

He pulls my face to him, and my breath catches in my throat. He uses his thumb, which grazed my cheek a few moments ago and pushes my head up from under my chin to expose my neck.

"*YOU. ARE. MINE.*" He kisses slowly down my neck, growling each word in between kisses, making his way to the mark. Grabbing onto his shirt, I'm full-on panting by the time Tyler places the final kiss square on the mark, and goosebumps cover my whole body.

His free hand moves to my lower back and pulls me closer, my back arching, my boobs flush against his chest. I moan loudly, surprising myself, his cock growing harder under me. This man is driving me crazy.

I want to lower my head to look at him, but he keeps me in place, his mouth on my neck, his breathing heavy. Tyler doesn't move, his hands shaking slightly. He kisses me again, and his canines scrape against my neck, sending shivers down my spine.

"Ty-Tyler," I pant, my boobs moving against his chest as I breathe, the friction on my nipples making me gasp, and I grip him tighter.

"Fuck Abby, you feel so good. I'm struggling not to rip your clothes off your body and claim you here and now," he rasps near the shell of my ear, making me tingle all over, my hips grinding down on him on their own accord.

Tyler lets out a harsh hiss, and his hold on me gets tighter. His hand in my hair and under my chin moves over my body and grips my hips along with his other hand on my lower back, and he pushes my hips down on him as I grind my core against his now rock-hard cock.

Tyler groans and consumes my mouth, his kiss hard and desperate. His breathing is harsh, and his eyes, full of lust when he looks at me, are black as the darkest night.

I push my hands up his shoulders and into his hair, gripping tight and biting his lower lip.

Tyler moves his hands under my ass, lifts me off him, and turns us so I fall on my back on the bed. We move so fast that I don't have time to react. He pulls his shirt up and over his head and is on top of me in two seconds, kissing me again and pushing his tongue into my mouth. The taste of him is intoxicating.

He pulls back slightly, both of us panting. "Do you want to do this?" he asks between breaths.

My heart skips a beat; this man is so lust-driven, and he still takes the time to ask me if I am ready.

I nod slowly. "Please just take it slow. I'm scared I will freak out otherwise."

"My love, if you aren't ready, we don't have to do this." He is the ultimate gentleman, placing my needs above his own. This is so weird; I am still so surprised when he does that.

"No, I-I am okay, just take it slow."

"Tell me to stop if it gets too much, okay?"

I nod, and he gives me the most handsome smile I've ever seen, his semi-elongated canines showing. "Have I told you how sexy you look in my shirt?"

"I didn't think you noticed," I say, blushing bright red. "I had nothing else to wear after I took a shower."

He closes his eyes and groans again, "Fuck, and I laid here fucked up with you in my shower, I can't believe I missed that."

I laugh at his statement. "You weren't fucked up, you were sick." I blush again. "We will need to do something about it then, won't we?"

Tyler growls, claiming my mouth again, his hands roaming my body, and comes to a stop on my boobs. He pinches my nipples through my shirt and rolls them between his fingers. The feeling shoots pleasure through my body, my breath hitching in my throat, and my back arches off the bed, wanting to get my body closer to him.

Tyler seems to love this reaction as he does it again, getting the same result. I'm panting now. The corner of his mouth pulls up, and it feels like my core will explode. He slips his hands underneath my shirt and pulls it over my head. Next, he slips the shorts Layla gave me down slowly, taking in all of me. Tyler inhales sharply, and his eyes darken as he takes in every inch of me. "Fuck, my love, you are so beautiful," he hums as I lie naked on his bed, blushing still.

He places small butterfly kisses from the bottom of my foot up to my inner thigh before looking up at me and smiling, and he kisses me on my now wet core.

I gasp and throw my head back, grabbing onto the covers. Tyler flicks his tongue over my clit, and I bite down on my lip to stop myself from moaning, drawing blood. Suddenly, his heavy body pins me to the bed, his eyes fixed on my bleeding lip. He bends down and licks the blood off my lip, closing his eyes, his half smile on his face again. When he opens his eyes, the hunger for me has multiplied by ten.

"Don't you dare keep quiet, my love. I want to hear your pleasure. Do you understand me?"

I nod at his words, and he smiles mischievously. "I want you to use your words, Abby."

I gulp, and he raises his eyebrow, tracing small circles on my body, and makes agonizingly slow movements toward my core.

"I understand," I gulp.

"Good girl." He smiles triumphantly at me. "Now, where was I," he says between kisses moving down my body.

He stops at my nipple, takes it into his mouth, sucking on it, and then flicks it with his tongue, making me moan aloud. He smiles around my nipple and does it again and again. Fuck, this is going to be the death of me.

I'm breathless when he eventually leaves my nipples and moves down my stomach, licking and kissing towards my clit. He flicks my clit a few times with his tongue before he takes me into his mouth.

"Fuck, Tyler," I moan as he ravishes me.

He comes up for a breath as another moan leaves my mouth. "That's the sexiest my name has ever sounded," he chuckles. He uses a finger and slides it through my wetness, and I groan, earning me one of those sexy, naughty smiles of his. His eyes never leaving me. "Say it again," he growls at the exact moment he pushes two fingers into me.

"Ahh, Tyler," I moan his name again, my back arching off the bed.

He starts to move his fingers slowly at first, watching me. His intense stare adds to the pleasure that's building in my body. He moves a little bit faster, the pressure building.

"Are you going to come for me, my love?" His voice hoarse.

I nod, and he slows his pace. "I told you to use your words, Abbygail."

"Yes, please, Tyler, don't stop," I almost beg, and he doesn't disappoint.

His pace picks up—I can feel my pleasure building again—and then he curls his finger up ever so slightly, hitting my g-spot and throwing me over the edge. I scream his name as I climax over his fingers and his hand. His movement slows as I come down from my climax. He pulls his fingers from me as I open my eyes. Smiling, he places them in his mouth and sucking my pleasure off his fingers.

I blush again when he hums with pleasure. "Oh, my love, if you just knew how good you tasted." He tilts his head at me and pulls down his pants. His massive cock springs free, and my eyes widen. *Oh fuck.*

"Babe, are you okay?" he asks, concerned as he moves between my legs, his hand on my raised knee.

"I-I," I start. There I go, stuttering again. It's so pathetic. "I, um, haven't..." I trail off.

Tyler tilts his head, frowning at me. "You haven't what?"

I swallow, not knowing how to put it into words. This is so fucking embarrassing; I cover my eyes with my arm. "I haven't been with anyone before." My voice is barely above a whisper as I eventually get the courage to tell him.

His grip tightens on my knee, and he sighs heavily. "How is that possible?" he asks, and I know exactly what he refers to.

Suddenly, I feel so damned exposed. I sit up and try to cover my whole body with my hands, which, of course, is impossible. I look up at Tyler, pleading.

"Um, I-I, um-"

His eyes soften as he watches me. The mood is totally ruined, and I'm to blame. This man had just given me the most mind-blowing orgasm, and I had to ruin it because of my "virgin state of mind." I roll my eyes mentally. I should have expected this to happen to me, naturally.

CHAPTER TWENTY-THREE

KAYDEN

We leave Tyler's room as he bellows for us to get out. The mate bond got him good. Tyler's protectiveness over Abby is admirable, but this issue with the mate bond curse bothers me more than I care to admit.

We have a severe problem on our hands. I don't mind taking over the Alpha duties for a while, but people are starting to ask for Tyler and getting suspicious. He and I need to sit down and get some of the shit sorted out. Luckily, the festival is running smoothly and without a hitch for once—and secondly, to my delight, it's almost over.

I sigh, working through the scenarios in my mind, with everything else that needs to be done, when Layla sobs behind me. *Fuck*, this issue with her brother is really getting to her. I feel horrible for not noticing my mate is upset, and I want to kick my ass for not being more supportive.

"Lay, babe, are you okay?" I ask, concerned, as I turn to her.

She's crouching down, her head in her hands, and her body shakes as she cries.

My heart breaks when Layla looks up at me with her tear-stained cheeks. I walk back to her, crouching in front of her, opening my arms, and she almost falls into them.

Layla wraps her arms around my neck and buries her face on my chest. I fold my arms around her, rubbing my hand on her back soothingly, the other cupping her head until she can find her composure.

Sebastian looks unimpressed and a little uncomfortable as he lingers to one side. On the other hand, the worry is clear on Julia's face. I don't like the fact that they're seeing my mate vulnerable. "Why don't you guys give us some privacy?"

Sebastian nods, relief washes over his features, and turns on his heel, making his way up the hall, turning a corner out of sight. Julia frowns; the look on her face is one of uncertainty. She shifts her weight from one foot to the other as she rubs her hand up her arm.

"I don't know where to go. I don't think I'm safe returning to the Timber pack with everything that happened. What I did is a betrayal, especially with their Alpha," Julia's voice is soft as she mutters her response, a hint of fear in her voice.

"She's right," Layla agrees, pulling away from me. Sitting back on her knees, she sniffs and wipes her nose on her sleeve. "Julia isn't safe near the Timber pack. She should stay here."

"Babe, you know I can't make that decision. That's up to your brother, our Alpha," I say, frowning at her.

"Don't worry; I know there needs to be a vote. I understand that. May I please ask if there's a room where I can stay which is far from my previous pack? I know Jace and Owen are locked up, but I can never be too careful," Julia expresses as she looks at me.

That's right, we locked those two fuckers in the dungeon. I need to check on that situation when I'm done here. I look back down at Layla, stroking her cheek and, in the process, swiping a stray tear from it.

She gives me a small smile before I look back at Julia, and I take my phone from my back pocket, calling Sebastian.

He's going to be pissed.

"Hey, yeah… I know, man… Listen, Julia needs a room far from the Timber pack… Okay… See you in a few…" I disconnect the call, placing my phone back in my pocket. "Sebastian will be here in a few minutes. He'll show you to your room."

Julia nods once and slowly walks up the hallway as Sebastian rounds the corner. I give him a grateful nod, and he returns my gesture.

I turn my attention back to Layla, her face still wet from the tears.

"Talk to me, babe," I tell her.

"Kay, I can't lose my brother too. I've already lost my father, and if something were to happen to Tyler, I don't think my mother would be able to handle it. It will surely kill her, and then what will happen to me?" she sobs again.

I watch her as she talks, listening to the sadness that overshadows her usually carefree, mysterious, and playful personality. I want to burn the world just to make her smile and take away her grief.

"Layla, listen to me, okay?" I say, lifting her face so she can look at me. "Everything is going to be okay, I promise. Your brother is the most stubborn hybrid I have ever met…" I trail off, tilting my head. "Shit, sorry, let me correct myself. We met someone more stubborn than him," I say with a knowing smile, and Layla frowns.

"What are you getting at?"

"Listen, Abby's not going to let him die. She may have been through hell and back, but that girl bounces back so quickly it's astonishing. She's the perfect mate for Tyler."

"I know, but what bothers me is, what if he marks her and she dies…" Layla trails off, and I know exactly what she's thinking.

For a normal wolf, it's unbearable to lose your mate. We don't know what will happen to Tyler if he has to lose his mate so soon after finding her and not even mentioning if he's the one who took her life to save his own.

I sigh, not knowing what else to tell Layla. "We just need to have faith, babe. Unless you can find out more about this?"

"There is nothing more to research, Kay. We have exhausted all our resources. Melissa even went to the other Elders, and they didn't have much knowledge about this. She says that's why the Elders always ensured that the prophecies are done in private, so something like this can be avoided," Layla renders.

"Fuck," I huff out a sigh shaking my head. "Leave it to Tyler to have a difficult mate bond."

"Yeah, sounds about right," Layla mutters under her breath.

I get up from the floor, pulling her up with me. "Come on, Lay."

"Where are we going?"

"You haven't had any sleep in the last day or so. Maybe we'll be able to think clearly after a warm shower and a good night's rest."

She nods, sniffing again, and I bend down to pick her up, bridal style. The squeal I get when I have her in my arms makes me smile broadly at her as I make my way to our suite.

CHAPTER TWENTY-FOUR

TYLER

TWO WEEKS LATER...

"Where is the other part of this map and the reports we got yesterday?" Kayden asks, frustration evident in his tone. I, of course, am not listening to a word he or anyone else is saying. All I can think of is the hatred building in my heart. I'm not sure towards whom exactly, but at this stage in time, Abby is getting the blunt force of it.

The past two weeks were exhausting with the festival and everything that happened. One thing that's a blessing is that the festival is over and was an enormous success.

I am currently seated in my office. Kayden sits opposite me, discussing the situation we find ourselves in with the warrior wolves and bringing them up to speed.

The same night Kayden saved Abby from Jace and Owen, they escaped and made a run for it. We discovered this when Sebastian went down to check on them and to take them some water.

I have a zero-tolerance policy for attacks against my pack, not to mention against my mate, but I will not be cruel unless it's called for. Jace and Owen had absolutely called for it, yet Abby had convinced me not to stoop to their level. I can't bring myself to tell her that he escaped.

Resting with my elbow on the armrest of my chair, I rub at my temple, watching Kayden. My head hurts from overthinking the whole situation. I pinch the bridge of my nose as my thoughts go back to Abby each time, and I clench my jaw out of frustration.

The thought of the night Abby was brought to me to save me from this fucking curse makes me think of our—almost—first time together.

I truly fucked up there. I couldn't think straight with her there looking so good, her stubborn nature only adding to the attraction. I should've asked her first if she'd had sex before. I just assumed Jace took advantage of her, and I wanted to fix it: claim her and make her forget what happened. I know it sounds ridiculous, but when the bond is this strong, filling you with lust, it drives you and your wolf to the point of thinking about nothing else than to claim what's yours.

I still have to feed from Abby regularly, although I try to avoid some of the feeding times. I don't know what's happened between us. There's a new tension—not the good kind—that wasn't there before, and I don't know how to fix it.

After Abby moved away from me and covered herself with the blanket—the look in her eyes still haunts me—it seemed as if our bond weakened slightly. The calm I felt when she touched me isn't working the same way it did before.

I'm struggling to rein in my temper more than I did before. I'm feeling resentful towards Abby. It's absurd. I know this isn't her fault, but I can't help feeling that my whole life has gone up in flames since I met her. Sometimes, I think I would have been better off if I had never met her.

What the hell is wrong with me?

I drag my hand through my hair as the alarm on my phone goes off, showing that I need to find Abby for my next fucking feeding. My anger is rising to the point where my heart is pounding. I growl defeatedly. I am getting tired of this.

We haven't had the chance to talk much after that night. The fear on her face and the slight hint of embarrassment in her scent was like a slap to my face. She got dressed and didn't really talk to me after that. Don't get me wrong, she's not avoiding me, and she definitely doesn't shrink away from her duty to make sure I'm able to lead my pack and protect them, but therein lies my problem. The fact that it feels like she's doing this to repay me somehow. Or maybe that she feels guilty. I don't know, but when I feed, we don't say a word to each other. She doesn't even look at me. I can blame *my* stubborn ass for that. I thank her after each feeding and then leave the room.

This whole ordeal has been a total mess. A mate bond is supposed to get stronger, not weaker. The fact that Jace marked her so many times undoubtedly plays a crucial role in this. I clench my jaw so tight I swear my teeth will crack under the pressure, thinking about the mark on her neck that isn't mine; that's another thing I'm struggling with. It makes me livid to know my mate is marked by another, and I can't correct this because she could *die* from it.

"FUCK!" I slam my fists on my desk, and everyone around me quiets down. I look around, realizing what I just did as Kayden looks up from the map he's examining on my desk. He raises his brows, looking unimpressed.

"You okay, man?"

I ball my fists, and my jaw ticks as I try to rein in my temper. I close my eyes and take a few breaths, forcing all thoughts of Abbygail out of my head—or at least I try to. "Yeah, just give me a minute," I force through my clenched jaw.

"Guys, give me and our Alpha here a few minutes, won't you?" Kayden utters as he turns to look at Sebastian and the other warriors in the room. They nod and make their way out of the room, closing the door behind them.

"Thanks," I breathe out when we are alone in my office.

"What's going on, man? You seem off. I thought you had control of your temper since you met Abby."

"I did, but now I don't know. Something is wrong between us." I rise from my chair and approach the window, leaning forward and resting my hands on both sides. The thunder cracks outside, lighting up my office. The sky is dark, and the clouds loom overhead. The weather looks as gloomy as I feel in my heart and soul.

"I am resentful towards Abbygail. That's not supposed to happen. Whenever I see her with Jace's mark on her neck, my anger rises in my chest, which drives me insane. I know it's absurd, but it's like my wolf's losing it because I can't mark her and claim her as mine and as the Luna of our pack. Every day that passes, the anger and resentment get worse," I confess. The sigh leaves my chest in a huff as I drop my head.

Kayden shifts in his chair and just stares at me without saying anything. The one time I need him to assure me that I'm being stupid, he says nothing. I look over my shoulder, and he shrugs. "Tyler, you need to talk to her about this. For normal wolves, it's painful if they don't seal the bond within a few days of finding their mate. You and Abby met over two weeks ago, and it makes sense that your wolf feels the way he does. He feels rejected. The problem comes with your vampire side. Aren't vampires possessive of what's theirs? I think the two sides of you are at war."

I sigh again, feeling perplexed. "Perhaps you're right. I am being unreasonable towards Abby. She's been through so much, and now she must deal with me not knowing how to handle this kind of shit, taking it out on her. I know she cares about me. I just hate that I'm dependent on her blood, which adds to the fact."

"Speaking of which, aren't you supposed to have your feeding right about now?" Kayden asks, sounding concerned as he folds his arms across his chest.

I clench my jaw again, my lip pulling up as I suppress a snarl. "No! I can't keep doing this. I need to focus and get myself to work through this. What kind of Alpha am I if I need to be dependent on my woman?"

"You are *so* being a dude right now, and you know you're being an asshole, right? You need her as much as she needs you. The fact that you haven't sealed the bond is fucking with your mind. Don't let Abby hear you, or you will scar her for life." Kayden is right, and I know it. It's a hot mess in my mind, I need Abby more than I need to breathe, but I can't shake these shitty feelings.

It's as if my body wants to remind me that my stubbornness is useless when my legs start shaking where I stand. I know I've waited too long *again*. I grip onto the windowpane and try to steady myself. My heart slams against my chest, I'm struggling to catch my breath, and I let out a snarl as the pain shoots through my head.

Kayden jumps up from his seat, screaming for Sebastian as I sink to my knees. I'm fucking pathetic. Kayden runs to me as Sebastian comes crashing through the door.

"Oh, for fuck's sake, Tyler, your stubborn ass is going to get you killed and, in turn, make us vulnerable," Sebastian states, annoyance and irritation dripping from his tone as he kneels beside me.

"Careful, Sebastian," I warn with a relatively weak growl.

He snorts as he and Kayden place my arms over their necks, pulling me up from the floor and taking me to the couch I have in the office. Before Abby, I used to work long nights, and then I would just sleep here. Who am I kidding? I've been sleeping here for two weeks after the mess between us.

Kayden whistles through his teeth to get the attention of one of the wolves outside the office.

"Go get Abbygail, NOW!"

The wolf nods quickly and runs from my office. I hate this. My strength drains from me with every breath I take. I squeeze my eyes shut, concentrating the remainder of my energy on trying to slow my ragged breathing. It's not working.

"Tyler, just keep still. Abby should be here any minute," Kayden asserts.

Sebastian leans against the fireplace, his arms crossed over his chest, the same annoyed look on his face. I know he's worried. He's just showing it differently. He's my Gamma and all, and sometimes he makes me want to rip his throat out, but he speaks the truth even though I don't like to hear it. He doesn't say much—but when he does, he's usually right, and that pisses me off. Fifteen minutes go by, and Abby's still not here. My consciousness slips in and out. I haven't felt this weak since she started giving me her blood.

"Where—" I struggle to speak when the pain crushes down on my chest and splits my skull. "Abby—"

"I don't know, man. I'll call Layla to go and see if she can find her."

"No—" I breathe out. I don't need a lecture from my sister right now.

The wolf Kayden sent to get Abby comes running back into my office, catching his breath, and shakes his head grimly.

"I can't find her, Beta Kayden," he huffs between breaths.

"What? What do you mean you can't find her? She's supposed to be in Alpha Tyler's room," Kayden snaps irritably at the guy, who backs away slowly.

I use all my strength to turn on my side to get off the couch. I need to find her, but Kayden stops me, pushing against my shoulder. My strength is now almost completely gone. My consciousness fails me miserably as my world goes black.

"How is this even possible?" Kayden barks.

I open my eyes weakly, taking in a strained breath. What the fuck is going on? What happened? My office is darker than it was, and I realize I must've passed out. *Damn it!*

"Kayden, he's awake," Sebastian's strained voice fills my ears, but it sounds far away.

"Tyler, bud… Shit. You scared the shit out of me. Listen, we can't find Abby, and I don't know where the hell she could've gone. I'm calling Layla right now. I'm not hiding this from her," Kayden insists, a sense of urgency in his voice as he takes his phone out and calls my sister. "Lay… Shit… Yeah… It's Tyler… He doesn't look good… Don't yell at me, babe… Fuck, Layla, you know how full of shit he can get… I don't know where she is. We can't find her… She went where?... Shit!... I'll send Sebastian… Yeah, bye." Kayden curses and almost crushes his phone in his hand when he hangs up.

"Kay—" I groan in agony, as the pain I felt earlier is back with a vengeance. I swear this is what it feels like to be impaled on a sword or a spear.

"Fuck, Tyler," Kayden's voice is panicked, and he stumbles over his words. "Sebastian, Abby went for a run, and I think she might have gotten lost in the woods. Please find her and bring her here."

Sebastian curses violently and sprints out of the office just as Kayden finishes his sentence. Defeat, along with helplessness, snakes its way through my body. I'm so pathetic; my mate's lost in the woods somewhere, and I can't even feel if she's panicked or if she needs me.

Why would she even want me to find her after our weird atmosphere these last few weeks? I'm pushing her away, and I'm sure she feels the rejection, which isn't my intention, but it just happened.

My chest feels like it's about to crush in on itself as I struggle to breathe. The sound of it comes out in short huffs. I'm officially worried.

This is worse than the first time. Maybe Abby decided she had had enough of my bullshit, unpleasant demeanor, and behavior and took off. A sadness fills me at that thought. I'm such a piece of shit. How could I have let this get so out of hand?

I hiss when the agonizing pain shoots through me again, and the realization hits me that this is really going to kill me. I didn't think it was possible. Abby had me convinced she would not let me die, and what did I do? I refused to do *my* part and go to her.

Layla comes running into my office a few minutes later, and she glares at Kayden as she takes my hand and kneels by my head. I smile at her weakly as she feels my pulse and curses. "Fuck, Kayden, how could you let this happen?" Layla snaps at Kayden, looking over her shoulder at him.

"You're fucking kidding right?" Kayden is fuming now. "You blame me for this, really? You know your brother better than anyone in this fucking pack, and you think I have a say when he sets his mind on something?"

"You promised me, Kayden, you promised everything would be okay, and now look at where we are!" Layla screams.

I squeeze Layla's hand, not knowing if she even feels it, but she turns to me quickly.

"Please—" I struggle to form the words. "Don't... not... Kayden's... fault," I pant, trying to speak in between short breaths.

"Tyler, don't talk, please. Save your strength," Layla sobs as she wipes the sweat from my face. "I'm sorry, babe, please just help my brother," she pleads desperately to Kayden.

Kayden starts pacing before pulling his phone from his pocket again and calls Sebastian.

"Where the fuck are you, man!... No!... It's getting worse... Just get your ass here. We need to move him to the hospital,"

Kayden snarls at Sebastian and then throws his phone against the wall, smashing it instantly.

"Kay, please calm down," Layla gets up and walks to Kayden, but he backs away from her, shaking his head in warning. "Babe, I said I'm sorry. Why are you doing this?"

"Lay, stay there!" he growls at her. "Just give me a minute to get a hold of my wolf, okay?"

I've never heard him growl at Layla. This must be taking its toll on Kayden just as it is on my sister and the rest of the pack. I'm destroying my family and my pack from the inside.

That fucking bastard must've known I would do this: be stubborn, and place Abby's wellbeing in front of my own and the pack's. He's probably counting on it, wherever he is. Sebastian comes sprinting into the office, looking at Layla and then at Kayden, confused, before looking at me.

"Whatever I'm interrupting can wait. I've already called Adam, since you don't answer your phone," he utters as he spots the smashed phone on the floor. "And now I know why. We don't have time to lose our heads, kids. There are more pressing matters at hand."

Kayden shoots Sebastian a look that can kill as he moves towards the couch. He and Sebastian each take one of my arms and place it over their necks, pulling me up and lifting me off the couch. I hiss out in pain as they drag me to the hospital.

They make their way through the hall with me hanging from them at an agonizingly slow pace. I can't take this for much longer. "Argh- please stop-" I beseech desperately, my voice barely audible.

"Ty, you need to hold on. We're almost there. Please just hold on," Layla cries as she walks beside Kayden.

The pain is so unbearable, I'll welcome death at this stage. I don't even care anymore.

CHAPTER TWENTY-FIVE

ABBYGAIL

"I'm going to lose my damn mind," I growl aloud, pacing the floor of Tyler's room, raking a hand through my hair. I need to get out of this fucking Packhouse. This place is enormous, but it's suffocating me. The way things are between me and Tyler is unbearable. I don't know what went wrong. One moment, we were like two teens in love, unable to keep our hands off one another—and then, *boom*, nothing.

I'm lying to myself; I know exactly what went wrong.

Cringing, I think about the night Tyler and I almost had sex. It was a disaster. I can't believe he made me experience the best and only orgasm I've ever felt, and then I had to ruin it with my damn insecurities. He was so gentle with me, and then—*yeah, then*. I want to scream from frustration. Damn it, the one good thing that happens to me, and I fucking ruin it.

That's it. I can't stay here a moment longer. I pull on the running shoes Layla's given me and walk out of my room. Tyler and I haven't spoken about anything real since that night. I feel so broken inside. I didn't think it was possible, but hey, here we are.

Of course, the main problem was that we still haven't sealed our mate bond. I understand that ours is exceptionally unique—and fragile, if you ask me. Look at how fast everything went sour. Aren't hybrid mate bonds supposed to be stronger than any other wolf bond? Well, maybe the prophecy's mistaken. Seems like it.

I walk out of the front door, and to my surprise, no one has tried to stop me. I take a deep breath and step onto the gravel surrounding the mansion. I look around, taking in the astonishing scenery for the first time since I arrived. It's gorgeous.

Tall, thick trees with brilliant green leaves surround the mansion, and if I listen carefully, I can hear a stream of water running somewhere.

I inhale deeply and take off running in the direction of the woods. It's been so long since I was outside and on my own; the throbbing drive in my chest pushes me to run even faster. I run nonstop, pushing my limits like I haven't done in forever until I'm forced to stop and catch my breath. I bend over, my hands on my knees, and I breathe harshly.

It takes a few minutes to calm my racing heart and to catch my breath completely. Smiling from the exhilarating feeling, I scan the beautiful forest surrounding me and then the realization hits—I'm lost.

Shit, I didn't pay any attention to where I was going, and now don't know where I am.

"Great, Abbygail," I scold myself, scanning my surroundings again. Well, this is as good a time as any to bond with my wolf.

I close my eyes and concentrate on my senses and my surroundings. I inhale deeply and get a whiff of the oak trees and the damp ground with the fallen leaves. A beaming smile forms on my lips when I smell the rain in the air before it has even fallen. This is amazing, and I can feel my wolf making her presence known. This feeling is astounding, the power running through me, the strong connection with my wolf. Opening my eyes, my canines push past my lips, and I inhale the air around me. My senses homing in, knowing exactly what to do, I take off running again, tracking my own way back to the Packhouse.

The speed at which I'm running is thrilling, and the wind in my hair makes me feel free. I run, and the heavens open as the rain pours down, soaking me thoroughly. A delighted shriek escapes my mouth when the mansion appears in the distance.

I'm elated as I jog up and open the front door. Nothing can wipe this smile from my face.

I'm sorely mistaken.

I make my way through the hall, still smiling like a silly schoolgirl, before I sense the discord in the air. The scents lingering in there are mixed with panic, pain, and smell foreign. I frown as I follow the panicked scent that stings my nose. What the hell is going on?

I round the corner of the hallway I'm strolling down, leading me to Tyler's office, and my heart drops to my stomach. I stop dead in my tracks, not being able to move. The panic I smell manifests in my chest, soon replaced by fear at the sight before me.

Kayden and Sebastian walk toward me slowly, Tyler draping over their shoulders with his feet dragging behind him. I sniff the air again, and a horror-filled gasp escapes my lips.

The stench of death is hanging in the air, and the absolute fear it instills in me turns my world upside down.

No, no, no.

How did this happen? How can I forget about our arrangement? *Shit.*

I get control of my body again, and I run to him. "ABBYGAIL, WHERE THE FUCK HAVE YOU BEEN?" Layla yells at me, and I wince as shame adds to all the existing feelings.

"I-I'm, I—" I stutter as I halt in front of Tyler. I cup his face in my hands and lift his head. Tyler's eyelids are heavy, and his breathing is almost nonexistent. I listen intently to his heartbeat, and I can barely hear it. "I got lost, I'm so sorry, I-"

"I don't care for your excuses, Abbygail-" Layla barks.

"Layla! That's enough. We don't need this right now," Kayden growls at Layla and then looks expectantly at me. I am still soaking wet, the water dripping off me. "Abby, I don't care where you've been. I only care if you are willing to help him, please. I know you guys are in a bad space, but he needs you now."

"Of course, Kayden. I didn't do this on purpose." I feel hurt that they think I will purposely withhold my blood from Tyler. "He didn't come to me when he was supposed to feed, so I went for a run. I didn't have the strength to fight with him again, and the house was starting to suffocate me."

"I understand, but please, there's no time to spare."

"Please, lie him down," I tell Kayden and Sebastian.

They do as I ask, and I kneel next to him. "Tyler, my love." My heart aches as I use the same endearment he used for me for the first time, and he can't even hear me. "I'm here. Please don't leave me." A tear runs down my cheek as I stroke his.

Kayden backs away from us and moves to Layla, taking her into his arms. Sebastian moves to stand behind me.

I look up at Layla. "I'm so sorry, Layla. I need a favor from you, please." Layla nods hesitantly, and I continue, "Don't stop him. If he kills me with the amount of blood he needs, then let him take it."

Layla's eyes widen, and she shakes her head frantically. "No, Abby, I can't do that. The consequences could be catastrophic."

As she speaks, I bring my wrist to my mouth, and my fangs protrude past my lips, biting down hard, tasting blood. I bring it to Tyler's mouth, and he doesn't move at first. I pull at his chin, opening his mouth slightly. I place my wrist at his mouth, letting my blood drip into it, and after a while, he swallows slowly.

With every gulp, I feel the energy flow from me to him. Tyler groans and sucks harder. Raising a shaking hand, he pins my wrist to his mouth.

I look at Layla, my eyes pleading. "Please, Layla, let him take as much as he needs—even if I pass out from the blood loss."

The tears form in Layla's eyes as she nods. I give her a small appreciative smile as Tyler's grip on me tightens. He growls low in his chest, and his eyes flutter open as he sucks harder still. My blood leaves my body at an alarming speed as he drinks from me, and it's not long before I start to feel lightheaded.

Shit, I can't pass out now, he needs more—and if I lose consciousness, he won't take what he needs. I know Layla promised me, but there's no way she will let her brother suffer because he killed his mate.

I'm starting to sway, and my eyes feel heavy. Tyler bites deeper into my wrist, making me hiss.

I don't feel so good, and I'm getting cold from the amount of blood he is taking from me. To be honest, I don't care. He needs this.

As I'm trying my best to stay upright but failing miserably, Layla moves to my side quickly and catches me before I hit the ground. I didn't even feel myself falling.

"Kayden! Fuck! You need to stop him," Sebastian exclaims from behind me.

"TYLER," Kayden bellows, his voice reverberating off the walls as he moves closer to us. Tyler's gaze jumps to Kayden's, and he narrows his eyes.

"You're killing your mate," Kayden growls at Tyler, gripping his shoulder tightly.

Tyler's eyes widen, and he stops immediately, pulling my wrist from his mouth and inhaling deeply. Kayden's words sink in, and he turns on his side on the floor quickly, seeing me lying in Layla's lap. I feel so weak. I don't think Tyler has ever taken so much from me, but he looks better from what I can make out. My vision blurs, and I try to keep from blacking out.

Tyler scrambles to his feet and moves to me.

"Are you fucking insane, Abbygail?" Tyler exclaims, his words more worried than scolding.

He bends down, picks me up from the floor, and walks towards his room, clearly not worried about the rest of the crowd who's watching him leave. "Layla, get her some water and something to eat, please," Tyler calls over his shoulder.

This is the closest I've been to him in over two weeks. I lean against his chest, feeling his body's warmth seep into mine as he moves effortlessly through the halls until we reach his room.

I'm drifting in and out of consciousness when Tyler gets to his room and kicks open the door. The heat from his body is so welcoming, making it extremely difficult to stay awake.

He walks to his bed, lays me down, and sits beside me. Tyler rakes his hands roughly through his hair, watching me with narrowed eyes. The stubble visible on his face makes him look scruffy but still handsome as hell. "What were you thinking?" he asks, annoyed now.

I don't know how to answer him. All I want is to make sure he's okay. I'm not letting him die, not because of me. The reality of this situation sets in, and I know what is expected of me. We need to mark each other. There is no time to decide anymore. The next time this happens, one of us might not survive. I just don't know how I'll react when he marks me—and then, there's the looming fact that I could die.

"Didn't think," I mutter, my eyelids feeling heavy, not having the strength for complete sentences. Maybe I can just rest for a little bit before we address this issue. "I'm so tired," I whisper, closing my eyes.

"No, Abby. You need to stay awake." He shakes me lightly, and I groan, opening my eyes.

"Please, just a little bit." Closing my eyes again.

"*No*, Abbygail," he commands in his Alpha voice. I crack open one of my eyes and eye him. Did he really try that? "Please, my love. You need to stay awake. Eat something, and then we can talk about sleeping." His tone softens a little.

Tyler lifts his hand and brings it to my face, pausing just before he softly cups it. I frown. Why did he hesitate? Have I made this man doubt my feelings for him? I huff as I realize we haven't talked about our feelings. Everything is still so awkward.

I lean into his touch, sighing. "We need to talk, Tyler."

He closes his eyes and clenches his jaw. He stays like this for what feels like forever. Tyler breathes out harshly as he opens his eyes slowly, taking his hand away from my face.

I'm instantly cold where his hand was just seconds ago, and I wince inwardly. "Um, we-" I begin, but Layla interrupts me when she walks around the bed with a sandwich and a glass of water.

I have no appetite, but you bet your ass Tyler isn't going to take no for an answer. I move to sit up, and his arm wraps around my waist as his other hand cups the back of my head and moves me upwards. "Thanks, it wasn't necessary, though. I can manage on my own."

His face falls for a second before he composes himself, letting go of me.

Layla approaches me, hands me the plate with the sandwich, and sets the glass on the bedside table. "Thank you." I give her a small smile as she steps back from the bed.

"It's my pleasure," she says, rocking back and forth on her heels. "I owe you an apology, Abby."

"For what?"

"For talking to you like I did, I had no right, and I feel bad about my outburst."

"You don't need to apologize. I deserved it. I left when I had a duty. I can't believe I'm so stupid," I say, embarrassed, not looking at either of them.

"The only stupid thing you've done was to let me take so much blood from you," Tyler accuses.

I wince at the tone of his voice and feel annoyed by it.

"What would you have had me do, then?"

Tyler looks taken aback by my question. He frowns after a few seconds and his jaw locks. He huffs out air through his nose, glaring at me. I place the plate with the sandwich on the bed next to me, folding my arms across my chest as I raise my eyebrows at him. "I'm waiting, Tyler. Tell me what you wanted me to do, then?"

Layla's eyes jump from me to Tyler, clearly sensing our tension. She clears her throat, still rocking back and forth on her heels.

"Hey, guys. This is not something to be fighting about," Layla says and turns to Tyler. "Abby did what she thought was right at that moment. You were dying, Ty."

Tyler's face twitches from the anger he is trying to suppress. He balls his fists and stands abruptly, then turns and storms out of the room without another word or glance.

A heavy sigh pushes through my mouth, and I let my head fall against the headboard, closing my eyes.

The bed moves as Layla sits where Tyler was just a few seconds ago. I don't lift my head. I just open my eyes a little to look at her. "I can't argue about this with him anymore, Layla. It's exhausting," I tell her, covering my face with my hands.

"I know the feeling. Tyler isn't one of the easiest wolves to work with. He is *so* set in his ways and always gets what he wants. I think it's because Tyler feels responsible. If things get out of his control and something bad happens, it will destroy him. He got like this after our father died and had to take over as Alpha. You need to remember it's already a tough job to be an Alpha to a pack, but he's the leader of all of them. To be King is sometimes soul-crushing," Layla says encouragingly.

"I know, and therein lies my problem. Tyler needs a strong Luna who can carry that burden with him, someone with leadership capabilities and who is caring and stubborn like him. I'm none of those things, and I know that he will realize that along the way—and then he will leave me when I've given him my heart and soul. I will not be able to handle that kind of rejection."

Layla watches me as I talk, and she tilts her head frowning. A huge smile spreads across her face as I finish, and I'm confused. "What's so funny?"

"When are you going to see that the wolf you're describing, the one who has to be next to my brother, is you, exactly?"

"No, it's not." I shake my head. "I'm broken, Layla. I have too many issues. How can you even consider me a leader of a strong pack when I don't even feel that strength in myself? I'm just now connecting with my wolf where you all did when you were young."

"Abby, do you think anyone would dare stand up to my brother like you do? They don't dare to defy him. A lot of people are afraid of him," Layla tells me, resting her hand on my knee. "The way you just challenged him is something I thought I would never live to see."

"Why are they afraid of him? I don't understand?"

"Let's just say Tyler has a zero-tolerance policy. He doesn't think twice to act if someone is threatening our pack. He will burn the world down to ensure his people are safe and cared for. And don't get me started on the fact that some wolves don't understand what a hybrid is. That alone terrifies them, and his temper isn't helping much," she laughs dryly as she rolls her eyes, "as you have just seen."

I snort at the last part of her sentence. Yeah, I've seen that a lot, but I don't see me *not* taking shit from him the same way Layla does. I shake my head as my stomach growls loudly, and a giggle slips from Layla's mouth. "You better eat something, Tyler will surely lose his shit if he returns and you didn't eat." Layla nudges her head in the direction of the plate as she stands. "If you need anything, just call me, okay?"

I nod, and she turns to leave. "Layla."

"Yeah?" Glancing at me over her shoulder.

"Can you please tell Tyler that I need to talk to him?"

Layla looks worried for a second and then nods. "Yeah, sure."

"Thanks."

Eyeing the plate next to me, I take the sandwich from it and take a bite. "Hmmm." This is really good. I didn't realize how hungry I was until I took a bite from the sandwich.

I finish it quickly and lie back down after drinking some water, feeling my strength return slowly. I sigh happily and sink further into the pillow as I close my eyes.

CHAPTER TWENTY-SIX

TYLER

I storm out of my bedroom, down the hall, and to the kitchen. I need an outlet, but the limit on my strength is driving me insane. I wish I could spar with Kayden or some of the warrior wolves and get back to training. I'm on the edge. One more thing and the scales will tip, and it won't be good. My emotions are getting the better of me, driving me up the wall.

No, let's clarify, not so much my emotions as my mate. That damn woman is going to be the death of me, I swear. Why can't she do as she's told? Why can't she listen to me?

Why does she need to go against me every fucking time?

I violently push my hair out of my face; I still haven't gotten it cut. Not that I've had a chance with everything that's happened. I must look like something you pulled from a trash can. I rub my cheek, feeling the stubble scratch against my fingers. It's getting out of control. Fuck it, I don't care.

I fume, thinking of how weak she was after I drank from her. I could've killed her, for fuck's sake. Her defiance afterward, and how she challenges me when I'm trying to protect her, make me see red. This going back and forth is taking its toll on me. A roar rips through me, and I punch the wall once. Twice. Three times.

"Jeez, Tyler, don't tear the house down. I actually like living here," Layla remarks as she strolls into the kitchen. She stops in the doorway, crosses her arms over her chest, and leans against the door frame.

Glaring at her, I push my hair out of my face again. "Now is not the time, little sister."

I turn my back on her, walk to the window, and grip the counter beneath it, leaning forward. My grip tightens, making my knuckles turn white.

"Why is she getting to you like this?" Layla frowns as she walks up next to me, jumping up to sit on the counter where I stand.

"I don't know." I let out an exaggerated breath. "I can't do this back and forth with her. I get weak when the sickness reclaims me, close to dying, and she feeds me her blood to the point of almost dying herself. It's like a vicious cycle. My wolf's getting impatient; he wants our mate and can't handle this distance between me and her."

Layla pierces her lips as she swings her legs back and forth. "Well, the solution is clear. You need to seal the bond and mark her Tyler."

"Really, Lay, you don't say," sarcasm drips from my voice, and I roll my eyes at her. "You know it's not that easy. If it were, I would already have done it. Abby has trust issues, and the fact that she's never been with someone, and with everything Jace had done, makes it somewhat difficult. I don't want to force this."

"Damn it, brother. You can be so dense sometimes. Fix that, then! Show her she can trust you! Show her that you will never hurt her! Be the man she needs, and the man I know you are. You know you are better with her than without her," Layla tells me as she jumps off the counter.

"Oh, and Abby's asking for you," she adds, walking out of the kitchen, and I stare after her.

I shake my head at the thought of my whirlwind sister and look down at my hands still gripping the countertop. I roll my eyes, huffing out a frustrated breath through my nose. My knuckles from the hand that connected with the wall are cracked and bleeding. Great, it looks like my healing is screwed with this bloody curse.

I grab a dish towel from the drawer and wrap it around my hand. This is going to be interesting. I just know Abby's going to be pissed at me. I frown at that thought. Since when does it bother me how pissed someone will get when I do something?

I groan as I walk out of the kitchen.

As I walk into my room, I make a knot in the palm of my hand with the two ends of the towel wrapped around my knuckles. Looking up, I see Abby on her side facing the door, pulled up into a ball, fast asleep, her chest moving up and down peacefully.

The sight of her in my bed warms my heart and wakes up a particular member—whose presence isn't wanted now. We need to address specific issues between us first before anything remotely sexy can happen.

I walk over to the bed as quietly as I can. I don't want to disturb her and wake her up. The last feeding has taken a lot out of her. I sigh as defeat creeps into my chest. When will this ever end? The threat of either mine or Abby's death, the danger of Jace and Owen—who we still can't find. When I eventually get my hands on that bastard, I will tear him limb from fucking limb.

Slowly.

I'm going to make him suffer.

My lips pull up in a silent snarl as the thought of Jace angers my wolf. Abby still doesn't know they escaped, and the idea of her alone in the woods earlier with those two on the loose makes my skin crawl. What if he got to her when I was in that state? He could've killed her.

I take a deep breath and push the thoughts out of my mind; I can't think about this now. I need some distance, even if it's just across the room from her. I'm agitated and can't seem to rid myself of the feeling, so I sit against the wall on the floor opposite the bed, facing Abby.

The room is dark, the moon semi-covered with the clouds still looming in the sky. Small rays of moonlight pool into my room, but the little amount that shines through the window falls on her face, illuminating her features.

Fuck, she's gorgeous.

Her waist-length, black, wavy hair pools around her as she sleeps, her frame small but strong.

I pull my knees up to rest my forearms on them as I lean against the wall, still watching her. This beautiful specimen is mine, and I treat her like the plague. I am being so unfair towards her, and it's killing me.

We seriously need to fix things. All this time wasted, we could've bonded more, but no—I, Tyler Storm, had to be a world-class dick.

I snort at myself, and Abby stirs. *Shit.*

She stretches her limbs and opens her eyes, scanning the dark room. Her eyes fall on me, and she jumps. "Fuck, Tyler. You scared me." I stay quiet, my eyes never leaving hers. She frowns and sits up on my bed. "Tyler?" There's uncertainty in her voice.

She gets off the bed and walks over to me slowly. Abby's steady on her feet, and the relief rushing through me makes me inhale deeply. I watch her still as she approaches me cautiously.

"My love," she whispers hesitantly.

I inhale sharply, and I swear my heart makes a fucking summersault in my chest as the words hit my ears. She kneels before me, lightly tracing her fingers over my arm—the electric current runs through me, intoxicating—to where the dish towel is wrapped around my hand.

She looks up at me, taking my injured hand in hers. Abby frowns and then looks back down at my hand. "What happened?"

"Oh, nothing much. The kitchen wall and I had a misunderstanding." I smirk at her, not moving from my position. Abby tilts her head and frowns again; she grips the towel tightly and pulls it off my hand. She gasps when she sees my bloody knuckles and now-swollen hand.

I flex my fingers. Shit, this is a new feeling. I usually heal so fast I don't feel the pain. I've had a few misunderstandings with some hard surfaces, but my hand has never looked this bad.

The worry in her eyes sets me on edge. I don't need her to worry about small shit like this. Abby softly touches the wounds on my knuckles, and I hiss, pulling my hand from her grip. "Leave it, Abby," I command harshly.

I don't want her covered in my blood; the irony doesn't escape me.

She drops her hands to her lap, staring at me. I see the inner turmoil raging in her eyes. I guess she settles on annoyance. "Really, Tyler, it's a childish move, don't you think? And now that I want to take care of it, you act like a bloody sour wolf." She places her hands on her hips and narrows her eyes at me.

"You sound like my sister," I chuckle half-heartedly.

Abby huffs, still watching me through her narrowed eyes. She licks over her lips in frustration, but it has the opposite effect on me, and a groan slips past my lips as I watch the action intently.

She eyes me suspiciously like she's not sure her action was the reason for my groan.

The corner of her mouth pulls up in a half smile, looking sexy as hell, and she licks her bottom lip before biting down on the corner of it, pulling it into her mouth torturously slowly. My breath hitches in my throat, and there's triumph in those beautiful emerald eyes of hers as she cocks her head. "Is something wrong, my love?" Her voice is low, filled with seduction.

I feel my dick harden in my pants—*fuck*. We need to talk first. We need to sort out the shit between us before we have playtime.

Playtime, what the fuck. *Nice one, Tyler*, I cringe inwardly.

"Abby," my voice is hoarse, and she smiles broadly, knowing full well what she's doing to me. "We need to talk first." She crawls closer to me, the slow and deliberate motion making her hips sway, moving between my legs and placing both hands on my chest. She dips her head down to my neck, leaving small kisses after every nibble reaching my ear.

"Then talk," she whispers, her breath brushing against my skin. I close my eyes as my breathing quickens. If I don't stop Abby now, I won't be able to control myself for much longer. Her hold on me is terrifying but in a good way. I swallow hard, my hands shaking. I grip her face as lightly as possible, leaning forward and pushing her back on her heels.

"You are making it exceedingly difficult to keep a hold on my damn control, I can't think clearly. I'm fighting the urge not to act on my instincts and the thoughts playing in my head." I grit my teeth. Her eyes move from my lips and land on mine, her emerald eyes almost glowing. I know mine is as black as the night sky.

"What instincts?" she teases as her hand moves down my chest and pauses on my abdomen.

"Abbygail," I warn, growling.

She looks at me through her lashes and gives me an innocent smile. Her fangs are visible, just slightly longer than her regular teeth line. "What do you want to do to me?" Again, slow and full of seduction, she licks over her fang with her tongue and slowly pulls it into her mouth, letting out a small moan.

I clench my jaw, and my grip on her face tightens when my hands shake. She's driving me insane.

"Are you going to tell me?" Her hand moves down towards my dick a little more.

I take in a shaking breath, closing my eyes. "It's proving exceedingly difficult to control the urge to dominate you and to pin you to this fucking floor. I'm fighting with everything in me, not to be rough with you, not to take you and fuck you until you scream."

Opening my eyes, I find that irresistible smile pulling at her lips. "Then dominate me..." she tells me, still smiling, her hand moving over my length, and as she grips me through my pants, she whispers, "*Alpha.*"

I hiss, and all my control shatters. I move fast as I get up off the floor, pushing her backward and pinning her to the floor with my body. A growl rips through my chest as my wolf claws to the surface. Taking her hands, I pin them above her head, and a gasping moan escapes her mouth. My mouth crashes onto hers, and I kiss her possessively, not allowing her to breathe properly as I consume her, my tongue ravishing her mouth. Abby moans into me, which drives my hunger for her even more.

I push up from her, and she gasps for air as I grab the hem of her shirt and tear it off her, exposing her beautiful, full breasts. I also have no mercy for her shorts as I rip them off her.

"Don't move," I growl at her, my fangs exposed, and she nods, her mouth a little open as she pants.

I pull my shirt over my head and shove my pants down, releasing my throbbing member.

I spread her legs and move between them; I take one second to look at her eyes for fear or uncertainty. Her eyes show nothing but need as she pants and squirms beneath me. "Remember what I told you?" She nods again. "Words, Abby," my voice low.

"Yes."

"Yes, what?"

"Yes." She smiles mischievously. "*Alpha.*"

I groan, "You are driving me fucking mad."

I place my index and middle finger at her mouth, pulling at her lip and urging her to open her mouth. "Suck."

She frowns, and I raise my brow at her. Abby opens, and I place my fingers in her mouth. She swirls her tongue around my fingers and then sucks on them. I pull them from her mouth and place them at her entrance, sliding them over her clit. I can feel just how wet she is.

I groan as I smile at her, my fangs scraping my bottom lip. "Fuck, my love, you are so wet."

My dick twitches as my fingers slide into her, and her back arches off the floor. Her hands move to my arms, and I pull my fingers out of her, making her groan in protest. "Didn't I tell you not to move?"

Abby shivers as she nods. "Yes, Alpha," she breathes. I know she does it on purpose to drive me over the edge.

"Fuck Abby, you are going to make me come before I've even had my fun with you."

"Hmmm, sounds like a challenge," she teases.

I push my hand through her hair to the back of her head, gripping tight in the nape of her neck, and she whimpers. I pull her face to mine, and I bite down on her bottom lip. She inhales sharply, and one of those sexy moans leaves her throat.

"You have no idea what you're doing to me, do you?"

"No, but I can always find out," she breathes against my mouth, her hand slipping between her legs and gripping my dick firmly. I hiss, closing my eyes. The feeling of her hand on me makes me shudder. Abby moves her hand slowly down my length, and I grip her hair tighter, resisting the urge to thrust into her hand. "Ah, F-Fuck."

My body tenses from the pure pleasure running through me. My head is a muddled horny mess. She grips me tighter, and her rhythm tortures me, slowly moving up and down my length.

I'm trembling at her touch and her hold on me. Abby looks up at me with those stunning eyes, a hint of brilliant white around her iris, the rest vibrant green.

I swallow hard before kissing her again, her movement picking up, but not by much. I am going to lose my mind.

I break away from her mouth, panting, both of us breathless, her rhythm still steady. I rest my head against hers, and I can feel her smile at my trembling body. "I want to consume every part of you," I growl at her.

"What are you waiting for, *Alpha*?" That fucking word has never sounded so sexy before, and it will never sound the same after tonight. Of that, I'm sure.

I close my eyes as her hand moves faster. I groan as I take in a shaky breath, and I swear she just giggled. Releasing her hair, I push her back down to the floor. "Hands above your head."

Abby tilts her head, giving me the same seductive smile as before. Her grip on my dick tightens in defiance as she keeps her pace, not faltering once.

My lip curls up, bearing my canines at her slightly. "You are playing a dangerous game, my love."

"Whatever are you talking about?" Abby licks over her bottom lip slowly.

"Fuck, Abby," I growl out, gripping her wrists. I pin them above her head roughly. I slide my fingers through her wetness before pushing them into her, not holding back.

Her ass lifts off the floor, and she grinds onto my fingers as she gasps and moans, "Shit."

Abby keeps surprising me with her actions. She moans again as I move my hand, curling my fingers up slightly. I feel her shudder as she gasps—*jackpot*—hitting her g-spot each time. "Keep your hands above your head, my love, or I will stop."

"Yes, Alpha," she pants.

Letting go of her hands, I move down to her nipples, latching onto one with my mouth and pinching and rolling the other with my free hand. "Yes, oh yes, please-" she moans. Reveling at how my touch melts her body, I graze my fangs over her nipple in my mouth. Abby inhales sharply, and her back arches when my movements pick up. She's whimpering now, her orgasm not far, making me smirk when her body trembles.

Just before her orgasm hits her, I pull my fingers from her, and she whines.

"No, please, Tyler, why did you stop?"

I give her a playful smile as I kiss her, positioning my dick at her entrance, pausing as I whisper on her lips, "You are not going to come on my hand. I want you to come all over me inside of you."

Her breath hitches, her eyes widen slightly, and she nods.

I push into her slowly, barely keeping a grip on my self-control. I pause again, letting her get used to me inside her. "Are you okay?" I don't dare take my eyes off her.

She swallows and then nods. "Just go slow, please."

"Oh, you will be begging me for more later." I kiss her again, sliding into her until she can take me fully. Tilting my head when I hear her breathing coming in short puffs, I wait until Abby nods reassuringly to me.

I start to move slowly, letting her get used to the movement until I feel her legs wrap around me, lifting her ass, making me go impossibly deeper. My rhythm doesn't falter once.

I cup the back of her neck with one hand and her ass with the other, lifting her more, and she gasps, her eyes rolling to the back of her head when I hit her g-spot again. My pace is steady as I grip her tighter. She whimpers as I move in and out of her.

"Tyler," she lets out a breathless moan. "Please."

My pace is still slow and steady, enough to bring her just to the brink of her orgasm but not enough to push her over the edge. Don't get me wrong, this pace is driving me just as insane as it's driving her, but I can't let go of my wolf and lose control. The incredible power I feel from having this type of control over her makes me drunk. If the roles are reversed, she will have the same control over me, which excites me. "Please, what, my love?"

"I need more, please."

"All you have to do is ask."

"Please, *my Alpha*. I need you to go faster. I can't take this slow torture, please," she pants as she begs me. Closing my eyes at her words, I can't keep the groan from rumbling in my chest, my control really slipping now. Picking up my pace, I slam into her. Fuck, this has never felt so good before.

Abby's eyes are hooded, and her breath comes in short, sexy puffs just before her body stiffens when her orgasm hits. Her back arches, and she screams my name over and over again. I slow my pace to control my wolf, who is now clawing to be let out. I keep moving as she rides out her orgasm, picking up my pace again when she is spent.

The urge to mark her at this very moment is so strong I can't think of anything else. A growl rips through my chest, and I halt my movements as I squeeze my eyes shut. My breathing is harsh and ragged as I struggle to keep my wolf at bay—which isn't sitting well with him, and now I must fight to keep him in the background.

"Is something wrong?" Abby breathes.

"I need to get control of my wolf. Just give me a second. If not, I am going to mark you." I grit out through my clenched jaw.

Abby's breath hitches in her throat, and I don't dare move, not feeling confident that my wolf won't take advantage of my vulnerability now. I feel her hand on my heart, making me shiver at her touch, and I open my eyes, looking down into hers, which is so open and vulnerable. "Then mark me." Abby's voice is so sincere it caresses my ears with the whisper, and she turns her head to expose her neck to me.

"No, Abby, I can't-" I force through my clenched jaw.

She turns her head back to me, her eyes sad for a split second before she grabs onto my back, grinding herself on me.

I hiss out, the sensation sending my want for her into overdrive, overpowering every rational thought, and I start to move harder this time, making her gasp at every thrust. My pleasure builds, and I slam into her harder, wanting to go deeper, chasing the high of my own release.

I feel her orgasm building again as her nails dig into my back. That will leave some marks, but I don't care. I will wear them with pride.

I grunt as I feel myself near my release. Abby's almost at the peak of her next orgasm when she lifts her head to me and bites down in the crease between my neck and shoulder, *marking me.*

I don't have time to react before the mark burns up my neck and down my chest and shoulder.

A roar leaves my throat as my wolf takes control, my canines pushing further past my lips.

I grab her face roughly, turning it to the side, exposing her neck. Thrusting into her as my pleasure releases, I sink my teeth into the mark Jace has left on her neck. Her back arches, and a scream rips through her chest, her nails digging deeper into my back before she slumps back to the floor, panting.

My wolf retreats to the back of my mind, content with marking our mate, and I regain control of my senses.

Fuck!

No!

No!

NO! WHAT HAVE I Done?

How did I lose control like that? Abby marked me first, which fueled my wolf—the damn prophecy. My heart slams against my chest as panic takes root in me.

I pull myself from her quickly, looking down at her. She smiles at me weakly, and her breathing is short and quick as I touch her cheek. She's burning up, and her body starts to shake.

I get up from the floor quickly, pulling up my sweatpants. Grabbing a blanket from the bed, I rush back to Abby. Her breathing is getting shallow and rapid as she shakes.

Wrapping the blanket around her body, I pick her up from the floor, pressing her to me as I walk to the bed.

"Fuck Abby, why did you do that? *Why?!*" I almost yell at her as I lie her down on the bed.

"W-We n-needed to seal… the bond for you t-to get b-better, remember?" she stutters, her face contorting with pain.

"ARE YOU FUCKING INSANE?" Now I *am* yelling at her, the panic in my chest making me act irrationally. "YOU COULD DIE, AND YOU DIDN'T EVEN CONSIDER WHAT THAT WOULD DO TO ME."

She flinches, a tear running down her cheek. "You're the Alpha King; you can't be held back by someone like me. If I die, I know you will be okay. You will find the person from the prophecy, and you will barely even remember me or my name after a while."

I stagger back, retreating from her as if she slapped me. My wolf whines as he feels the weight of what we will lose if we don't act now. "THIS IS SO MUCH BULLSHIT. YOU ARE MY MATE ABBYGAIL. I DON'T WANT ANYBODY ELSE BUT YOU—I LOVE YOU," I bellow with ferocity.

The panic turns into anger. This is the first time I've told her I loved her, which means nothing if she dies.

Abby smiles at me weakly, my words sinking in. I distinctly note that she doesn't say she loves me back, which rips my heart to shreds. "P-please, Tyler, please don't be angry. I'm sorry-"

she groans, pulling into herself, her breathing irregular. Abby grabs at her neck, a blood-curdling scream leaves her lips, and she convulses.

I grab my phone from my bedside table and dial Layla's number. "Lay, please help!" I scream into the phone when I hear her voice.

I don't even know if my sister hears me as I throw my phone down and run to Abby's side, picking her up in my arms to do—I don't even know what to do—as the last of the attack on her body dies out, and she lies unconscious in my arms.

CHAPTER TWENTY-SEVEN

LAYLA

"I wonder if those two have worked out their differences already," I say never-mindedly, more to myself than to Kayden. We are in the kitchen, and I'm sitting at the table while Kayden is busy making us something to eat. I love this man with everything in me. He spoils me rotten, and I know that.

Kayden turns and walks over to where I'm sitting, two plates in his hands. I close my eyes and inhale deeply as the aroma from the flapjacks and bacon hits my nose. "Hmmm, comfort food. What did I do to deserve someone like you?"

"Who says you deserve me?" Kayden chuckles as he sets the plates down on the table.

I slap his hand playfully. "Hey! That's mean."

"Babe, if you're going to ask stupid questions, expect stupid answers."

I laugh at him as I pick up a piece of crispy bacon, taking a bite and savoring the taste in my mouth. I catch Kayden staring at me, his hands folded in front of him and resting his chin on them. He's giving me one of those "eat me up" smiles.

Giggling like a bloody schoolgirl, I cover my mouth and swallow the food. "What?"

"Nothing." He shrugs, still smiling at me. "I'm just appreciating the fact that you are mine."

"Always and forever, babe. I love you so much."

"I love you more." He winks at me.

"Dream on, lover boy," I laugh.

Kayden chuckles as Sebastian and Julia walk into the kitchen. They walk around the table, Julia sitting next to me and Sebastian taking one next to Kayden.

"You two seem lighthearted, that's something new," Sebastian mocks, grabbing a flapjack from Kayden's plate.

"Hey! Make your own damn food," Kayden scolds Sebastian, grabbing at the piece of food but missing it as Sebastian shoves the whole thing in his mouth.

"Come on, kids, there's enough to share, no need to fight," I laugh.

Kayden whips his head to me, the look on his face brings me to tears as I laugh at him. It's almost the same as when you take a bone from a dog, which isn't so far off from being true if you think about it. Sebastian seizes this moment to sneak a piece of bacon, but Kayden catches him in the act.

"Now, now, boys, let's play nice," Julia playfully scolds, lifting her brow with a smile on her face as they argue about the bacon.

"Coffee, anyone?" Sebastian chuckles as he gets up from the table, walks to the coffee station, and takes out four cups as we all say yes please.

"I'm sorry to spoil the mood, but have you had any luck finding Jace and Owen yet?" Julia asks somberly, looking at Kayden as he takes a big bite of his flapjack with bacon on top.

I sigh when the whole mood changes in the room. Well, it was nice while it lasted. Julia fiddles with her hands as she waits for Kayden to answer her. Kayden narrows his eyes as he chews and holds up a finger, indicating to wait a second. He swallows and clears his throat.

"No, nothing yet. I'm getting worried. We know Jace's plan, and the fact that we can't pinpoint where they are and when they might attack is working on my nerves."

"I know the feeling. It's like you're waiting for the pin to drop. It really is nerve-wracking." Julia agrees.

"I'll send out a team of warriors to patrol the border of our territory and another to search the neutral area beyond our borders for a clue. Maybe they can pick up their scent," Sebastian comments as he walks back from the coffee counter with our coffee in hand.

I listen to them discussing the plans to get a lead on Jace and Owen, feeling worried. It's been two weeks since their escape, and there is no news, no attack—nothing.

I'm wracking my brain to think of what Jace's strategy can be when my phone rings in my jeans pocket. I take it out absent-mindedly, not really looking at the screen as I answer the phone.

"Hello, Layla, speak-"

I don't have time to finish my greeting when Tyler's screaming voice comes over the phone. My face pales as I hear him cry for me to help.

Everybody's attention is on me and the noticeably short call. We all jump to our feet at once, running out of the kitchen, almost falling over each other making our way to Tyler's room.

I burst through the door, and I'm stopped dead at the sight of Tyler clutching onto Abby's unconscious body, rocking back and forth, tears streaming down his face. Kayden slams into my back, and so does the others, forcing me to stumble further into the room—making Tyler aware of our presence.

I catch myself before I hit the ground, using the momentum to run to Tyler's side. The look on my face must be mirrored on Kayden's as he stands next to me, looking horrified.

"What the fuck happened?" Kayden all but spits.

Tyler doesn't answer immediately, and I understand why when he looks at us. His irises red from anger, the normal color almost totally drowned out, his jaw clenched, his breathing heavy.

He clutches Abby tightly to his chest, his fingers digging into her exposed skin.

I kneel next to him, placing my hand on his arm softly. I don't understand what's happening. Did Abby not heal from the last feeding? I look her over, not seeing anything wrong, and I turn my attention to my brother. My breath gets lodged in my throat when my eyes fall on his neck.

He's marked.

The mark on his neck is still bloody, but already healed. What the hell happened?

"You need to help her, Lay, please!" Tyler's voice sounds broken and hoarse when he finally speaks. It doesn't sound like him.

"I will, I promise. You need to tell me what happened so I know how to help Abby."

Tyler snarls at the memory, his hands turning claw-like as he holds onto Abby. "Lay, you need to take her from me. My wolf is about to take over, and I don't know if I can stop him."

"Babe, I need your help. I don't think this will be as easy as it looks. You need to hold Tyler at bay when we take Abby from him," I say over my shoulder, eyeing my brother, knowing full well that in this state, he will not let her go so easily. "Julia, I need your help. Sebastian, I think Kayden's going to need yours."

Both of them nod as they move to us quickly. Tyler's head drops, and he starts to shake, a growl building deep in his chest. Making eye contact with each of them, I nod slightly, indicating for them to move. Kayden and Sebastian grab Tyler's arms, forcing them behind his back as Julia and I gently take Abby from Tyler's lap.

The moment we remove Abby from Tyler, he thrashes against Kayden and Sebastian's hold on him, snarling and baring his canines at us.

They pull him off the bed and push him to the floor, pinning him down. Sebastian pushes down with a knee on his back and Kayden on the back of his neck, still holding a death grip on his arms.

I wrap the blanket tighter around Abby's body, realizing she's completely naked. Scanning over her face quickly, not finding anything wrong, I shift my attention to the rest of her. The sight of the very fresh, unhealed mark sitting at the base of her neck makes me gasp as I realize what happened.

"Julia! We need to move her to the hospital now!" I yell, pointing to the mark on Abby's neck as the hysterics crash over me. Julia curses, tears in her eyes as she looks at me, terrified. We carefully pick Abby up from the floor, making our way out of the room.

Tyler lets out a vicious roar, and I hear Kayden and Sebastian curse simultaneously as something crashes to the floor.

"We need to move, Julia. I don't think my brother has a hold of his wolf. Everything is going to look like a threat to him now. Hopefully, the guys can subdue Tyler long enough for us to get Abby to the doctor."

"I hope so, too," she sobs, as we move down the hall.

CHAPTER TWENTY-EIGHT

KAYDEN

"**D**AMN IT! WATCH OUT SEBASTIAN!" I yell as Tyler swings a claw at his head. Luckily, Sebastian is a fast wolf. That's why he's in charge of training the warriors. Sebastian ducks the next two swings from Tyler, then he rushes him and tackles Tyler to the ground with brute force.

Tyler snarls at Sebastian as his head hits the ground, disorienting him momentarily, which gives Sebastian enough time to jump to his feet. Tyler gets to a crouching position, ready to attack the person in front of him. I take this moment of distraction and move behind Tyler, grabbing him around the neck in a chokehold. Sebastian notices my movements before I move and grabs Tyler's hands as soon as my arm winds around his neck, pulling him up.

Squeezing tightly, I feel Tyler thrashing against us. This isn't working. He's not going down.

Tyler pulls from Sebastian's grasp and pushes his right claw backward past his ribs and into my side deeply. I roar in pain as blood spills down my side and leg. I let go of Tyler, and he spins to face me, stalking closer as I retreat. My hands are on my wound, pressing down to stop the bleeding. *Fuck... Not good.*

I forgot that a wound sustained from a hybrid doesn't heal like any other injury. It takes a few weeks. I don't know if it's because of the vampire gene or the fact that it's the two different venoms mixing. No one can figure out why, when you sustain a wound from a hybrid in battle, it doesn't heal. "Tyler, please," I plead, still moving backward until my back slams into the wall.

Tyler stalks closer, his claw raised above his head, and the next moment, he brings it down, swiping at my jugular. I dodge the onslaught and push myself off the wall, tackling him to the floor again.

Not waiting another second, Sebastian punches Tyler twice in the face, knocking him out cold.

"Fuck," I grunt, stumbling to my feet.

"Damn it, Kayden. I thought I had him pinned. We need to get that checked out." Sebastian grabs a shirt from Tyler's closet and hands it to me so I can try and stop the bleeding.

"Urgh... Don't worry, man. I keep forgetting how resilient he gets and his raw strength when he's like this."

"Do you think we need to chain him up in his office again? If this is going to be a regular occurrence, we're going to have a problem. He's out of control, and the other packs will use this to get him dethroned if they find out," Sebastian says, clearly frustrated.

"No, I don't think it's necessary to chain him up in his office. Maybe just some wolfsbane-soaked ropes to tie his hands until he wakes up. Hopefully, he will have regained control by then," I huff as I put more pressure on the wound on my side.

"Okay, sounds good. I'll get right on that. You go and get that checked out."

"Yeah, on it," I grunt as I leave the room and make my way towards the hospital.

LAYLA

"What's going on, Lady Layla?" Adam rushes to us as we enter the emergency room, his eyes widening in shock before calling over his shoulder to the nearest nurse and then turning his attention back to us. "Put her down on the gurney. Nurse, close the curtains and give us some privacy."

"May I please get something to cover her? She's naked, and my brother will lose his mind if he finds out anyone saw her naked."

"I understand. Please take one of the hospital gowns and dress Abbygail quickly so I can examine her. What happened?" he questions, handing me the gown before turning his back to us. I open the blanket around Abby, and Julia helps me to get her dressed. I brush some of Abby's hair from her face as I turn and call Adam to us.

"She's decent, doc. Please help her. I think Tyler marked her. He almost died last night when we couldn't find Abby to feed him, and he took a lot of her blood. When I saw her last night, she said she was tired of arguing with my brother. So, I assume she marked him so he can be cured."

I rush through my words as Adam takes out his stethoscope, pressing it to her chest, and frowns as he listens to me and her heartbeat. He removes it from his ears and hangs it back around his neck. Taking out his flashlight, he checks her pupil response before he examines the bite on her neck.

"How do you know she marked him first?"

"I can absolutely guarantee you she marked him first. I know my brother. He won't put his life and needs above those he loves, especially not his mate. He would rather die."

"Yes, I do agree, and it makes sense. This dilemma might count in our favor," Adam says cryptically.

I frown and look in Julia's direction. She must be feeling the same level of confusion as me as she shakes her head, shrugging. You can add a bit of bloody frustration to it because I am so over this cryptic shit we deal with. *Why can't something about this whole shitty situation be simple for once, ugh!*

"Please, Doc, I can't handle any more cryptic shit. Just say what you want to or explain yourself, either way, out with it."

"In a minute." Adam cuts me off, the panic in his voice sending a chill down my back when Abby's body starts to shake lightly before a total onslaught of convulsion hits her small frame.

"NURSE!" Adam yells as he pushes Abby to the bed to stop her from hurting herself.

Three nurses come running into the room as Adam barks out commands to what he needs from them. Abby's body is still trashing in his hold. Two minutes pass before the attack leaves her, and she slumps to the bed again. *Fuck! Please, please let her survive this.*

"Lady Layla, Lady Julia, please wait outside so we can attend to our future Luna. We will inform you of what's going on as soon as we have answers," one of the nurses in the room tells us.

I can't take my eyes off Abby as she lies motionless on the bed. The nurse clears her throat. She looks at me expectantly, and I frown. The nurse gives me a soft smile, and I notice her kind eyes, the worry evident on her face as she tries to hide it not to upset us. "I'm sorry, what did you say?"

"I asked you and Lady Julia to please wait outside so we can attend to our Luna," she repeats, ushering us to the door. "I will inform you personally with any news if the doctor doesn't do it himself, I promise."

I nod hesitantly and make my way to the waiting area. *What am I going to do?* I turn to see if Julia is okay, but she's not with me. *Shit, where is she?*

Looking around me in a panic, I spot her sitting on the floor just outside the room where we left Abby, sobbing.

"Julia, hey, come on. Let's take a seat in the waiting area. We can't stay here. We don't want unnecessary attention," I say softly as I crouch down next to her, taking her hand to help her off the floor.

Julia looks up at me, and I give her an encouraging nod as she gets up and follows me to the waiting area. We both take a seat on—or rather, fall into—the soft chairs. The cushioned seats are welcoming, and so needed.

I push my hands through my hair as I sigh. I really can't handle this anymore. All this crap needs to end.

"What do you think Adam meant?" I startle when Julia's voice breaks the silence of the waiting area. I didn't expect her to talk.

"I don't know. I hope with everything in me that Adam found a solution, because I cannot take any more bad news."

I lean back in my chair, closing my eyes. Tiredness completely envelops me. I hope Kayden and Sebastian are all right. My brother is a force to be reckoned with in his normal form, but when his wolf comes to play, nothing can stop him.

A crashing sound coming from the hallway brings me out of my thoughts, and I look to Julia, who is already on her feet and on her way to the door. "SHIT! Layla, it's Kayden-"

"WHAT?"

I'm out of the door before Julia can finish her sentence, gasping when I spot my mate slumped against the wall on the floor, blood covering his side and his hands. "KAYDEN!"

"Lay," he groans breathlessly, looking up at me and smiling weakly.

He's pale from the blood loss, and that gash in his side does not look pretty.

"What the hell happened?" I almost squeak as panic takes hold of my heart and chest.

"Calm down, babe, I'm okay-" he grunts as he hunches over coughing. "Tyler was too quick for us, and I let my guard down for just a second, and he shoved his fucking claws into my side."

"Damn it, Kayden, how can you be so negligent? You know what Tyler is capable of! How many times have you been in battle beside him? You should've been more careful."

"I know, babe, no need to lecture me. I thought at least you would be worried, but no, you're mad that I wasn't fast enough." Kayden rolls his eyes at me as the nurse from behind the reception desk approaches us with a gurney.

"I *am* worried, you idiot," I mutter. "Now get off your ass and onto the bloody gurney so they can look at that wound of yours."

Julia comes to Kayden's other side and wraps his arm around her neck as I take his injured side. We pull him up and help him onto the gurney. Kayden groans in pain as he lies down before smiling up at me again.

"Why the hell are you smiling?" I'm annoyed with him. He made a stupid mistake, and it could've turned out even worse than it did.

"You're so cute when you're angry. Do you know that?"

"You are delusional, babe. Shut up and get healed up so I can kick your ass for being stupid." I roll my eyes at him as they take him into another room to get cleaned up.

"This stupid, delusional fool loves you regardless," he calls to me just before the door shuts behind him.

I rub my hands frustratedly over my face, inhaling deeply and letting out a strained sigh.

Julia places a caring hand on my shoulder. "We'll get through this, Layla. We must; otherwise, everything we know and love will crumble to the ground. If Abby doesn't survive this, we will not be able to avoid a war. I don't think Tyler will be able to think straight, and I think he will act on loss and the hurt that will follow."

"You are absolutely correct, Julia. The little humanity my brother has left will be lost forever if Abby isn't strong enough to pull through, and when he finds out what he did to his best friend…" I trail off, not wanting to finish the sentence.

Julia sighs, obviously knowing exactly what I did not say. She moves towards the waiting room again, stepping inside, and holds the door open for me to join her.

"You go ahead, Jules. I think I'll call Sebastian. I'm worried about Tyler."

"Okay, let me know what he says. I'll wait for the doctor or the nurse."

"Thank you."

"No need to thank me, Layla. I will do anything to help you guys. I feel somewhat guilty about everything—and I know you're going to say that this isn't my fault—but I feel partially responsible for what Jace managed to do."

"Julia, you need to stop that shit now. Look at everything you have done for Abby and afterward." I walk to her and hug her. "I'm grateful that we have you here. I will make sure you stay and become part of this pack. Damn anybody who says something different."

Julia laughs at my statement as she hugs me back. I know this is an unlikely friendship, but I am relieved that I don't have to go through all of this on my own and that I have a friend like her. I will be forever grateful for Julia.

"Go, call Sebastian and find out about Tyler. Otherwise, it will bug you the whole time," Julia says as she pulls away from the hug.

I let out a nervous laugh as I take my phone from my pocket. Julia is very perceptive. She will definitely be an asset for this pack. Tyler will be stupid to refuse her, and Abby will not be happy with him if he decides to kick her out.

I walk just beyond the hospital doors and dial Sebastian's number. I hope Tyler is okay. I sigh in frustration when there is no answer. Where the hell can the damn Gamma be? I huff as I redial the number.

"Yeah?" Sebastian's curt voice cuts through the line.

"Really, Sebastian, how many times do I need to tell you that answering a phone so crudely pisses me off. You are the bloody Gamma of this pack. Act like it."

"Layla, how many times do *I* need to tell *you* that how I answer the fucking phone has nothing to do with you? Is there something you need from me?"

"Yes." My frustration turns into irritation. "What happened with Tyler and Kayden?"

"Kayden and I tried to subdue Tyler, but he got away from me and slashed Kayden with his claws," he sighs irritably.

"Fuck. Where is Tyler now?"

"I managed to knock him out. Kayden and I decided to restrain him with wolfsbane-soaked ropes. Just until he knows he can rein in his wolf. I just finished up with that. He's still in his room." The way Sebastian relays the information is so matter-of-fact, like there's nothing weird about it.

This guy knows how to push someone's buttons. I don't know if he adopted this persona to deal with the battles and the bad part of being a Gamma. Maybe this is his coping mechanism.

"Fine, Kayden was taken to get cleaned up and stitched up. Hopefully, the damn wounds don't take forever to heal," I tell him, I know that will be his question to me next.

"Okay, that's good to hear, and Abbygail?"

"No word yet. She had another seizure."

"Layla, you know we-"

"I know, Sebastian, I can't deal with that now. She will be fine. We need to believe that. If not, I will lose my brother. So please drop this topic for now. Call me when Tyler comes, too."

Sebastian huffs his response and the call disconnects.

Ugh, I'm gritting my teeth. Sebastian is the best wolf for this position and one of my brother's most loyal friends, but I wish I could buy a bloody personality for the asshole.

Shoving my phone in my pocket again, I return to the hospital. The nurse who worked on Kayden is behind the reception desk again. I walk over to her, and she looks at me with a warm smile. "Lady Layla, I wondered where you had gone. Beta Kayden is doing well. The wound is deep, but we managed to stop the bleeding and got him stitched up. He's in Room D if you want to go see him."

"I had to make a call. Are you sure Kayden is fine?"

"Yes, absolutely." The nurse hesitates, but after a few seconds, she frowns and asks, "How did Beta Kayden sustain the wound because he's not healed yet? I have my suspicions, but it's better to hear than assume?"

Shit, how am I supposed to tell the nurse that her Alpha is out of control and attacked his Beta? This will cause problems we don't need now.

"I can't divulge the information now; please forgive me. Just know we appreciate your discretion."

The nurse watches me for a few seconds. Usually, they need to know precisely what happened to report it to Kayden or Sebastian, but since it's Kayden who's been injured and the fact that I'm Tyler's sister, she doesn't push the subject. "Very well, Lady Layla." She bows her head to me and sits behind the computer, continuing with whatever she was busy with before Kayden.

I sigh before pursing my lips as I watch her. I hate lying to our people or being so mysterious, and she's only doing her job. It's clear that she is offended by my statement, but I can do nothing to change it.

I turn and walk to Room D of the hospital wing. Rounding the corner, I hear cursing filter into the hallway, and a tray crashes to the floor just before a monitor screams.

My heart drops as I realize the commotion comes from Kayden's room. I take off running to the room, expecting to see him worse off, but as soon as I burst in the door, I'm met with a semi-naked Kayden and a handful of nurses around him trying to keep him in bed.

Naturally, it's to no avail, as he is ten times stronger than the five nurses combined trying to get him to lie down.

I stop in the doorway, watching the commotion in front of me. It's damn near funny if you ask me. Kayden is trying to yank out the drip they placed in his arm. The cables from the heart monitor are pulled from the machine—hence the constant screeching—dangling from his chest.

"Please, Beta Kayden, you need to lie down. Your movements are not good for the wound you sustained. You need to rest, please."

"Damn you, woman, unhand me now. I don't have time to lie down," he snarls at the nurse, pulling on his arm before he topples backward onto the bed.

I bite down on my fist to stop myself from laughing. It doesn't work as the laughter spills from my mouth. Every single wolf in the room freezes as they turn to see me in the door. I catch Kayden's eyes, and the look on his face makes me double over with laughter. "This. Isn't. Funny," Kayden grits through his teeth, glaring at me. He shrugs the five nurses still clinging to him off as he gets to his feet again.

"Oh, babe. It's bloody hilarious. Will you please listen to the nurses? Don't be a baby and get your ass back on that bed. You need to take it easy for a couple of days. With all this struggling, you've opened the damn wound again." I point to his side and fold my arms across my chest as I raise my brow at him.

"FUCK!" he bellows and sits back down, looking defeated.

"No need to be so short-tempered. We already have a stubborn ass Alpha. What happened to your laid-back nature?" I ask as I walk closer to him.

"You know very well what happened to my laid-back nature- OW DAMN IT, WOMAN!" he flinches at the nurse now cleaning his wound, *again*, to dress it with clean bandages.

I sigh as I shake my head. Men can be such babies. They will go to war and don't show anything, but try to clean the damn wounds and they bitch like they are two years old.

I wait until the nurse finishes tying the bandage around Kayden's ribs before I sit beside him.

The nurse turns to me, clearly pissed off at Kayden and tired from all the struggling. "Lady Layla, please keep your mate in bed. He needs to give that wound time to heal, as it's not healing as it should. The nurse at the front desk said you don't want to give details, and that's fine, but with the limited information this is all we can do for now. He needs to do his part and stay still," the nurse says firmly, directing the last part at Kayden, and then promptly turns on her heel and marches out the door.

"Really? Do you need to be so damned stubborn?"

Kayden grunts as he lies back down, clutching his side. I know he must be in a lot of pain, but of course, he will try to hide it. "I'm not stubborn, babe. I'm not too fond of hospitals, and you know that. I have a lot to do. Sebastian is alone with Tyler, and I'm afraid his wolf will still be in control if he comes to."

"Look, there is not much you can do now. I spoke to Sebastian about fifteen minutes ago. Tyler is still out cold, and he will call me when Tyler wakes up. So, stop being a bitch and heal up. I still owe you an ass-kicking, remember?"

Kayden narrows his eyes at me before he lies his head back down on the pillow and closes them as he accepts his defeat. "Fine, but just know you will pay for calling me a bitch," he mutters, his eyes still closed—but that 'eat me up' grin of his is ever-present.

"I'll hold you to that. You know I like a challenge." I laugh, relieved, as I get up from the bed and kiss him on his forehead.

"I'm going to check on Julia and see if there's news about Abby. Please stay in the bloody bed."

"Hmmm, can't promise anything," he hums just before drifting off to sleep.

I smile warmly at the beast of a man lying on the small hospital bed—unnecessarily stubborn, but I love him to death.

Turning, I make my way to the waiting area and find Julia sitting on the edge of the soft, comfortable chairs, bouncing her knee and wringing her fingers. "What's wrong? Did something happen?" I ask quickly, making her head snap to me. Relief covers her face.

"No, nothing happened. It's an unnerving feeling not knowing what is happening, and I'm worried about you and Kayden. How is he?"

I roll my eyes, sighing tiredly, "Unnecessarily stubborn, but he's okay. He's resting. Eventually. Took an army of nurses to get him back to bed, and I'm not sure it would've worked if I didn't step in." I laugh a little at the memory of my mate and the nurses trying their absolute best to get him on the bed.

"Sounds like he is going to be a difficult patient."

"Ha, difficult is putting it lightly. Kayden drives me fucking crazy. He wants to get back to his duties and doesn't think of the consequences." Julia laughs wholeheartedly at my exasperated statement, and I smile, amused. It feels good, and it lightens the mood.

CHAPTER TWENTY-NINE

TYLER

My burning wrists wake me, along with the extreme discomfort. What the hell happened? My mind feels fuzzy, and nothing comes to mind. I open my eyes slightly, looking around. I'm still in my room but on the bloody floor. I groan, and the sound of a chair sliding on the wooden floor from someone standing up grounds me somewhat. I follow the noise, and my eyes fall on Sebastian. His face is laced with irritation, which isn't anything new, and worry. Now, *that's* new.

Sebastian approaches me slowly, not saying a word. The silence is deafening.

I move my hands again and hiss, feeling the burning around my wrists intensify. I look up at my hands—that are tied to my own fucking bedpost—and anger flares through my entire body as I snap my head back to Sebastian. "What is the fucking meaning of this?" I snarl.

Sebastian stops a few feet from me and folds his arms across his chest. The worrying look intensifies. That really is an odd look for him. I've never really seen worry on his face. "Your wolf?"

"What about my wolf?"

"Is it under control, Alpha?" he demands.

I frown. What the hell is he talking about? I roll my shoulders and feel for my wolf. He's pacing in my mind, agitated, but somewhat calm. "Yes, but not for long if you don't release me and tell me what the hell is going on," I grumble, my jaw clenched so tight I might crack some of my teeth if I don't calm myself.

Sebastian doesn't move for a while, his brows pulled down, contemplating if I'm telling the truth. He curses under his breath and moves to me, taking the damn wolfsbane rope off me. I huff a breath through my nose, watching my wrists heal, but the burning feeling still lingers as I rub them. *I hate wolfsbane!*

"What do you remember of last night?" Sebastian curtly asks as he retreats from me quickly, looking careful and weary. Don't get me wrong, there is no hint of fear anywhere on him.

"I- uh-" I narrow my eyes as I wrack my brain, coming up short. Clearly, my wolf is trying to keep me from remembering. I don't know if it's for his sake or my own, but I need to remember.

Sebastian watches me, his eyebrows raised. He is quiet the whole time, not trying to help at all.

"Spit it out, Sebastian," I snap, getting up from my seat on the floor.

My body aches. It feels like I've been in a fight recently. I tilt my head when a flash of a memory of me and Kayden fighting springs to mind.

I groan again, holding my head. Suddenly, all the events from last night hit me at once, and my head spins. "Fuck... Abbygail," I whisper, grabbing at my neck where she marked me. The mark is healed, but slightly raised.

I look up at Sebastian, searching his eyes for confirmation, and find more than that. I close my eyes and remember calling Layla as Abby suffered from a seizure after I marked her. My face pales, and I snap my eyes open.

"Where is she?" My voice barely above a whisper now, dreading the answer. "Please, my friend, tell me I didn't kill my mate."

My heart sinks to my stomach as I watch the different emotions play over Sebastian's face, coming to the very last one, which is a mixture of concern and sympathy.

"No." I drop to my knees, not having the strength to keep standing.

Sebastian comes to kneel in front of me, and he places his hand on my shoulder. "You did not kill your mate. Abbygail is in the hospital, but I'm afraid it's a dire situation. I don't know if she will last through this day. She's been getting seizure after seizure. Layla and Julia are still waiting for Adam to come and speak to them."

I look up at him, my breathing rugged as the panic grips my insides from his words. *What have I done? How could I have been so careless?* I should've had more control. I push my hands into my hair and grab at the roots, pulling hard as a soul-wrenching scream leaves my throat.

"There's more," Sebastian says carefully after the scream dies out. I look up at him, my chest constricting from worry. He hesitates, and I can see he's unsure if he should tell me, probably concerned that my self-control is fragile.

It could be. I don't even know anymore. Did I ever really have control of my wolf? Every other wolf in my pack seems to have more of a handle on their wolves than their stupid Alpha.

"Just tell me, please," I plead, dropping my hands to my knees.

"Kayden," he hesitates again, not saying anything for a few minutes.

"What about Kayden?" I ask quietly, as the tension builds.

"You put him in the hospital as well. We tried to keep you from killing all of us when Layla and Julia took Abby from you. Kayden was stupid and distracted." He rolls his eyes. "He grabbed you from behind in a chokehold, and I grabbed your hands, but you got out of my hold, and you…"

"Fuck, Sebastian, just spit it out!"

"You shoved your claws into his side. He'll survive, though," he renders, seeing the horrified look on my face.

"What?" I ask, mortified, dropping my head. *Fuck. I am a monster.* What kind of Alpha attacks his best friend? What Alpha is so weak he can't control his wolf? I cover my face with my hands as defeat and self-hatred crash over me, along with a morbid realization: I can't lead this pack, let alone all the packs in the territory.

I will find Jace and Owen and ensure they are taken care of, and then I'm stepping down. My people deserve better than me. I'm a danger to everybody around me. The fear they all have isn't uncalled for. I thought my being a hybrid was a good thing, helping me protect everything and everyone I love, but I was wrong.

Sebastian taps my shoulder, bringing me out of my mind.

Looking up at him, I see his frowning face. I can't tell him what I'm thinking. They will try and deny it, but the evidence is clear, and I can't hide it anymore. If the pack finds out, they will surely turn against me. I can't handle the disappointment from my people, let alone the fear they will have for me more than what they already do.

"Come on," Sebastian says, taking hold of my arm and pulling me up. "Let's go see Kayden and find out what's going on with your mate. You need peace of mind because I can see the war inside you. Please don't make hasty and irrational decisions, now."

I'm silent as I get up and walk to the spot on the floor where I discarded my shirt when Abby and I mated. My heart aches as I remember, the pain in it almost crippling. Our mating bond was supposed to be unique and heavenly. Instead, I'm plagued with horror and worry.

Bursting through the hospital's front door, I march past the reception desk. Everyone around me scatters and no one is saying or doing anything to stop me. I look around the hallway, and everyone I make eye contact with bows, then looks away quickly. The fear coming from them is bothering me more than it used to.

"ADAM!" I bellow in the middle of the hallway, causing more fear to spike, and the scent hits my nose. The smell of fear is disturbing, it has a tinge of metal to it, almost like blood. It puts me on edge, making me think of Abby again. "ADAM!" I roar this time, the windows and door rattling with the force of my voice.

Now is *not* the time to fucking ignore me.

The whole hallway is chaotic as wolves come to see why their Alpha is roaring in the middle of the hospital hallway. The ones that are already there duck into rooms which I'm sure aren't theirs.

"Alpha Tyler." The nurse hurries to me, bowing low. "Please calm down. I know you must be worried. Doctor Adam is still attending to Abbygail."

"That's *Luna Abbygail*," I snarl at the poor woman, and she steps back from me, trembling.

Looking over her head and around the hallway for Adam again, my eye catches my reflection in the large mirror on the wall next to me, and I know exactly why she's trembling. The sight of me isn't very welcoming. I have a snarl on my face, baring canines, and my damned eyes are a mixture of black and red.

That's new, I think to myself as I sigh, feeling increasingly frustrated. Closing my eyes, I inhale deeply, letting out my breath slowly. Panic and worry clearly don't work well with my short temper and temperamental wolf.

"Please forgive me, nurse. I didn't mean to frighten you," I grit through my teeth, my eyes still closed, not trusting that they've returned to their normal color. I can still feel my canines, sharp and long, in my mouth.

"I-I understand, Alpha, no need to apologize-" she stutters, regaining her professional composure. "I'll call the emergency room and see what is taking so long."

I give her a slight nod, slowly opening my eyes. Her face reacts to mine, but she walks away quickly, not wanting to set me off again. I sigh heavily, my canines retracting again, as Sebastian clears his throat behind me. Fuck. I forgot he was still with me.

Looking over my shoulder, I see his stance, and I feel irritated about it. I can smell the wolfsbane in his jean's back pocket. The asshole is hovering, never taking his eyes off me. I can't blame him, though. I've been unable to handle my wolf without the poison, so I guess it's good he's here—doesn't mean it doesn't bug the shit out of me.

"Tyler?"

I hear my sister's voice come from down the hall where the waiting area is. I cringe as I look at her, the guilt of what I did to Kayden washing over me. I shove my hands in my pockets as I walk to her.

"Hi, little sister," I clear my throat as I see the worry in her eyes mixed with exhaustion. "I'm so sorry, I-"

"Don't, Tyler, please don't apologize. We know it was an—accident, if you will. Kayden doesn't blame you, neither do I."

I frown at her. Yeah, that's what she says now, but if Kayden's injury were worse, she would be singing a different tune. I lower my head, not wanting to see the hurt she's trying to hide because she thinks like me. "Where is he?"

"Room D, but he's sleeping. Please don't wake him. I already had to threaten him to keep him in bed. It's a nasty wound."

Shoving a hand through my hair, I huff, knowing that Kayden—although he wants people to think he is chilled and nothing fazes him—is quite stubborn, to say the least. He is duty-driven, just like me. That's why I always knew he would be the best Beta any pack can ask for. Maybe even a better Alpha than the one the pack is stuck with.

That's it, I've made up my mind. I will hand everything to Kayden when I step down. He won't be happy, but hey, it's either him or a stranger.

Layla frowns at me, picking up on my change of mood. I won't be able to hide my plan for long. My sister is very perceptive about the people in her life, even more those she loves. I swear it's her special kind of magic to know precisely what people are up to.

"Tyler, what's going on? You seem off. The calm coming from you is unnerving. These situations normally mess with your wolf. You haven't even asked me about Abby yet," she accuses as she approaches me.

I move back a few steps, keeping enough space between us. Calm? Me, calm? I must be hiding it well. I laugh sarcastically. Okay, maybe Layla's perceptiveness is slipping, or she is overlooking stuff because of what's happening.

Abby... My heart aches at the thought of her. I can't bring myself to ask Layla. I'm too afraid of the answer, but I can't put this off any longer. I need to know even if I don't want to. My wolf is demanding it.

"Where is she?" My voice barely above a whisper.

"She's stable, Alpha Tyler," Adam says from behind me, and I growl at him as I jump.

That doesn't happen often. Nobody can sneak up on me. I hate the fucking feeling, and besides, if anyone can sneak up on a King, there's a problem.

Well, soon-to-be ex-King.

Adam raises his brow at me but realizes his mistake and clears his throat. I feel Sebastian stepping closer to me, his hand in his pocket. My lip pulls up slightly as I snarl at him. He just shrugs, never removing his hand from his pocket.

"I'm afraid the news isn't good, Alpha. I wish I could have given you better news. The best I can give you is that she did not die. Unfortunately, the bite and the seizures are too much for her body to handle. She has fallen into a coma." He maintains eye contact while he speaks, trying not to set me off with the news he needs to give me.

I, on the other hand, need to keep calm, so I close my eyes as my hands shake. I take a shaking breath, folding my arms over my chest, hiding my trembling hands. The tensions are high, and everybody's on edge, waiting for me to lose it.

Okay, I know that when it comes to Abby, my control over my wolf is fleeting, but fuck, give me some credit. I think I am getting the hang of it, not all of it, but some of it.

I release my breath, not noticing that I am holding it in. It, too, comes out shaking. I'm so fucking pathetic. Opening my eyes, I'm taken aback at everyone around me. Sebastian has taken an attack stance. Adam is holding his hand out in front of him, eyeing me suspiciously. Layla and Julia have moved to flank Sebastian, and the nurses who were here a minute ago are nowhere to be seen now.

"Really?" I drop my hands to my sides as I watch them. "I'm in control, you can back the fuck off," I snap irritably at them.

"Sorry, Alpha, if the situations are reversed, you would do the same. We are in a public place, and if you are going to lose control, it will be devastating for the pack. We don't need them to fear you more," Sebastian says cautiously as he slowly rises, removing his hand from his pocket.

"I. Don't. Care," I grit out. "You won't need to worry about me for long."

"What does *that* mean?!" Layla narrows her eyes at me.

"No concern of yours, little sister," I state in my Alpha voice, letting her understand that this topic isn't up for discussion.

However, it won't keep her off it, and she will pursue it later. On to Abby. "May I see her?" I ask Adam flatly as he lowers his hand.

"Are you sure you're fine, Tyler? Because there's more we need to discuss before you go to see her," Adam cautions in a lowered tone. I roll my eyes; there's always more, isn't there? Ugh, just get to the point.

"Yes, Adam, say what you need to."

"Well, as I said earlier to Layla and Julia, I have done my own research and need to ask you a few questions about your mating night. Do you mind?"

"What the hell has that to do with anything?" I huff, annoyed now. I'm calm and in control still, but this line of questioning is pushing it.

"Please, just listen. I need this information from you. It could change everything," Adam inquires, and I narrow my eyes at him before I give him a short nod.

"Which one of you initiated the marking? Meaning, who bit first?"

My jaw clenches as my wolf gets agitated by divulging our intimate doings with our mate. He growls in my head, and the sound reverberates through me as I ball my fists.

"Tyler," Sebastian warns me.

"Just give me a second," I snap angrily at Sebastian. "You aren't helping, buddy. Back the fuck off, will you? Your whole attitude is pissing us off. You are antagonizing my wolf, never mind me."

Sebastian narrows his eyes at me and steps back: not much, but giving me space to breathe. I take a slow, deep breath as I scold my wolf. *Can you please stop making it difficult? If you weren't such an overbearing asshole that kept taking over and making me lose my shit, we'd be able to handle these situations better. So, stop it, please.* My wolf whines in my head, but I can feel him backing off.

I relax my hands and look at Adam. "She bit me first."

Relieve washes over his face as a small smile spreads on his mouth. Hope glints in his eyes, which wasn't there before.

"What?" I frown at him.

"Well, Alpha. There is hope, then. I have come upon some very, very rare folklore. It says that if a hybrid meets an already-marked mate, the marked mate must initiate the mating ritual first, as this will seal the bond and break the curse of the one who bit them before they met their mate. This proves trust and submission from the pure to the tainted one."

"I don't understand, Adam. I did not submit to anything." He frowns at me as he opens his mouth to repeat what he said, but I cut him off. "Fuck, Adam, I understand the words you just spoke. What I meant was, I don't understand what this means for me and Abbygail."

"Ah, so you need to consider that it's folklore, but I figure that myths must start somewhere, don't they? What I'm getting at is that our Luna might pull through. What concerns me is that Jace marked her so many times, and that surely will play its role in this," Adam admits.

"Adam, are you sure about this? Please don't let me get my hopes up for nothing."

"I am relaying what I found, Alpha. I thought it best you know that there might be hope. Our Luna is comatose at this stage, and I can't tell you if and when she will wake up. I hope that your mate bond is stronger than this curse, and it will pull her through the darkness," Adam utters, looking over his shoulder as one of the nurses approaches us.

"Doctor, you are needed in Room A," she tells Adam before she turns and bows to me. "Alpha."

"We moved her to the private wing of the hospital, with security. I wasn't sure how many people knew about her and the fact that she's our future Luna. You are welcome to go and see her." Adam bows to me. "Now, if you will excuse me."

"Come on, Ty, let's go see Abby. I've read somewhere that some patients have woken up from their loved ones talking to them. Maybe the fact that you sealed the bond will also help. The pull to be with one another is strong," Layla says, hope evident in her tone as she takes my hand, pulling me towards the private wing.

CHAPTER THIRTY

TYLER

SIX MONTHS LATER...

It's been six months, and Abby still hasn't awakened from her coma. I was by her side every day for the first three months straight. Talking to her, reading to her, willing her to open her eyes; but she just lay there, never moving. I started to lose hope with every day that passed after the first three months.

Kayden healed up from the wound I inflicted on him. He says he's not angry with me; he was stupid and should have known better. I still blame myself.

On a positive note, my control has improved immensely. My wolf and I are moving as one. We have one purpose in mind: to find the bastard who placed us in this dilemma in the first place.

I haven't been to see Abby in weeks; it makes me feel guilty, but I can't look at her lying in that bed wasting away. So I decided I would be more productive in the field, searching for Jace and Owen.

I can't sit there and watch my mate. The haunting thoughts that play in my head are driving me insane: thoughts of her never waking up, of her staying in this state for the rest of our lives.

Layla isn't happy that I decided not to see Abby anymore, and she's worried that my humanity will be lost if I don't hold on to the small tether my mate provides.

With every day that passes, I care less and less about anything that's good and pure. I don't have an appetite anymore. I eat when I feel my strength leave me, and I don't really talk to anyone anymore. I lock myself in my office, shutting everything out. It suits me; this way, no one can get harmed because of me. Kayden and Sebastian are the only ones allowed in my office.

Keeping my head busy is the only thing I can do, so we've been going through information and recon that our scouts brought in. We are leaving in a few days. We got a lead that Jace and Owen fled to the Northern mountains. There are rumors that he is building an army to attack my pack and territory. Over my dead body; he will need the whole damn world, not just an army.

I've also heard rumors that he's trying to recruit other supernatural beings to join him. He hasn't had much success, though. My name and reputation are known far and wide. They will be stupid to get into bed with that piece of shit and think I will not retaliate. Those who think they are going to join forces with Jace and attack us will surely pay the piper. I will not show any mercy. *Never again.*

The thought of going into battle excites me, bringing a wicked smile to my face. I can already feel how I'll rip Jace limb from limb. I shake my head at myself. I know precisely why Layla is worried: my thoughts are becoming darker with every passing day without Abby by my side.

"What's with the disturbing grin?" I startle when Kaden's voice brings me out of my wicked thoughts. He's staring at me over his phone, brows raised. Kayden is arranging with the neighboring packs for our arrival later this week. We are passing through their territory. I don't need their permission—I'm just being polite. I don't need bad vibes from the rest of the packs when we are nearing a war. The less I worry about another pack attacking us, the better.

"The very vivid images I see make me smile, that's all." I laugh darkly.

"You are worrying me, Tyler. Are you sure you're up for this? Your humanity is delicate, and I'm afraid that if something happens, you will lose it forever."

"Fuck, Kayden, since when have you become a mother hen? I'm fine. What do you expect me to do? Sit by that fucking bed the rest of my life?" My playful tone turns dark as my anger sears through my veins.

"Hey, no need to get upset. What kind of friend am I if I don't say anything to you? You need to hear it." Kayden shrugs, the worry on his face not fading.

"It sounds to me that you've given up on Abbygail waking up," Sebastian accuses. He's by the window leaning against the wall beside it, his arms folded over his chest, looking out at the night sky before turning to me.

"Sebastian!" I growl. "Know your fucking place."

"Humph, growl as much as you want, Alpha. I just know that if you go into battle with a distracted or defeated wolf, you will surely be killed or get someone killed," Sebastian states, pushing himself off the wall and walking toward me. He's correct, as usual. The bastard is always right. I wouldn't call myself distracted; I haven't been this focused in quite some time. I know what I want and what I need to do.

"You are driven, Alpha, but by what? You have one goal in mind and will do anything to see it through. That is one of the reasons why I will follow you into battle, but this time it feels different.

What is your plan afterward? You have always done things for a greater purpose. What's that purpose now?"

My eyes darken at his words, and he nods in acknowledgment. I have always been grateful that my Beta and Gamma can read my emotions and actions, but now I don't know if that is a good thing anymore. "Hmmm, I thought as much," Sebastian sighs, shaking his head.

"You have two fucking choices here," I grit out through my clenched jaw. "Either you are with me in this, or you step down as the Gamma of this fucking pack."

"Fuck, Tyler, are you losing your mind?" Kayden asks, perplexed.

I snap my head to him, staring him down. I don't need my two trusted friends and pack members lecturing me and trying to get in my way. If they aren't with me, I will do this alone.

"No, it's fine, Kayden," Sebastian says, before turning to me. "You know I will always have your back, my friend; I just want you to think of the fallout of your vendetta. Don't get me wrong, all of us want to tear Jace and Owen's throats out for what they did to you and our Luna, and they will pay with their lives. But what will happen to you after we deal with them?"

"That's none of your concern. Now, can we please get back to our strategizing, or am I doing this on my own?" I state, rather harshly. Both of them eye me warily, not saying another word. I prefer that, actually. I know I'm not the Alpha and friend they are used to, but I can't be what they need. I have nothing left to give. "I'm waiting." My tone is still sharp and harsh.

"As you wish, Alpha," they say in unison, bowing to me. A pang of regret shoots through me, but I push it aside. I can't let these feelings of me hurting my friends' feelings take precedence in my mind. I must focus on what is to come and what I need to do.

Bending over and leaning with both my hands on my desk, I look down at the map, taking a deep breath, and huffing it out through my nose. I hope the intel we received is worth the amount we paid. I can't take any more disappointment. I've had my fair share.

RING... RING... RING...

I huff at the sound, but nobody moves to stop it.

RING... RING... RING...

With every ring, my nerve endings are curling in on themselves, and now I'm glaring at the phone.

RING... RING... RING...

"Just answer your fucking phone, Kayden!" I snap at my Beta. "It's the seventh time it rang in five minutes, and it's working on my last nerve."

"I thought you wanted to focus on planning when we leave."

"Kayden," I warn as the phone begins to ring again.

"Fine," he concedes, taking his phone from my desk and answering it.

"Yeah-, oh hi babe... No, I can't talk now... You know where I am.... No... nothing's changed... Yes, worse."

I eye Kayden as I listen to his conversation with Layla. I can hear everything she's asking him, and it's pissing me off. I'm not a bloody child. Why the hell can't she just understand to back off? I don't need to be told what to do. I have duties and priorities. She knows this. "No babe, that's not a good idea, and you know that... Of course, he's listening... Yes, what did you expect, though, has been biting off our heads at the slightest mention of..." Kayden clears his throat at the last words as he looks into my eyes.

I don't look away. I just narrow mine and fold my arms over my chest, and my lip pulls into a snarl. Kayden rolls his eyes at me as he listens to Layla. "Listen, babe, I need to go... No, I can't talk about this now... He's snarling at me... No!... Don't Layla-"

I sigh, knowing exactly what's coming. I unfold my one hand and show three fingers in the air.

"Three."

"Two."

"One."

On cue, Layla bursts through my office door, the look on her face menacing. She scans the room until her eyes fall on mine.

"Leave," she snaps to her mate and Sebastian.

"No, Layla, I am terribly busy and don't have time for one of your 'chats,'" I state, annoyed now.

"Tyler, so help me," Layla says slowly.

"Babe, please. Not now; this day is already too long. I know you want to help-" Kayden starts to say but stops as soon as Layla shoots him one of her looks. I must admit, my sister is a sweetheart, but she can really be scary if she wants to be. Who am I kidding? She's *my* sister, so it shouldn't come as a shock. Unlike me, you don't see her bad side as often as mine, but you better listen when you do see it.

"Fuck! Fine, leave us," I sigh bitterly, sitting in my chair.

Kayden and Sebastian look from Layla to me; they look hesitant, but Layla's impatience is clearly felt in the room. They grimace at me and leave my office, closing the door as they go.

CHAPTER THIRTY-ONE

LAYLA

I'm livid, fuming, mad beyond recognition. Pick one.

I can't believe my brother is so arrogant and bloody stupid. He's declaring war on Jace while his mate lies in a coma. He should be by her side and make sure she wakes up, but no, he thinks the solution is battle and getting himself killed. This path he follows is worrying me, and there is something he's not telling me. It's this nagging feeling I can't get rid of. Ugh, well, he will get an ear full, if nothing else.

My face is red from the anger that's bubbling in me. I place my hands on my hips, and Tyler raises an eyebrow.

"Are you going to say something or just waste my time?" Tyler asks, annoyed.

"Brother, don't push my fucking buttons at this stage. I'm trying to calm down so I don't yell at you; all you do is make it difficult. I know exactly what you're trying to do, and it won't work."

"What do you want, Layla?"

"What the hell are you doing, declaring war?"

"This is a need-to-know situation, and you don't need to know," Tyler says bluntly.

"What about Abbygail?"

"What about her?"

"Are you fucking kidding me?"

"No, Layla, what are you expecting of me? Do you want me to sit at that fucking hospital bed for the rest of my life?"

"YES!" I almost scream.

"And do what exactly?" Tyler forces a bored look on his face, thinking I'm going to miss the wince that goes with it. My mouth hangs open at his words. Did he lose his damn mind, or am I hallucinating? I frown at Tyler, shaking my head in disbelief.

"Did you really just ask me that?"

"Yes, Layla, I did. If you want, you can sit there and ruin your life. I have accepted my fate, and I accepted that the woman lying in that bed isn't my mate. It's an empty vessel. My mate died the night I marked her," Tyler says bitterly. I'm gaping at Tyler's words like an idiot.

There is silence for quite some time between us after his last word dies out, and it just gets louder. I clear my throat, knowing he won't speak first. *Stubborn bastard!* "You truly are giving up on her, aren't you?"

"I don't see it as giving up. I'm merely accepting what no one else apparently can. I'm not destined to be happy and loved. Everything that happened in the last six months is just a cruel joke," Tyler scoffs, his whole mood and voice darkens at the latter part.

I recognize it as soon as my brother meets my gaze again. He's hurting, mourning his mate. Tyler thinks he's already lost her, and he can't show anyone how he feels and that this is tearing him apart. I also know that he will never admit it. The only one who can save him is Abbygail, and I'm afraid if she doesn't wake up soon, there will be nothing left to save.

I laugh at the irony. Here in front of me stands a man feared by so many. He's strong and resilient. He's capable of burning the world with a single command, but the only one that can keep him from giving in to the dark is a feisty black-haired beauty.

"Something funny about this? Care to enlighten me?"

"No, it's more of an observation than anything else."

Tyler pulls one brow up, expecting me to tell him what I'm thinking of, but he will not be so lucky to know tonight. I know the moment I tell him, he will lose his shit, which might push him even further away instead of getting him away from the edge that's his hell.

"I'm waiting, Layla."

I huff as he uses my full name. Gone are the days when he calls me Lay. Any affection he had left is long gone now, and it left with Abby's consciousness. "No, Tyler, I will not elaborate or enlighten you. I will tell you the day you are yourself again with Abby by your side, but not a moment sooner."

Tyler laughs bitterly, the sound breaking my heart. "You will be waiting till your death. *Abbygail. Is. Not. Coming. Back.*"

"Ty, please don't-" I say softly. My eyes soften as the hurt I thought I saw earlier shows on Tyler's face.

I walk towards him, and he jumps up from his chair, angry now. "Fuck, Layla, can't you stop prying? I don't need your sympathy, nor do I need your pity," he growls as he walks to his window, his back to me now. "I'm done. I've given you your audience. Now please leave."

"But-"

"GET OUT," he bellows, his office shaking from his voice's raw power and heartbreak.

I watch my brother for a few seconds more and decide that pursuing this now will help no one, so I turn on my heel and leave his office, hearing a guttural sob as I close the door behind me. It's so challenging to be there for him.

I remember how he struggled when our father died. No one was allowed near him. He saw his heartbreak as a weakness, which is so far from it. I can just imagine what he must be feeling, and the fact that he is powerless to get Abby back must drive him mad.

I sigh as my heart threatens to break more when I spot Kayden leaning with his back against the wall just outside the office. The man has been constantly on his phone for the last few months. It irritates me, but I know he must do it. It's his job. Tyler relies on him more than he knows.

"Hey babe, are you okay?" Kayden asks when I come to a stop next to him. He looks concerned: my face betraying me like always.

"Yeah," I sigh deeply. "I'm really worried, babe. Tyler has given up completely, and I don't know how to reach him. He is acting as if Abby died, and that's so far from the truth."

"I think Tyler's struggling more than he is showing us, and he decided to go with this idea because it's easier than to hold out hope for something that might never happen. Your brother has never been the patient type, babe, you know that. Don't get me wrong, I'm not saying he's impatient now. I think he has a plan he wants to execute, and if he cuts ties, it's easier," Kayden says, trying to reassure me.

"That plan he wants to execute is my biggest worry, though. Something feels off. It's not that he has just given up on Abby; it's like he has given up on all of it, which will make him vulnerable. Tyler won't be heading into this fight with a clear head. He won't be vigilant like always, and Jace will get the upper hand. Not only that, he will place you and the rest of the pack in danger."

Kayden pushes himself off the wall and pulls me into his arms, tightly crushing me to his chest. He kisses my forehead lightly, never pulling away. "I will ensure his head isn't too far up his ass, babe. I promise you that," he speaks against my skin, and I know he will do anything in his power to protect my brother—but at what cost?

CHAPTER THIRTY-TWO

JACE

There's excitement in the air, like static electricity vibrating through my body. I have found some kindred souls that are invested in my cause. Who knew so many wolves and other supernatural beings wanted to see the Storm Empire fall?

I must admit, we were lucky, Owen and I. If that twat of a Beta and his pathetic Gamma weren't so distracted with Abbygail, we wouldn't have escaped that damn place. My brow pulls down as I think of the narrow escape. The thought only makes the anger pool in my stomach. *Shit!*

My whole bloody empire is to waste because of this fucking prophecy. Hopefully, this wasn't for nothing. I have gathered a sizable army, if I have to say so myself.

When we ran from the Lunar Packhouse, we made our way to the Northern mountains and found shelter and solace there. We went out looking for reinforcements the moment we proved dominance in the territories surrounding the mountains.

I'm surprised at the turnout of the warriors we collected. Some didn't have an issue with the current Alpha King but did with the earlier one, and that alone made them join. I let them believe he was still alive and aiding the current one; not my problem if they believe whatever bullshit I tell them.

I laugh as I picture Tyler on his knees before me, begging me to spare his pack. Oh, and when I get my hands on my little slut again…

My thoughts become even more dark and glorious as she pops up. I will have my way with her this time, and she will beg for mercy, which she will never receive. I lick my lips as the image of her on her knees in front of me trails through my mind, her looking up at me as her mate lies dead beside her.

"Ahh, how fucking pretty," I sigh, and my member twitches in my pants.

"Something you want to share with the class?" Owen asks, and I am ripped from my fantasies.

I forgot I was in a meeting with the warriors and other supernatural beings' leaders. Well, at least my reputation precedes me, so what do I care what they think?

"None of your damn business Owen!" I snap at my Beta.

"Hey, don't get mad at me. You are the one moaning in the middle of the bloody meeting." Owen shrugs and turns to talk to the vamp next to him.

I rub my hand over my face and let out a frustrating growl. I didn't realize I was being verbal with my fantasies. *Just great.* Turning my attention back to the people sitting in front of me, I curse aloud, but everyone seems not to be fazed at the least.

I rub my hands together and clear my throat. "Welcome, everyone. I hope your stay in the caves isn't too bad. I know it takes some getting used to, but this is all for the greater good. A little sacrifice of uncomfortable sleeping will not go unnoticed, I can assure you." I'm speaking loud enough so everyone can hear clearly: I hate repeating myself.

"Alpha Jace, we have been here for almost a year, and nothing has happened yet. When are we planning to attack the Lunar pack and overthrow the bastard in that throne room? I am getting impatient, and so are my men—and I think I can speak for all of us when I say this," Alec, the ruler from the vampire clan, says as he taps his long fingernails on the rock he is sitting on.

"Alec, I hear your concern and understand the need to get this over with, but we can't storm the damn Packhouse of the Lunar pack like we don't know better. You, of all people, know how lethal they are. Look at what happened to more than fifty percent of your clan back when you thought you could take them on alone," I state, and I can see the anger mixed with sorrow flash behind his eyes, making his jaw tick.

Guess Alec decided it's best not to challenge me further: he stays silent.

"As I was saying." I look intimidatingly across the open space of the cave, seeing who will dare to interrupt me again. "You don't need to worry about when our attack will occur because that is why I asked for this meeting. I am here to tell you that we are ready. We need to tie up a few loose ends before leaving, but you can let your men know to get themselves ready for a vicious and bloody fight. I know every single one of them, and you, are craving it just like us," I say, gesturing to Owen and then to myself.

As soon as I stop speaking, cheering rings out from every person in the room. I smile wickedly as the enthusiasm spreads through me as well. I have waited exceptionally long for this time to come, and it's finally within my grasp.

"We leave in a week, so make sure everything is as planned and discussed over the last few months. I will not tolerate any mistakes, and failure on your part will lead to punishment. We have all wanted retribution for most of our lives, and we are going to get it."

Okay, I don't need retribution, but they don't need to know that, do they? As long as they fight for my cause, I will feed them any lie I can think of. One of Owen's main worries has been, well, what if someone finds out? It's been lingering in the back of my mind, too.

I huff, shaking my head. Well, I will eliminate those who dare to defy me or stand in my way, and get what rightfully belongs to me.

"You are dismissed," I say, loudly again, and the hoards of werewolves and vampires stand and begin to move out of the cave mouth, chatting amongst themselves.

Within a few minutes, the whole campsite is buzzing with excitement. I don't know if most of these soldiers know precisely what they are fighting for. Knowing most of the leaders, they probably don't. What do I care, though? Just as long as Tyler dies a slow and torturous death.

Come to think of it, the most torture I can inflict on him is if I take his mate right there in front of him as he lies dying, unable to do anything to save her.

That thought brings a wicked smile to my mouth, and I make a mental note of it. I will need to keep control and not let my rage and hunger for power cloud my judgment. Otherwise, I will not let Tyler suffer but grant him a merciful death, and I simply can't allow that. "Come, Owen, we need to discuss some separate and additional planning of our own," I tell him, as I walk past the remaining vampires lingering in the cave mouth.

CHAPTER THIRTY-THREE

TYLER

I wish someone could come and rip my damn heart from my chest. I can't take the aching and throbbing pain anymore. I wish I could turn it off. It's the only reason I throw myself into this war so much. I need something to distract me from the absolute destruction that is my life. And Layla is only making it worse. I have almost succeeded in ridding myself of some images of my mate lying lifeless in that bed. I know she's not dead, but it's only a matter of time if you ask me. Why on earth would I get the chance of love and happiness?

A sob rips through my chest, and I curse myself for letting it happen.

This is an absolute disgrace. I laugh bitterly at my pathetic self. Suppose my father could see me now. He would be so disappointed. His grown-ass son is crying for a mate he never got the chance to love. I can't stop the damn tears that spill from my eyes. I cover my face with my hands as the sobs come one after another as I stand crying, my whole frame shaking.

My sister's words run through my mind, and I know she speaks the truth. I am distracted and will never forgive myself if anything happens to my men because I am selfish and careless.

Taking a deep breath, I wipe the tears from my face and move to my desk. I take the maps from it and study them again. I will place my focus where it's needed the most, and now it's required here. We need to find Jace and end him and his misguided plans to rule this kingdom. I'm still the reigning King, and as long as I'm in this seat, he will never get the chance to harm anyone again. If I have to give my life to stop him, I will surely do so. I have nothing left to lose.

The creak of my office door opening makes me look up, and Kayden enters cautiously. The look on his face mirrors the feeling in my chest, but I will not let myself show it. "Are you feeling alright?" he asks me, sounding worried, and I know the tear stains are still visible on my face.

Sighing heavily, I contemplate if I genuinely want to answer his question. Given that Kayden has been my best friend since childhood, he knows everything about me. It's a curse and a blessing.

In battle, he can read me from a distance, and I never even have to say one word for him to know what I am planning or to act just as I am going to, but the rest of the time, he's a pain in my ass because of it.

"Yes. Why wouldn't I be?" My voice is harsher than I intend it to be.

Kayden lets out a tired sigh, his eyes sad, and I know exactly what he's thinking, but he keeps it to himself, and I have never been more grateful to him. I cannot handle another conversation about Abby; my heart simply can't take any more of this.

"How are you planning on doing this, then?" He gestures to the maps in my hand.

"I think we should leave tomorrow at first light so we can arrive when it's dark," I state, returning to the maps as I study the path we want to travel. "It's better to do it when the rest of the world is sleeping. We don't want to draw unnecessary attention."

"Hmm, sounds about right," Kayden agrees as he comes to stand next to me and study the same path I am. "Maybe just taking a turn here and not there." He points to two different spots on the map.

I study the new route he pointed out, frowning as I listen and rearrange some of the plans in my head. Yes, that is perfect. It will cut straight through the mountains and not around them. It will ensure that we don't walk into an ambush and will get the upper hand if they are hidden in a cave or something. "Perfect," I tell him, placing the maps back on the desk.

Sitting in my chair again, I gesture for Kayden to do the same. He nods and goes to sit in his usual chair. I interlock my fingers in front of me as I rest my elbows on the armrests.

"So, my plan is as follows: we need to surround the perimeter of Jace's hideout and whoever is with him. We cannot let anyone live who is against us. We must separate the misguided from the evil ones."

"And what do you want to do with the 'misguided ones,' as you call them?"

"Fuck, Kayden, we can keep them locked up and see what their intentions are before we make drastic discissions. We can't go on a bloody killing spree, now can we?"

"That's not what I'm implying, Tyler, damn it. You're making it difficult to talk strategy with you when your mind is not on the problem," Kayden growls at me, clearly struggling to keep his irritation concealed for much longer.

I raise my brow as I tighten my grip. It will not serve any purpose if we start to fight with each other now. We need to focus all our anger on the people that deserve it. To have inner turmoil will be our downfall, and I will not let that happen. "Kayden, please, I am not looking to fight with you. If I have to be honest, I haven't given much thought past the fact that I make Jace pay for the grief he has caused me and Abby." I sigh, closing my eyes and leaning my head back on my chair.

Silence follows my statement, and I don't have the strength for an argument. After what feels like an eternity, I lift my head and find Kayden watching me. The look on his face is something along the lines of sympathy and determination. I tilt my head, frowning.

"I know you think I don't understand what you are thinking and going through. I haven't lost my mate or had to go through what you did, but believe me when I say I will always have your back. *You* just need to understand that I will not let you do reckless things in order to settle this vendetta you have. My job and duty is to make sure my Alpha and, most importantly, my *friend* doesn't get harmed in doing so," Kayden states sternly.

There is no use in arguing with his logic because it is his job, and I know he will not let anything happen to me if he can help it. I can't ask for a greater Beta than him. I am proud to have him by my side, even for the brief time I have left being the Alpha King. "I know, my friend, and I appreciate you more than you will ever know. I will always be thankful for you, and when this all ends, this pack will be forever grateful that they have you." The cryptic message is vague, but it can't be overlooked.

Kayden tilts his head, frowning, and narrows his eyes at me. Clearly, my words don't sit well with him. He sits forward in his chair and starts bouncing his knee. The frown on his face now turns to anger. "Excuse me? What do you mean when all this ends?"

"Don't worry about it, okay? I'm just being dramatic." I smile half-heartedly, rolling my eyes, hoping to throw him off, but I should know better.

"You have never been dramatic. Batshit crazy, yes, but never dramatic. Layla may tease that you are, but we both know this is bullshit. Don't you dare sit there and tell me lies and think I am going to fall for them or that you will distract me from the fact that you are planning a *suicide mission!*"

"Kay, please just calm down. I am not planning a suicide mission. I promise, scouts honor."

Kayden laughs angrily as he gets up from his chair and slams his hands down on my desk. The sound reverberates through the office. His eyes flash with the fury behind them.

"I. Am. Not. Fighting. A. Lost. Cause." Kayden's anger builds as he grits out each word.

"It's not a lost cause, my friend." I sigh, feeling defeated as I drop my hands to my lap and lower my head.

Kayden will not be happy with my decision, but he has the right to know. I can't expect him to walk into this battle with me without having all the information. There will be no chance to turn back when I utter these words. I need to be strong enough for my people to let this happen. What I will do after I step down is beyond me. It's all I have ever known.

"Please sit down. I need to tell you something," I tell Kayden firmly, gesturing to his chair again. He shakes his head, his jaw clenched.

"I think it better that I stand."

"Fine, have it your way." I inhale deeply, letting it huff out from my nose. "After we kill Jace and Owen and everything is safe for the pack and all the territories, I will step down as Alpha and King and recommend you to the council for my successor." Talking slowly, I watch his face go from shock to disbelief to disgust to pure rage again.

Some might think the Elders have a say in the matter, but it's up to the council: every Alpha in our territory.

Kayden doesn't say anything as he balls his fists, his chest heaving as he tries to calm himself and his wolf. He slams his fists down on my desk again as a roar rips through his chest. With no effort at all, Kayden picks up the chair he had sat on and hurls it across the room.

He turns to me, chest still heaving heavily, his eyes dark, and his lip pulled up in a snarl, baring his teeth at me. Clearly, I was right about his reaction to my plan. My wolf stirs in my mind as I take in the sight of my friend.

Not happy is more of an understatement.

I get up from my seat slowly and am genuinely astonished that I am this calm in this situation. I walk over to Kayden and place my hand on his shoulder. He snarls at me but doesn't move. I look him dead in the eyes, pleading for him to understand why I have to do this, but he will not see reason.

"I stand corrected," he growls. "Clearly, you know exactly how to be dramatic."

"Humph, don't you sound like your mate," I roll my eyes. "Please understand, my friend, I cannot bear to let anyone else be hurt because of my poor leadership skills. For the better part of the year, everything went up in flames, and that alone should be enough evidence for you to look at. Look at what happened just seeing my mate and everything happening afterward. You had to run all my duties as an Alpha while I was incapacitated just from a silly mate bond. What kind of Alpha King is so weak? The people need someone as strong and capable as you," I say, lowering my eyes, unable to look into his livid ones anymore.

Kayden will never take this gesture as a weakness. Alphas aren't allowed to lower their eyes to anyone, but I can trust my friend, and I know he sees the rawness of what this is doing to me. I, too, will lose my shit if he tells me he's leaving my side, but this is different. I don't *want* to abandon them, but I have to for the sake of this kingdom and its people.

"Tyler, please tell me you are joking or tell me this is just something to get a rise out of me because I am struggling here," he sighs desperately as he places his hand on my shoulder.

"No, I'm dead serious, my friend. I cannot take this anymore. Didn't you see the people's faces in the hospital? And whenever I take a walk, they scatter before me. I'm not a leader; I'm a fucking dictator... just *like Jace*."

Jace's name comes out in a growl. I never in my life thought I would ever compare myself to him, but it's true. Even Kayden told me to rein in my temper so the people wouldn't fear me.

"You truly have lost your damn mind. That's the only thing that makes sense. The old Tyler will never have said what you just did. He would never have backed down this easily."

"This isn't easy-"

"Seems pretty easy to me," he cuts me off and steps away with a scowl on his face.

"Kayden-"

"No, Tyler, fuck this. Pull your head out of your fucking ass, will you? I can't go into battle with a pussy." The anger from earlier returns just as quickly as it left him. "I'm done talking about this. I will inform Sebastian of your plans for tomorrow morning and the strategy to get to Jace. It will give you enough time to get rid of this bullshit you are spewing," he snaps at me and turns on his heel, storming out of the office and slamming the door shut so hard it whines under brute force.

"Damn it!" I breathe out in frustration, rubbing my hand roughly across my forehead and dragging it down my face.

I lie in bed, staring out the massive window as the sun rises. It's almost time to get up, and I couldn't sleep last night with the argument that is left unresolved between me and Kayden. I even tried calling him to no avail.

He is pissed at me, and I don't blame him—but like he says, we cannot afford to be distracted.

Groaning, I curse at my lack of self-preservation. I needed to sleep to be prepared for the long journey ahead, but no, my mind decided it best to be tired and run disturbing scenarios through it all night.

I throw the covers off myself and get out of bed. I'm not sleeping in my room. I couldn't bring myself to sleep or spend one minute there without *her*. Her scent is still so overwhelming it chokes me each time I walk into the room where I destroyed my life.

I push my hair back and out of my face. It has grown out of its initially sleek style I loved to wear. I just didn't want to make any effort.

My insides feel just as disheveled as my outsides look, so who the hell cares? I certainly don't.

Making my way to the bathroom, I open the shower so the water can run hot before I step into it. Usually, I take cold showers to cool my extreme body heat, but lately, it feels like I can't keep the heat in. Come to think of it, it's ever since I lost Abby.

Everything I have ever known about myself is now long gone, and I am left with an empty space in my heart and mind.

I take a long, hard look in the mirror. I look horrible. My hair is messy, my beard has grown out, and my eyes look empty. I scoff at my appearance. Well, at least now, I genuinely look scary.

Steam builds in the room, and I move to the shower again. I step into the scalding water, never opening the cold water to reduce the temperature. I hiss as the water hits my back. The pain shoots through me, feeling good like I deserve it for what I did to my mate.

I stay under the blistering hot water until it starts to run cold. Turning, I feel the uncomfortable sting in my back as I basically cooked my flesh, but I can feel it healing, so I don't pay it any attention.

I wash every inch of my body and then rinse it under the icy water. This has been my ritual for the past six months. I let the water run over my hair and face, hoping to wash away my emptiness, but it never does. I'm wasting time standing here, so I might as well get out and get this over with.

Grabbing a towel from the rack, I step out, drying myself off quickly. I walk to the closet naked and hear a shriek coming from the bed as I'm halfway across the room. I turn to the sound and roll my eyes when I see my sister sitting on the bed.

I grunt at her and continue to where I need to go. Layla knows better than to come into my room, especially when I shower. I take a pair of jeans from the top rack of my closet and pull them on after covering my ass with boxers. "What do you want?" Grabbing a shirt from the bottom rack of the closet, I pull it over my head and onto my body.

"Is it safe to look now?" Layla peaks through her fingers, clearly flustered.

"Yes, Layla, tell me what you are doing here?"

She avoids my question, tilting her head as she stares at me. "Why is your back looking like you just got off the barbeque?"

"Fuck, Layla, I don't have time for twenty questions. Either you tell me what you want, or you get the hell out."

Layla narrows her eyes at me. She doesn't like the "new me." Her words, not mine.

I don't even know the real me anymore, so I don't argue with anyone who tells me I'm not myself. It's pointless.

"I came to see if you are going to go see Abby before you leave on your trip."

"No," I say bluntly.

"Tyler, don't be an asshole, please. She needs you."

"She doesn't need anybody, Layla. She's in a fucking coma."

Layla stares at me, her face still displaying disbelief before turning dark. "I thought you might still say that so..." she trails off, takes her phone, and holds it to her ear as it rings after she dialed a number. "Yup, still the same... Okay, I'll wait here. Love you."

"What the fuck are you doing Layla? Calling Kayden will not change my mind. You are such a nosey little bitch, and I am tired of it-"

"Tyler Alexander Storm, have you forgotten your manners?"

I pale as I hear my mother's voice come from behind me. I spin to find her standing in my doorway, her hands on her hips and scowling at me. She is the spitting image of my sister, just with a few more wrinkles and wisdom behind those eyes. "Mother," I say, surprised.

My sister jumps off the bed and hurries to my mother's side, a satisfied smile on her face as she hugs her.

"Mommy, you made it. Thanks so much for coming. As you can see, we have a genuine problem with this one," Layla claims as she gestures to me with her thumb.

"Layla! *So help me.*" My tone is venomous.

"Tyler!" My mother scolds me again. "Your father would be ashamed of how you speak to your sister."

I narrow my eyes at my sister before looking at my mother. My jaw ticks as I try to keep myself from lashing out, and I nod at my mother. It takes about five minutes for me to get a hold of my temper, and my mother patiently waits for me to come and greet her.

As soon as I feel my shoulders relax, I walk to her and kiss her on the cheeks before bowing my head to hers so our foreheads touch. The gesture is the ultimate sign of respect. "Please forgive my rudeness." Stepping back, I bow to my mother.

"Aww, you're forgiven, brother. I love you too," Layla says sarcastically, and I feel the snarl pull at my mouth, but I manage to stop myself.

"Will you two please behave yourselves?" My mother asks, annoyed now.

"Sure, mommy, so as you can see, this *beast* standing before you isn't your beloved son. I never thought my brother would be the kind of man who would abandon his mate in a time of need," Layla tells my mother, eyeing me every few seconds.

I growl at Layla, unable to keep it in this time. She is pushing her boundaries with me today. Does she want me to be infuriated and distracted before I leave for battle?

My mother shoots me one of her disapproving looks, and I avert my eyes. She clears her throat and turns to me. She walks closer, takes my face in her hands, and I close my eyes at her soft touch. I inhale the familiar scent that brings back perfect childhood memories. My mother's scent is strong, smelling of wild peppermint.

She grips my face a little harder and turns my head from side to side, inspecting me as she looks me over. I open my eyes and frown at her. I know better than to question her methods, so I keep quiet and let her do what she needs to.

She pulls her fingers through my hair and down to my beard, rubbing her fingers in it and then pulling on it slightly until I grunt. She chuckles softly, and her eyes grow sad. "You look so much like your father. A little more disheveled than him, but not by much."

"Mom, please." I lightly place my hand over hers on my cheek. "Don't do this to yourself."

"Do what, precisely?" My mother sounds unimpressed, her brow raised. "Remember your father? The wonderful man who gave me all the love I could have asked for? The father most children dream of, and the man you cherished."

Sighing sadly, I purse my lips, aching to have my father here with us. He would have been the perfect person to tell me what I needed to do to handle the shit show I am in now. Maybe none of this would have happened if he was still alive and ruling as the Alpha King.

"Don't you dare, Tyler," my mother scolds me.

"Dare what, Mom?" My voice betrays me as it shakes, and I try to hide the sadness and self-loathing but fail miserably.

"I told you this already: your father would be enormously proud of the wolf you've become. I know *I* am. I don't see a beast or a monster. I see my beautiful boy who just lost his way."

I close my eyes and feel the ache grow stronger in my shattered heart. A tear escapes my cheek, and the brokenness I pushed so far down now trying to make its way out of my chest, but I can't let it happen.

I cannot let my emotions get the better of me, not now, not anymore. I need to be as cold as steel to do what is required.

Sighing, I pull from my mother's grasp and step away from her and my nosey-ass sister, harshly wiping the tear from my face. Why the hell did Layla have to pull our mother into this? She knows our mother can talk me out of most of my dumb-ass ideas, but it will not work this time.

"Mother, please." My voice hoarse from the ache in my chest. "I can't do this now. I need to go. My men are waiting for me."

"Oh, my dear boy, you need to face the hurt I hear raging in your heart and mind. You cannot face off with someone who has one goal in mind, and nothing will distract him from carrying out his mission. Your mind is at war with your heart, which *will* get you seriously injured or killed."

"Mother, I truly don't have time for this. Please excuse me. I love you very much. Always remember that." I try my best to dismiss this subject as I kiss her on her cheek quickly and push past her.

My mother doesn't fall for my bullshit, though, bless her heart. She grabs my arm and tightens her grip on me. I stop, not turning to her, lowering my head in frustration.

"Your men can wait. I am not done talking to you, and you will listen to me before you go off to get yourself killed. I know I can't stop you from doing that, but you have enough respect for me not to turn your back on me."

I simply nod, keeping my stance. "I'm listening."

"Your mate is lying in a damn hospital bed. She needs you just as much as you need her. You are acting truly selfish. How can you justify this war, but you cannot even fight for her as you fight for your people?"

"*I am doing this for her,*" I growl each word slowly, trying to keep my composure as I look at my mother. My wolf didn't like the accusation much; it was the first time he showed displeasure in three months.

My mother narrows her eyes at me as she studies my eyes. I realize they must have changed color again to a mixture of black and red. *Fuck.* I turn my eyes away when I realize what happened.

"Look at me, Tyler," she commands.

I huff out a breath and turn to look at her. Letting her take in the monster version of her son that she said did not exist.

"How long have your eyes been changing to this color?"

"I'm not sure," I huff irritably.

"After the mate bond when Abby fell into the coma," Layla chimes in from the side.

"Hmm… Let me see the mark," my mother expectantly says as she reaches for my shirt.

"NO!" I snarl at her, and she pulls her hand from me quickly.

Realizing my mistake, I bow my head at her, the regret running through me more than I can take. The one woman who has always been by my side and looks out for me, and I just snarled at her. My father would genuinely be disappointed in me. It's something I would never have done in the past. Maybe my humanity is slipping.

My eyes soften, and they return to my normal mismatched ones. I take my mother's hands in mine and bring them to my mouth, kissing them. "Please forgive me. I didn't mean to lose my temper with you. I can't bear to talk about Abbygail anymore. She is lost to me forever. Can't you understand that?"

"Show me your mark, Tyler. Now," my mother commands in the same stern voice as before, this time waiting for me to show her as she removes her hands from mine.

I sigh at her command and pull my shirt away from my neck, exposing the mark Abby left on me. She frowns and steps closer to me. My wolf starts to pace in my mind, impatience radiating from him. He notices something, and it's agitating him.

"What is it?"

"Are you sure you completed the bond?"

"Yes, why do you think she lies in that coma?"

My mother looks up at me, and she shakes her head. Seeing her eyes dart between mine as she thinks.

"There's something off about this," she adds but doesn't elaborate.

"What do you mean?"

Why I'm surprised by her statement is beyond me. When, in this whole experience, has anything *not* been off?

My mother looks from me to my sister and then back to me again. Smiling lovingly, she brushes my cheek and reaches up to take my face in her hands again, pulling me down to her and kissing my forehead. "Never you mind. Please be safe out there. You better come back to me, or there will be hell to pay, do you hear me?"

"Yes, ma'am."

I'm so utterly confused right now. What the hell was all that? My mother will not take this topic further even if I beg, so I don't even ask her to. She smiles at me again before she looks at my sister. "Come on, my nosey daughter, let's get out of here and go for some breakfast," she proclaims and drags my sister from the room as Layla starts to protest, leaving me alone, still unable to wrap my head around what just happened.

My wolf also noticed the change in my mother's mood. There's something there, and I know she's deliberately keeping it from me.

I scoff as I grab my boots by the door and make my way to where Kayden and the rest of the warriors are waiting for me. I am already more than an hour late.

Stepping in front of my men, I feel the pressure looming. If they know what I am planning after this mission, they may think twice before going into battle with an Alpha who will abandon them.

Kayden is standing on the step below me; his demeanor towards me is strained, and if we aren't careful, the rest of the warriors will notice.

I clear my throat, trying not to show the worry creeping through my body and soul. I need my men to believe in me one last time. Knowing they will also not approve of my decision to step down, but this is how it needs to be. "Good morning, everyone."

The troops in front of me at once yell *hoo-rah* like they are in the army. Well, they aren't far off from a human army, so it's fitting.

"I know all of you are fixing for this fight, and I want you all to know that I appreciate each and every one of you being here." Every eye is on me, and I think it's time they know why we are declaring war on the Timber packs' Alpha and Beta. "There is something I need all of you to know, seeing as you will fight for this cause."

Kayden's head snaps to me, and his eyes widen. It looks like he's not ignoring me anymore.

I stare ahead of me; I can't face his criticizing look now. "I found my mate. Unfortunately, Jace held her captive and enslaved her. He marked her, and when we eventually sealed our bond, it nearly killed her. She is lying in a coma in the protected wing of the hospital."

The collective gasps and growls that reach me make me feel almost guilty for not telling them sooner. "Alpha, what does this mean, exactly?" Roy asks as the rest of the troops whisper amongst themselves.

I frown at Roy. Did he not hear what I told him mere seconds ago?

"Are you telling us that Jace purposely had our Luna enslaved and caused harm to her?" he elaborates when he sees me frown.

"That's exactly what your Alpha is telling you. We need to settle a score. Your Alpha almost died because Jace marked his mate. Jace knew she was destined for Alpha Tyler, and he spat on that sacred bond," Kayden's voice booms out before I can say anything.

The whispering turns into aggressive growls and snarls as the troops listen to Kayden speak. The anticipation hangs in the air, almost charging it. It drives my wolf to the edge of my mind. I let out a thunderous howl, and the rest of the men follow suit.

I look at Kayden, and the sadness and betrayal behind his eyes make me cringe. He will not understand my reasoning, but I hope he will come around one day.

"Move out. We can't waste any more time. Our scouts are giving us the all-clear, and the sooner we get there, the better."

The troops let out three *hoo-rahs* before taking their positions, and we move into the forest.

It will be me or Jace tonight, and only one of us will survive—and I can promise it won't be Jace.

CHAPTER THIRTY-FOUR

KAYDEN

Tyler walks in front of us, with me and Sebastian following close behind. We are traveling down the hidden path to the forest's edge, where the mountains begin. All of us are on edge, listening for the slightest sound of movement or feeling the air for change.

Tyler stops dead in front of me, making me almost slam into his back again. He pulls his fist up to show the troops to halt as he turns his head and closes his eyes.

He must hear something; it doesn't take long for me to pick up on the faint crushing of twigs. It sounds like someone running. Fuck, they *are* running, and it's moving towards us, *fast*.

I sniff the air and catch Tyler and Sebastian doing the same. Tyler turns to us and motions for us to move next to him. His claws grow as the sound gets louder and louder.

We don't hesitate to move and take our places next to our Alpha. We all take an attack stance as the rest of the warriors silently move out and position themselves around the perimeter. Tyler sniffs the air again, and a low growl rumbles through his chest as his lip pulls up in a silent snarl, exposing his very long canines. I must admit, having a hybrid for an Alpha is the best weapon we can ask for. Don't get me wrong, a wolf can hold his own, but having a hybrid on your side doesn't hurt.

The crushing of leaves and fallen branches get so close it sounds like it's on top of us. We steady ourselves and get ready to lunge at whomever or whatever comes through that tree line.

Tyler rolls his head on his shoulders, showing that the time is now, but we hold our attack as one of our scouts comes crashing through the tree line, falling to his knees in front of us when he realizes it's his own pack.

"Jack, what the hell happened?" Tyler growls, kneeling in front of the young wolf.

Jack heaves for air, the look on his face terrified. It makes me shiver as I look at the kid on his knees. Something feels off. The atmosphere is changing. It feels charged somehow. I turn my head to listen.

Nothing.

"Gone-" he huffs as he struggles to pull air into his lungs.

"What do you mean gone?" A sense of urgency consumes me.

He swallows hard, and I wave one of the warriors over. "Get him some water now," I snap at the warrior, who walks to Jack and hands him his flask.

Jack gulps down the water like he hasn't had any in a long time. He catches his breath and looks from me to Tyler—the same frightened look on his face. "I don't understand, Alpha. When I checked a few hours ago, they were still in the cave, but it was empty when I moved in to take one last look."

"What?" Tyler exclaims exasperatedly. "Fuck!"

Tyler gets to his feet when we hear the roar of wolves come at us from all directions. Tyler's eyes widen as he looks at me, and I know we're in trouble. "Sebastian, move!" Tyler yells at Sebastian, who knows precisely what the strategy is.

"Kayden, my friend..." he's cut off when I grab him by the neck and push him down as a claw swipes at his head.

I quickly move, jumping over Tyler's back and kicking the wolf in the chest who tried to kill my Alpha—and friend—mere seconds ago. He goes down with a thud, whining as his head bounces off the forest floor. Tyler jumps up, his eyes crimson red and his canines pushing past his lips as he nods his thanks to me before a deafening roar leaves his chest.

Within seconds, the rest of the warrior wolves move around the enemy as they are trained, fighting to protect their Alpha.

Tyler grabs a nearby enemy wolf, who's trying to slash at him with his claws, by the throat and crushes his windpipe with no effort. Tyler lets his dead body fall to the ground, moving towards some warriors surrounded by too many enemies.

Tyler plows through the attackers with ease, making sure no one lives. I admire my friend, but I need to keep my head in the game as a pair of claws dig into my shoulder. I grab at the wolf just in time as he comes for my jugular with his teeth. I snarl viciously at him before snapping his neck like a twig.

When I drop the lifeless body to the ground, I hear a high-pitched scream, and look around quickly, seeing a lot of bodies on the ground and many injured wolves—luckily, not many of ours. This fuels my drive, and I lunge at a pair of oncoming wolves when I hear an Alpha wolf howl in the distance.

Fuck, Jace!

I rip through the two in front of me efficiently, then turn to look for Tyler. He won't be thinking clearly. I need to stop him. This is precisely what Jace would be planning. He knows the legends of the hybrids, and once they taste blood in a fight, the haze takes over. Knowing Tyler and the state he is in it worries me.

I call for Sebastian, who runs to me, taking down four more enemy wolves in his path, his face covered in blood splatter and a malicious grin—typical Sebastian, always eager for a fight and in his best element.

"Where is Tyler?" I yell at him above the roars around us.

He frowns, spinning to look around at the chaos when the same howl from earlier rings again through the forest. Sebastian's eyes widen as he realizes who the howl belongs to, and he takes off running after it. A growl leaves my lips as I take off after him. Sniffing the air, I catch Tyler's scent, mixed with so much rage it is choking me. I push myself to run faster as Jace and Owen's scents hit my nose next.

Damn it, Tyler!

I hear Sebastian snarl from my left as Tyler's roar comes from straight ahead.

Running into a clearing ahead of me, I know precisely why Sebastian is snarling. Ten wolves surround him, but Sebastian looks bored. A vicious smile creeps on his lips as he hunches down into an attack stance. Lifting a hand, he beckons them with his index finger to attack him.

The wolves roar and run at him all at once. He laughs excitedly as he jumps into the air and lands outside the circle as the enemy wolves run into each other. He tsks, wagging his finger from left to right, agitating them even more.

I turn my attention back to Tyler, now facing off with a clan of vampires, as Jace and Owen stand on a flat rock bed looking at the fight. My anger gets the better of me, and I stalk toward Owen, who has now stepped off the rock and is circling Tyler outside the clan of vamps.

I recognize the leader of the clan as Alec. He once was an ally to our pack, but then his lust for power grew so much that he attacked us. More than half of his clan got wiped out that night. This happened just before Tyler's father suffered from a heart attack and died.

I stalk closer and closer to Owen, my anger building in my chest. Tonight, this fucker will die, his last heartbeat in my hand as I rip his heart from his chest. I snarl and lunge at him, only to be tackled to the ground. The hit I suffer causes three ribs to snap, one puncturing my lung as I struggle to breathe.

Grunting, I get up, stumbling, looking for the thing that knocked me to the ground, and I see Jace laughing at me as he moves into the darkness of the trees. A frustrated growl leaves my throat as I grip a hand over my broken ribs.

I look back to where Tyler is, and the picture is horrifying.

The full moon is shining directly into the clearing, illuminating everything eerily. I cough, retaking a deep breath, this one a bit easier, as my ribs and lungs start to heal.

"Are you going to stand around like a fucking pussy, Beta Kayden, or are we finishing this?" Owen snickers at his pathetic punch line. I look to where Tyler is still fighting the horde of vamps, but this time Jace is moving between them like a fucking snake weaving his way closer and closer to Tyler.

What pisses me off is the fact that he does this behind Tyler's back, knowing full well that he is distracted. Only a coward attacks from behind.

I howl at Tyler to warn him just as Jace lunges for him, but it's too late. Jace's claws plunge deep into Tyler's side and back. Tyler roars out in pain, sinking to his knees. I turn to run to him, but Owen tackles me to the ground again.

I slap away his claws as he tries to swipe them across my throat and kick him off me. He hits a tree with so much force his wind gets knocked out of him, the tree cracking and shedding bark from the impact.

It gives me enough time to get to my feet, and I run into the circle of vampires who have stopped to watch the two Alphas. Four vamps turn to me as I plow through the most of them.

Tyler is on his knees in front of Jace, hunched over from the pain and bleeding profusely. Jace is elated with the turn of events, and he laughs maniacally. The vamps grab me and pin me to the ground. In a fight where I'm at full strength, there would be no way these fuckers could pin me down—but when I'm injured, they are just as strong, if not more. An injured wolf is no match for one of them, let alone four.

Fuck, we are in *serious* trouble.

Jace hooks his claws under Tyler's chin, forcing his head up to look at him, drawing blood as his claws puncture Tyler's flesh. I snarl at the vampires holding me down as I struggle, but they laugh viciously.

No, no, fuck.

CHAPTER THIRTY-FIVE

ABBYGAIL

Everything is fuzzy. I can't seem to grasp reality. I don't know where I am. I feel lost in this world surrounding me. Nothing sticks. It plays out like movie scenes before disappearing just as quickly as it starts. I squeeze my eyes shut, grabbing at my head; I'm losing my fucking mind. Hearing a roar so loud it makes my ears hurt, I snap my eyes back open. The scene playing out in front of me feels a lot more real than anything else I have seen.

Jace lunges at Tyler and plunges his claws into Tyler's back.

Tyler roars out in pain as he slumps down to his knees, the blood pouring out of him like a tap left open.

Vampires pin down Kayden as he struggles against their hold.

Jace hooks his claw under Tyler's chin, forcing it up so that his claw digs into his flesh.

A scream rips through my whole body as I see Jace lifting his other claw-like hand to land the death blow.

The scream I hear in my head comes to my ears as I open my eyes and shoot upright. A blinding, burning pain crawls slowly from the nape of my neck to my shoulder, up my neck to just below my ear, and then down my back.

I throw what I think are sheets from me and get out of bed too quickly. My legs are too weak to carry my weight, and I fall to my knees, screaming again.

The door bursts open as people come barreling into the room. My vision is blurry, and I feel my cheeks are wet. I must be crying. What the fuck is going on?

"Abbygail!"

I hear my name being called but struggle to separate the dream realm from reality. I grab my head as more voices call out my name. I whimper. It's all too loud, and it feels like my skin is burning.

"Abby, hey. You're okay, just relax. You are going to be fine. Take a deep breath. There you go," the voice that called my name tells me as I inhale deeply, letting it out shakingly. I frown as the sounds in the room become more apparent through the fuzziness in my mind with every breath I take.

Beeping from one side of me and screeching from the other echoes around the room, irritating my ears. Is this a hospital? I don't remember going to a hospital. I shake my head slowly from side to side, tears still streaming down my face.

I gasp as another flash from the fight I saw enters my mind, and I scream again. Firm but gentle hands grab my shoulders, bringing me out of the haze my mind didn't want to let me escape.

"Abby, it's Layla. You are safe. I promise. Hey..." she trails off when I look up at her, and she smiles softly at me.

The relief washing over me makes me slump back on my ass, my body feeling weaker than before. I focus on Layla and see worry behind her eyes, but her smile is warm and welcoming.

Some more sounds filter through now that I have some focus back, and looking around, I see Dr. Adam as he calls the nurses to help me up. Behind him is a beautiful gray-haired woman. She resembles Layla closely, but her eyes draw me in. She has the same eye shape as Tyler.

My eyes widen when I realize who she is, and I drop my gaze back to Layla, who clearly has seen the shock on my face when the realization sets in. It's Tyler and Layla's mother. The former Luna to the pack.

Shit, I wish I could meet her under better circumstances.

Wait, now that I think of it, what circumstances are these? I frown, not being able to pinpoint exactly how it is that I ended up here. Layla naturally notices my confusion, since she hasn't taken her eyes off me.

She pauses, frowning, tilts her head, and turns to her mother, who looks just as shocked as her.

"Do you see that?" Layla asks her mother, who in turn nods and hums her acknowledgment.

"That is what I was looking for when I asked to see his mark," the former Luna reveals.

The conversation between Layla and her mother confuses me so much that I don't notice the nurses kneeling at my side, and when one of them grips my arm to help me up, I yelp, and my breathing escalates as I look at them in fear. I'm still freaked out, and I don't like that they are touching me.

"Hey, don't freak out, okay? Let them look at you, and then I will tell you everything," Layla assures me as she gets up and out of the way.

"It's fine, I'll do it," Adam says as he walks and kneels beside me. The nurses get up and move to the other end of the room. Adam takes my wrist and places his index and middle finger on it while I watch him, my eyes still wide from fear. He stays like this for a few minutes before turning to me, slowly placing my hand on my lap. "I need to look at your neck, okay?" He waits patiently, and I give him a quick nod after a few seconds. Adam smiles reassuringly, grips my chin softly, slightly pushing my head to the right, and frowns before looking at me again.

"I'm going to pick you up now, and there is nothing to fear, okay?" he tells me, and I nod slowly. Adam picks me up from the floor and puts me back on the bed I jumped out of.

Relaxing into the pillow, I let them do what they need to do. The sooner they finish, the sooner I can find out what is going on.

It takes about thirty minutes for them to check my vitals and re-attach the monitors. I feel my strength return, but not as fast as I want. Adam gives me the all clear under the circumstances—which I still don't understand. I thank them as they leave, then turn my eyes back to Layla.

"Okay, so firstly, I'm going to hug you," she says slowly as she approaches me. This only confuses me more.

I nod at her, still frowning. She walks closer and hugs me tight. A sob rips through Layla's chest as she cries on my shoulder, holding on like I might disappear. It takes her a couple of minutes to compose herself again, her mother coming over and rubbing her back. "Come on, dear, you don't want to suffocate the poor girl," she says softly as she smiles at me again.

Layla lets go of me and steps back, pulling a chair to the bed and sitting down. She wipes her nose on her sleeve, and her mother wipes the tears from her face.

"What happened?" I croak, frowning at the sound of my voice; it's hoarse, and my throat is scratchy.

I clear it, and Layla hands me a cup of water. I take a sip and wince when it hurts going down. It must be from all the screaming. *That dream was so vivid.*

"Well," Layla says as she bounces her knee. "What do you remember?"

"I don't remember much, Layla. Did something happen to me?"

"Do you remember Tyler marking you?"

I shake my head slowly, frowning again. I wrack my brain. Why can't I remember? My wolf whines weakly in my mind before the images from our lovemaking and mating bond slam into my mind, making me groan from the headache it's giving me.

I recall Tyler being sick from the mate bond curse, and all that would save him was to seal the bond. I remember how we made sweet love, and I just couldn't let him die, so I marked him first—which triggered his wolf to do the same.

The prophecy comes to my memory next, and I look at Layla, still confused. "I remember marking Tyler so he would seal the bond, and it worked. How am I still alive, though?"

"Well, your body didn't handle the marking very well with all the shit Jace had put you through, but I knew you were strong enough to overcome this."

"Overcome what, exactly?"

"Adam found some myths and very ancient folklore that basically says you needed to mark my brother first, which you did, and that ensured the bond was sealed correctly."

Surprise washes through me. I am so tired of prophecies and all these kinds of bullshit. It makes my stomach churn. Don't get me wrong, I am thrilled that there was information available that could help them, but I am done now.

I touch where Tyler marked me, and a smile form on my mouth. Layla and her mother exchange glances again as they watch my every move.

"What?"

"It's too difficult to explain, so I'll just show you."

She takes her phone from her pocket and tells me to tilt my head to the right. I frown again. My poor forehead will look like the Grand Canyon if I don't stop with all the confusion. She takes a picture and hands me the phone.

I gasp and cover my mouth with my hand when I see the tattoo on my body. It all stems from the mark. I have never seen anything so intricate like it before. It's so beautifully elegant.

It runs to just below my ear, and it looks like plant veins with flowers lacing it as it curls everywhere, a crescent moon at the bite mark. The veins run down my back and shoulder from it, forming flowers at the ends and curving here and there. Butterflies lace some of the flowers, and it immediately lets me think of the freedom that Tyler had given me.

I touch my neck lightly, feeling the tattoo, and it's slightly elevated. I feel fully content for the first time in my life. Can this really be over? Can we have our happily ever after now?

"Does Tyler have one too? Is he okay? Did the bonding cure him?"

Layla looks uncomfortable as she looks at her mother, who gives her an encouraging nod as she smiles warmly again. "Yes, the bonding cured him, and, um—you could say he is getting by, but he will be ecstatic when he sees you."

"What do you mean he's getting by? How long have I been out?"

"Well, you fell into a coma after the last batch of seizures your body went through and…" Layla trails off, looking extremely uncomfortable now.

"Layla. How long?"

"Six months," she cringes as she answers me.

"SIX MONTHS?" I yell. Well, I didn't mean to yell. It just came out that way.

"Calm down, dear, please," Tyler's mother tells me as she places her hand softly on my leg, and I feel myself calming instantly.

Layla sees me frowning again, and she smiles brightly. "Abby, this is my mother, Alice, the former Luna of the Lunar pack."

"Nice to meet you, Luna Alice-"

"No, no. I will have none of those formalities from my new daughter. Besides, I am no longer Luna. That would be you," she says excitedly, the same warm smile still on her face.

I blush at her words as I fidget with the covers on me. Guess the stupid prophecy was right, then. "Layla, please tell me you are joking about the six months."

"I wish I were Abby, but unfortunately, I'm not."

"Shit." The curse leaves my mouth before I can stop it, and my eyes snap to Alice when I realize what I said. "I'm so sorry. Please forgive my poor manners."

"Abbygail, stop apologizing. I would react the same way if I found out I was in a coma for so long."

"How is he? Where is he? I need to see him, Layla." I sound desperate, but that is precisely how I'm feeling. Thinking he is the one that placed me in the coma must break him.

"He didn't take it very well, to be honest. He sat at your bedside for three months straight, reading and talking to you, willing you to wake up. He lost hope, and hasn't been here in the last three months."

Tears build in my eyes at the thought of my mate broken. Why does he always have to be so hard on himself? He grinds my gears sometimes. Marking him was my choice, not his.

Alice sees the hurt on my face and takes my hand in hers. I can't believe he gave up so quickly—but then again, from the little time I've had to know him, I know it isn't giving up but coping with the grief.

"Dear child, if you just know how much Tyler has grown to love you in the brief time he's known you. He grieved for you more than he did for his father." The endearing in Alice's tone warms my heart as she rubs my hand softly.

"Please call him for me. I desperately need to see him." Layla looks at Alice again and then back at me. A worried look creeps on her face. The same expression is mirrored on her mother's face as well.

I don't like the feeling I'm getting from them. Why isn't Layla calling him? The same sense of dread takes hold of my heart that I got from the dream the longer she stays silent. "Layla, please," I plead now, feeling the tears stinging my eyes again.

"I'm afraid he's not here, Abby."

"What? Where is he?"

"Tyler lost all hope of you returning to him, so he turned to the only thing he knew how to control. He went to look for Jace and Owen—"

"Wait, wait. Aren't they locked in the dungeon?" I cut her off.

"They escaped the same night Kayden found you with them," she says, guilt coming off her.

"Are you shitting me?" I'm baffled at what she's telling me. "Why didn't anyone tell me this?"

"Tyler didn't want you to worry."

"So, the bastard lied to me," I snap at her.

"Abby dear, please understand where he comes from with his reasoning."

"I do understand, Alice, but trust is important, and it's a fragile thing. I am going to kick his ass when I get my hands on him—right after I kiss him," I laugh softly. My emotions are all over the place, but one thing I know for sure is my love for that stubborn asshole.

They smile at me before their faces turn serious again, spiking the feeling of uneasiness in my chest.

"They left about two days ago, and no one has heard from them," Layla confesses.

My face pales as all the blood drains from it. This surely can't be true, can it? "The dream," I whisper as I touch my mark.

"What dream?"

"I was trapped for so long with images that did not make sense, but then I saw a dream which felt so real. All the scenes were so vivid..." I trail off as the image of Tyler on his knees, bleeding in front of Jace, comes to mind. "Fuck!" I exclaim, and I throw the cover off me again.

Getting out of bed, I pull the wires from my chest that are connected to the monitors. My legs are still weak, and I sway just as Layla catches me.

"Damn it, Abby, will you please just stay in the bed."

"I can't, he's in danger. I need to get to him, Layla. NOW!"

"What do you mean-" Layla stops talking when she sees my face and the utter fear behind my eyes. "Abby, you can barely stand. How will you be able to help him?"

"I..." I trail off, not having an answer.

"You're a hybrid, aren't you?" I hear Alice's voice come from across the room.

"Yes."

"Then part of you needs blood to heal faster, here drink this," she insists, handing me a blood bag. "It's Tyler's. He thought it best to have a backup if you needed any. Guess it's as good a time as any to use it."

"No. Wait. I can't drink this," I say, pulling a face in disgust.

"Abbygail, you are hell-bent on going after my son, so please just think this through. It's the only way you will heal and get your true hybrid strength back," Alice tells me, pushing the bag toward me again.

"Fuck." She's right. I take the bag from Alice and put it to my lips. Biting off the top piece, I squeeze too tight and blood pushes out of the bag. Gasping, I lick it off my hand, and the surge of energy and power pushing through my body catches me off guard. I close my eyes as the feeling settles in me. My fangs push out, and I drink more of the sticky liquid.

Shit, this feels so good. I finish all the blood and open my eyes. Alice and Layla watch me intently. I inhale deeply as I lick the last of the blood off my lips, and I feel myself heal wholly and quickly.

"How do you feel?" Layla asks me, and a bright smile forms on my lips.

"I've never felt so powerful before. It's intoxicating."

"That's good. Do you still want to go after Tyler?" Layla cracks her knuckles, knowing what my answer will be. She's fixing for a fight, which strengthens the urge to rip someone's head off their body.

"Oh, hell yes!" As my eyes flash, a growl leaves my chest, and Layla laughs elatedly.

"Then let's get going."

"Before we leave, I have to get a sword."

Layla looks at me confused, tilting her head at my request. Alice smiles widely as she understands my train of thought. "She wants to be poetic, my dear," Alice tells Layla. Turning to me, Alice places her hands on my shoulders. "You will be a great asset to this pack, young lady. I am profoundly grateful that my son has you as a mate."

"Thank you so much." I hug her. "Now, if you will excuse me, I need to get dressed for the occasion, and I need my accessories."

"This is going to be so much fun," Layla exclaims, clapping her hands together and jumping up and down. "I'm getting Julia. No one will be able to mess with us."

I smile at her as I walk past her and out of my hospital room, the nurses looking at me dumbstruck. I woke up from a six-month coma only two hours ago, and now I am walking out of the hospital like nothing ever happened.

Strolling into Layla's room with her trailing behind me, I look around. It's light and airy here, the total opposite of Tyler's. Layla smiles, "Let's get you dressed, yeah?" She walks straight to her closet, throws open the door, and pulls out black jeans and a tight-fitted tank top, also black. She hands them to me, and I smile broadly. This is fitting; I take off the hospital gown and get dressed.

I braid my long hair to the opposite side to leave my mark visible for everyone to see. The power I feel pulsing through my veins is enhanced by the knowledge that the most powerful Alpha hybrid marked me and that he is *mine*. I grab a pair of combat boots from Layla's closet and pull them on.

Julia enters the room, looking fierce and ready for what's coming. She whistles low, looking me over, and I grin at her. "Well, look at you now. You look ready for the part." Julia wanders over to me and hands me the elegantly designed silver sword. My wolf senses the silver, and I can feel her wariness as I reach out to touch the pommel. One cut with this… Jace won't know what hit him.

The hilt is engraved with wolves in battle, and the blade is smooth with only the words JUSTICE WILL PROSPER engraved on the edge in gold.

"Where did you find this?" I ask Julia, unable to take my eyes off it.

"Oh, I told Julia to go get it from the mantle in my brother's office. It's just a family heirloom passed down through the centuries. If I remember correctly, it was used to liberate our people in some other stupid battle. I never really listened when it was told to us as kids," Layla says, shrugging, looking very bored by the subject.

Smiling, I run my fingers over it, remembering the times my father and I had trained together. I never thought they would be helpful, but I know whose blood will be staining it today.

I hope we aren't too late because if my mate dies because I can't save him, I will burn this fucking kingdom to the ground and anyone who stands in my way.

I turn to face Layla, dressed in something similar to what I am wearing. Layla and Julia tied their hair up in high ponytails, and the war makeup they painted on their faces made them look fierce. Their faces remind me of pictures I used to see in our history books of ancient warriors.

I contemplate painting my face as well but decide against it. Jace will look into *my* face when he dies, not one hidden behind paint. "Ready?"

They nod, growling low in their throats.

Just as I am about to turn and move out of the door, it bursts open as one of the warrior wolves that stayed behind to protect the territory comes running in.

He stops dead at the sight of us, and the energy in the room also seems to seep into him. His eyes flash when he inhales our scents, and the same determined growl comes from his chest.

"What?" I snap.

"Luna," he sinks to one knee, bowing to me. "We received word. Alpha Tyler and the rest of the group that left two days ago are nearing the pack territory, but they got cut off, and it's not good. Our Alpha is seriously injured. Beta Kayden and Gamma Sebastian are trying to keep Jace from killing him, but they are outnumbered."

"Fuck." I look at Layla and Julia, whose canines are showing as they snarl at the news.

I turn back to the wolf on his knee. "We need to move *now*. Get the second line of defense ready. We need to leave some to protect the Packhouse but get as many as possible to fight with us."

"Yes, Luna Abbygail." He smiles excitedly as he rises. Bowing to us once more, he quickly moves out of the room to do what I ordered.

"Come on, girls. Some heads are about to roll, and I can't wait," I say darkly. With Layla flanking my right and Julia on my left, we walk out into the hall and make our way to the front door, where my army stands, waiting for my next order.

CHAPTER THIRTY-SIX

TYLER

I charge the wolves who have my men surrounded, and I make short work of them. My vision the same color as the blood covering my hands. I must admit, my wolf is ecstatic with the fight. It helps eliminate some of those pent-up feelings and shitty experiences we must deal with.

Two wolves charge me, claws swiping toward my head and chest, I duck and spin, dropping down and slicing their Achilles tendons, making them drop to the ground, whelping.

Getting to my feet quickly, I grab each of them by the throat and feel their windpipes crush under my tightening grip as I snarl viciously at them. It's a ruthless way to die, but I no longer care. They will pay the price if they want to challenge me and go against the kingdom and my people.

My head snaps to the left as a piercing howl echoes into the night sky.

Recognizing the sound instantly, I turn toward the howl, baring my teeth as I sniff the air. Sure enough, Jace and Owen's scents hit my nose, and I take off running into the woods. It ends now before anyone else dies.

My wolf is so lost in the haze of the blood lust that we don't even think of backup. Hopefully, Kayden hears the howl as it rings out a second time.

I push myself to run faster, following their scent. Not long after running off, thundering footsteps fill the air behind me. I sniff the air again and catch Sebastian's scent. I smile, knowing that my backup is almost here. Not that I would need any.

I run into a clearing and am stopped dead by the sight in front of me. Jace stands on a large open slab of rock, expanding the width of the clearing. Owen and a whole horde of vampires flank him.

Is that Alec? The fucking bastard did not learn his lesson the first time, it seems. To get into bed with a psycho to stand against me? That's a new low, even for him. Well, I guess I will have to wipe out his whole fucking clan this time, to make a statement.

I scan the enemy line, and I know I am highly outnumbered. I inhale deeply, holding my breath as I calculate a plan of attack in my mind, letting the air out slowly, setting my sights on Jace.

"So nice of you to finally join us, your majesty?" Jace opens his arms wide, and his condescending laugh cuts through the night. "So glad you can join your own death party."

"Stop spewing bullshit, you piece of shit, and come fight me," I grit my teeth, my nostrils flaring.

"Now, now. Don't be so eager to meet your death." He shakes his head at me as he snickers, "Tell me, how is my little slut doing?"

A roar leaves my throat, and I bare my teeth, snapping at Jace when he mentions Abbygail, and I charge at him. He laughs wickedly, pointing to me, and screams, "ATTACK!"

The horde of vampires at his sides comes barreling towards me, and within seconds, I'm surrounded. I fight off every single assault that comes my way, but something seems off. They aren't attacking me all at once. It's like they are playing tag. Each one getting a turn to fight me, mocking me. It's not difficult to fight them off, but every time I am going to land a death blow, they switch.

They are trying to tire me out for when that coward Jace wants to kill me. Well, I have news for him: my wolf is starving for a good fight, and his little setup will not get to me that easily.

I grab the vamp that has his turn with me by the front of his shirt, pulling him towards me quickly, the look on his face covered with surprise. He didn't think I was this fast. Guess they don't know I'm half vampire.

I snarl at him, baring my fangs, my fingers snaking around his neck. I twist my wrist slightly and snap his neck, then pull his head from his body. Throwing his lifeless body to the ground, I look at Alec, challenging him, and he hisses angrily at me.

Alec charges me, his long nails out and ready to cause serious bodily harm. I sidestep him, turning fast as he comes for my throat. I hear Kayden's roar, and it distracts me. Alec slices his nails across my face, cutting a deep gash from just above my brow over my eye and down to my cheek, which burns like crazy—

—and then claws push into my side and back.

A roar leaves my mouth as I fall to my knees on the forest floor. Pain consumes me, and I grab at my side, trying to stop the bleeding.

The vampires around us back off as Jace stands before me, his hands drenched in my blood. Hunched over from the pain, I'm trying to push down on my side wound and feel the blood run down my back. I curse as the blood spills past my hands over the gaping wound, and I hear Jace's triumphant laughter.

In my peripheral vision, I see Kayden kick Owen off him and run to me, but four vampires tackle him to the ground and pin him there. His eyes widen with fear as I feel Jace's claw push my chin up to look at him, drawing more blood as it pierces my skin. I snarl weakly at Jace. The amount of blood pooling at my knees is alarming, to say the least, and I feel my power and energy slip away with every drop that falls on the ground.

Jace smirks when he looks down his nose at me on my knees in front of him. "Well, isn't this a pretty sight? The Alpha King is on his knees in front of the *true* ruler of this kingdom. My day has finally come." He lets out an evil laugh. "I had other plans to make you suffer, but seeing that you brought the fight to me, this will have to do."

The clearing is quiet, and the moonlight shines brightly on us as Jace lifts his clawed hand to land the fatal blow. The look of pleasure on his face is unmissable.

This isn't how I planned tonight to go either. But, like my mate lying in a coma, not everything is in my hands—and I don't even fear death as I stare it in the face now. I lift my chin, preparing for the strike, when Sebastian comes barreling through a gap in the circle. He has quite a few wolves with him.

Jace curses as Sebastian tackles him to the ground and goes for his throat. Owen comes out of nowhere and kicks Sebasian off of Jace. Sebastian slides across the floor, getting to his feet mid-slide and snarling at Owen.

"Fall back!" Jace yells as he and Owen make a run for it.

The vampires holding Kayden down hiss and almost vanish into thin air, moving so fast, and we are left alone in the clearing. Breathing a sigh of relief, I fall forward and brace for impact, my hands still clutching my side, but Kayden catches me before I hit the ground.

"Fuck, Tyler, why did you have to run in here without backup?" he yells. "If it weren't for Sebastian, we would be dead!"

I groan as the blood keeps running past my hands. I cannot understand why I haven't healed yet or even started.

"Fucking Alec!" I hear Sebastian curse, then grab my face and turn it to look at the slash marks. "Looks like he got you good, and by the looks of it, he dipped his bloody nails in wolfsbane."

Sebastian pulls my hands away from the wound at my side and then turns me to the side to inspect the one on my back.

"This will surely scar, fuck," Sebastian snarls.

"Scarring... isn't my biggest worry at the moment," I groan, clutching my side again.

"If that is true, we are truly fucked. You need to heal, and the path back to our territory will be difficult. Damn it, Tyler! You really do have a death wish." Kayden scolds me, ignoring my statement, and I try to laugh at him, feeling too weak to argue.

"We need to..." I say slowly as I concentrate on my words. "Move... they can come back..."

"No shit, Sherlock." Kayden scoffs, rolling his eyes.

"I'll take this side." Sebastian grabs my arm and pulls it over his shoulder.

I grunt and scream as the pain hits me. What's eerie is that it's not the pain in my side or back that makes me scream. It's coming from the mark in the crook of my neck. It burns like hellfire, and I can't seem to suppress the scream that rips through me.

Pulling my arm from Sebastian, I fall to my knees again, and they stare at me like I am losing my mind. My wolf is howling in my mind so loud it feels like my ears will explode. He's weak from the wolfsbane and the blood loss. My wolf whines as the howl dies out, and I feel him retreat into the back of my mind.

"Mark..." I grit through my teeth, my breathing shallow and quick.

Before I can understand what's happening, the burn intensifies, running from the mark down to my shoulder and down my left pec.

I grab my shirt, ripping it open, and I hear Kayden and Sebastian gasp as they step back.

What the fuck is going on? I have never felt wolfsbane like this before.

The burning is gone just as fast as it started, and I fall forward again, wincing from the gaping tears in my side and back. Panting, I touch my mark and feel something slightly elevated there. Guess it wasn't the wolfsbane, then.

"I thought it was only a myth, but color me pink..." Kayden trails off as he walks to me.

"What is it?" I ask him, still trying to catch my breath.

"It's a hybrid mate bond tattoo." Kayden sounds confused and surprised at the same time. "But how is this possible?"

Howling rings through the quiet forest and snaps us back to the looming danger. How can I forget where we are and the fact that Jace is going to come for my head now that I am not able to protect myself? We need to get back to our territory fast.

"Let's get out of here," I grunt and stagger to my feet.

"As soon as we get cell signal, call for backup. We are going to need it. Jace is circling us like a fucking vulture," Kayden tells Sebastian, who nods in return as he swings my arm over his neck again.

The walk back to the Lunar territory is slow and painful. Every once in a while, we hear growling, and howls ring out as we move. They are toying with us. That much is clear. Jace and his misfits have the upper hand, and he's using it to the best of his abilities. I don't know how he knew we were coming for him in the first place—unless he has other magic beings, besides Alec's clan, working with him.

Stumbling through the forest at an agonizing pace, I struggle to keep from passing out. The amount of blood I've lost is alarming. We have to stop regularly, and it pisses me off. I am holding my pack back and, in doing so, placing them in even more danger.

I tried to convince Kayden and Sebastian to leave me and save themselves and the rest of the pack, but they cursed me out.

I should know better, but I had to try.

"Argh, stop please, I can't-" I groan when my feet drag, and I can't seem to get one foot in front of the other.

"Come on, Tyler, just a little bit more. We're almost there," Kayden pleads with me.

"Let me catch my breath, please."

"Fine, five minutes, then we move again," Sebastian tells me crudely.

They lower me down and let me rest with my back against a massive tree trunk. The pain in my side is worse than the one in my back. Luckily, the bleeding has slowed. Looking at how soaked my clothes are, it doesn't surprise me.

"Guys, please. You need to leave me and go-" I start to say, but a coughing fit racks through my body, and I hear Sebastian curse.

Wiping my mouth, seeing blood on my hand, I know precisely why Sebastian reacts this way. Shit, this isn't what you want to see with wounds like mine.

Letting out a strained laugh, I lean my head against the tree trunk, and the movement makes me groan.

"Don't worry about it, okay?" I wipe my hand on my pants—not that it helps much. Everything is covered in blood.

Howling rings out again, this time closer, and my Beta and Gamma's heads whip to the sound, growling low as their warrior modes kick in. They bend down, grab my arms, and hurl me off the ground, making me curse at the sudden action on my broken body.

"Fuck!" Kayden exclaims.

"Time to move." Sebastian orders, and the remaining wolves move quickly, surrounding us keeping a tight circle. "On three, we step as one."

"Tyler, so help me. You better not fucking die on me, do you understand me? We need to work together. We need to move, and we need to move now." Kayden grunts next to me as he adjusts my arm around his neck.

Knowing I am not one of the lightest people to carry, I pity my friends. Kayden and Sebastian are doing their best here, but I know they are tired and worn out. They've been carrying me for most of the night. I wish they would leave me. It's not helping anyone if all of us get killed.

"Yeah, I know," I groan, trying to take some of my own weight on my left leg since my right one is useless with the gash just above my hip.

They wait for me to get my balance sorted out and adjust my weight, nodding to them when I feel ready to move. We step as one being, which makes my body surge with adrenaline. My pack gives me the power to get to our territory.

We move forward for another thirty minutes without incident when I see my pack territory line ahead of us. A sigh comes through my pursed lips.

My relief is short-lived when snarling and growls erupt from all directions. Fuck, my territory is just within our reach, and the fuckers waited for this precise moment, knowing that this is no man's land. This neutral part of the territory means that anything goes here. If Jace kills me here, he won't be in the same amount of shit he would be if he killed me in any other territory.

The realization sends a chill running down my spine. I can feel the bastard's eyes on us already, seeing his smile in my mind and his malicious aura drift in and out while he toys with us.

"We aren't going to make it, Kayden. You need to leave me. You must get a layout of where we stand so we can set up a perimeter. Sebastian, run for backup," I grit through my clenched jaw.

"I told you I will not leave your side until you are safe in the Packhouse," Kayden tells me, not moving from my side, holding my wrist tighter around his shoulder.

"Fuck Kayden, *leave*," I snarl in my Alpha voice, and I feel his back go rigid when the command hits him.

Kayden turns his gaze to me slowly, his body shaking slightly as he tries to fight the command I just gave him, shaking his head at me as he presses his lips into a thin line. "No," he forces out.

The adrenaline running through my veins gets another spike when he refuses to obey my command, feeling my canines elongate and seeing red. "Now!" Placing more force behind the command.

Kayden doesn't have a choice, and he drops my arm from his shoulder as my second command rings out. It's deafening.

The warriors flinch along with Sebastian once my voice bellows over all the noise in the forest.

"Do as you're told, Sebastian," I command him as well. An extremely dangerous, low growl comes from his chest as he lets me go. Sebastian watches me to see if I am able to stand on my own before he takes off towards the Packhouse.

The silence that follows when they leave is unnerving.

Someone clears their throat, and I sigh, lifting my head and staring into Jack's concerned face.

"Alpha, are you sure sending them away is a good idea? I assure you we will protect you with our lives, but it would have spared a lot more of us if they stayed." Jack's head snaps to the left when snarling comes just a few feet from us.

"Yes, you take the rest of the wolves and spread out. You need to make sure we are the ones surrounding them if we want to survive this attack," I grunt, limping towards the nearest tree, leaning with my shoulder against it and placing pressure on my side again. "And of course, we need some bait, don't we?" I force a smile as I gesture to myself as the bait.

The horrified look on Jack's face makes my stomach clench, but I push it aside. He opens his mouth to protest, but I growl low, making him think twice about arguing with me now. He's not sold on this plan, but he has no choice. He turns and tells the rest of the wolves what my plan is. They don't move, and I sense their hesitation as they look at each other.

"Why does everybody choose tonight of all nights to second guess their Alpha and not obey direct orders?" I snarl at them.

It only takes a few seconds for me to be left entirely alone, as they don't wait for me to say anything else.

I push myself away from the tree and limp slowly towards the territory line again.

Knowing Jace, he isn't too far behind and probably heard the exchange with my men, giving him the opportune moment—as I am alone and unprotected.

Right on cue, a foot on my back kicks me forward, making me fall with so much force my head hits the ground, disorienting me. Laughter rings out as I grunt and shake my head, pushing myself up from the ground but failing to stand.

I will fight until my last breath—which won't take long, if I'm honest.

Regret fills my heart at the thought that I wanted this; now, I'm not so sure anymore. I have been a martyr for the last six months, and have given up on myself and my people. How I wish to change that and show them—I could be what they need me to be.

Groaning, I push myself up from the forest floor again, my arms shaking from being too weak, staggering as I stand and turn to face him. I'm seeing double, but I don't care. "Oh, very courageous of you, but I would have preferred to kill some to get to you," Owen snickers, and Jace's laughter rings in my ears.

"I don't have the strength to do small talk tonight. Let's just get this over with," I spit at them. I am obviously not steady on my feet as I sway and stagger again.

"I was hoping for more banter like in the fight scenes you see in movies, but hey, I'm down for just ripping your throat out," Jace admits playfully.

"Come on then," I pant, and beckon for him to come at me. "I really don't have all day."

Jace clearly doesn't like my condescending remark, because he snarls with so much ferocity that saliva spews from his mouth.

"Look who's the one who can't control their temper now," I laugh darkly, then wince when my side wound aches from being jolted. I resist the urge to hold my side, not wanting to give Jace the satisfaction of seeing me crippled.

"You are dead, Tyler Storm. I will wipe your memory away to the extent that people will think you were a myth."

"You can try." Grunting, I smirk as I flip him off.

A roar leaves his and Owen's chests as they run towards me, canines bared and claws ready to strike.

I brace myself for impact, slapping away Jace's hand when he swings for my chest, but I'm not quite fast enough for Owen's swing. Lucky for me, only his fist connects with my jaw. It doesn't mean it didn't hurt like a bitch, though.

My head swings to the side from the blow, and I lose my balance, hitting the ground with a painful thud. A scream rips its way out of my throat from the pain shooting through my body.

The moment I hit the ground, Jace kicks me in the ribs twice, quickly. The air gets knocked out of my lungs, and the pain keeps me from breathing back in. My side is screaming at me, as well as the gash on my back, as I'm collecting dirt and leaves in the open wounds.

I'm still struggling to take in air as Jace squats down next to me. He tilts his head, watching me struggle, patiently waiting for me to drag air into my lungs. As soon as I do, he snakes his fingers around my throat and hauls me off the ground. My feet barely touch the forest floor.

He tightens his grip on my throat and places the claws of his free hand at my heart, pushing them into me, just piercing my flesh.

I bare my teeth from the onslaught of added pain while he chokes the life out of me. He will never give me a mercy killing: I know better than that. No, Jace wants me to suffer. He brings my face closer to him, his sickening smile sending waves of anger through my body.

I try my best to lure my wolf out. I won't be able to do this without him. *Please, I need you, please come back. Your overbearing ass is always trying to tear shit apart, and now that I need you the most, you retreat like a pussy. I know we are injured badly, but we are stronger than this.*

Nothing, not even a growl. I guess I am on my own.

Jace tilts his head, pushing his claws deeper inch by inch. I can't help but choke out a strangled scream when his claws scrape against my rib cage.

"I told you that you would regret meeting me, and look at you now. I bet you wish your Beta killed me the night he took my little slut from me," Jace snarls, baring his canines.

Looking down at him, I manage a smile just before I spit in his face. "Fuck... You," I force out of my tightened throat.

Jace's eyes flash with anger, and he pushes his claws even deeper into my chest, cracking my ribs under the pressure he places on them while he squeezes my throat tighter, making it impossible for me to breathe or even make a sound.

Black spots appear in my vision, my ears are ringing, and the pain consumes me. Jace is about to take the last step and push through my rib cage to my heart to kill me, when he stops and turns his head quickly.

"Did you hear that?" he asks Owen.

"Yes," Owen sounds surprised as he looks around frantically.

"Where are the clans?"

"Surrounding the perimeter, like you ordered."

"Good, let them know we have company." Owen nods and runs into the forest again.

Where the hell is *my* backup? I can't think straight with the lack of oxygen. Jace loosens his grip on my throat slightly, and the air comes rushing in, making me lightheaded. My hearing clears up with the air flowing through me, and the crunching of leaves pierces my ears.

It sounds like fighting is happening not far from here, and by the look on Jace's face, he is worried.

Owen comes sprinting back to where Jace is still holding me in the air. His hands are still on my throat and almost at my heart.

"Shit, more than half of the vampires fled. They say they will not fight in this war. They don't want the hybrid coming for them, not after what they saw in the clearing." Owen's face is pale while he relays the message.

If what Owen says is true, he must know how outnumbered they are. Jace no longer stands a chance if more than half his army fled. Even if he kills me now, he will perish tonight.

"Aww, poor Alpha needs saving, looks like your pathetic pack is coming for you after you so valiantly sent them away." Jace looks back at me. The snarky tone in his voice from earlier is gone, and the panic in it is apparent.

"Just kill him already, Jace." Owen sounds impatient but looks nervous as his eyes dart around occasionally, his shoulders tense.

"*You* don't tell me what I should do," Jace growls at Owen.

"You are going to get us both killed. I thought you wanted to rule this kingdom. It's within your grasp, and now you're playing with our future-"

"*My* future, Owen. Never forget that. You can always be replaced if you don't fit into *my* vision of what I want."

Owen looks like Jace just struck him with a whip as he steps back, but the shock is soon replaced by anger. "Let's make it easy. I renounce you as my Alpha," Owen grits out. "I have done everything you ever asked of me. Not anymore. I will not die here tonight." With that, he turns on his heel and runs.

I choke out a snort, and Jace glares at me.

"I don't need him. I can do this on my own. You can snort as much as you like, but you will never know what happens to your beloved kingdom and your people. I will grant you the courtesy to tell you what will happen to your mate, though. I will bed her and have my pups grow within her. She will submit to me, and I *will* break her."

I choke out a weak snarl when his words filter through my mind's cloudiness, but I don't have time to react before a mighty roar comes from the right side of the forest, making my ears ring.

The sound is foreign. Apart from my own, I haven't heard a roar that powerful before.

Jace's head whips toward the roar, and he frowns before he smiles wickedly.

"You better stay back, princess, or I *will* rip his heart out." Jace's grip on my throat tightens again, and he pushes his claws past the bones of my ribcage, scraping against my heart. I choke out a painful grunt.

CHAPTER THIRTY-SEVEN

ABBYGAIL

"Does anybody have word on Alpha Tyler?" Julia asks as we close in on the territory border.

No one answers, making my already-shot nerves feel like they are about to tear apart.

Just as I think we might be too late, I see Sebastian walking up to us, and I frown. He looks venomous, but his eyes widen in surprise when he sees me. I wave at him, and his eyes trail over every inch of me, resting on the tattoo on my neck. Sebastian frowns, and a mixture of confusion and recognition mars his face.

"What's going on?" Layla asks from beside me.

"Your fucking brother has a death wish. He ordered me and Kayden away. Jace wasn't far behind us." Sebastian narrows his eyes at me while answering Layla.

"Are you fucking kidding me? How can he do that?" Layla growls.

My heart sinks to my boots. Why would Tyler deliberately place himself in more danger? The urgency to get to him now rises in my chest.

"Fuck, Sebastian, didn't your mother teach you it's rude to stare?" Layla snaps.

Her words bring Sebastian back to reality, and he frowns at me again.

"What do you mean?" I ask him.

"Like I said, our Alpha ordered us to leave him. He wanted us to leave him behind. He's injured badly and isn't healing, meaning he cannot protect himself," Sebastian snarls, irritation lacing his voice. Without missing a beat, he says, "I'm sorry, but how the hell are you standing here?"

Sebastian's question throws me off guard for a second.

"Sebastian!" Layla yells at him, but I put my hand up to stop her from scolding him.

There is no time for this. If Jace was on their heels and Tyler sent all his best protection in different directions, he will be in serious trouble. "Later, it's not the place nor the time for this. Your Alpha, my mate, is in danger, and we need to get to him before it's too late."

"Yes, Luna," Sebastian says, smiling, clearly the authority in my voice showing my status. "What's with the sword?"

"Poetic justice," I shrug as I smile.

"Sounds perfect."

"Take me to him."

Sebastian nods, and he takes off running into the forest.

The anticipation vibrates through me. Tonight, I get my justice and eliminate the monster that terrorized my every waking moment for six years. I place my hand in the air and show the troops to follow Sebastian.

We haven't moved far into the neutral zone when the first attack hits us from three sides.

We stand our ground, fighting and killing anyone who dares to strike. I'd never been in battle before, and I thought it would be difficult at first—but my wolf is excellent, and it comes as easy as breathing.

"Make sure none of them make it into our circle. As long as we stand firm, they don't stand a chance," Julia yells above the fighting. "And as soon as you see a gap, Abby, you need to take it and get to Tyler."

"Got it," I yell back.

My canines push past my lips, and my eyes change color as one vampire lunges at Layla while she is distracted fighting another. "Oh no, you don't," I snarl at the idiot, tripping him before he gets to her. He falls to the ground, and Sebastian rips his throat out.

I smile my thanks at him, and he comes to fight at my side with Layla and Julia—seeing that many of them have spotted me.

"That's the Luna, by the looks of it. Kill her, and we defeat the Alpha King!" Another vampire calls to his comrades.

"You need to get her to Tyler," Layla yells at Sebastian.

"On it."

Three vampires come for me the moment I step out of the circle. One swipes at me, cutting the flesh on my arm, as the other two try to grab my wrists. I yelp from the sting it leaves and narrow my eyes at the assholes. Their nostrils flare when they catch the scent of my blood and the rarity of it. They hiss, and I smirk. Perfect, it will distract them long enough for me to take them down.

I duck down, moving between them, ripping the one's heart from his chest. He turns and sees the pumping heart in my hand as I whirl to face him. He frowns at me, and then looks down at the gaping hole in his chest before he falls to his knees and collapses to the ground, dead.

The two remaining vamps look at their fallen friend and then angrily at me. "You fucking bitch!" they screech.

A haughty smile forms on my lips, and I tilt my head at them, throwing my weight from one hip to the other, taunting them with the heart still in my hand. "Did he need this?" I feign innocence, batting my lashes. "Oh, sorry, here, you can take it."

They stalk toward me menacingly, their fangs bared.

Looking from one to the other, my wolf growls in my mind, and the sound comes to my mouth; she's reading their movements, knowing exactly what they are planning to do.

They strike simultaneously but are too slow for us, and I grab both by the throat. I snarl at them. Moving fast, I rip their hearts from their chests without any effort and drop their corpses to the ground. The remaining vampires flee when they witness what I did to three of their strongest fighters.

The pure adrenaline mixed with hybrid power and Tyler's blood running through my veins makes me someone you don't want to mess with tonight. I never knew I had so much power and resilience.

Whistling to Sebastian, I motion for him to come to me. Our time is running out, and I can feel it.

"Which way?"

"Northeast." He points in that direction, and I nod.

"Let's get going."

"Where's Kayden?" Layla asks as she runs to me and Sebastian, Julia following closely behind her.

"Not sure, he was supposed to see how far the enemy hordes are spreading. I haven't heard from him in a while," Sebastian states, worried.

The look on Layla's face is unnerving, and it mirrors my feelings exactly.

"Lay, I will be fine. Take Julia and the warriors and go find your mate." I place my hand on her shoulder.

"Are you sure you will be okay?" Layla asks, hesitating. The pull to get to Kayden must be wearing on her. I know because I feel it, too. The uneasiness is very unsettling.

"Go, please, make sure he's okay. I'll make sure your brother comes home safe. I promise."

Layla gives me a quick nod, tears rimming her eyes. She wipes her eyes quickly, turning to Julia.

"Ready?"

"Hell yeah, let's rip some heads off," Julia growls.

I smile at my two friends, watching them run off in the opposite direction, feeling so unbelievably blessed despite the grim situation.

"Abby." The urgency in Sebastian's voice pulls me back to the looming danger still ahead of us.

"Sorry."

Sebastian nods, and we run deeper into the forest, him leading us toward the place where they left Tyler. *Please, don't let me be too late.* I won't be able to survive this if Tyler doesn't. I just made a promise to Layla, and I intend to keep it.

I sniff the air, and my breath catches in my throat as Tyler's scent hits my nose, but it shoots panic throughout my whole being. Pain, mixed with a hint of death, coating the night. *No!*

I push myself to run faster, my wolf snarling in my mind as she drives us forward, picking up on the other scent mixed in with Tyler's. His scent is forced into my memory, and I will always recognize the triumphant smell he lets off when he is about to conquer. *Fuck!*

I run into a semi-cleared area in the forest, and what I see makes me want to throw up.

CHAPTER THIRTY-EIGHT

LAYLA

"Did you see Abby back there?" I ask Julia, still feeling surprised at her drive and fighting technique.

"Yeah, I can't believe it's the same girl from almost a year ago," she laughs.

The absolute warrior Abby turned into is a breath of fresh air. She went from being scared and broken to a true-born leader. The moment we enter the forest and the vampires attack us, I see just how strong she is. The raw power, coupled with the speed and agility she possesses, is astounding. I will fight by her side any day.

She will be everything from the prophecy and so much more. But Abby needs to get to Tyler in time, or we will lose her too.

The moment I get time to scan the scene through the fighting, I notice that Kayden isn't anywhere to be seen. Worry ebbs my mind and heart. Sebastian said he had to survey the enemy hordes, but they're busy attacking us, and I couldn't smell or feel his presence. The fact that Sebastian hasn't heard anything from him makes me go into full-on panic mode. I need to find him, but don't know how to leave Abby.

"Go, please, make sure he is okay." Abby notices my dilemma. I nod quickly, thankful that she has my back. Julia and I turn and run off in the opposite direction as Abby and Sebastian.

It feels like a lifetime before I catch a hint of Kayden's scent, but the fear I am trying to push down spreads when I do.

Changing course, Julia follows close behind with the troops. My ears catch the battle that's ongoing just ahead of us.

"Move out," I command, pointing to my left and right.

Without having to look back, I know they split with accuracy.

I run into the heart of the fight and see my mate fighting at least ten vampires, but he's losing.

The cuts on his arms, back, and chest are alarmingly deep. Luckily, I can see them heal, but the blows fall so consistently that the next slice is delivered just as another one heals.

It ensures that he keeps losing blood and his body can't recuperate.

I run towards him, a snarl ripping through me as one asshole swings his claws at Kayden's throat.

Kayden jumps back, but his speed fails him, he knows he won't be able to get out of the way fast enough. The claws make contact just as he turns his head to the side so the blow falls on the side of his neck. They cut deep, and he groans, falling to his knees just as I reach him.

I jump into the air, coming down hard on the vampire who's responsible for the attack on my mate. Grabbing hold of his head, I twist it sideways and up, ripping his head from his shoulders.

Within seconds, his head is in my hands, his body falls to the ground, and I land crouching.

Rising slowly, I throw the head at the remaining nine vampires, who in turn hiss at me, but they don't attack. Their eyes are wide, and I look around at the vampires who have stopped fighting.

The troops are stalking closer, killing anyone who attacks.

"I will give you one chance," I growl, baring my teeth. "Leave now, and we will forgive your mistakes against the Lunar pack and the kingdom, but know this: if you stay and fight, I will have *no* mercy."

The collective snarls echoing through the forest from our pack warriors make the vamps think twice about their assault. "We will go," one of the nine vampires before me speaks up, bowing to me.

"Excellent choice," I smirk, and they disappear.

I don't waste another second and spin to see Kayden on his back, Julia's hands on his neck, trying to stop the bleeding.

"Babe!" Failing to hide the panic in my voice.

"Impressive, ba—" Kayden starts, but the blood gurgles in his throat.

"Please, don't talk," I almost sob, not having any control of my voice as the panic manifests. We are too far from the Packhouse to get him to Adam, and I don't know what to do.

Julia presses down harder on his neck, and he squeezes his eyes shut. "He's going to be okay, Layla. I just need to stop the bleeding. He's healing, but very slowly because of all his injuries."

"Thank goodness."

Kayden opens his eyes after a while and smiles at me as he reaches for my hand. I grab it like it's my only lifeline. He snorts and then grunts from the pain it's causing. "You are a bloody idiot, do you know that?" I tell him through kisses on his forehead.

Kayden squeezes my hand, shaking his head slowly. I'm glad he's not talking, but I desperately want to hear his voice speak my name and tell me he loves me.

Julia lifts her hands from the wound, smiling reassuringly at me, and returns the pressure on his neck.

"How's it looking?"

"He's going to be fine. He'll be weak, but that can be fixed with rest and recuperation."

"I don't have time to rest." Kayden's voice is raspy but firm.

He frowns at Julia and pushes her hands away from his neck, trying to get up.

I growl at him, and he looks at me surprised. Kayden will be the death of me, I swear. The vampire nearly ripped out his throat, and he is still too stubborn for his own good. "Please, babe," I say. "Could you not do this to me? I need you to listen for once and not be stubborn. Give your wounds time to heal, please."

Kayden watches me for a few seconds, his eyes narrowed. He sighs and rolls his eyes at me, lying back down. "This bossy nature of yours is a lot like Tyler's. It's fucking annoying..." he trails off, smirking at me.

"I don't care if it's annoying, and if it's a lot like Tyler's, then you should be used to it by now."

"Guys, can we leave the banter for when we are safe at home, please?" Julia asks, amused.

"Fine, is it safe to move him?" Looking to Julia when she examines the wound again.

"Yeah, he should be able to stand and walk with some assistance."

"With no assistance, thank you very much." Kayden's annoyance at Julia is uncalled for.

"I'm sorry, but what exactly is your problem with me?" she asks him, sounding annoyed herself.

"Your fucking mate is the cause of all this-"

"Babe! That's enough. You know she has nothing to do with Jace's shit. When are you going to realize that she is fighting with us? She risked her life for us tonight—for this pack—and she didn't hesitate to come to help me find you, placing herself at risk."

"Ex." Julia folds her arms over her chest, glaring at Kayden.

"What?" Kayden's head snaps to Julia. His face shows little to no emotion.

"*Ex*-mate. It seems you forgot that I renounced Jace."

Folding my arms over my chest, I raise my brows at Kayden when he looks at me.

"I'm sorry, Julia. Force of habit, I guess. Thank you for helping Layla tonight," he concedes after a few moments of silence.

"Don't worry about it," Julia says as she gets up.

Kayden looks back at me, and I shake my head at him. He can be so fucking rude sometimes. "Come on, let's get you up and out of here. Julia, do you mind helping?" I look directly at Kayden when I ask for her help. I swear I'll hit him on one of his wounds if he protests.

Lucky for him, he doesn't, and we get him up from the ground. He hooks his arm over my shoulders, and we walk to the Packhouse. "I take it Tyler is safe and well if you are this calm and taking me back home," he smiles.

"Well, not exactly."

Kayden frowns at my words and stops walking. "What?!"

"Just chill, okay? Abby and Sebastian went to go get him."

"Are you fucking insane, Layla? Jace is after Tyler, and if Abby is anywhere near them, he will use her to get to him," Kayden bellows and pushes away from me.

"Babe," I warn him. "Do not speak to me like you do one of your soldiers. I know it slips your mind now and again, but I got trained in the same manner my brother was. I can hold my own, and I know when someone isn't capable, too," I tell him, trying not to lose my temper with him.

"Wait, hold on one minute, did you say Abby, like Abbygail, who's in a coma?" Kayden frowns as he comprehends my words.

"Took you a while to catch that, hey?" I laugh. "Yes, Abby. She woke up from their mate bond tattoo and a vision of you and Tyler getting attacked."

"How the hell is she fighting if she just woke up?"

"My mother gave her the blood Tyler left if it was needed to save her. It healed her instantly, and you have to see her. She's fierce and strong and determined." Kayden's mouth hangs open, and I laugh again. A thought comes to me which makes me doubt my earlier decision, and the smile fades quickly. "Okay, maybe—we should go to them in case they need us."

Julia nods in agreement, and we change our course to make our way to where Sebastian pointed earlier.

CHAPTER THIRTY-NINE

ABBYGAIL

My body feels frozen to my current spot when I see Jace's long, snakelike fingers around Tyler's neck and the other pushed into his chest at his heart two knuckles deep. The strangled choking and groans leave Tyler's throat as Jace forces his hand deeper into Tyler's chest, causing bile to rise in mine.

A low growl vibrates from Sebastian's chest, and he moves forward, teeth bared.

I grab his arm, and he snaps his head to me, frowning. I place my finger over my mouth when Jace doesn't pick up on us being there, probably too focused on his primary goal. As much as it breaks me, and I want to get to Tyler, we have to use this to our advantage.

"Move to the other side and wait for my signal," I whisper to him low enough so only he can hear me.

Sebastian nods and turns to creep to the opposite side of Jace.

Inhaling deeply, I mask my scent. I walk to the edge of the darkness so my face can stay hidden as the sun rises, deliberately stepping on a twig and making it snap under my feet.

Jace's head snaps in my direction, and he smiles wickedly at me. My heart is pounding, and my nerves decide it's a fun time to go haywire.

"You better stay back, princess, or I am going to rip his heart out," Jace snickers and pushes his claws deeper into Tyler's chest, reaching the three-knuckle mark.

I take another deep breath, realizing he thinks I am Layla. I can't wait to see his face when he sees mine.

"Come to play and watch your brother die?" he taunts.

I walk closer, still keeping my face and upper body in the shadows, and he squints. I tilt my head when I hear his heartbeat pick up. Maybe I should screw with his mind a little. I let out a high-pitched giggle, one you might hear in a horror movie.

Jace frowns, unsure who stands mere feet from him as the sound dies out. I pull the sword from its covering, and the *schwing* sound coming from it makes Jace's face pale.

I look at Tyler's injuries, and the panic threatens to overwhelm me. His blood drenches his clothes. There's an extremely deep gash on his side, and the gaping one on his back looks painful. The torn wounds are large enough to expose the bone. The one that worries me the most is where Jace's claws almost wrap around Tyler's heart.

"You better show yourself. This horror game you are trying to play is just making my patience wear thin," he growls, and Tyler screams when Jace closes his grip on Tyler's heart.

I gasp, and the sound makes Jace's face pull into a very twisted look—one of uncertainty and anger. "I'll give you to the count of three, and then I will show our King here what his black heart looks like."

My wolf paces my mind, but I keep her back. We can't show him our hand just yet.

"One," he sneers, squeezing harder, making Tyler whimper.

"No need for theatrics, Jace. Here I am." Talking slowly and controlled, trying to keep my voice from shaking as I step into the light.

Jace freezes when he sees me. His eyes widen in surprise, and his jaw drops open. "Haven't you changed, little slut—"

The words grate in my mind, and my wolf lets out a fierce roar at the mention of the degrading nickname he uses for me. I smile as I see him stiffen, and the fear running over his face, however briefly, makes him look pathetic.

"You will never call me that again. You will address me by my rightful title."

Jace seems to regain his composure and narrows his eyes at me. "Is that so? And what would that title be exactly?"

I smirk at him as I trail my fingers slowly over the mark on my neck, the smirk turning into a broad smile when his eyes follow my finger's movement and I see them darken. "*Queen.*" Dragging out the word, laced with venom.

Jace almost chokes on a snarl, and I can't help but laugh. Maybe I should not push his buttons, with him still having a death grip on my mate, but it feels right.

My suspicion is confirmed when I see his grip loosen on Tyler's neck and hear Tyler start to take short, painful breaths. *That's it, Jace, you fucking bastard. Focus on me.* Sebastian can get Tyler out of here as soon as I can get Jace away from Tyler, and I can finally finish this.

"What?" he spits, the anger in his voice making it shake.

"You heard me, bastard. *You* will call me 'Queen'—or 'Your Highness,' whichever one you prefer," I say, still smiling and stepping closer slowly, hoping my witty responses distract him from my advance.

I make sure my walk is slow, seductive, powerful, and full of confidence. Jace will not be able to resist the urge to overpower or dominate me. That much has always been clear, his obsession with me submitting taking precedence over everything else in his life.

He growls, looking from me to Tyler. An evil smile spreads across his face, and he tugs on Tyler's heart. "You are playing a perilous game here, little slut," he grits out as Tyler groans and his face contorts from the pain.

"Nope, I haven't started the game just yet. How about you come and face me, coward? Then the dangerous games can start," I tell him, swinging the sword playfully.

"Are you seriously challenging me?" Jace sounds surprised as the anger creeps into his tone.

"Well..." I shrug. "Not that it will be a challenge now, will it? For this to be a challenge, you'd have to be worthy, and we both know you are nothing of the sort. You aren't even worth the air you breathe."

"Trying the insult approach, are we?" he snorts, narrowing his eyes at me.

"I would love to insult you, but I'm afraid I won't do it as well as nature did..." I trail off with a smirk, resting the sword on my shoulder and my free hand on my hip, now standing within striking distance.

Jace's face grows dark as I trail off, and I can see he struggles to keep his composure. I keep eye contact with him, and after a few seconds, I can't control the laughter from bubbling out.

I keep playing on that part of his self-righteous ego, pushing all the right buttons. Jace forgot that with all the shit he put me through, I learned exactly what his weak spots are, and now I can use them against him.

The next few seconds happen fast, but it's like I can slow it down. Jace rips his hand from Tyler's chest and lets him fall to the ground. I look at Sebastian in the shadows and nod to him as Jace rushes me.

Sebastian bolts to Tyler's side, placing one of his arms around his neck and pulling him up from the ground, and Tyler moans.

"You fucking bitch," Jace bellows.

He swings his claws at me, and I jump backward, landing in a crouching position. I look up at him, smiling. I rise slowly, dusting the dirt on my pants off.

"Is that all you got?" I ask mockingly.

Jace roars and stampedes towards me. He swings at me again, and I dodge his assault, slapping him in the face as I move past his hand. This action gets me another roar, and he tackles me to the ground.

I hit the ground harder than I thought, and the wind gets momentarily knocked out of my lunges. Tyler's blood still running through me makes for a quick recovery, and I kick him off with ease as I jump to my feet again. "Really?" I ask, raising my brow at him. "This is just pathetic. I can't for the life of me understand why I was ever afraid of you. You suck."

Jace's nostrils flare at my mockery, and he lunges for me again. I turn out of the way again, bringing the sword down and slicing it across his back. He falls to the ground, screaming. Rising, he spins to me, lunging again. Clearly, his composure is failing, and he is attacking me in a blind rage and not with any kind of strategy.

I jump back, slicing the sword over his arm, quickly bringing the blade up and cutting him across the face. Jace screams when the edge makes contact. "You are hiding behind that fucking blade, little slut," he pants, getting to his feet again.

Attacking again, he grabs my arm and pulls me to him before wrapping his hand around my throat, glaring at me and baring his teeth in a wide, triumphant grin.

"Got you," he barks out a laugh as he tightens his grip on my throat.

"You sure about that?" My voice is calm, as I smile back at him. Jace's expression turns from surprised to livid in mere seconds, not getting the reaction from me he wants. *Stupid fuck.*

"I am no longer stained by the fear of you haunting me. I know my worth, and no one is taking that from me again."

Swinging the sword, I connect it with his side, driving the blade deep into him and making him roar. He loosens his grip slightly, giving me ample movement as I pull the sword from him and kick him in the chest, and he stumbles backward and falls on his back.

His body hits the ground with a loud thud, causing the earth to shake slightly and me to burst out laughing as the image of the giant falling from the beanstalk comes to mind.

"You think you are clever with that fucking thing, don't you. Meanwhile, you are too scared to face me without it," Jace grunts, spitting blood to the ground as he slowly gets to his feet.

"That's not how I see it. I just don't want your filthy blood to stain me anymore," I say, pulling the blade up and looking at Jace over it, seeing his blood dripping from it.

"Don't flatter yourself. I know you will never be able to fight me without that blade," he taunts me.

"Okay, fine, come at me. I promise I will leave the blade at my side," I say, batting my lashes.

The moment Jace reaches me, I swing the sword out in front of me, stopping him in his tracks as the tip of the blade pushes against his throat, a trickle of blood running down his neck where it pierces his flesh.

Tilting my head, I smirk at Jace, who growls at me, his anger almost consuming him.

"On your knees," I say playfully, pushing the sword deeper into his flesh. Jace winces and lowers to his knees, his hands in the air as his lips pull up into a harsh snarl. "Aww, poor baby. You don't like it if someone is degrading *you*. The feeling of helplessness isn't nice, is it? You thought I would let you come anywhere near me with those filthy fucking hands of yours?"

"You're going to regret this," he bites out, his jaw ticking, his eyes deadly as he glares at me.

"Hmmm, I don't think so, no. *You*, on the other hand, will never know if I actually did regret anything." I lean forward, stopping mere inches from his face. "Take a good look, you fucking coward. My face will be the last thing you ever see," I sneer, and slowly, I drive the blade into his throat.

Jace's eyes widen in shock, gasping. He grabs his throat when I pull the blade from it. I smile down at him as he falls to the ground, blood gurgling from the wound and out of his mouth.

"Karma's a bitch, isn't it?" I ask him as I crouch down next to him. Jace grabs at my ankle weakly, and I slap his hand away.

I stay like this until the last air leaves his body, and his chest doesn't move. Tilting my head, I listen to his heartbeat until no sound comes from his chest. I watch for movement, not wanting to leave it up to chance, but there is none. Sighing, I close my eyes when the burden that was Jace lifts from me.

"Abby!" Layla's voice comes from behind me, and I get up slowly.

She walks to my side, looking down at Jace's body, a sigh of relief coming out of her in a huff. "You did it," she mutters softly. "I can't believe you did it."

Julia slowly walks to my other side, looking down at the man who terrorized both of us.

"I'm so sorry, Julia," I say softly, and she looks at me.

"You never apologize for this, Abby. He deserved this and so much more. You didn't just free yourself from him. You also freed me—and I can never tell you how much I appreciate that," she adds tearfully, a sad smile on her face.

"Thank you, Julia," I huff, turning to see Tyler on the ground.

Sebastian is applying pressure on the gaping wound in Tyler's chest, making him grunt weakly. Kayden rushes to his side, cursing violently.

"Look what happens when you don't fucking listen to me," Kayden scolds him as he lifts Tyler's body to look at the overall damage.

The sword drops from my hand when Tyler turns his head to me slowly and frowns. He watches me, and the look on his face is one of utter disbelief as he mutters my name.

Tyler pushes Kayden and Sebastian's hands from him and tries to get up, the look on his face now covered with raw determination like he needs to ensure that what is standing in front of him isn't an apparition.

Moving quickly to his side, I drop to my knees, pushing lightly on his chest to keep him from getting up. "Hi, my love, long time no see," I laugh through the tears streaming down my face, making my vision blurry.

Tyler huffs his dismay at my lame-ass joke but lifts his hand to my face, stroking the tears from my cheek. "Is it really you?"

"Yeah, my love, it's me. I came to save you."

"I've never in my life been so happy to be the damsel in distress. It brought you back to me."

I laugh at his shitty statement, but the pure joy exploding in my chest makes me feel like I can soar above anything. Our bond solidifies, and the power running through me makes me feel I can be everything he needs and so much more.

EPILOGUE

TYLER

Lying on the couch, bare-chested and in my most comfortable sweats, in the living room with Abby in my arms, watching a movie—which is long overdue if you ask me—I absentmindedly trace my fingertips up and down Abby's arm. I will never get used to her body against mine. Sometimes, the disbelief hits me hard, and the need to touch her just to make sure I'm not dreaming overwhelms me. She's mine, and that alone makes my heart soar.

My fingers trail over the mark on her neck, tracing every inch of it, smiling absentmindedly, thinking of how special this is, how lucky we are, and how far we've come. My thoughts go to the night Abby killed Jace.

Sebastian frowns as he looks at Jace's seemingly lifeless body. He gets up slowly, moving like a cautious cat about to pounce on his prey. "I'm not taking chances," Sebastian snarls when he approaches the body. He picks the sword up from the ground where Abby left it and swings it down, severing Jace's head from his body.

The memory of Jace's demise plays in my mind, and I realize what day it is.

Today, three years ago, my precious Luna saved me from myself and that fucking bastard who almost succeeded in separating us and taking over my kingdom. I close my eyes as that night plays in my mind in a loop.

"I can't believe it's you."

The disbelief I feel must be evident as Abby kneels beside me. She smiles at me and touches my face softly.

Immediately, the sparks flow through me, giving me a sense of power. Abby caresses my cheek again, watching me, the worry in her eyes unmistakable. "We are going to have a lengthy discussion about what happened here tonight," *she tells me, her eyebrow raised slightly.*

I swallow hard. Kayden could not have told her what my plan was, could he? When did he get the time?

"First, we need to discuss what happened with you," *I insist.*

I'm lying in the protected wing of the hospital, in the same bed where I came to visit my heart's desire when she was so close but yet unreachable.

Abby looks around the room, the irony not slipping by her. She laughs softly, and I quirk my brow.

"Something funny?"

"Yeah, actually. Isn't this where you were supposed to sit when I was in a coma, but you decided to give up on me?"

"Hey, that's unfair. I sat by your side every day for three months straight."

"And after that? Because if I understand correctly, I was out cold for six," *her brow raised now.*

I huff a sigh, and the action causes me to almost double over from the pain in my chest, side, and back. Fucking wolfsbane. I have a good mind to ban the damn flower from ever being grown again. It has caused me more trouble in the last year than it should. I think I will make it punishable by death to use it on your own kind.

Abby still watches me as I get my breathing back under control, and I look at her from the corner of my eye, feeling guilty. She laughs at me again, gets up from the chair she was sitting in, walks over to me, leans down, and kisses me on my forehead.

I grab her arm when she starts to move away from me. "And where do you think you are going? I had to endure fucking forever without you, and now you think a small kiss on my forehead will suffice?" I growl playfully.

"Oh, we are quite a demanding Alpha, aren't we?" Abby watches me, the desire pools in her eyes, and it feels like hours before she leans down too damn slowly to kiss me, a seductive grin on her face.

She's doing this spitefully slowly, knowing precisely how impatient I am.

I grab the front of her shirt and pull her to me, growling. I smash my lips to hers, and that earns me the most lustful, beautiful moan I have ever heard coming from that pretty mouth of hers.

"Alpha Storm. Where is your mind at?" Abby's voice pulls me from the memory. I smile at the formality she uses when she feels amused or wants to tease me, looking down at the beautiful smile that reaches her eyes. She's lying between my legs and in my arms, where she belongs.

These last three years have been incredible, to say the least. Abby has been by my side with every decision, every order, and every move I had to make. She challenges me in all the right ways and has no fear of calling me out on my bullshit, even if I don't like it.

"Oh, my beautiful Luna—with you, always." I wink at her.

She raises her brows at me, looking amused as she turns on her stomach, leaning with her chin on her hands on my chest. She looks up at me, her eyes dancing with playful mischievousness.

"I bet it is, yeah. And the fact that it's been three years is not plaguing you at all," Abby counters with a small smile, but her eyes look sad for a moment, and she traces the scar over my eye.

Looking down, I follow her eyes as they rest on my chest, where the scar is visible over my heart. Abby brushes over it lightly as if she's afraid it might still hurt.

The fucking wolfsbane made sure I scarred beautifully after everything healed.

Pulling her face up to look at me, I smile at her. I don't want her to feel bad about them. I will wear them with pride like she does hers. "There's that, but what stands out the most is my badass Luna. The memory of you with that sword, fucking up that bastard, still turns me on," I smirk. My cock hard and twitching in my pants against her chest.

A playful smile spreads across her face as she looks down at my dick.

Abby sits up on her knees on the couch and looks around to see if she can spot anyone coming or going and then grabs the hem on my pants and yanks it down, letting my member spring free.

Watching her eagerness makes me even more turned on. I can feel myself getting even harder for her.

"Hmmm, aren't you all excited for me," she says, licking her tongue slowly over her bottom lip.

Bending down, she takes me into her mouth, scraping her teeth against my length as she goes down and sucking as she comes up.

I hiss as pure pleasure pushes through my body, and my hips thrust upwards without permission as my head kicks back, my eyes rolling back in my head. She pushes them down and looks up at me with those deep emerald eyes full of desire.

It's always a play at dominance if she lets me. Like I said, she challenges me, and it drives me insane. Sometimes in a good way and others in an "I want to pull my hair from my head" way.

I grab a fist full of her hair, holding her in place as she licks at my head, and it sends shivers down my spine. "Fuck, my love." I'm growling the words.

She smiles at my profanity and takes me into her mouth again, picking up her pace this time.

Damn it, this feels so good. I'm nearing my climax, and if Abby doesn't stop now, I'm going to come in her mouth—and that will just not do.

I pull at her hair, and she releases me, her eyes dark with desire. "Something wrong, my love?"

"If you are going to continue with this, I won't be a gentleman."

She laughs at my subtle remark and sits back on her heels, tilting her head to the side as she narrows her eyes at me. "Who says I want a gentleman tonight?" she purrs so low it sends shivers running through me, and I swallow hard.

"Fuck Abbygail, you are going to send me and my beast to the edge of never being a gentleman again," I growl as I get up and pin her on the couch beneath my body.

"So then take me like you want... *Alpha,*" she purrs, and that does it.

I rip her shirt from her body, tearing it in half, making her gasp and laugh at my aggressiveness. "You are so going to buy me a new one of those," she taunts.

"Baby, you can have the whole fucking shop," I growl again, ripping her pants from her as well, which makes her squeal. I laugh throatily, bending down to her lace underwear and ripping them off her with my teeth.

She gasps, now breathless, and pushes her hands into my hair, gripping it tight as I lower to her core, licking at her wetness. She bucks her hips as a moan leaves her mouth. Oh fuck, the sounds of pleasure coming from her will make me come, and I haven't even entered her yet.

I suck on her clit as I push two of my fingers into her, making her gasp loudly, and she grips my hair tighter and moans my name.

I work her to the edge of her climax and then add a third, which pushes her over. Abby screams as the orgasm rips through her body, my name echoing through the house.

I'm in awe of this gorgeous woman, watching her when she comes down from her pleasure. Her hooded eyes makes me want to fuck her so she won't be able to walk for at least a few days. "More?"

"Yes, please, *Alpha*," she smiles, playing with the title, knowing it drives me wild.

Grabbing her hips, I pull us both up and sit so she straddles my hips, not yet entering her. The squeal I get from moving us so fast makes me laugh, and she lightly slaps me across my chest.

"You creep," she chuckles playfully.

"What? You said you want more, and we both know this is what you mean."

Abby smiles slyly and lifts her hips so I can position myself at her entrance. She lowers herself onto me, throwing her head back as she takes me entirely, moaning again. She starts to move slowly, my hands on her hips as she rocks them back and forth. She traces my mark with her fingers like always before she clasps her hands behind my neck.

Moving my hand up to her shoulder and into the back of her hair, I pull her to me, kissing her passionately with every fiber in my body while she rides me. Her orgasm builds again with mine this time, and she rides me faster and harder until we both are breathless when we reach our climaxes simultaneously.

Abby collapses against my chest as we pant, sweat covering every inch of our satisfied bodies.

Pushing up from me, she retraces my mark, and I frown at her. "What's wrong, my love?"

"Nothing. When I look at your mark and how it fits perfectly with mine, it still blows my mind."

The first time I saw my mark was when I was in the hospital, and she took a picture to show me, then pulled her shirt off to show me hers.

Abby's mark is delicate and exquisitely crafted from her neck down to her shoulder and back. I, too, can't stop myself from tracing hers every time I see it. It calms my beast more than anything ever could. Mine, on the other hand, is bulky, almost tribal. It's one of a wolf howling. At the center of its open mouth is the bite Abby gave me. The wolf's head and neck are decorated by thick swirls running down my shoulder and left pec.

It still makes me do a double-take every time I see it.

"Of course it will. We are made to fit perfectly." I say, sounding corny.

Abby laughs at me, as she probably thinks the same thing. "You can be such a dork." She giggles and kisses me. "I love you so much." Placing my arms around her, I pull her to my chest and deepen the kiss. Abby moans into my mouth, and I smile against hers, feeling pride and love fill every inch of my being.

To think this little feisty she-wolf could tame my beast makes us both happy. "I love you most," I sigh into her mouth, realizing that happiness and contentment walk hand in hand in my life now.

THE END

ACKNOWLEDGMENTS

My rock and my safe place, my husband, David. How do I start to thank you for all your support and late nights listening to what I wrote that day? Even if sometimes you couldn't stay awake coming home from a hard day's work. Without you I probably would never have started writing or thought I was any good. Your belief in me is something I will always cherish. Thank you for pushing me to finish my story and bringing it to life. You and our beautiful girls drive me, and I thank the Lord daily for you. I love you the most, baby.

To my support system, who is always ready when I need you, Natasha Oosthuizen, my friend, thank you. You haven't stopped encouraging me from the first moment you read my story. Thank you so much for brainstorming with me, even if we are now a world apart.

Jeni Olivier, you have become a pillar of support from day one, and I can't thank you enough for your input and insight. You helped shape my story and backstories in a way I never thought could be brought to life. Thank you for the coffee dates and advice. It means the world to me.

Cleany, Jessica Kuhn, thank you so much for your support and love for my first-ever novel. I could not have been more blessed with you in my life.

To my beta readers, Karien, Helen, JP, Cornelle, Engela, Jessica, Natasha, Jeni, Thea, and my lovely mommy. You are the reason I still write. Thank you for reading and re-reading my story.

To my editor, Erica Rodgers. Thank you for helping me make my story better.

My team at FriesenPress, thank you for taking a chance and helping me to publish my book baby. I am thankful to work with people with the same love for storytelling as I have.

To my readers, thank you for taking a chance on my story and the world living rent-free in my head. You are why we write, and the support we, as authors, receive from our book community makes this worthwhile.

To my mom, Henriette Havenga: I left yours for last because if it weren't for you, Mommy, I would not have been the strong person I am today. Thank you for being there every step of the way. I know it was challenging when we moved to Canada, but I love you so much and am so happy to have a mom with whom I can share anything, even the spicy parts of my stories, haha.

ABOUT THE AUTHOR

Mianke Fourie couldn't find the book she wanted to read—so instead, she sat down and wrote it. And then, well, she was hooked.

Mianke always had a fondness for fantasy, especially shifter stories like this one. She has a passion for shaping new worlds in her imagination, and when she's out and about in ours, she's a hair and makeup stylist, a hiker, and a painter.

She was inspired by the experience of coming back from the brink and doing things you'd once thought were impossible. She hopes you'll find the courage to heal your own wounds, no matter how deep they run, inside these pages—and maybe a bit of a thrill on top of that.

Mianke lives in British Columbia, Canada, with the love of her life, their two beautiful daughters, and their German Shepherd. You can find her on Instagram and TikTok at MiankeFourieAuthor.

Printed in Canada